THE CURSE OF THE SEELIE KING

THE CURSE OF THE SEELIE KING
OUR TWISTED FATES
BOOK ONE

CHLOE EVERHART

Copyright © 2023 by Chloe Everhart

All rights reserved.

No part of this book may be reproduced in any form or by any electronic or mechanical means, including information storage and retrieval systems, without written permission from the author, except for the use of brief quotations in a book review.

Cover Design by Maria Spada

For those with dreams they refuse to give up.

Content Warnings

This book contains dark themes including: bone breaking, death in childbirth (mentioned), death of a parent (mentioned), genocide (mentioned), gore, kidnapping, mature language, misogyny, murder, possessive male love interest, self-harm, sexual harassment (no depictions of rape), sexually explicit scenes, suicide, thalassophia, violence

If you believe I'm missing a specific warning, please contact me.

I want everyone to enjoy *The Curse of the Seelie King* safely and with the most accurate information possible.

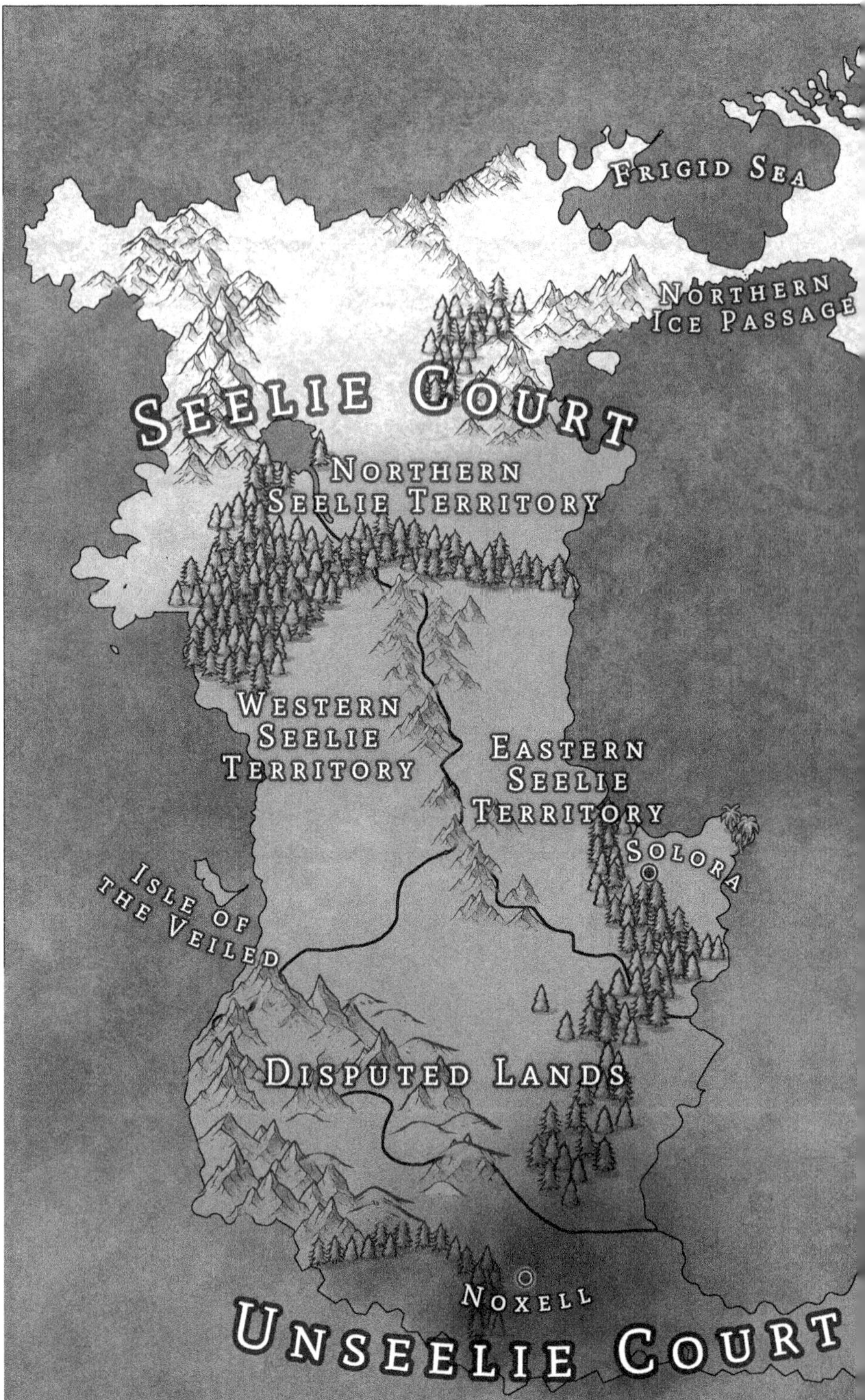
Frigid Sea
Northern
Ice Passage
Seelie Court
Northern
Seelie Territory
Western
Seelie
Territory
Eastern
Seelie
Territory
Solora
Isle of
the Veiled
Disputed Lands
Noxell
Unseelie Court

Unclaimed Frozen Waste
Aular
Althene
Quoruus
Scorched Desert
Dreaming Sea
Elspeth
Idle Islands

I
ROSELYNE

The King of Althene's dark eyes narrowed from across the table, watching and assessing me for the most important trait a daughter should possess—*obedience*.

"Do you understand, Roselyne?" my father asked quietly.

It wasn't truly a question. A command lingered between his words.

The entire table averted their eyes, instead opting to pierce their roasted carrots and pheasant with their forks. Their silence was their complicity in my death.

I ground my teeth and dug my fingers into the hard wood of the dining table to bite back a scream. The wood gave way as my nails carved tiny half-moons into the veneer, my knuckles white and nails threatening to split.

I nodded once and fought against the tears that threatened to spill over my cheeks. With this betrothal, my father set me up for a life of pain and suffering, all to strengthen his own seat as the King of Althene. He'd marry me to a monster for *gold*. I forced away the unshed tears.

Marrying for love was never an expectation for me. My

power as a princess didn't lie in the swing of an ax or the clanging of steel in battle. I was no conqueror. Instead, any semblance of influence I wielded stemmed solely from what my marriage would grant a neighboring kingdom. Like all women of nobility, I was tasked to birth future kings, and nothing more. I'd made my peace with this reality years ago after one crushing heartbreak, but what my father was now insisting would mean my death.

My father droned on, the rest of his words and explanation drowned out by a dull buzzing in my ears. Panic filled me as his meaning sank true and took root in my chest, choking me. My eyes flicked around the table, searching for someone to come to my aid. It was crucial that someone to speak some *sense* into the king—but my father's advisors were all puppets, and my two brothers would not meet my eyes. *Cowards.*

My father's stern voice broke through the haze of my barraging thoughts, and my gaze snapped back to him. He dabbed at his mouth with a pristine napkin as he spoke, entirely missing the brown grease at the corners of his lips.

"Be prepared to leave in two weeks. Part of my guard and an emissary will escort you to the faelands through the Northern Ice Passage. By the faeland's first snowfall of the season, you will be the fae king's bride, and Althene will prosper for it." He turned back to face his advisors, and it was done. My father's attention was elsewhere, and I was betrothed to the King of the Seelie Fae.

The Ruthless King.

I shuddered. The Seelie King was infamous among the human kingdoms for his cruelty. Knowing this, my father still promised me to this monster. What use could a fae king have for a human bride?

My corset was too tight, and my breaths too rapid and shallow. The room began to spin. With shaking hands, I brought my wineglass to my lips, but did not swallow. My stomach churned uncomfortably, as if snakes slithered inside me, squeezing my lungs and waiting to burst forth from my chest.

My chair screeched against the tile as I pushed up from my seat, desperate to expand my lungs in a bid for more air. My wine goblet slipped from my hands and shattered against the floor in thousands of tiny shards. Everyone at the table snapped their gaze to me as burgundy liquid pooled against the cream-colored tile. Two servants silently rushed forward, cleaning the mess.

"I cannot marry the Ruthless King!" I pleaded in some desperate attempt to my father.

My voice was shrill and sounded far away. My hands shook, sweaty where they clasped the edge of the large wooden table. A different liquid splashed onto the tile, swirling and mixing with the spilled wine. I winced at the sight of blood blossoming along a slice down my palm. My father's face flashed with anger before he schooled it back to his expressionless mask, ever the dutiful monarch of Althene.

"You can, and you will," he said simply before drinking deeply from his goblet, throat bobbing with every swallow of the wine. "I accepted the fae king's terms as they were sent to me. It's already done, secured by his perverse fae magic."

This was no negotiation. This was my duty, what I was born and bred to do—marry a monster to secure riches for the family. I could do nothing but stare, mouth agape, at my father.

My eyes swept down the table once more but found no aid. No one dared to defy the king—not even for this madness. The entirety of the human kingdoms knew the fae held disdain for humans. They'd use their power against us.

That is why we were separated by the sea as was agreed long ago.

I stood still, palm dripping blood onto the tile. "He will kill me," I said, half choking, begging my father to see reason. "With this betrothal, you sentence me to death."

A few of the royal advisors shifted uncomfortably in their seats, refusing to acknowledge the truth of my words. There was a reason the fae and humans did not intermingle. After centuries of separation, humans still remembered the stories of our ancestors—tales of the fae's savagery and cruelty toward them. Only a few fae generations separated the wars between our peoples. What were mere centuries to turn the heart of near-immortal beings?

My brothers, Corbin and Wallace, kept their eyes low, each pushing their half-forgotten food around their gilded dinnerware, not wanting to draw our father's ire. Only my future sister-in-law dared to watch me.

Ariadni snaked an arm through Corbin's and hooked around him possessively before assessing me beneath her long lashes. Her head cocked in question, full lips slightly parted as if she considered speaking but thought better of it. Thick black waves cascaded over her bronze shoulders as she studied me, but said nothing. I tore my gaze away from my brother's fiancé and turned back to my father.

My legs trembled. "Why him? Please choose someone else for me," I begged. "Surely there is someone else, some lord or—"

The king slammed a fist against the table, making everyone's place settings clatter noisily. He took in a deep inhale and pointed a finger toward me. The visible patch of skin beneath his black hair flushed red with anger.

"Sit down, you insolent child!" he spat. My knees threatened to buckle beneath me. His lips curled into a snarl. "You wasted these years I've allowed you a choice, spurning every match brought to you waiting on—what? *Love?*" He barked a laugh. "Don't you see? This is the best thing that could happen to this family. You're lucky news of your tryst with that squire boy didn't reach more ears and spoil you for everyone."

The mention of my previous lover was ice in my veins—his betrayal a still-tender bruise on my heart. I sniffed indignantly, willing the tears lining my eyes to not fall, irritated that my father would bring up Nolan in front of everyone.

Father gestured with his hand, beckoning me to sit back down. A flush crept across my cheeks, and I was suddenly ashamed by my outburst despite my justification. That was not how well-bred ladies were expected to behave. I lowered myself into my chair.

The king's features softened with my compliance. He drained his glass and addressed me once more, gentler this time.

"Your marriage will open up trade and goodwill between humans and fae for the first time in centuries. Once you are wed, the Seelie King will send ships filled with gold to our kingdom. Thousands will prosper all because of your selflessness. Your sacrifice will be historic—they'll sing songs of it in the years to come as Althene grows stronger than any other kingdom in the east."

My sacrifice. Hot tears pricked at the corners of my eyes. I quickly wiped them away, face burning from embarrassment. I wanted to sink below the table and disappear, but I needed to be strong. I swallowed the lump that had formed in my throat and nodded, accepting. There was no other choice. I never had a choice.

"Two weeks' time?" I asked, my voice sniffly.

My father eyed me suspiciously, but then nodded his head,

clearly pleased with my acquiescence. "Yes, you'll remain in Althene through Corbin and Ariadni's engagement ball, their wedding, and then you will depart. You're to be married before the first snow, as was agreed."

I shivered as waves of disbelief wracked through me. Two weeks was all I had left of my time in Althene. My stomach churned uncomfortably, the dinner I had previously picked at threatening to reappear. Two weeks to pack my bags and say goodbye to my life as I knew it, before marrying a monster.

As quickly as my life had been upended, my father changed the subject. We would spend no more time on my problems. Just like that, everyone moved on. It was decided.

The rest of the dinner I sat numb, eyes glazed over and barely hearing a word anyone said. My tablemates talked of frivolity and the upcoming ball to honor Corbin and Ariadni's engagement as if my entire life hadn't been pulled from beneath my feet in an instant. I played the part perfectly, nodding politely and eating my food daintily. I was the perfect princess—too bad I was doomed to die.

"No," Dove whispered. She slapped her small hand over her mouth. "You can't mean that!" Dove's bright blue eyes went round with horror. "The king cannot marry you off to that *killer!* Isn't that what they call him? The—"

"Ruthless King," I finished, grimacing. The fae king's reputation preceded him all the way across the sea. Even in the far reaches of the human kingdoms, news had spread of how the Seelie King used his powers of torture to murder his own father and take his throne.

I would be wed to a monster, and there was nothing to be done of it.

"You're to live across the sea? And worship all their strange gods?"

"The three-headed goddess hasn't done much good for me." I plopped my body down against the plush white chair in my bedchambers and sank into the cushion. "Maybe the fae gods will be more generous," I replied, trying to keep the bitterness from my tone.

My lady's maid sat beside me; her arms wrapped around her knees as she stared at me in abject horror.

"I'll be fine, Dove," I lied. "We knew this day would come eventually."

I smiled weakly at my closest friend. Her eyebrows knit together, but she didn't object, seeming to sense I didn't wish to discuss the matter further.

I dug into the sweet treats stacked on the silver tray before us, refusing to sink into the chasm of despair now torn open within me. I didn't want Dove to worry. We only had two weeks left together, and I wanted to make the most of our time. I studied her face, committing every aspect of my friend to memory. Her small, heart-shaped face, bright blue eyes, and wild red hair. My father supplied Dove to me at age sixteen when it was decided that I required a proper lady-in-waiting. She was chosen, plucked from her life as a trainee at one of Althene's brothels, and we've been together every day since.

After a decade of companionship, we were to be separated. I pushed down the wave of bitterness that threatened to overtake me. Dove was my one true friend at Castle Althene. It was a slight comfort that at least one other person was as horrified as I was at the prospect of my upcoming nuptials.

Dove and I lounged together in my bedchamber eating

sweets and drinking bubbly wine while playing cards. It was so typical of us, but the knowledge of my departure loomed in the shadows at the corners of the room, threatening to pull me under. She scooped up a card and laid out her hand, grinning. Dove shook her loose red hair happily as she shimmied her shoulders toward me.

"I win again!" she trilled.

I rolled my eyes, but couldn't help the smile that tugged at my lips. Dove was naturally good at everything, but lacked the arrogance to make that irritating. Until she arrived at the castle, she hadn't been given much in her life, but she was tenacious and took advantage of every opportunity presented to her. Dove's parents died when she was still a child, leaving her in the care of a distant relative. Her aunt subsequently sold Dove to The Divine Lily to work as a maid until she was old enough to train for the type of work the brothel was known for. I quickly shuffled the deck of cards and dealt them out evenly.

When Dove arrived at the castle a decade ago, she quickly acclimated to life at court, mastering horseback riding, needlepoint, dancing, and gardening. By all accounts, she was more equipped for the life of a princess than me. Where I floundered, she excelled, but it had never been a competition between us, and I felt nothing but beaming pride for all her accomplishments.

Dove drew a card from the neatly stacked pile and wrinkled her nose before playing her turn.

Besides being married off to an evil fae king and leaving the only home I've ever known, I was most upset about the prospect of leaving Dove behind. Our card game went on for a few more minutes, each taking turns discarding and retrieving face-down cards, working to make our pairs.

THE CURSE OF THE SEELIE KING

"What do you think he'll be like?" Dove asked, breaking the silence.

I knew who she meant.

I sighed and slumped against the back of the sofa, resigned. "Evil? Murderous? Take your pick."

I hadn't much hope for my betrothed's temperament. I threw down a pair of cards a little too roughly and jostled the table, knocking over the large pile of cards. With a groan, I slipped off the sofa onto my knees and began picking them up one by one.

Dove bit her lip and joined me on the floor, helping me pick up the discarded playing cards. She peeked at me through pale eyelashes as she scooped up a handful.

"The Seelie King wanted to marry you for a reason. Do you suppose he's only bad to his enemies?"

She gazed at me with all the hope in the world, her blue eyes brimming with unshed tears. I pressed my lips together. I desperately wished her words could be true, but I knew they were not.

I closed my eyes and took in a deep breath, steadying myself. My fingers curled into a fist, gripping the familiar fibers of the rug to keep from collapsing. It's true some men in this world were virtuous and kind, but my betrothed was no *human man*.

A *fae* like the Seelie King, didn't earn his brutal reputation erroneously.

I reached forward and squeezed Dove's hand. It would do no good to upset her further and sour what little time we had together.

"Yes, maybe so. Maybe he'll be kind to me," I lied.

"And handsome?" she asked.

I paused for a moment. Although I'd never seen a fae—I

knew the common traits. Long of height and limb with huge batlike ears. Some were even said to possess elongated teeth to pierce the skin of the prey they hunted.

I shivered.

"Yes." I laughed, albeit stiffly, not wanting to worry Dove further. "Maybe he'll be handsome."

2

DECLAN

The *Andromeda* sat in the capital city of Althene's harbor, bobbing with the wake of other ships, disguised as a human merchant vessel. Here in the northernmost human kingdom, the water was gray and full of foam, and the shores rocky and uninviting—unlike the Seelie Court's turquoise coastal waters. From my place at the ship's railing, I could see down the crisscrossing narrow alleyways of squished together thatched roof dwellings that made up the bulk of the capital city. The King of Althene's stone castle fortress sat atop a large hill, surrounded by a spiked gate, imposing over the outer city.

My salvation waited for me inside the gray stone castle. My unsuspecting princess. I flexed my hands, pulling my lessened power to the surface. The witches' curse would be broken soon, and I'd return to the height of my power with none—save for my council—any the wiser to my weakening magic.

Kera stalked up behind me on silent feet and placed a hand on my shoulder. I turned and faced my spy. Her expression was grim, dark eyes distant and observing the humans busily working in the port.

"Are you sure you want to do this?" Her small mouth turned down at the corners.

"What choice do I have? I need her, and you know it."

She bristled.

"Her father arranged transportation for her to take the Northern Ice Passage. We could have waited. This seems—rash." Kera grimaced as a soft wave of gray water sloshed at the side of the ship, rocking it slightly. "We could have avoided the Lyssan Sea and waited for the princess to arrive herself."

"And have her freeze to death on the way to the faelands before she can be of use to me?" I shook my head, and dark strands fell into my eyes. I ran a hand through my hair, pushing it from my face, my fingers catching on the tangles courtesy of nearly two weeks at sea. "No, better to get her myself. I wouldn't trust the Althenean King to not send a decoy in her place in an attempt to fool me." My eyes traveled to the crowded, dirty streets, full of shushing mothers and barefooted human children. "You know what the humans think of us."

Kera gripped the side of the ship's railing and peered into the murky sea below.

"I defer to you, Declan," Kera said.

I leaned again over the railing. "Do you sense the magic now? Her magic?"

Kera chewed the side of her mouth. "I don't sense anything." She glanced at the large hill and the gray stone castle atop it. "We're too far away. But I am certain, Declan. The human princess has magic in her veins. I felt it during my time in the castle."

"And she's a witch?" I asked.

Kera wrinkled her nose. "I've read the prophecy as you have. I am assuming so, Declan. What else could she be?"

My mind wandered to the bedtime stories my mother told

me as a child as I rocked in her arms—to those filled with more legend than truth. Tales of Dedric the Brave, with his double-edged blade, a great fae warrior who slew demon-kind and banished them to the Otherrealm. Of Siobhan and her flaming sword, a human marked by the stars and blessed with the gods' own divine powers of light and shadow. Of Sibyl, the mer seer who *saw* the demise of this realm, and who single-handedly halted the course of fate. Those stories were fiction, myths created to teach moral lessons to young fae children, not rooted in any actual history. The witches, however, were very real, and their demise haunted me every day of my life—their screams filled my ears when I closed my eyes to sleep.

Kera shifted on her heels. "I tracked Roselyne during my time in the castle. I sensed the magic stirring beneath the surface of her skin. She's oblivious to her nature."

"The human princess is a witch," I said.

"Perhaps the last." Kera nodded, a note of sadness in her voice. "Do what you must Declan, but remember—get in, get the girl, and get out."

It was embarrassingly easy to gain access to the Althenean crown prince's engagement ball. The humans were ill-equipped for any sort of magical approach; I felt almost guilty for crashing the event. With only a simple glamour, the guards believed I was the human lord of some local township and waved me through the gates. No one questioned me further.

The noise of the ball reached my ears, even from my spot deep within the confines of the castle's gardens. Tiny glass baubles lined the garden pathway, some sort of glowing beetle propped inside each orb, a poor imitation of the fae's magical everlights. Kera waited for me aboard *The Andromeda* alongside the rest of the crew, with plans to set sail as soon as I arrived with the princess to begin our journey back across the sea.

Kera gave me a concise description to identify the princess—tall for a woman, light brown hair with nearly white streaks framing her face on either side, and a general air of haughtiness expected by those of her social standing. That should be enough to identify her.

I heard approaching heavy footsteps and slunk into the shadows off the garden path.

A blond man in formalwear strode by, chest puffed out, heading for what appeared to be the castle's greenhouse.

I should have turned away and entered the thick of the party. I was here to find the princess and leave, but something called to me, bidding me to follow the man to his destination. I skulked deeper into the shadows and away from the lit path.

The man stood in front of the ivy-covered glass building and smoothed his pants before swinging the door open and walking inside. I concentrated and listened closely. After a few moments another voice mixed with his. This other voice was feminine and enticing, drawing me nearer, although their words were too low to be deciphered. Filled with curiosity, I entered the greenhouse, staying in the shadows to remain concealed, not realizing this action was the first of many decisions setting my long-promised fate into motion.

3
ROSELYNE

My hair was plastered to the back of my neck, Dove's intricate styling wasted and undone by sweat. It was ungodly stifling inside the ballroom. Although it was a relatively mild night for the middle of summer, the swarming press of bodies inside the castle mixed with the stench of alcohol had me quickly overheating and needing refuge.

The musicians on the stage paused between songs. I utilized the absence of the music to yell over the crowd to Dove, who was already drunk on sweet wine and spinning merrily, pressed into the body of some nobleman I didn't recognize. She seemed happy enough where she danced, her canary yellow skirts swishing from the movement, and her red hair a wreath of fire as she twirled.

Corbin and Ariadni sat across the room atop a large dais, two future monarchs clasped hand in hand, assessing the revelers celebrating their engagement.

Ariadni was dressed exquisitely, as usual. She wore a deep purple gown with tiny beaded silver whorls sewn into the skirt. My oldest brother sat beside her in a matching suit and cape, the two of them a shining image of premarital bliss and the future leadership of Althene. My eyes trailed back to my lady's maid, whose arms were now wrapped around her dance partner's shoulders, neck craned up to his ear with a devilish smirk on her face.

"I'm going outside!" I called over the dull roar of the crowd, my voice muffled by the chattering of voices around me.

Dove grinned lazily before nodding toward me and grinding her body into her dance partner, hips swaying to the beginnings of a new song.

Shameless flirt.

I rolled my eyes but couldn't help but grin. I wished I could be as carefree as Dove. She didn't let inhibitions or self-consciousness hinder her—she simply did what she enjoyed without apology, something I'd tried once with devastating consequences.

Just outside the double doors to the lawn and gardens, the full moon hung low in the sky and thousands of stars twinkled mischievously overhead. I exhaled deeply for the first time since arriving at the ball and let the knot of anxiety inside my chest loosen slightly. Only a few partygoers had spilled over into the stone garden pathways, most preferring instead to enjoy the ball indoors. The air was thick and oppressive, still hot although the sun had disappeared hours ago. Even so, it was a relief from the horde of people inside. The sweet smell of the garden flowers drifted through the air, jasmines, gardenias, and roses—a welcome contrast to the scents found inside the ballroom.

Small glass orbs filled with the soft blue light of the glowbugs lined the pathways, illuminating the dim walkway for the out-of-town guests. Instead of following the marked trail deeper into the gardens, I diverted left and meandered through the unlit pathway leading away from the celebration. I approached the small greenhouse where I'd sometimes keep Dove company while she worked the soft earth. A breeze blew and rustled my hair, unsticking it from my neck. I encountered no one else as I walked in the darkness, the heels of my shoes wobbly on the uneven stone.

I finally allowed myself to think about what was to come in only one week's time. No one deigned to speak about my fate to my face. Everyone knew nothing good could come from my union—and yet my father had agreed to the fae king's proposal. The gossip would keep the courtiers fed for months.

I glanced over my shoulder toward the ballroom. Through the large windows, I watched the hundreds of nobles pressed together, celebrating their crown prince while uncaring what was to befall their princess. Did the fae across the sea celebrate the royal engagements as we did? Did they too honor the three-headed goddess, or did they pray instead to whatever evil demon created them? I stumbled on a loose stone, but caught myself before I fell to the ground, wobbling on my ankle.

I knew little about my future home or its culture. I huffed a bitter laugh as I continued walking, my mood growing darker with every step.

The Seelie King could bring me to the faelands only to kill me for sport. Or perhaps I'd be one of ten wives—his newest plaything until he tired of me and threw me onto the street.

I entered the dark greenhouse and breathed in the comforting smell of damp soil and fresh herbs. Dove spent much of her free time inside of this greenhouse, toiling with the earth, and I accompanied her most days despite my intrinsic inability to coax the plants to grow. Everything I touched withered and died, despite Dove's patient instruction.

After years of failures, I began opting to sit and read books on a small bench placed in the center of the room while Dove dug into the soil with her bare hands, creating life from nothing more than seedlings. I surveyed the thriving nature created by my friend's hand, and smiled at the memories we'd shared here, away from the prying eyes of courtiers. I dug my ornate shoe against a loosened lichen-covered stone and turned it over.

I sat on the bench with my chin placed in my hand, resting against my knee. The sound of the musicians' stringed instruments were absent all the way out here past the royal gardens, secluded away from the guests. Alone in the darkness, I let loose a few tears, finally allowing myself to feel the despair clawing at me that I'd hidden in front of others for the past week.

I didn't want to go to the faelands, but I was duty bound. I breathed in deeply a few times, the fresh air cleansing my lungs and calming my fears.

The top of the metal bench bit into my neck as I slumped in the seat with a sigh. I wasn't ready to return to the party and face the smiling crowd. *They* didn't have to marry a monster. *They* didn't have to upend their entire life and move away from the only home they'd ever known. *They* hadn't woken up in the night drenched in sweat from dreaming about the bloodthirsty fae with silver eyes tearing into their throat with his fangs. I'd wake each night, clasping at my neck, sweating and unable to drift back to sleep.

The scrape of heavy footsteps on the rough stone made me stiffen and sit upright. No one else should be this far off the lit path. A familiar voice sounded out in the greenhouse's dimness as Duke Eugan stepped into my line of sight. I slumped in relief.

"Princess," he drawled as he approached me.

Since I was of marriageable age, Duke Eugan made it clear that he was interested in pursuing me, although I never returned his affections. Now the prospect wasn't an option—I belonged to someone else.

When I was twenty-one, he'd proposed marriage to me, and my father had refused, citing his station as a duke not befitting a princess. For that, I would be eternally grateful. There was nothing *wrong* with the duke, but at the time of his proposal, I was still reeling over my first and only heartbreak.

I assessed Duke Eugan as he approached me. He was no more than ten years my senior and classically handsome, with short, cropped hair on either side of his square jaw and loose golden curls stacked on top of his head.

I smoothed my gown as Duke Eugan entered the small circle of dim light at the center of the greenhouse and quickly wiped my eyes.

"Duke Eugan," I murmured, as he pulled me to stand and placed a wet kiss against the back of my hand. My skin prickled at the touch as I wrenched my hand away and wiped it on the skirt of my lilac-colored gown.

"I'm so glad I ran into you here," he said in an oily voice that made me shiver, motioning around the dim greenhouse.

Broken pots and dirt littered the rough stone flooring. Cobwebs glistened in the corners of the ceiling, too high and out of reach of Dove or any other caretaker. This area of the grounds was not marked for the party, unadorned with the garlands of greenery and effervescent orbs of glowbugs.

I crossed my arms over my body, suddenly uneasy and all too aware of my isolation from the rest of the guests.

Duke Eugan shifted on his feet.

"I've been wanting to offer you my congratulations

regarding your brother and his new bride's betrothal," he said, sucking in through his teeth.

His eyes lingered for a moment at the low neckline of my gown before he licked his lips and addressed me once more.

"I still despair that it is not others congratulating *us* instead—" He took a step toward me, and I moved away on instinct.

Bile rose in my throat.

He didn't notice, and continued his line of thought.

"I, of course, harbor no ill will toward the king, but choosing to align Althene with the *fae*?"

He spat the last word, and his beautiful face twisted into something ugly. He took another step toward me, his normally blue eyes darkened to black, his irises swallowed whole. I backed myself against a wall, trying to put space between us as he continued in my direction, shaking his head.

"It's such a shame we couldn't be together, that we never got to act on our—*baser* urges." He moved closer still.

Only a few paces separated us now. I smelled the alcohol lingering on his breath. Trembling, I held out my palms facing the duke, creating space between us.

My voice shook slightly when I spoke, unnerved by his boldness.

"I assure you, Duke Eugan, there were no urges for me." I turned to leave. "Now if you'll excuse me—"

He cut my words off, caging me within the confines of his body and the wall. He stunk of ale, and I was running out of patience for his behavior. In the past, the duke had made many attempts at my favor, but never had stepped so far as to harm me, always acting the part of a gentleman.

"You're drunk. Let me go," I said, more bravely than I felt.

Instead, he leaned forward and breathed in deeply near my face. I shuddered.

"I wasn't good enough for you? But some beast of a man is?" He laughed and shifted his body closer to mine, and I squirmed, trying to get away. "You would have made such a lovely bride for me," he slurred.

Duke Eugan reached out his hand and gently cupped my cheek in his palm. I jerked my face away, no longer interested in being polite or touched by some man who believed I owed him my favor.

The duke was a drunk man with a bruised ego, and I wanted no part in being near him. His fingertips dug into my jaw as he wrenched my head back to face him, the scent of alcohol hot on his breath.

"My lord," I said harshly, attempting to break his hold and duck beneath the confines of his arms. It was no use. The duke grabbed onto my arm and twisted tightly, burning my skin.

"Please let me go," I said as I worked to wrench away from him.

He held steady and jerked my body toward his. Pain radiated up my arm.

He meant to harm me.

The gleam in Duke Eugan's eyes was unlike anything I'd seen before—animalistic and cruel.

The men of the human world were just as monstrous as the fae abroad.

My heart thundered wildly against my chest. The greenhouse was empty. The duke and I were alone. He was larger and stronger than me, and I was at his mercy. Fear bubbled inside of me, threatening to boil over.

I struggled to break free of his grip, but he twisted harder and pushed me up against the wall, knocking the air from my lungs with the impact. A clay pot jostled from an overhead shelf and clattered to the ground, shattering into hundreds of tiny shards. I screamed.

"Stop fighting me," he grunted as he pushed my head to the side.

I closed my eyes, working to muster enough strength to throw him off me. I twisted my leg free and kicked wildly, aiming for anything that would disarm him.

As my knee struck the duke's groin, the fresh fragrance of cedar cut through the familiar damp scent of the greenhouse.

"You little *bitch*," the duke said. He raised a hand to strike me, and I closed my eyes, preparing for the impact.

A loud crack echoed throughout the greenhouse, but I felt no pain.

The weight of the duke's body no longer pinned me against the wall. I took advantage of my newfound freedom and opened my eyes, breathing in deeply and gulping down lungfuls of air I desperately needed.

Duke Eugan shrieked and backed away from me, clutching the wrist he'd been poised to strike me with.

I clamped a hand over my mouth to suppress a scream.

His hand was a ruin of flesh and bone.

Something snapped the duke's wrist entirely, the delicate bone protruding through his skin in a bloody slash of ivory. The hand hung limp and useless as dark streams of blood dripped down his arm and onto the dirty stone floor underfoot. His fingers each sat twisted at grotesque angles, flattened as if an object of considerable weight had crushed them.

My stomach roiled at the sight. *The three-headed goddess has finally intervened on my behalf.*

The duke's face morphed into an expression of pure agony and horror as he turned and bolted from the greenhouse, leaving me alone.

4
DECLAN

The princess scampered out of the greenhouse. She rounded the corner and disappeared into the darkness of the gardens, no doubt heading toward the safety guaranteed by the crowd of nobles in her father's halls.

But she couldn't outrun fate.

I dragged a hand down my face with a groan. So much for staying covert. I don't know what possessed me to get involved. I didn't give a shit about this bratty princess. She was purely a necessity—a way to restore my magic.

Seeing her struggle against that bastard lit something inside of me—some dormant pool of rage I hadn't realized existed—and I'd been inclined to act. It meant nothing.

She meant nothing.

I padded along the path, concealed by night, and followed closely as she made her way back toward the party. She was oblivious to the shadow on her heels.

Kera's steady instruction echoed in my mind. *Get in, get the girl, get out. Don't cause a scene.*

The reserve of my power was more drained than it ought to

be from that small show of power. Far from home, the normal swell of magic sputtered in my veins, unable to rise to its expected levels. I turned my face up to the sky, silently cursing the witches who damned me in this way.

I felt naked and exposed. This princess better be the answer to my prayers.

I ducked beneath a canopy of pale moon-wisteria, following Roselyne as she cut across the yard and reentered the lit path of the palace gardens. *Good girl. Stay out of trouble. Go back to the party.*

I watched as the princess waved politely to a couple sipping their drinks in the gardens—powdered and stuffed Althenean nobility undoubtedly, embellished with colorful baubles and beads around their necks. When the princess was out of earshot, they put their heads together, gossiping in hushed tones. The wind carried the woman's words to my ears.

"Have you heard? She's to be married to the Ruthless King. Do you think he'll kill her like he killed his father and stole his crown?" The woman could barely contain the glee on her face. The man laughed. I curled my hands into fists. They knew nothing.

The man replied, "I hear the Seelie King delights in torture, and finds pleasure in the act. *That's* what he wants her for—to warm his bed and engage in his wicked perversities." The two laughed together at that.

Irritated, I maneuvered past the man and woman. I considered killing them, but thought better of it. I needn't waste any more of my magic. *Get in, get the girl, get out.* They made no notice of me as I crept through the long shadows created by the towering flora of the royal gardens. Princess Roselyne hadn't seemed to have heard their jabs and moved quickly toward the large double doors.

My eyes trailed over the princess' body, trying not to notice the luscious curve of her hips in her gown. She slipped inside the doorway, and I followed close behind, akin to a predator. Though something inside of me recognized that this princess was anything but meek prey.

I ducked inside the ballroom for the first time tonight and was immediately immersed into a crowd of drunk human nobility. A servant handed me a flute of champagne. The blush-colored liquid went down easily, but was much less potent than the fae variety and did nothing to damper the growing nerves inside of me.

Get in, get the girl, get out.

My eyes scanned the room until I found her. The beads of her light purple gown shimmered in the candlelight lining the walls, throwing sparkling reflections on every surface. I found myself transfixed, like a moth to a flame.

She opened her mouth to speak with some plump redhaired woman I didn't recognize and a man who could only be one of the princess' brothers. The man laughed at something the other woman said. His resemblance to Roselyne was striking save for his thick black hair as opposed to the honey-colored tone of the princess'. He also lacked the striking palm-width sections of silver hair that framed her face. I saw the silver strands better than I had in the greenhouse, tied away from the rest of her curls as if she were ashamed of it.

Roselyne's brows drew together, her head angled toward her two companions as if speaking in secrets. Her mouth moved with urgency—but I saw no trace of fear in her evergreen gaze.

As if being compelled to do so, I pushed through the crowd, closing the distance between the princess and myself. She threw her head back in laughter and my breath caught in my throat, the radiant beauty of her taking me unaware. I balled my fist, my nails digging into my palms. Who was this woman I was destined to wed, and why was I so intrigued?

I drew nearer, still concealed by the press of bodies all around. The inane urge to ask her to dance took root inside of me. I wasn't done learning about the woman who I'd be taking to my court to marry. For now, she would think me merely some minor lord at yet another extravagant ball. I approached her from behind.

"My lady, would you care for a dance?" I asked quietly, feeling a curl of delight as I watched tiny pinpricks sweep over her neck and shoulders. *Humans are all the same. Easily delighted and easily frightened.*

She inhaled as she turned to face me, and her eyes widened. Her full lips parted as she appraised me, and I was suddenly uneasy with my new plan. She swiftly schooled her features into the practiced, polite expression that all women of court could produce on command. In that way, humans and fae were not dissimilar.

Her hair spilled forward across her shoulders in a cascade of waves as Roselyne nodded her head once and offered me her hand. I took it in mine and kissed lightly. Her skin smelled faintly of jasmine, and my mind conjured the white flowers and green ivy that climbed up the pale stone towers of my home. The princess' cheeks pinked from the contact, and she withdrew her fingers from my palm. I felt a rush of satisfaction despite my indifference toward her.

At that moment, the musicians on stage struck up a slower melody, one meant as a couple's dance. *Perfect.* She eyed me warily, then offered me her hand once more, which I gladly took in mine. Her palm was delicate, her skin creamy and unmarred. She'd certainly never worked hard labor or swung a weapon in battle.

She smiled demurely, fanning her lashes against her cheeks as I placed a hand at her lower back and began the dance. The steps were the same in the human kingdoms as they were in the faelands, and we both expertly moved in time with the music, gliding along the dance floor as if we were on ice.

"I've never seen you before tonight. What is your name, my lord?" she asked politely, her eyes sparkling with innocent curiosity.

"Declan," I said without elaboration, before spinning her out toward the crowd, then back cradled against my chest.

"Declan." She repeated my name slowly, as if tasting each individual letter in her mouth. "And from which kingdom are you visiting, *Declan*?"

"Far away," I said dismissively, already regretting the sliver of truth I'd granted her.

She scowled, and I bit back a grin as satisfaction licked through me. She was easy to rile.

"Do you wish to know who your current dance partner is?" she asked, attempting to goad me.

Shit.

I'd forgotten to address the princess with proper Althenean etiquette when I approached her, unpracticed to their customs. The silence between us grew heavy, but not oppressive. The moderate tempo of the strings guided our feet beneath us.

I spun her in a circle. My future bride was an excellent dancer, it appeared, her movements practiced and fluid. It was clear she had been brought up as I had, and made to master all the common dance variations nobility was sure to encounter in any court.

It was such a shame I was about to uproot her entire life, but if one human princess' happiness was the cost to restore my magic, I'd do it time and time again. She eyed me warily, and I plastered on a warm smile in return, hoping the expression appeared genuine.

"I'm aware of who you are, Princess Roselyne of Althene," I said.

She arched a brow in response, her face skeptical.

"Well," she said coolly, "then perhaps you're also aware of *who* I am newly betrothed to."

"I am," I replied.

Her eyes narrowed and flashed dangerously in my direction. She kept an arm on my shoulder and took a few steps, trailing around my body. I whipped around to keep her in my line of sight and took her back up into my arms.

She tilted her head, appraising me.

"And yet, you've asked me to dance tonight. Such boldness is rarely found in a man."

The princess smirked and blatantly eyed me up and down again as we swayed together, and the burn of her scrutiny seared me down to my bones. She drew closer to me—her face barely inches from my own. She was reckless. I held her gaze. I would not balk before this human. She drew back and cocked her head as we continued to move to the soft songs supplied by the musician's stringed instruments.

"Since my upcoming nuptials were announced, most men won't even meet my eye for fear of the Ruthless King's wrath," she said wryly.

The Ruthless King. The moniker I was gifted one century ago sent a ripple of displeasure through me. How little the humans knew and yet they were righteous in their disdain toward me.

She chewed her lip for a moment before adding, "But I

welcome his ire." She didn't notice my bitterness and laughed at her own words, a pleasant sound similar to tinkling bells. Her full lips curved upward, full of mischief as she swept her hands across my shoulders, resuming a proper dance position. She winked, and we began to dance once more. "It's the least I am owed for the fate forced upon me. What say you, Declan? Shall we defy the Seelie King together?"

My skin prickled, not unpleasantly, from the sound of my name on her lips. It was too tempting. Too dangerous. This princess wasn't anything as I expected.

She held her gaze firm on mine as she waited for my answer.

Who are you, Roselyne Vaughn?

By all accounts, this woman should be on edge and unnerved, having witnessed what transpired in the greenhouse. But instead, she possessed only a cool, unaffected demeanor and seemed entirely intent on acting purely on impulse.

She was willing to defy her betrothed, me, a man she thought of as a monster, to dance with some minor lord at a party. If she craved mischief so desperately, I'd give it to her.

I could be the demon the humans thought me to be.

No one paid any attention to us, everyone else in the ballroom much too involved in their own dalliances.

I splayed my hand across the small of her back, earning a small gasp from her lips.

The sound stirred something low within my body.

My hands trailed lower, testing how far her boundaries would allow a stranger to traverse, cloaked by anonymity among a crowd of hundreds. She didn't flinch or move away, and instead arched her back, pressing her chest into mine, daring me to proceed. We continued the dance, our bodies rubbing in tandem and eliciting a dangerous friction between us.

Energy crackled in the air, suspended all around us, ripe with potential to spark. My fingers swept against the curve of her ass, before bunching the fabric in my fist and twisting.

The rough beading of her gown bit into my palms, bringing me back from the brink of delirium.

The buzz of the crowd faded away into a distant hum. Although we were surrounded by the crowd of glittering party guests, Roselyne was my sole focus, and the only subject in my line of sight.

How interesting this princess has turned out to be.

Our bodies were affixed together in dance, moving together as one entity. The proximity was natural—comfortable, as if the forebears of the prophecy guided us together themselves.

I brought my face closer to hers, and watched in wicked delight as the pulse point of her neck thrummed rapidly, growing more frantic as I drew nearer. She tipped her head back, granting me access to the creamy skin of her neck with no regard for who could be watching.

I trailed my mouth against the delicate flesh of her throat, the floral scent of her skin heady and alluring, before navigating my lips to the shell of her ear and whispering low.

"I think you'll find, *Princess*, that I am not a man who scares easily."

Gooseflesh rippled across her skin. She turned her face toward me, eyes heavily lidded beneath thick lashes, her lips barely parted. Some invisible force urged me to close the gap between our mouths and bring my lips to hers. I was lost in a haze of lust, with a deep unmistakable ache growing below my belt.

Would it be so terrible to enjoy the one destined to save my magic?

There was movement in my periphery. From his gaudy

throne upon the high dais, the King of Althene stood, and the crowd grew quiet, turning their attention to their reigning monarch. Roselyne stiffened in my hands and quickly moved to create space between our bodies.

The spell cast between us was broken.

I released my grip on the princess' gown and slipped away into the crowd without a word, flexing my hand as if to remove the sensation of her skin against my palm.

5

ROSELYNE

My father's voice rang out through the large ballroom. The chatter of the crowd died down immediately, and all turned to face their king. The musicians abruptly pulled away the bows of their stringed instruments, and I winced at the discordant sound of the sticks sliding from their positions in haste.

My attention snapped to the dais. My father stood in front of his ornate throne. Corbin and Ariadni sat to his left in smaller, less ornamental thrones of their own behind a handsome table. My father was a man in his fifth decade, wider than he had been in his youth but still formidable to behold.

The comforting presence of Declan's body against my own was suddenly absent, and I yearned for the sturdy press of the stranger I'd taken such delight in. I whipped my head around, searching for him in the crowd, but he was gone, disappeared into the sea of Althenean nobility. Declan never told me which territory he was from, but with bitterness, I remembered it was moot. I was duty bound to marry a monster-king.

Several servants glided through the crowd, armed with

mother-of-pearl crusted trays of fizzing liquid in crystalline glasses, right on cue for the king's speech and subsequent toast honoring Corbin and Ariadni's engagement.

"Welcome all." Father paused and took in the drunken faces of the adoring guests. "As we celebrate and give thanks to the goddess"—he gestured with his hand across the planes of his chest three times, and the rest of the crowd followed suit—"I also wish to celebrate the union of my eldest son, your Crown Prince of Althene, Corbin Vaughn, to his beautiful bride, Princess Ariadni of Elspeth."

The crowd roared and stomped, clapping wildly. My father held his goblet high. "I wish them many years of happiness together, and that when I am gone, Ariadni shall be a gracious queen to Corbin."

More polite applause sounded from the audience.

I allowed my eyes to sweep through the crowded room searching for the mysterious man I'd shared the dance with. I only caught glimpses of my father's speech as he addressed the excited crowd.

"...allow for a bountiful harvest...strengthen our relationship with the South..."

Bored, my eyes slid to my brother and Ariadni. They sat to the side of the king's larger throne—their dark wooden table inlaid with curving ornate carvings of forest fauna along the legs. The table was dressed with a deep green cloth and ornamented with ivory dinner and glassware with emeralds encrusted around the perimeter. Corbin's head was inclined toward his betrothed, his cropped brown hair mixing together with Ariadni's black tresses, as they sat close together, obviously in love. *Something I'll never have.*

My father continued his speech as the crowd began to grow restless, no doubt wanting more to drink. I scanned the sea of guests and found Dove and Wallace about twenty paces from me. Wallace had his arm slung around my lady's maid shoulders and leaned his hair against hers. My brother and my friend shared an airy casualness completely devoid of any romantic inclination, unlike the man Dove danced with earlier in the night. My father's voice droned on.

"...a marriage of love and duty and honor...so unlike the sacrifice the princess has undertaken concerning her betrothal to the monster we all know as the *Ruthless King*."

The crowd shuddered in unison, and my eyes snapped back to my father at the mention of my own forthcoming betrothal.

My face grew hot, and the crowd's combined gazes burned like hot brands against my skin. Relief would only find me if the ground deigned to swallow me whole. Unfortunately, my father seemed not to notice my discomfort and continued. My hands grew slick, and I wiped them against the lilac skirt of my gown, the tiny hand-stitched beads rough against my palms.

A familiar male voice rose above the crowd, quiet and controlled, but effectively cutting off the words of my father.

"The princess' sacrifice?" He chuckled low, and a thrill shot down my spine at the rumbling sound. "A *burden*?" the man asked, sounding more amused than anything.

My father closed his mouth and began scanning the room for the intrusion.

Everyone in the ballroom quieted—the room crackling with wary anticipation. I could not see him, but I heard the thud of his footsteps in the silent ballroom as the madman stalked closer to the dais. The crowd parted around him like wilting flowers, wanting to separate themselves from this fool who'd dare incite their king's ire. I still could not see him, even as he continued speaking, making his way toward the high stage. My father waited there, eyes filled with fury and mouth pressed together in a tight line.

"Well, *I* think the princess is rather lucky," the man called out, loud enough his voice carried throughout the ballroom. His boots clicked against the tile as the crowd held their collective breath. "I've heard the Seelie King is more handsome than any human man and a very formidable lover."

Scandalized gasps filled the room before turning to hushed whispers. My father was not a man who accepted being interrupted, especially in his own home, at an event of his hosting. The king's entire head grew red and his jaw set in obvious irritation as he scanned the crowd for the man responsible for the disruption.

A man dressed in all black approached the high dais. He carried himself with the familiar body language of a man who was aware of his own power, chest out and head held high. My brows knit together in confusion as I took in the features of the man I'd shared a dance with mere minutes ago.

Declan?

A small gasp escaped my lips as he stalked past me without any regard, and the scent of cedar and citrus wrapped around me in a heady caress. My hand slapped across my mouth in horror as realization slammed into me.

Declan, the man I'd danced with, is the Ruthless King.

I don't know how it was possible, but I was certain. My heart hammered wildly in my chest, as if it would burst through completely. He'd come for me early, toyed with my emotions, and now planned—what exactly? The crowd tittered nervously at the interruption, unaware of the monster in their midst, thinking the man before them only some drunk fool.

My father sneered at Declan, and Ariadni's dark eyes flashed. She tapped on the table with her fingernails before gripping Corbin by the shoulder and whispering urgently into his ear.

Declan stood before the dais and smoothed his shirt, completely at ease despite the waves of antagonistic energy rolling off my father. Declan appeared the exact same as he had while we danced, tall, shoulder-length dark hair, undeniably handsome—but something about how he carried himself was different now. Some sort of vibrational shift occurred since we spoke last, clearly marking him as inhuman. How could the others not sense it?

The two swordsmen guarding my father at the base of the stage withdrew their blades and readied them, waiting on the command from their king to cut down the intruder.

I wanted to cry out, to warn them, but my scream died in my throat. If Declan was the Seelie King, and the stories were true, he would slaughter them all if he pleased.

Declan smirked, clearly amused with the disturbance created by his own design.

"A *burden*?" Declan repeated with a click of his tongue, addressing the stage loudly enough for his voice to carry across the expanse of the room. "See, I'd actually call it an *honor* for Princess Roselyne to come rule beside me in the Seelie Court."

He laughed, sending shivers skittering across my skin.

The crowd tittered nervously, unsure if he was joking or some baseless drunkard, and began to back away from the stage, separating themselves from what would certainly end in bloodshed. The guests that had previously been near me shrank away, effectively deserting me. Only a few paces remained between me and the Seelie King. I stood open-mouthed and red-faced, and at that moment, I hated him.

He'd made a fool of me, presenting himself as caring and kind in some sort of cruel fae trick before revealing his true nature. He grinned at my father, catlike and dripping with condescension. I scoffed.

Declan relished this, the asshole. He turned his face away from my father for the first time since revealing himself and appraised me up and down, seemingly unimpressed with the bride he'd chosen for himself. He turned back to face my father.

I scowled, thinking of how I'd felt in his arms.

How could I have ever enjoyed his company, even for a dance?

"I do what's best for my kingdom," the Seelie King said, shaking his head. "Do you truly believe if I had my choice of bride, this human brat would be my chosen?" Before I could make sense of that, he jerked his head in my direction, indicating me. "But alas," he said, "the Seelie Court's deal with Althene is signed, and I have use of her."

The swordsman with their blades drawn eyed each other nervously. I noticed Corbin move to grip the pommel of his sword, ready to pull the family blade from its place at his hip. My eyes darted to the nearly imperceptible movement as Ariadni's hand trailed beneath the multiple layers of her swishing skirt as if she were also readying a weapon.

Hundreds of eyes pressed against my back.

My father's face contorted, his dark eyes bulging from their sockets as if they would burst from his head. Declan turned and winked at me. No one else reacted.

Had I imagined it?

I blinked, then began to tremble as some terrible combination of fear and rage pumped through my veins as the realization of what was happening sank in.

My father sneered at Declan, still unaware of the threat inside his halls.

"Get this drunkard out of my sight! How *dare* you interrupt your king!"

"*My king*?" Declan laughed, and his features began to morph.

Where previously Declan's ears were rounded like a human's, they elongated before my eyes. Tanned pointed tips stuck through his curtain of dark hair, marking him as otherworldly. As fae. Every person inside the room stilled, unsure if they could trust their eyes.

Declan's appearance continued to change, more subtly now. He was slightly taller and broader of chest, towering completely over most men inside the ballroom. His clothing pulled taut against the muscles of his body. My eyes drifted toward his broad back where the dark fabric threatened to rip under the newfound tension. I quickly averted my eyes.

I hated him.

"Who do you think you are?" my father roared, his face red with anger, oblivious to the changes in Declan's appearance and blinded by his own rage.

Declan rolled his eyes, grinning lazily. "I thought it was obvious."

He began ticking off his titles on his fingers. "I am Declan Danchev, King of the Seelie Fae, although you may know me by another name: *The Ruthless King*. I've come to collect what is mine."

My father paled as he realized who stood before him. "We- we're sending Roselyne in one week's time! By way of the Northern Ice Passage," he said. "You were never supposed to come to Althene, that is not what was agreed. You have no right to be here!"

Declan rolled his eyes. "Why would I give you time to concoct some ruse and send some poor common girl across the ice, and keep your pretty princess locked up in your castle? We share no love between our kingdoms. I'd never trust you to deliver her to me." He shrugged. "Besides, by fae law, Roselyne belongs to me now. It's my choice what I do with my possessions, and I intend to take her *now*."

My fists balled at my sides. I wanted nothing more than to pummel him.

Spittle flew from my father's mouth from his place on the stage.

"I will not be talked to like this in my own hall by some fae bastard—"

The thousands of flickering ivory candles that covered every flat surface inside the great hall extinguished at once, plunging the gilded ballroom into darkness. A moment later, they reignited in unison. Someone screamed, and panic set into the crowd. People began pushing and shoving, clawing at each other and fighting to exit the two double doors at the back of the ballroom to avoid the Seelie King's wrath. I stood transfixed.

Other soldiers stationed around the room worked against the crowd, struggling to get near enough to defend their king from the monster in their midst.

Declan picked at his nails absently, unaffected by the men advancing toward him with blades drawn and seemingly unaware of the general chaos that had broken out around him.

"I'd be careful how you speak to me, King of Althene. The tepid peace between fae and humankind rests precariously between the legs of your daughter," Declan purred, golden eyes shining in the flickering of the candlelight. A bitter taste coated my tongue.

He smiled wider. The guards pushed their way through the thick throng of people more frantically, trying to reach their king before violence erupted. I couldn't find Wallace or Dove in the crowd, and prayed to the goddess they'd already exited the ballroom. I glanced to see my brother, Corbin, squeezing his future-wife's hand, his face frozen in an expression of uncertain agony.

One of my father's men burst free from the crowd and charged the Seelie King.

Declan didn't even deign a passing glance at the man, unconcerned with the attacker. He instead addressed the King of Althene in a voice of calm control.

"Call off your rabid dog, or you will find out why I am called ruthless."

"Kill him," my father snarled. The soldier ran for Declan, his sword aimed high as if to cleave the Seelie King in half.

Declan flicked two fingers in a barely perceptible gesture.

The soldier's body was hoisted into the air by some invisible force, and his sword clattered to the ground. Rooted to the spot, I could do nothing but gape at the horrific scene playing out before me.

The soldier's legs kicked wildly, scrambling to find purchase against the air. He screamed as his body contorted violently, spine twisting and limbs bending backward. There was a sickening crunch, and the man's body hung limply in the air.

A moment later, the dead soldier's heart burst forth through layers of armor and flesh and soared into Declan's outstretched palm.

Bile rose in the back of my throat. No one should be capable of such power.

The organ pumped a few sluggish beats, leaking out a trickle of dark blood that flowed over Declan's hand onto the pristine marble floor. The soldier's corpse slammed into the ground in a flaccid heap. Declan carelessly tossed the heart back into its cavity with an uncaring smirk—the Ruthless King's power on display for us all.

More soldiers surrounded the fae king, who let out an exaggerated yawn.

Declan eyed the dead body at the foot of the dais. "That was your doing, Althenean King." Declan said my father's title like it was an insult, then scoffed.

A small squeak slipped from my lips, and through the mass of long black hair, Declan's pointed ears pricked at the small sound.

"You have no right to be here!" my father yelled out, barely audible over the screams of the crowd as they fought to exit the room, beating on each other's backs in a wild frenzy trying to escape the Seelie King's wrath.

I don't know why my legs didn't carry me away screaming with the rest of the guests. My feet would not lift from the ground. My fear had planted roots, immobilizing me in this spot.

Declan *tsked* once and shook his head in mock disappointment. His eyes flickered with amusement, as if he took joy in the fear and bloodshed that surrounded him.

"I'm here to collect my bride," he said simply, gesturing toward me and flexing his hand. "All this—*nastiness* is unfortunate but can end right now if you wish." He paused for a moment, then shrugged. "Or I can destroy you all. Your choice."

None of the guards motioned to attack Declan, immobilized in their position, trapped in his impenetrable thrall.

"You think I'm going to let Roselyne go with you now? After you've killed one of my own men? You're as insane as they say. Fuck the agreement."

My father sneered at the Seelie King, but his eyes betrayed his fear. He was outmatched, and he knew it.

"I don't believe you have a choice," Declan said coldly. "The princess belongs to *me* now—the agreement signed and stamped by you, the promise of our union by the first snowfall sealed in irreversible magic for the promise of gold. Live with your decision you've made for your daughter, or die now. I'm taking her, regardless."

I trembled at the command in his tone. Disgust and anger twisted in my gut as hot tears threatened to spill over onto my cheeks. I was nothing more than a bargaining chip in a world ruled by powerful men and their desires.

My father opened his mouth to retort, but before he could get a word out, he began sputtering and choking. He clawed at his face, which turned red as he gasped for air. Declan stood with relaxed posture and plucked an abandoned wine goblet from a table, eyeing it disdainfully before swirling and sipping the liquid with an air of indifference.

My father was trapped under the spell of Declan's power like some invisible noose was tied around his neck. Declan turned to face Corbin, who stood with his own sword drawn, chair kicked away. Corbin stood in front of Ariadni, shielding her with his body.

"You're the heir apparent, right? Do you desire to be King of Althene, *boy*?" Declan asked my eldest brother.

My father clawed uselessly at his neck as the life was choked out of him. Corbin moved to attack Declan, but was stopped by some invisible barrier, no doubt placed by the Seelie King himself.

Hate simmered behind Corbin's eyes as he stood motionless, pinned in place by the all-consuming power Declan possessed.

Declan cooed at my brother, antagonizing him.

"In one moment, I could end your father's miserable life." Declan cocked his head. "I could rip his spine directly from his body with a blink. He probably wouldn't even feel it. Shall we paint the halls red in preparation for your coronation?"

Corbin's expressions twisted in rage and agony, the only part of his body able to move. I couldn't take it anymore.

"*Stop it!*" I screamed.

Declan was visibly startled by my interjection.

My father's face progressed from red to purple as his eyes rolled to the back of his head. My feet began walking of their own accord, traitorously moving me closer toward the monster in my home.

"Stop!" I cried again as I reached the Seelie King and slammed my fists against his hard chest. He quirked a brow, clearly unbothered but surprised by the barrage of my fists.

The Seelie King rolled his eyes but acquiesced. My father slumped to the ground and coughed as he filled his lungs back with air. He was shaken, but alive.

"Anything for my betrothed," Declan said, voice dripping with derision.

I loathed him entirely. The stories were right. He was a monster—but I would go with him to end the attack on my family.

Declan turned away from my father atop his stage and faced me, offering me a hand.

"Come, Princess."

There was no choice.

I took a step toward my doom. I would not cry. There was no honor in tears. I exhaled shakily as I took a step, dragging my feet toward my captor—my husband-to-be.

The fae king took my hand in his as my first tear crested.

This was my duty to my kingdom, signed and sealed by my own father.

I reached for the Seelie King, and his own hand enveloped mine as softly as when we danced.

He tugged me against his body and gently held me in his arms. He touched a finger to my forehead. Blackness crept into my vision and swallowed me whole.

6

DECLAN

With a twinge of regret, I recalled how the princess' beautiful face had twisted into malice once she realized who I was—what I was. Cold spray from the ocean misted my face, plastering my dark hair to my forehead. I wiped it away.

I shouldn't have danced with her first. What had Kera told me?

Get in, get the girl, get out. I fucked that up spectacularly.

I shook my head, working to clear the thoughts warring in my mind. The stars glittered above, no doubt laughing at how horribly I'd botched my retrieval of the princess. I gripped the railing and stared into the black waves, disappointed with myself. I'd allowed my curiosity to override all rational parts of my brain when I saw her in that dress, and nearly killed the King of Althene as a result. *Ending the curse is all that matters.*

I shook my head again, erasing all thoughts about the human princess with moonlight face-framing hair and bright green eyes. Kera hadn't mentioned the princess' beauty when she described her before I set off to claim her. It didn't matter. Beauty is not what I needed her for.

The ship lurched, and a wave of deep green sea water crested the deck of the ship and pooled around my feet. I gripped the rough wooden railing as to not fall into the churning waters below. They were barely visible under the dim light of the moon, but even in the non-stormy season, the waters of the Lyssan Sea were ancient and unforgivable. No help would come to me if I found myself thrust below their depths.

With a groan, the ship righted itself once more as we sailed toward the faelands—toward home.

Captain Theitand Malobe of *The Andromeda* had answered the call for transport across the Lyssan Sea quickly, and most importantly—with discretion, although the journey did cost me a small fortune. Still, I'd pay the price tenfold to reverse the fade of my magic.

Soft footsteps padded against the deck of the ship, barely audible over the crashing of the waves. Kera approached me, emerging from the shadows like a wraith. She stood beside me, both her small hands gripped tightly against the railing as she grimaced and stared into the choppy water.

Her normally golden tanned skin was ashen and cast in a greenish hue, and her straight black hair was mussed and stuck up at odd angles as if she hadn't had the foresight to comb it properly.

She removed an orange ginger candy from the pocket of her pants and popped it into her mouth. She closed her eyes and chewed.

"I'm never setting foot on a ship again," she growled, then swallowed. "If you need company to cross the sea with you again, ask someone else."

THE CURSE OF THE SEELIE KING

"The wind is in our favor. A few more nights, and we'll be home," I said, as I turned toward Kera.

I released my grip from the rail, stepped away from the edge, and turned toward my friend. "How is she?"

There was only one person I could be asking about. The woman who hated me, the one I was destined to marry.

Kera shrugged and popped another candy into her mouth.

"The same as when you asked earlier today. Still asleep, or pretending to be."

We walked together toward my assigned cabin aboard the ship. The night crew we passed averted their gazes and did not acknowledge us—the Ruthless King and his Widowmaker. Instead, they busied themselves with their seafaring tasks in silence until we were out of earshot.

Kera and I slipped inside the sparse room I'd been staying aboard. The only furniture inside were a small bed, desk and sitting bench—but I didn't need anything else. Cobwebs hung in the corners, and a thick layer of dust covered the unused desk. Captain Malobe insisted the Seelie King have use of the best cabin aboard the ship, but I declined, offering it instead to the human princess.

I sank onto the hard mattress with a groan and ran my hands down my face. Kera wiped a finger through the thick layer of dust on the small chair and grimaced before perching herself on the edge of the seat.

"I want you there when she wakes up," I said, breaking the silence.

Kera narrowed her eyes. "And why not her betrothed?"

I exhaled, releasing all my pent-up energy in one breath.

"She'll hate me for what I've done—for taking her away. I need you to help—*acclimate* her to the faelands," I said.

Kera bristled. "The princess is not some new pet to be

house-trained." I opened my mouth to interject, but Kera cut me off with a wave of her small hand. "Besides, you know my skills are best served elsewhere—not as a chaperone for human women."

"Kera—"

She shook her head. "Are you asking me as a friend or commanding me as my king?"

I straightened my spine. She spoke again before I could answer.

"I will do as you wish, Declan. But I disagree with your methods."

"She only needs to know—"

"—what is strictly necessary," Kera finished. "Yes, yes. I know." The ship lurched again, and Kera's hand shot to her mouth. She groaned through her fingers. "We should have traveled by lunar ash."

I raised a brow. "You know we couldn't. Not this distance. Besides, we have only a limited amount." Kera clenched her stomach and bent at the waist, dangling her head between her legs.

"You could have brought Callum." She sniffed. "I detest the sea."

"You know he had to stay and oversee the city with the Daylight Guard," I said.

The sickly green pallor returned to Kera's skin. "Fine," she said, waving her arms in defeat. She retched once, and I stifled a laugh.

"Are we done?" she snapped as she righted herself in the chair. "I need to vomit, and I'd hate to do so in your lovely stateroom." She bared her teeth at me—her attempt at a simpering smile.

I nodded and with that, Kera swept out of my cabin and into the dark corridor beyond.

7
ROSELYNE

Sunlight streamed in through the expansive glass window across from the bed, stinging my eyes. The air smelled of salt and sorrow. My stomach grumbled, and I curled my body into a ball, wrapping my arms around my knees and bringing them to my chest. My head pounded relentlessly behind my eyes.

I remembered everything.

The room I found myself in was ornate and plush with pale wooden furniture and an overfilled bookcase lining the wall opposite a large window. A giant map of strange lands and seas hung across the entire length of one of the walls with marks and symbols I didn't understand scrawled across it in bright green ink.

The desk was stuffed with wrinkled papers, broken quills, and ink pots littered inside one of the drawers. I padded toward the window. Bright turquoise water stared back at me, vast and unending with no landmass or landmarks in sight.

They took me by sea.

My father had arranged my travel through the Northern Ice Passage as the Lyssan Sea was considered too temperamental. As a child in Althene, my father once brought Corbin, Wallace, and I on a trip to the seaside a few hours north of the castle. The shore was rocky and gray, the water the deepest of blues, and icy against my skin.

I shivered despite the heat radiating from the glass pane of the window. I wore only the same chemise I'd worn under my gown the night of the ball. My beaded lavender gown sat folded neatly on a bench, with my heeled shoes on top, and a clean, simple dress made of lightweight green fabric also folded beside it. I slipped it over my head. It was a little tight in the bust, but fit decently enough. My head pounded in my skull, a persistent dull ache behind my eyes.

"We reach the Seelie Court in two days."

My eyes went wide at the sound of a voice, and I whipped around to find myself face-to-face with a fae woman. My breath caught in my chest. I knew her. I recognized her small stature, sharp cheekbones, and nearly black eyes—but that was impossible. I blinked again, trying to make sense of the familiar face before me.

She set down the tray she was carrying on top of the wooden desk. She was slight of body, with elongated ears that stuck out through loosely plaited thick black hair she slung over one shoulder. Although I was over a head taller than this fae woman, something sinister simmered behind her eyes that led me to believe she would be a formidable enemy to have. She leaned against the open doorway, slowly chewing with eyebrows drawn together, seeming like she'd rather be anywhere else. At least we had that in common.

"Who are you?" I asked.

My voice was hoarse from disuse and my throat burned from the salt air. I cleared my throat as the woman crossed the room toward me and handed me a glass of water from the tray. I took it and sank back down into the bed before gulping it down. I cursed myself, remembering to never accept drink from the fae.

"It won't poison you," she said with a knowing smirk.

She lifted the empty glass from my trembling hands then poured more water into it. When she handed it back to me, I grasped it tightly in both hands and brought it up to my lips, clinking it softly against my teeth as I waited for her to speak again—to explain.

The fae woman sighed impatiently. "My name is Kera."

The name sent a rush of memory galloping back to me, and the glass slipped from my hands. Before it could shatter against the wooden floor of the cabin, Kera caught it in one hand with feline deftness.

I swayed slightly. Kera placed the glass on the desk and eyed me warily.

"Are you ill, Princess Roselyne?"

"I know you," I said. It sounded like a question.

"You do," she replied with a nod.

I assessed Kera once more. She stood with her arms crossed wearing a flowing tunic and loose pants, not unlike the men who labored in Althene's castle and grounds. She was different than she appeared when I first met her—resolutely fae where she previously hadn't been. I did know her.

Kera had entered in competition vying for my oldest brother's hand in marriage earlier this year. She'd left the contest early on, claiming sickness. Ariadni, the beauty of Elspeth had ultimately won Corbin's favor and his heart.

"From Corbin's betrothal tournament?" I asked.

"The very same." She sat down on my bed and crossed one slim leg over the other, the overstuffed mattress cradling her petite frame. She bounced on it slightly.

"*Gods*, this one is loads better than the ones in the other rooms," she commented. With a groan, she lay back and reclined completely against my bed. My mouth hung open as I sat and stared at her. Kera's eyes drifted closed. I'd been in close quarters with this woman and never known she was fae. How was that possible?

"A glamour," she answered the question before I even asked. "The same one Declan undoubtedly used at your brother's little party."

She quit her admiration of the mattress and sat upright to face me.

"It's easy to trick humans. You lot see what you want to see." She waved her hands and suddenly her ears no longer stuck out through her hair and the ever-present effervescence she exuded diminished slightly. She appeared like a human—like the young woman I'd met mere months ago.

A small gasp escaped my lips. Although I'd seen with my own eyes that Declan could change his appearance, it was hard to believe that I'd lived in such close proximity to a fae only a few months ago and been none the wiser. The next moment, she was back to normal, the glamour gone.

"Why were you—?"

"In Althene?" Her lips curved upward. "Certainly not to marry your brother," she said, snorting a laugh.

She didn't elaborate and instead pulled out a small, orange, bark-like object from her pants pocket and broke off a piece before popping it into her mouth. A large wave crashed against the window opposite the bed. Kera shuddered as she eyed the pane of glass separating us from the torrential sea. She swallowed. "I'm to help you adapt to life at the Seelie Court. Declan's orders."

Declan.

The Seelie King's name was a leaden weight twisting in my gut. I turned up my nose and turned away from Kera's intense gaze, but I still felt her eyes boring into me. Even though she'd been kind so far, it was all a ruse. She was one of them, a *fae*. They were evil. I'd seen it firsthand.

"I don't need help adapting." I said, narrowing my eyes. "I know all about the fae. The fae's disdain for humans is infamous."

My voice was unnaturally high, and I fought back the tears that threatened to spill as my voice grew shriller. I refused to cry in front of Kera. I didn't want to confirm what the fae all believed. Humans were weak. Pathetic. Easy to control.

My face twisted into a snarl.

"I've heard stories of the Seelie King's depravities. I know all about the perversities of your kind, how evil you are, blood drinking, the hatred—"

Kera interrupted with a laugh.

"You've got us confused with the Unseelie, and lucky for you, and all of us—they no longer exist." A shiver ran down my spine. "As far as Dec's depravities go?" She laughed again, as if she found this entire predicament hilarious. "I've never shared a bed with the Seelie King, and therefore I cannot personally attest to his *perversities*—he's definitely not my type."

How could he not be?

I shook my head, emptying it of my traitorous thoughts.

I frowned.

"I serve the king in other ways," Kera replied, tipping her

head toward me. "Information is the most valuable currency of them all. It's one of the many ways I make myself exceptionally useful to Declan."

"The other ways?" I asked.

"My charm and wit, of course." Kera scoffed with fake indignation.

Her gaze softened slightly as she placed a hand on my shoulder to steady me. "No one is going to harm you, least of all Declan. You're under his personal protection, and everyone knows it. If any of these crew members even looked at you wrong, he'd rip their heads off with a snap of his fingers," she said with a wryly.

I forced a scowl. "He hurt my father," I whispered. "Killed one of his men."

I thought of the soldier who's name I didn't know. Declan had ended his life as if it was child's play. The man would still be living if not for me and the stupid betrothal my father agreed to. The dead soldier probably had a family who mourned him.

"Your father would have done worse to Declan if he was capable. I think you know that." Kera abruptly stood. "Would you like to go stretch your legs after you eat? Although your stateroom is lovely, you've been in this cabin for days. Despite my hatred for the sea, the view is beautiful, and the air is fresher on deck."

I hesitated. Was this some fae trick? I sensed no deception from Kera, just perhaps a small prickle of irritation.

"I'm supposed to help you, remember?"

I chewed on the inside of my cheek.

"Am I to be a servant to the Seelie King once we arrive in the faelands?"

The fae were known for their tricks against humans and for

creating impossible loopholes in their contracts. It was well-known all over the human kingdoms that entering an agreement with the fae was asinine. The fact that my father did so confounded me. Was my only use to him as a bargaining chip for more gold in the crown's coffers?

Kera blinked. "I don't see how a human princess with no practical skills would be a particularly useful servant."

I frowned at that.

"No, Roselyne," she sighed. "You're to marry the King of the Seelie Fae, just as your father agreed. There are no tricks, and no fae deception. Nothing of the sort. You will live in the palace under the protection of the king."

A sudden thought entered my brain.

"How many wives does the king have?" I asked, insisting on finding the obvious catch in the situation and desperate to understand what my life would behold.

Kera pinched the bridge of her nose and mumbled something indiscernible.

"None," she said. "When you marry the king, you will be his only wife."

Another horrifying notion occurred.

"Will I be queen then?"

"Yes," she answered and elaborated no further.

"Why me?" I whined. It made no sense why the fae king would want me as his bride. Athene was the poorest of the human kingdoms, and not rich in any natural resources.

Kera's face revealed nothing.

"To secure an alliance between the faelands and human kingdoms, isn't that obvious?" she replied, speaking the clearly well-rehearsed words. I had the distinct notion she wasn't telling me the entire truth.

But despite that feeling, and against my better judgment, I allowed Kera to lead me from the darkness of my cabin to step into the sun as far away from home as I'd ever been.

8

DECLAN

The sweetest scent of jasmine cut through the stench of sweat and open sea, ensnaring me. I tore my eyes from my opponent to see *her*—Roselyne, standing next to Kera, casting my spy in shadow. For someone who wasn't interested in helping acclimate the princess to life among the fae, Kera was doing brilliantly.

The human princess' eyes were narrowed and locked on me. She wore her hair loose around her shoulders, tangled with salt air. I eyed her up and down, appreciating her figure beneath the fae clothing, her rounded ears a stark contrast to those who surrounded me.

Behind Roselyne, the sun began its nightly descent toward the horizon in an explosion of pink and orange. The light set her curvy silhouette in a glowing halo against the backdrop of the open turquoise colored sea. The human princess' mouth was tight and observing, intensity dancing behind those green eyes.

A hard punch struck the side of my cheek, and the metallic tang of blood filled my mouth as I bit into my tongue. The crowd of fae sailors surrounding the makeshift sparring ring cheered loudly. Through the buzzing of my vision, I saw a few hands exchanging copper coins. My bride-to-be's lips curled into a smug smile. I wiped my mouth and smirked, diverting my attention back to my sparring partner.

"Nice hit, Zak," I said grinning.

The scrawny sailor wasn't exceptionally strong, but he was quick, and with my momentary distraction, it had paid off for him. He had balls enough to strike the Seelie King, and I admired that.

I wiped my mouth with the back of my hand and a smear of blood came off on my skin.

Zak glowed. No one had been able to land a punch on me the entire trip to Althene or so far on the journey back. Only the diversion of my human bride's beauty distracted me enough to allow someone to capitalize and take advantage of the situation.

"If you used your magic, I wouldn't have been as lucky, Your Majesty!" Zak said. I hid a grimace as I considered my fading magic. I painted my face with a genial smile.

"Maybe so," I said, "but we agreed—fists only, and you did exceptionally."

Zak's grin took up the entirety of his face. I scanned the rest of the crowd of men, trying my hardest not to stare at Roselyne, standing at the fringes of the gathered crowd with Kera. Her arms were crossed with a haughty expression painted across her face. She hated me.

Remembering where I was, I quickly turned and addressed the gathered men.

"Who's next to fight our newest champion? I have some business to attend to."

With that, the sailors groaned, and I stepped out of the

throng of bodies making my way toward the captain's on-ship study. When I allowed myself the luxury of turning and searching for them among the crowd, Roselyne and Kera were already gone.

"We're making excellent time. Tonight's rainfall will be nothing but a blip. It's too early in the season for serious storms."

Captain Theitand Malobe stood confidently behind his handsome desk, arms stretched across a map covered in curved lines and hand scribbled notes. The ship's navigator predicted a storm tonight, and although this crew was supposed to be the best, the thought did instill a small amount of fear within me. There was a reason it took a highly specialized crew to cross the Lyssan Sea, and why they were paid handsomely for the journey.

The captain took a long puff from his pipe and a large cloud of spiced tobacco drifted through the room making my throat itch.

"We could reach the Seelie Court as quickly as the day after tomorrow if the wind allows."

Theitand was a human, probably less than a decade older than Roselyne, with tanned skin, and a bright copper mustache and beard that covered most of his face. His casual air was somewhat comforting to me as I glanced out the large window of his private study aboard *The Andromeda*. Theitand crossed the room and poured two generous servings of amber liquid into crystalline glasses.

"It's not often my crew is hired to assist royalty across the sea. Have a drink with me." He waved me over as he sank into the overstuffed leather chair behind his desk.

I took a seat across from him, accepting the glass, and sipped at the spiced liquid. The slightly sweet drink burned comfortably as it slid down my throat.

"How long have you been in the business?" I asked.

Studying the room, most of Theitand's furnishings were of excellent quality, generally reserved for only the extremely wealthy, with inlaid gems in most of his furniture. It was apparent he did well for a ship captain.

"I've been with the sea since I was a lad," he said, puffing out his chest. He took another drag from his long wooden pipe. "I got my start as a cabin boy with a—less than reputable sailing company."

I suppressed a smile. "So as a pirate?"

Theitand's face split into a huge grin, showcasing a golden canine tooth inlaid with one bead sized emerald. His laugh was a wheezing one, as if he couldn't get enough air. He waved a finger at me with false admonishment, each adorned with a variety of chunky rings that reflected the dim light of the room, a display to his extreme wealth.

"I'm not so unwise as to answer that," he said, laughing. "But you could say I got my start in some not quite legal ways—but it all worked out for me. I saved my coppers, worked up the line, and found myself with enough money to buy a small ship and start my own crew specializing in transporting goods across the sea. The business grew."

He tipped his glass and swallowed the rest of his rum with ease.

Now that I was slightly more comfortable considering the storm, we shared another drink before I bid the captain good night, and excused myself from his study.

"If you ever want to hire your own personal company, think of me!" Theitand called as I exited the doorway and found myself in the narrow residential hallway located near the bottom of the ship.

I turned to walk in the direction of Kera's quarters to inquire about how Roselyne was doing now that she was conscious.

At that moment, like she had been directly summoned to me, a particularly feisty, particularly angry human woman slammed into my back. I spun around and caught her in my arms before she hit to the ground.

9
ROSELYNE

"Am I in your way?" an amused voice said from above me.

I blinked open my eyes and found myself wrapped in the arms of my enemy—my husband-to-be.

Hot embarrassment crept up my neck. I wriggled free of his grip, smoothed my skirts, and offered him my best glower.

"Yes, you are," I snapped. "I'm trying to go back to my room."

The Seelie King stood in the middle of the hallway, taking up all the space so I could not pass without his allowance. His eyes crinkled at the corners, and I felt a sudden sinking sensation like I was caught in quicksand. His lips curved upward and my heartbeat accelerated.

"Is that an invitation?" he asked, with that stupid smirk on his face.

Hot white fury coursed through me at the presumption in his voice. Everything about this man irritated me. He was too beautiful, and it made him arrogant and charmless. I liked him when he was Declan—human minor lord. Seelie King Declan was an asshole.

I straightened my spine.

"I may be forced to marry you, but I'll *never* bed you," I spat. My voice did not tremble, and for that, I was grateful.

That's what these men cared about right? The Seelie King had said it himself to my father. The fate of the kingdom rested between my legs. My scowl deepened. To males like the Seelie King, women were only good for breeding little princelings to continue their legacy.

I'd do no such thing.

Declan smiled blithely at that, like he didn't believe me. The arrogant asshole. Although I did mean the words, I found myself thinking about how the fae lord would be in bed, with his hard body and wide frame, inhumane quickness...

I shook my head, ridding myself of those unwelcome thoughts.

"I have no need of unwilling bedmates, Princess—least of all dull human ones whose lovemaking is likely as uninspired and bland as the kingdom she hails from. I have enough tedium in my life."

I scowled, and he smirked in response to my obvious annoyance, baiting me to snap back. His dark eyes swept down my body, appraising me. He clicked his tongue disapprovingly.

His eyes snapped back up to mine. "No, Roselyne. I do not and *will* not, command you to bed me once I take you to wife."

I sagged in relief.

Declan leaned forward toward me. "But, do not be so sure it will not be *you* who crawls into my bed one night, legs spread, with a demand on your tongue, begging for release."

His eyes bore into mine, golden and molten. My breath hitched, and it took all of my concentration to break away from his sharp gaze. There was no reason for his words to incite any sort of desire within me, but they had.

"Stop with your fae seduction," I commanded.

His brow rose at that admission, and heat spread across my cheeks.

"I'd do nothing of the sort," he said, with a wince as if he was hurt by the accusation. "My magic doesn't work that way, and even if it did—I would never employ force to ensnare a lover."

He shook his head and leaned toward me. His voice was low and rough. I leaned toward him, a fly trapped in the spider's web, no longer struggling, merely awaiting my demise.

My breath hitched as I listened to his every word. I swallowed thickly, my throat suddenly dry.

"Princess Roselyne, *when* you enter into my bed, you will do so willingly, and you will beg for me to take you. To grant you the release you so *desperately* seek at my hand."

I took a step backward, legs slightly shaking. Despite my disdain for the fae king, I couldn't deny the wetness between my thighs. He inhaled deeply and raised a thick eyebrow. My nipples stiffened beneath the thin fabric of my supplied dress. He may claim he used no magic against me, but there was no denying the physical reaction of my body at his words.

Wanting to play no further part in his games, I inhaled once, and spat in the fae king's face. He only smiled at that, and I suppressed a shiver. With more bravery than I truly possessed, I stood tall and replied to his words.

"Seelie King, perhaps *you* will beg for me, and I will deny you again and again."

With that I nudged past the fae king with an elbow and stalked toward my room, heart thumping wildly and arousal buzzing throughout my body.

Stupid, handsome Seelie King.

I smacked the pillow with every word I thought, pummeling the luxurious linens on my bed with my fists. Declan swore he used no magic against me, but that didn't explain the sickly lust that roiled through my veins whenever I was in his presence. I sighed, thinking of the time before he revealed who he was, and what he was capable of, when we danced and I was weightless in his arms.

One more whack against the now-abused pillow and I felt a tiny bit better about my predicament. I turned over and sank onto the bed, seething. My door unlatched with a small click and swung open. I sat upright and gripped the blankets to my chest, warily assessing my room. A small black cat stalked into the room and perched itself upon the chair near me. I blinked, confused. I hadn't seen any animals aboard the ship.

"Where did you come from?" I questioned, as I crossed the small room and closed the door before reaching to scratch behind the cat's ears. It purred and nuzzled into my hand, before hopping down onto the floor and meowing. I turned around for a moment to latch my room back closed. When I turned back to face my new furry intruder, I screamed.

Where the black cat had been, Kera sat cross-legged on my floor.

"Surprise," she said as she stood, the shadow of a smile etched across her face.

Words failed me as I stared open-mouthed at the fae woman who, only moments ago, was a *cat*.

She flipped her braid over a shoulder and took a seat on my bed. "It's not a big deal. I can get around tight places easier in my animal form." She grinned. "Plus, I knew it'd freak you out."

Not even wanting to get into how this was feasible, I shook my head. Clearly anything was possible when it came to fae magic. I sat gingerly on the bed next to Kera.

"Why are you here?" I asked, my brow creasing.

She smirked. "I heard you and Declan had a little lovers' spat. I was checking in. You appear to be doing fine."

"We certainly aren't lovers, and we didn't have a *spat*," I said, crossing my arms. I wasn't sure who I was trying to convince, myself or Kera. Everything about Declan felt inevitable. I had to remain strong and remember who he was. I may be forced to marry him, but I didn't have to *be* with him. Kera rolled her eyes and stretched out, taking up most of the mattress considering her small size.

"Sure." She shrugged as she placed her hand behind her head, completely relaxed. "Not yet anyway," she added. I didn't dare ask why she said that. From her place lounged across my bed, she kept talking. "I was supposed to come and tell you there's supposed to be a little storm tonight. Declan asks that you remain in your cabin."

Irritation flared to life within me.

"Declan could have told me that himself," I snapped.

I saw the shadow of hurt flicker across Kera's face before she smoothed it over.

"I believe he didn't think you wished to speak with him again at the moment." She paused before turning her head to study me as she sat upright on her elbows. "I've known Dec for a long time. He has a reputation for being brutal in war and to his enemies. But he is a good man. He will not harm you. You're safe with him."

I made a noncommittal grunt and Kera rolled her eyes at that.

"We're to reach the faelands in another day or so. Then you can see the Seelie Court for yourself and make your judgments."

"Maybe I'll be the first human to do so," I said wistfully.

Kera sat upright on her elbows and assessed me, arching a brow. "Humans reside in the faelands. Many of them."

I sat up as well.

"Oh." I fidgeted with my hair, the silver strands twirled taut around my finger. "We were taught that humans are nothing but cattle to the fae and all fled long ago."

Kera shook her head and mumbled something that sounded a lot like 'Althenean propaganda.'

"There are entire settlements and villages of humans. Of course, some live in the major cities, but there's an all-human village outside Solora, only a few hours north along the main road."

I must have appeared as confused as I felt.

"Solora is the capital city and seat of the Seelie Court," she added.

I nodded slowly, but my mind was reeling. If humans lived peacefully among the fae, I could admit, it was *possible* some of my other beliefs regarding them may also be untrue. I assessed Kera. She was fae, and had been nothing but kind to me. Unease settled into my chest, oily and uncomfortable. Had I been wrong all this time?

Her expression softened slightly. "Stay in your cabin tonight, Princess."

With that instruction, Kera left me, and I sat in the dark of my room in contemplation.

10

ROSELYNE

I awoke to a boom of thunder and the sound of heavy rain pelting against the window. The storm had begun. I trembled under my blanket as the ship rocked back and forth from the violent waves, thrusting open the drawer of the desk opposite me, and spilling its contents onto the floor. Ink bottles smashed and thick green liquid leaked from the broken container, staining the floorboards.

Through the clashing of the sky and the shouting of the crew overhead on the deck, a clear crystalline voice called out to me in a language I couldn't quite understand. I startled, searching for the intruder in the darkness of my bedchamber.

"Hello?" I called out, my voice wavering slightly.

Lightning flashed and light flooded my stateroom. I was alone. Before I could question it, a sensation of cool relief washed over me and trickled down my body as someone began to sing. The ethereal chanting was reminiscent of songs sung to the three-headed goddess in Althenean temples, yet somehow more beautiful, *more otherworldly*. The voice transcended possibility, and I found the song next to me, far away, and inside my head all at once. Instead of unease, I only felt a refreshing sensation of relief. This song veiled my other senses, suppressing the sounds of storm noise. It was serenity. Peace. The promise of bliss—if only I could reach its singer.

The voice floated through the air all around me, caressing my senses and cutting through the cacophony of the storm. All thoughts of fear left my body. I only had one purpose, and it was to find the owner of this voice by any means necessary.

I slipped out of my bedroom door and began to walk down the hallway, stumbling and grabbing the walls to keep from falling from the rocking motion of the ship. Another loud crack of thunder boomed outside, but it didn't matter. Nothing was more important than finding the source of the song that had crawled into my skin and taken root. The ceiling dripped seawater onto the top of my head from the storm raging on the main deck, the floorboards slick against my bare feet as I padded through puddles of rainwater.

Everything was a pleasant buzz, my concentration focused on reaching the sweet silvery song calling to me. The voice led me up the stairs to the main deck, the song the softest silk caressing my senses. Nothing else mattered.

The rain on the main deck was torrential, plastering my hair to my head and immediately soaking through my white chemise. My body shivered as the rain pelted against my face, but I felt no cold. I searched the deck for the singer, but only found the sailors fighting against nature's storm. I glazed over them, unable to focus on anything except my mission to find the enchantress calling to me.

Puddles splashed underfoot as I made my way to the deck of the ship, and a singular tear slid down my cheek at the incomprehensible beauty of the song. The voice resonated through me, my heart pumping in time. It was the most captivating sound I'd ever heard, both mournful and a song of celebration at once. I *needed* to find who was singing. I had no choice. With the thick sheets of rain barreling down, none of the sailors noticed as I slipped through them in my search for the singer. I was a phantom, floating through the ship deck, as the crew battled the raging sea, mad with the urge to find the source of the song.

The ship tipped, the right side nearly parallel to the horizon, and seawater lapped onto the deck. Bodies sprawled across the floor. I stumbled, scraping a knee, before the ship corrected and righted itself. White bolts of lightning streaked through the sky, illuminating the deck as the crew worked tirelessly to battle the waves.

My body shivered again, but I still felt nothing but the urgent need to find the voice. My bare feet slapped against the slick wooden deck as I walked to the railing on the edge of the ship.

The call was louder—I was getting close. I held the rail and peered over into the angry black waves below me, churning and creating violent whirlpools. The silver song swelled as if in confirmation of what I must do. I stood on the edge a moment, my hair wild in the wind, whipping around my face. I closed my eyes and the sea sprayed against my cheeks. The song was encouraging and enticing, urging me nearer the edge.

The song reached a crescendo, louder than it had ever been, a rush in my ears commanding me to walk into the sea. Silently, I stepped off the side of the ship and plunged into the dark water below.

II

DECLAN

I ran a hand down my face as the first drops of rain began to fall. I'd pushed the princess too far and too soon. I should apologize for heckling her and causing a spat. Breaking the curse would be easier with a willing bride.

The fear of failure pulsed uncomfortably inside of me.

Roselyne and I hadn't truly spat though, and we weren't a couple. I sighed, turned to the horizon, and watched the crashing black waves topple into each other like mountains.

This could have been easier—the marriage. I'd ruined any chances of the princess and my relationship being anything other than political by being dishonest in the beginning—and then attacking her father.

My teeth ground together as thoughts of the King of Althene and my time in his banquet hall began to sour my already unpleasant mood. Droplets of water fell from the starless sky, heavier than before, splashing gently against the hard wood of the ship deck, reminding me of tears.

While undercover in Althene, Kera watched Roselyne and reported her findings back to me using the Reflection of

Geminus handheld twin mirrors. One such piece of intel Kera shared was the princess' abject fondness for books. According to Kera, if the princess wasn't with her lady's maid, Roselyne's nose was nearly always buried within the pages of a book.

In all her correspondence made to me, Kera reported Roselyne to be a perfectly average princess, trueborn of the royal family, and completely unaware of the incredible amount of magic she possessed.

Hoping to save myself from any would-be usurpers who scented my weakening magic, I extended my intent to marry her, a human woman I'd never seen or met before. Even as the Princess of Althene, she'd never receive a better offer than to marry the Seelie King and enter into the faelands.

Apologies had never been my forte, but for her, I'd try, if only to make my life a tiny bit easier. I enjoyed taunting her, but only because my unwanted physical attraction to her was becoming difficult to bear.

Roselyne's ferocity engaged and excited me. With every snarl of her lip and the furrow of her brow, my interest grew. I could admit that some part of me was interested in her for reasons other than breaking the curse. In the past, women always threw themselves at me, wanting my money, my power, my body—but not her. My teeth ground together uncomfortably, and my head radiated pain. My bride-to-be held nothing but disdain for every fiber of my being, and it is my own doing that made her this way.

I stepped out from beneath the cover of the awning and was peppered with the sprinkling of water. I wasn't one for sentimental gifts and apologies, and my heart thrashed wildly thinking of the potential rejection of the human princess. The sky opened up, and the rain hit the wrapping and expanded into larger wet spots, marring the delicate paper.

The wind howled, and a large wave capped over the left railing as the ship groaned in protest and leaned into the cataclysmic waves, spilling the seawater onto the ship. The wind whipped my hair wildly around my face and misted me with the salt of the ocean. I hadn't bothered to tie it back up behind my head and was regretting it now as it hung limp across the side of my face. Lightning lit up the sky in streaks of white, soon followed by a thunderous boom. The storm had arrived.

I crossed the main deck as the sailors battled the wind and sea, and entered the small staircase that winded down into the bottom of the ship.

I made it to Roselyne's cabin and steeled myself outside the door, irritated that I felt *nervous*. I would give her the package —a book I thought she might enjoy, although as I stood in front of her door, I felt like a fool. I took two full deep breaths. I heard another crack of thunder outside from my position in the residential hall as the sailor's called out to each other on the main deck.

There was no reason to be nervous. I was King of the Seelie Fae. I helped lead in the war against the Unseelie fae and won. The witches fled the faelands for fear of me. I'd survived numerous battles—but this human woman sent me to my knees with one singular frown. It was ridiculous.

I puffed out my chest, donning the mask of the arrogant king and rapped my knuckles harshly against the wooden door.

Only silence met me. I leaned my ear against the door and tried to listen for the telltale rhythm of Roselyne's heart. I frowned when the only answering sound was the squeaking of some small rodent within the walls.

The door swung open easily when I turned the knob with my free hand. Her cabin was completely unlocked. I assessed the room Roselyne had been occupying and breathed in the sweet smell of her jasmine scent. Moonlight shone through her window through a gap in the storm clouds, illuminating her cabin in a cool, pale light. The bed was unmade, with the covers thrown awry as if she rose in a hurry.

The storm noise probably scared her, and she went to Kera seeking comfort.

That scenario made the most sense, but that didn't stop the unease settling into my bones.

My feet flew against the wooden floorboards, the increasing intensity of the rainfall urging me faster. I found myself down the hall, in front of Kera's bedchamber, and pounded on the closed door. When Kera swung open the door, appearing slightly irritated, she noted my face and immediately softened her expression.

I craned my neck over my friend's shoulders and found no one behind her. My face must have betrayed my worry.

"What's going on?" Kera asked, her forehead creasing. She rubbed her eyes.

My mouth was dry, and my tongue thick in my mouth. Dread coursed through my veins. Something was very, very wrong.

"Is Roselyne with you?" I asked, and I could hear the slight quiver in my words.

"No," Kera replied uncertainly. "I warned her of the coming storm hours ago. I haven't seen her again."

A thread snapped taut within me, tugging urgently on one end. My heart rate spiked, and a rush of excitable energy pumped through me.

I knew for a fact Roselyne was in danger, and though I could not rationally explain it—at that moment, I sensed my human princess had entered the sea.

12

ROSELYNE

I hit the water feet first, and my mind was released from the song's spell. The dark water swallowed me whole, tearing me from the surface and carrying me into its dark depths. I kicked my legs upward, clambering in the violent water, working to make it back toward the ship. With a gasp, I breached the surface.

Water roared in my ears and heavy raindrops pelted my face, blinding me as wave after wave crashed over my body and dragged me below the surface. Water rushed into my mouth as waves toppled over each other, pushing me further away from the ship, twisting my body and disorienting me. I opened my eyes under the water but could see nothing but endless black, my eyes stinging from the salt. I clawed and grasped at the water, fighting in slow motion to reach the surface, but my hits never landed. I was alone in a void of black.

Here in the darkness below the waves, I heard no storm, no lightning, and no shouts from the ship. My chest burned with the overwhelming need to inhale, but I fought the urge, knowing a lungful of seawater was the only thing separating me from my death.

Something gripped my ankle and jerked me toward them—I was momentarily relieved believing I had been saved. Instead, my body was dragged deeper into the darkness by the invisible force, away from the ship and any hope of survival. My last reserves of air spilled from my mouth in dozens of tiny bubbles as I screamed.

A sense of tranquil calm washed over me, and I was no longer drowning, no longer dying, but still being dragged deeper into the sea. The pain searing inside of my chest was gone, and I breathed easily surrounded by nothing but leagues of sea. The salt in the water stung my eyes as I forced them open, shocked by the absence of burning in my chest. I was suspended alone in the darkness, whatever force drug me this deep, absent now.

A shadow moved in the water, just out of sight. I squinted, trying to see. A faint greenish glow drew nearer as I helplessly floated in the cool water.

Someone approached me, swimming quickly and easily, alit by the soft glow of the jewelry adorning their hair and body. My eyes bulged as the woman drew close enough for me to make out her features in the dark water.

Merfolk.

I gasped, but no water rushed into my mouth to drown me. Tales of the mer were told to young Althenean children, but always known to be fantastical and fictitious. The woman before me was as real and solid as any human or fae I'd seen.

She had dark, smooth skin, and wore layers of necklaces and stacks of bracelets that shimmered and glowed against her deep complexion. Her body was human in appearance from the waist up—willowy and lithe—but that is where our resemblance ended.

Below the navel, where a human's legs would have split, hers were conjoined into one large appendage, similar to any other sea creature. Thousands of glittering blue scales covered her fin.

The mer woman appeared to be about my age, with waist length dark hair styled in hundreds of rope-like twists cascading to her waist. Multicolored shells and beads adorned her hair, a shimmering embellishment every few inches that I imagined would tinkle pleasantly if she ever found herself on land. As she drew nearer to me, I noticed some of her hair shimmered like threads of bright blues and greens, similar to the glowbugs in Althene.

The mer woman's eyes were large and wide-set, their color a cloudy white with no discernible irises or pupils, as if a thick film had been pulled over them.

We don't have much time, Princess Roselyne of Althene.

Her voice was clear and crisp inside my own mind. Her lips did not move, but I knew she was who spoke to me.

Merfolk were real.

The woman shook her head, sorrow lining her beautiful face.

Do not be alarmed, Roselyne, Mortal Princess of Land. I am Maren, and I mean you no ill will.

She held her hand to her chest, then extended it in a welcoming gesture. I stared, suspended in the dark water beneath the violent, crashing waves as she spoke to me.

I had to sneak away to see you. To understand.

She frowned, almost in apology.

Visions plague me of your face and fate, although I cannot say why. I needed to see you—to see if you are truly what they say.

What the king believes...There is another, and I'm not yet sure which one you are.

I opened my mouth to speak, to question what the hell she was talking about, but tiny bubbles spewed from my mouth in lieu of spoken words. Maren shook her head, and her braids floated effortlessly around her head like a halo. She swam closer to me, her large fin pushing through the water with ease and propelling her forward. Just as she was about to reach me, the water surrounding us vibrated. Her expression transformed into one of abject terror.

Maren's eyes widened and her voice filled my head, urgent and commanding.

Get to the surface. Board your ship. It's not safe in the water any longer. A beast pursues. GO NOW!

Her voice shook slightly, the previous formality absent. She kicked her fin in my direction, sending a wall of water propelling me toward the surface before diving deeper and disappearing among the darkness.

Whatever power granted to me to breathe underwater left with the loss of proximity to the mer woman, and my lungs began to burn anew. Bright flashes of lightning let me know I was swimming toward the surface. My legs pumped wildly, and the urge to inhale was overwhelming. I fought it, so close to the sweet promise of fresh air.

A booming thunderclap rang out, and the water vibrated once more around me. I kept swimming. My vision began to blacken around the edges, my head growing fuzzy. My lungs burned like blades stabbed in between my ribs, begging me to stop and rest.

Gritting my teeth from the exertion, I pumped my legs harder against the water, forcing my way upward to the surface. My muscles screamed in protest, but I couldn't turn back.

Something rough scraped against my leg as I kicked them out, pushing myself forward. I heard the faint shouts of the crew and saw the dark outline of the ship looming over me—I was nearly there.

I breached the surface and threw my head back, gulping in a few lungfuls of air before a wave pushed me back underneath the water once more. I surfaced again, gasping for air, and surveyed my surroundings. The storm clouds had parted during my time under the sea, and with the coming morning, the sky began to lighten. Gentle drops of rain peppered against my face, a lingering effect of the departing storm.

I screamed at the crew to hear me, but the sounds of the receding rain muffled my calls to them. Something hard and scaled brush against my feet, and I froze. The bellow of a crew member cut through the noise of the departing storm as a huge serpentine beast, half the length of the ship, breached the water. The creature slammed its gnarled head against the wooden side of *The Andromeda* before disappearing into the black abyss once more, the singular blue dorsal fin along its back visible on the surface of the water. This was no shark or whale. One of the sailors called out, voice ripe with fear.

"SEA WYRM!"

Panic consumed me as I worked to tread the rough water. Shouts from the crew and sailors rang out as they readied weapons. A huge ballista was wheeled to the front edge of the ship and affixed with giant iron bolts. All the monsters I'd been told about as a young girl were real, and the beasts of my nightmares hunted for sport.

I needed to get out of the water as quickly as possible.

It appeared the beast hadn't noticed my presence in the water, but I didn't want to wait around until it did. I swam as fast as I could and reached the side of the ship, but no one heard my pleas. I slammed my fists against the sides of the ship, screaming for help as I tried to stay upright against the waves crashing into the ship. The crew were nocking arrows, preparing some sort of powder and lighting it in flame, oblivious to my screams.

The wyrm attacked the ship again, this time from the stern, breaching the water and leaping onto the deck, its maw wide and full of forearm-sized sharp teeth. The weight of the wyrm's body tilted the ship toward it, and one of the sailors rolled into the beast's gaping mouth. With a sickening crunch, the wyrm sank its teeth into the sailor as his screams quieted. The wyrm had no arms or legs, but propelled itself forward on its blue belly, snapping its jaws at the remaining crew who were shooting arrows at it. The arrows bounced off the wyrm's heavily armored body and clattered to the ground.

Kera's voice rang out among the commotion, full of rage and authority.

"AIM FOR ITS UNDERBELLY!"

The whoosh of a dozen arrows being fired whistled through the air. I helplessly gripped the sides of the ship as it rocked violently in the water, and as the crew battled the sea beast.

One of the sailor's arrows found purchase. The wyrm bellowed in anger and slithered off the deck of the ship leaving a trail of crimson before the beast vanished into the water. Without the weight of the beast, the ship jolted and righted itself. The smell of blood filled my nose, sharp and tangy. Whether it was the man's or beast's, I did not know.

My nails bled as I tried to climb the side of the ship, but the wooden surface was covered in slippery algae that made it too slick to grasp. Rough barnacles sliced open my palms as I tried. I only made it a few handbreadths up the ship before crashing back down into the sea. My head bobbed under the water and got a mouthful of seawater as the wake threatened to pull me beneath the bottom of the ship. I scrambled against the ship in a desperate attempt to remain above the waterline before the wyrm realized I was within its reach.

"WHERE IS SHE?"

The Seelie King's voice boomed as the tail of the wyrm whipped next to me, slicing into the skin of my thigh and breaking my grip on the side of the ship. With a cry, I plummeted back into the water. In its bloodlust, the wyrm lurched at the ship, ramming its face where I had been clinging moments before. The sun began to rise above the horizon, lighting the gruesome scene in a pale pink and tangerine sky.

I splashed in the water, trying to draw the crew's attention while fighting my fatigued muscles. Time slowed as the wyrm turned its massive head toward me, its yellow reptilian eyes homed in on me as prey.

I frantically tried to swim further out, away from the monster. I refused to die like this. I had too many questions left unanswered, so much life I wanted to live. A heavy splash sounded in the water. I turned toward the noise, expecting to see the fangs of the sea wyrm readying to swallow me whole.

The wyrm was distracted. My eyes grew round at the sight.

"Hold your fire!" Kera shouted from the deck.

The Seelie King had jumped into the sea, his arms gripping the beast's thick neck and legs kicking in the water. Declan hoisted himself upright and onto the wyrm's scaled body. With a roar, the wyrm bucked, attempting to throw Declan off, but it lacked any limbs and was unable to reach the fae king with his mouth to tear into him. The wyrm shot down below the surface with Declan still holding onto its back. The surface of the water turned a dark red all around me. I cried out in despair for something I didn't quite understand.

The wyrm breached the surface once more, and let out a thunderous roar of pain, thrashing its head and creating waves in the water. Declan was still gripped around the wyrm now with his thighs, with a dagger in his hand repeatedly stabbing into the beast's thick neck. Dark blood spurted from the wyrm's wounds as it shrieked and thrashed its giant head trying to dislodge the Seelie King from its back.

I was transfixed watching the scene unraveling before me. Kera's voice called out to me from the main deck, above the carnage happening in the water.

"Swim toward the ship, Roselyne!"

She threw down a rope, and it made a small splash in the water. To my left, Declan still battled the wyrm, riding its back like a knight atop a monstrous stallion. Declan hoisted himself higher onto the wyrm, his face smudged with dark red blood. He stabbed into the beast's eyes, blinding it.

The sea wyrm let out a hideous shriek as dark torrents of dark blood streamed from its eyes. With one last-ditch effort, the wyrm shook its head and dislodged Declan off its body. He landed with a dull splash ten paces away and motionlessly slipped below the surface.

The wyrm turned to face me, the landmark where its eyes had once been now dark hollows. Thick rivulets of blood streamed down its face. There was no movement where Declan disappeared below the waterline.

The wyrm raised its head completely out of the water and stuck out its tongue, tasting the air. Its body coiled, and it began to swim directly toward me. The shouts of the crew were only a background buzzing in my ears. I needed to get out of the sea.

I kicked out my legs trying to swim toward the rope Kera had sent down for me, but no matter how much I moved my legs, I wasn't getting any closer to the ship. My arms and legs gave out, all my energy expended. I began to sink below the waves, barely able to tread enough to keep my head above the water. I gasped for air once more, my eyes on the large serpentine beast before me, poised to strike. Something rammed into my body and knocked me from the beast's trajectory. Strong hands wrapped around my waist and pulled me against a hard body.

Of no work of my own, I glided through the water and toward the rope Kera had thrown down. I worked to keep my eyes open, but made no sense of my surroundings. My legs burned, muscles screaming from overuse. My vision was blurry, the world spinning as if I was drunk on sweet wines. Black crept in from the edges of my vision, the dark shadows threatening to beckon me to unconsciousness.

My lungs rattled as I tried to inhale, unable to inflate fully, no doubt full of seawater. I found myself being carried in strong arms.

I concentrated and opened my eyes to see Declan's own golden gaze hardened on me, his full lips set in a thin line and his thick brows drawn in an expression of worry.

He cradled my body in his arms, held tight against his chest, as the crew and Kera helped to lift us out of the water. My neck extended back from sheer exhaustion, my wet hair covering my face like a veil.

Suddenly, the solid hardness of the deck was beneath my body, and I shuddered in relief. Someone threw a blanket over my shivering body as I faded in and out of consciousness.

In the water, the blinded sea wyrm roared in anger, and I let out a helpless whimper. Declan stood near my body, as if guarding me, holding a longer blade above his head, poised to strike. The sea wyrm shot toward us on the deck, using its sense of smell to guide its trajectory. Its man-sized jaws were wide open, prepared to make a quick meal of us all, sharpened teeth on display, and painted with blood. The scent of rot and death reeked from its throat, as it advanced straight for us.

Before the monster could sink its teeth into our flesh, Declan drove his sword through the roof of the beast's mouth and into its brain. Declan withdrew his sword with a grunt of effort, unsheathing it from the skull of the beast. Steaming, thick blood coated the blade as the beast roared one last time and fell backward into the water with a loud splash, and sank below the water, finally dead.

The Seelie King threw his sword to the ground and scooped me up into his arms. The sounds of the crew and Kera buzzed around me, but I could barely keep my eyes open.

"Mer," I said, voice hoarse and half-delirious. "Mer are real."

Declan frowned. "Is there a healer onboard?" he asked, voice ripe with worry.

"No," a crew member answered.

Declan held me closer to his chest.

The comforting scent of cedar and citrus filled my senses, and I breathed deeply for the first time since jumping into the sea.

13

ROSELYNE

Why was it so damn *cold?* I shivered as I floated through the air, weightless and carried by someone else. I nuzzled my face toward the warmth, found a hard chest, and breathed in the comforting and familiar scent.

Someone murmured softly against my hair. "Mer lured you into the Lyssan Sea?"

The fogginess of my brain momentarily lifted, and I opened my eyes, as I remembered the glowing woman beneath the sea. "She was kind...and confusing."

Declan clenched his jaw. "Mer speak in riddles, their meanings layered and ambiguous. Give no credence to whatever words she spoke."

The Seelie King held my limp body like a doll. My hair hung loose and damp, my soaked chemise see-through, and clinging against my skin. I trembled in his arms as a searing pain radiated from my thigh. The storm was over, and I couldn't help but stare at the fluffy clouds as Declan carried me away from the gruesome scene on the deck. I wondered how this was truly the same sky that wreaked havoc only a few minutes ago.

My vision slipped in and out of focus as we passed the main deck and below into the residential barracks. Declan gingerly placed me onto my bed, and I allowed myself to be swallowed by the softness of the mattress. My eyes fluttered closed as my body began to shake uncontrollably. I was cold and so *tired*. A low voice shook me from my near-sleeping stupor.

"Roselyne. Look at me," Declan commanded.

Too tired to argue, I opened my eyes to find Declan's face mere inches from my own, his intense golden eyes studying me, and breath hot on my skin. *Gods, he was attractive. Why did he have to be such an asshole?* I held his gaze. I'd never realized before that his irises weren't all gold. Within each bright golden disk there was another color also, but not nearly as apparent. I shivered again as fever swept over my body. His eyes stayed pressed on me, dark brows drawn together in worry.

"Silvery flecks," I said, half-deliriously, reaching my hand toward his face and running my fingers along his cheek.

My gaze traveled lower. Black stubble lined his jaw. He frowned and pressed a hand to my forehead. His thumb gently swept against my hairline, and I shivered. "You're burning up," he said, frown deepening. "Did the wyrm's tail scratch you?"

Yes, I wanted to scream out, but my voice failed me. My mouth wouldn't form the correct shape to make noise. The sensation of sandpaper coated my tongue and my throat burned when I tried to speak. Every inhale was like knives stabbing into my chest in quick succession. I shook, large tremors that rocked the bed. My eyes rolled back of their own accord, my body completely limp and at the mercy of whatever illness had consumed me.

The hard press of a body straddled my waist. The frantic grasping of large hands turned my head both ways before palming down to my chest and tearing away the remains of my nightdress, exposing my breasts and assessing my skin. There was nothing sensual in Declan's touch—he was clinical, efficient, and searching. The weight of his body left me and I mourned the loss of the grounding contact. My connection to this world was dwindling. I was simultaneously freezing and burning all at once, hardly able to keep myself conscious.

With a ragged inhale, I realized I was dying.

Declan's fingers wrapped around my ankles, his grip hard enough to bruise. He brushed his fingers up my shins, checking my skin, then moved on to my knees, giving the same rapid judgment. I was barely able to open my eyes and see the fae king, stooped over my body with a pained expression on his face.

His face was wild, brows turned downward with concentration. He chewed at his lip as his frenzied gaze roamed all over my skin.

Without hesitation, Declan pushed up the hemline of my chemise, making it gather around my waist to reveal the damage inflicted by the tail of the sea wyrm. My body was completely bare before him, but I didn't possess enough strength to be embarrassed by my nudity.

He grabbed me by the thighs, his fingers digging in slightly and making me wince.

In one fluid motion, he pushed my thighs apart. The air hit my skin, and I noticed the inexplicable sting of sliced skin marring my upper thigh.

He sucked in a breath. "The sea wyrm's tail is venomous," he said softly.

His finger pressed lightly to the skin of my thigh, almost reverently, near the crease where leg meets hip. I arched my back, reaching into the tiny slice of pleasure mixed among the terrible pain. Writhing and groaning, my hand fisted the first object within reach in an attempt to dampen the agony from the venom as it began to spread through my body.

My eyes rolled backward, and I closed them unwittingly as the pain became unbearable. The Seelie King bent my knees to better assess the wound, baring the flesh between my legs fully to him.

Electricity skittered through my veins at his touch, a welcome distraction from the wyrm's burning venom as it spread through my blood with every sluggish beat of my heart.

He lowered his face to my skin, and his hot breath exhaled against my sensitive flesh. The fae king placed his mouth against the deep cut inflicted by the beast. The rough stubble of his jaw brushed against the skin of my thigh, and I sucked in a sharp inhale. With his lips around the wound, he began to suck in slow rhythmic pulses, drawing the venom from my body.

I whimpered and bucked against the sting of pain, but his hands splayed against my thighs, holding me in place. As he sucked against my skin, the pain ebbed, and I was able to open my eyes and focus more easily. My breathing grew more regular and the blackness surrounding my vision receded as the pain ebbed away. I no longer needed to grip my fist for fear of screaming out in pain. I peered down the length of my body and realized I had hold of the fae king's hair between my fingers of one hand instead of the blankets. His dark wavy locks twisted throughout my fingers. I quickly released him from my hold, snatching my hand away, as I studied the vision of Declan on his knees before me.

Tiny pinpricks spread all across my skin at the sight. Declan raised his head from my thigh and met my gaze, lips swollen and red.

As if realizing the precariousness of our positioning, he

rose from his knees, looking anywhere but me. I snapped my legs shut and hastily lowered my ruined nightdress, despite knowing he'd seen all of me. My body continued to tremble, but the venom was gone. The Seelie King wiped his mouth with the back of his hand, turned, and silently left my room.

14

DECLAN

"This wasn't your fault," Kera said gently. "From what you say, it sounds as if Roselyne was lured beneath the Lyssan." Kera's hands gripped tightly against my shoulders, but I was shaking, all my energy used up from the rescue of the princess. My body was close to heaving, to collapsing.

Kera's voice was far away and tinny, despite being only inches from me. "Roselyne is fine. You saved her. We can still break the curse." Her words didn't help placate the guilt that swirled inside me. Roselyne was mine to protect, and under my watch had entered the Lyssan Sea during a storm, beckoned there by interfering mer or not. Everyone knew the sea was the Merfolk's domain—it would be unwise to provoke them while in their territory. Although I was angry, Roselyne said who she spoke to was kind, and I had enough enemies in my midst with no intention of creating more.

Kera and I sat beside each other on the small wooden bench of my cabin. She was curled up into the seat with knees tucked near her pointed chin. She took my fist in her hands and unfurled it slowly. My hand had been clenched so tightly, my nails cut through the skin.

"I was supposed to keep her safe," I said, burying my head into my hands.

"You did," Kera insisted.

She patted my back awkwardly, never having had to comfort me in this way before. There was a strange combination of emotions running through my mind. I needed the princess alive to serve my own purpose, but another part of me felt fear for her mortality when I saw her in the water, despite how insufferable she'd found me.

Kera shifted on the bench. "Your witch is safe, Declan." I nodded. "Your power can still be restored."

"Yes," I said. "That's what truly matters." I'm not sure who I was trying to convince, Kera or myself. I sighed. "The tail of the wyrm could have killed her, if not it's jaws," I said. "She could have *died*."

Kera's face softened. She squeezed lightly against my shoulders. Her voice came out in a whisper.

"But she didn't. Thanks to you, she lived."

In the hours after the attack, thoughts of Roselyne's safety had consumed me. Memories of her bleeding and feverish in my arms swam in my mind as I sat, waiting for us to set sail once again. Despite the damage done to the hull, the sailors repaired the ship in only a few hours. Captain Malobe swore we'd make it to the faelands only slightly later than previously expected.

I tried to convince myself I only cared about the princess' safety because she was the potential savior to my magic, but another thought coexisted at the back of my mind, unwelcome and persistent.

The unwelcome notion slammed into me like a fist to the

face. I shook it away. I had no time for *feelings*, especially for human princesses.

"The princess hates me," I said with another sigh. Too much rested on this fickle woman. "Am I fucking this up, Kera?"

She chewed her lip. "You did attack her father."

"He insulted me. I can't allow that."

Kera shrugged. "That's your prerogative, Declan. I know you'd prefer her agreeable."

She narrowed her dark eyes on me. *As always, Kera was correct, and I was an asshole.*

"You're still positive she's the one we need?"

"Absolutely. I still sense the magic in her veins pulsing and trying to escape."

"And she's definitely a human witch, not some sort of half-fae or—succubus?" I asked, thinking of the ways in which the Princess of Althene enraptured me so quickly.

Kera appeared to follow my line of thought and smirked. "Look at her. Look at her family. Yes—she's human."

I nodded, resolute. If news of my lessened power ever reached the Lords of the Seelie Territories, there'd surely be contenders vying to usurp me. I needed to charm this princess and make her my wife. My crown depended on it.

15

ROSELYNE

I've learned much about the faelands in the short time since I arrived.

Once we docked and exited *The Andromeda*, Kera pulled a half-filled glass vial of shimmering silver flakes from a hidden pocket in her pants and uncorked it. Instead of explaining to me what would happen next, she threw a handful of the substance over her, Declan, and me without a word.

The sensation of travel by the ash hadn't been entirely unpleasant, but instead felt as if someone looped rope around my midsection and yanked hard in every direction at once.

It worked though, and only after a few seconds of discomfort, my feet were no longer on the rocky shores of the port we'd docked at. We landed against green grass and soft earth before I collapsed to my knees, unaccustomed to the strange method of travel.

"We won't use the ash again," Declan said to Kera in a clipped tone. "Only to get her to the palace uninterrupted."

I stood, grumbling and dusting dirt from my skirt. For the first time, my eyes darted around and assessed the grounds of my new home. No squall of gulls or smell of the sea could be found. We'd traveled miles in only an instant.

"*What was that?*" I asked, breathless and full of the expected incredulity and wonderment of a human never exposed to fae magic.

Declan quickly stalked away before I'd even completed my question, leaving Kera and me alone on the expansive green yard of my new home.

"Lunar ash," Kera answered with a feline grin, slipping the near-empty small vial back into the pocket where she'd retrieved it. "Extremely expensive and difficult to procure." She paused. "Those who create it are gone, so the supply is finite." She patted her hip. "This is the last of Declan's reserves. It's only to be used only in cases of dire need—and to transport human princesses apparently. Come on, let's go get you settled. Gods knows I could use a bath."

She steered me toward a large golden palace and walked beside me. The sturdy earth underfoot was a welcome change after over a week rocking at sea. As we approached, I gazed upward and took in the view of my new home.

The exterior of the palace wasn't made of solid gold, as I'd originally thought. As we drew closer, I realized the walls were made of a shimmering white stone, with thick gold-colored rivulets shining in the sunlight and running through the exterior. Bright green ivy clung to the sides, scaling the height of the palace, with tiny white flowers blooming among the leaves. The Seelie Court's palace was smaller than the castle in Althene, but appeared warmer, and more welcoming. A large sun was carved into the front facade, its face watching as Kera and I walked through the entrance and into the courtyard. A set of curved double doors swung open, and I stepped into my new home. The interior of the palace was as ornate as I'd expected. The walls were painted an array of warm golds and reds, with suns and the occasional moon embossed on walls, carved into mantles and doors, and embroidered on tapestries lining the walls.

"The Seelie Court really appreciates the sun," I said as we passed some sort of sitting room with a massive golden glass orb in the center of the ceiling.

Kera grunted in affirmation, then led me up two flights of stairs and down a corridor toward a large intricately carved wooden door. She gestured toward the closed door.

"These will be your personal chambers until you are married, then you will be expected to share quarters with the Seelie King."

I swallowed hard.

"What do I do now?" I asked, glancing around the corridor.

Rows of similar doors lined the hallway. I'd grown up in a castle of similar elegance, but knew nothing of my new home except for the location of my bedchamber.

"Whatever you want," Kera replied unhelpfully. "I'll come by later and see how you've settled in."

With that, she strode away.

Tired of standing in the corridor, I swung open the door to my new rooms and shrieked.

A pretty fae woman sat on a small cream-colored sofa facing me. She stood and crossed over to me in one fluid movement, her blonde hair swishing as she did.

"Oh, wonderful! You've arrived!" she said with a smile. "It feels like I've been waiting for *hours*!"

She threw her arms around my shoulders and squeezed. I stiffened. She relaxed her grip and backed up a step, beaming at me with straight white teeth.

"I'm Essi," she said, bouncing on her heels. She spoke quickly, and I had to concentrate to keep up with the barrage of words as they tumbled out of her mouth in rapid succession. "I've volunteered to be your lady-in-waiting at the Seelie Court. The king, of course, has sent most of the staff and other courtiers away so you'd be more comfortable here."

She blinked her large brown eyes at me as if waiting for a response.

"Uhh, thank you," I replied, rubbing my arm. "The fae king sent everyone away?"

She waved her hand. "Mostly the courtiers. The king's brother's chambers remain empty, as he's away traveling. The spy, Kera, comes and goes, and only the best cooks and servants remain." She bounced animatedly as she spoke. "Everyone is ecstatic that you've joined us. It's high time the king married. *Everyone* agrees."

I nodded as she dragged me further into the room and sat me down on the sofa beside her. I glanced around the room and took in the fine furnishings. The fabric of the sofa was unlike anything I'd ever touched before—nearly liquid in softness. Essi continued talking.

"My father is Lord of the Western Seelie Territory," she said brightly. "I'd always dreamed about coming to live at the Seelie Court's capital. The city hosts the most lavish markets and traveling entertainment. You're going to *love* it in Solora. King Declan keeps the court small, but the grounds are lovely, and Solora always has festivals and parties to attend." She tossed her fluffy golden hair over her shoulder. "Your wedding will dwarf them all, though! I've already started planning everything! First of course, we'll have the customary fae betrothal ceremony. It will be the most extravagant—"

I coughed, interrupting my new lady-in-waiting.

"I'm sorry, Essi, I just really need to rest. It's been a long journey to get here." I smiled sheepishly.

The last thing I wanted to do was offend my first acquaintance at court. If fae courtiers were similar to their human counterparts, any affront could cause tension, but I needed to rinse the stink of the sea from my body. Essi didn't seem aggrieved whatsoever.

"I thought you'd want some alone time! I had a servant draw you a nice relaxing bath and perfume the water. The king wants to see you for dinner at sunset." She sighed dreamily. "It's *so* romantic."

A stone sank into my stomach and settled.

Dinner? Alone with the Seelie King?

Once Essi left my room, I climbed into the large copper bathing tub and sank below the water. My thoughts traveled back to the sensation of the Seelie King's mouth against my skin while I was feverish from the wyrm venom. The bathwater burned, singeing away all traces of Declan's mouth on my thighs. Gooseflesh broke out across my skin at the memory. I scrubbed myself clean in the scalding water, erasing all traces of my time at sea, and of the touch of the man who'd stolen me away.

After my bath, I padded out into the bedchamber, naked, forgetting I had no items of my own in this godsforsaken court.

Luckily, my closet was stocked with all sorts of colorful silk and satin gowns, and the simple pale blue dress I'd chosen slipped over me with ease. I cinched the waist. It was hotter in the Seelie Court than my home in Althene, and their fabrics lighter. The fae appeared to favor loose flowing garments with exposed skin as opposed to the thicker, more structured fashion I was accustomed to.

Without much else to do, I sat at the provided vanity and

applied cosmetics to my face in an attempt at normalcy. Despite my terrible time at sea, my skin glowed in the faelands, perhaps some remnant of the magic imbued in the air.

A gentle knock rapped against my door and I jolted in my seat. A glance outside the large window told me the sun hadn't set yet—it wasn't time to dine.

Had Essi come back in an attempt to primp me for dinner?

I groaned to myself. I'd need to have a talk with the fae woman about boundaries and my need for privacy.

The door swung open to reveal Kera, black hair damp and already fastened in a long loose braid, dressed in all black with a mischievous expression on her face. She stalked into my room before I could wave her in and shut the door with the heel of her boot once she was inside.

"Nice room," she said, glancing around my new bedchamber and rifling through the trinkets placed on the furniture before stopping to scan my body up and down. "Fae fashion suits you."

"I'd be flattered, but I'm afraid I didn't do any of the decorating myself—or choose the clothing," I said from my spot in front of the vanity as I blended dots of rouge across my cheeks.

Kera wiped a thin layer of dust off a decorative ceramic bowl and inspected her finger. "I'm seeing how you've settled in so far."

She plopped down on the sofa and outstretched her legs.

"I've got to leave on official court business, and I wanted to let you know that I'll be away for a few days." She closed her eyes for a moment. "Although I have an apartment in the city, I stay in the palace much of the time. Being on the council keeps me fairly busy, as well as all of Declan's other business he has me tend to."

"Sure," I said, not really knowing exactly what sort of other business she referred to.

"I assume you met the lady-in-waiting?" Kera asked. Her lip lifted at one corner.

"Essi? Yeah, she seems—nice." I thought of my own attendant back home, and a pang of homesickness hit me as I thought of Dove and my brothers. "How long does correspondence take between the faelands and the human kingdoms?" I asked.

"I don't know," Kera said with a shrug. "Declan paid handsomely to send his betrothal terms to your father. I would think simple letters would still take multiple weeks during storm season. There's not much reason for the continents to write to each other, and there aren't many ships willing to take the job. Fae do not openly trade with the humans." She smirked as she assessed me. "Until now, apparently."

I scrunched my face. "You told me you communicated with Declan while in Althene."

"Oh, well yes. We used a relic of Declan's family. Made it much easier."

I nodded, but didn't press further, and Kera didn't elaborate.

"Can I have some parchment and ink to write to my family back home?"

I'd been gone from home only a week, and I missed Dove more than I'd realized. I hadn't gotten to say a proper goodbye to her, and I'd likely never see her again. The Seelie King made sure of that when he ripped me away in the middle of the ball.

"Take it up with your husband-to-be," Kera replied, not meeting my eye.

I curled my hands into fists, ready to lash out when another knock sounded at my door.

"Come in!" Kera called out.

A broad muscular fae male stepped into the room and tentatively eyed the furnishings before his gaze snapped to Kera, completely outstretched on the sofa. The man was dressed in golden metal armor with a sword slung over his back. The same sun that was etched into the exterior of the palace was also embossed in the center of his chest plate. He was nearly as tall as Declan, but wider in the shoulders. His blond hair hung in loose clumps of waves that reached his chin. His gaze caught mine, and I was momentarily dazed by the deep blues of his irises. Upon seeing me, he knelt down on one knee and held a hand to his chest.

"My lady," he said, eyes blazing as I sat in stunned silence. He looked from his place kneeling before me, and I squirmed uncomfortably in my seat.

"I am Callum, Commander of the Daylight Guard and member of the king's royal council, and I—"

Kera's forceful snort through her nose interrupted Callum's spiel. The fae man frowned and snapped his head toward Kera with a question in his eyes.

"Callum, you're going to scare her with the formalities." Kera said.

Callum mumbled something where he stood and ran a hand through his blond hair before crossing his arms across his chest.

"How was I supposed to know? Dec said to treat her with respect," he whined.

A reluctant grin tugged at my lips.

Kera rolled her eyes. "She's not made of glass, treat her like you treat me."

I stood up from the couch. "Thank you, Callum. It's nice to meet you."

I curtsied and Kera snickered behind me. A quick glance out my bedchamber window told me the sun had begun to set. "I'm actually supposed to meet Declan for dinner right now, so if you could just tell me the direction of the dining room?"

"I'll escort you," Callum said, beaming. I swore if he was a dog, his tail would be wagging.

Kera also stood from her place on the sofa, exhibiting much more grace than I'd ever possess. "It's time for me to leave also." Kera tipped her head toward Callum. "Someone's got to work around here," she said, pulling me into a tight hug. Kera spoke low against my ear, although I'm sure with his fae hearing, Callum heard her words. "I've grown fond of you, human princess. Stay safe while I'm gone. I'll be back before the betrothal ceremony."

Kera slunk out of the room and I only then noticed the plethora of knives and bladed weapons strapped across her hips.

My heart thundered in my chest as I reeled from the last words Kera spoke to me as they echoed in my mind. *Betrothal ceremony.* I shook my head. My situation felt more akin to a lamb being led to slaughter than the lead up to a royal wedding. My shock must have been written all over my face because Callum spoke, snapping me from my trance.

"Don't worry, Princess Roselyne. Kera will be back soon."

Not wanting to correct Callum on the direction of my thoughts, I nodded blithely in his direction. He offered me an elbow. I slipped my arm through Callum's, feeling the cool bite of the metal armor against my skin as he led me out of my new bedroom and into the hallway.

16

ROSELYNE

The Seelie King's private dining room was—intimate. I'd expected ornate, perhaps even garish decorations considering the wealth of the Seelie fae and the rich, embellished architecture of the rest of the palace.

We sat at opposite ends of a plain table in uncomfortable silence as the palace cook, Pamylla, served our dishes before slipping out of the room by a doorway hidden in the walls. Roasted duck and some sort of root vegetable sat before me on a solid gold plate, staring at me. Although the food smelled as savory and rich as anything I'd eaten in Althene, my gut twisted uncomfortably. Declan speared some food on his fork and popped it into his mouth.

"Why am I here?" I asked, breaking the silence.

Declan chewed slowly, then swallowed.

"I thought you'd be hungry. I was under the impression humans eat as often and on a similar schedule as fae."

"No," I said, irritated. "Why am I *here?*" I waved my arms. "In the *faelands*?"

Declan blinked, then continued cutting into his meat as he

spoke. "Our meal has barely begun. Let's start with other things."

I narrowed my eyes, but Declan didn't shrink away from my stare, instead holding my gaze as if we were playing some game. He'd shaved his face since I last saw him, and vague memories of his stubble against my thigh had my cheeks heating.

I looked away, breaking eye contact. My foot tapped wildly underneath the table. Something in his words did not ring true, but what reason could he have to lie?

"It was you in the greenhouse," I said.

It wasn't a question, but I realized it sometime on the ship on the way to the faelands. The three-headed goddess hadn't intervened on my behalf with Duke Eugan, as I'd originally believed. It was the Seelie King's torturous magic that broke the duke's hand and sent him running in fear.

"Yes, it was," he said, solemnly.

"Why?"

He put down his knife and fork and laced his fingers together. "Why do you think?" he asked.

"How am I supposed to know?" I snapped.

"The man touched what is mine." I bared my teeth at him, but the Seelie King's words sent a shiver of electricity dancing down my spine. "Any other questions, Princess?"

"The marriage," I said, and one of his brows rose. "Is it some fae trick? Do marriages and betrothals mean something else entirely to the fae, and I'm actually to be a servant or one of many concubines you keep?"

He laughed, and the sound warmed me to my very core. I squirmed in my seat.

Declan leaned forward. "Do you feel like a servant?" He shook his head, and still-damp dark tendrils of hair fell into his eyes before he pushed them back. "No, I assure you, Roselyne. Marriage is the very same in the faelands as the human kingdoms. I will take only one wife—you." Nervous flutters filled my stomach.

Declan continued, "As my future queen, I will answer any of your questions and grant you anything in my power to make you more comfortable."

"Can I have ink and parchment to write to my family?"

"No," he answered, and my heart sank.

"You said—"

"Correspondence by letter is not secure over such a great distance, and I can't have you inadvertently spreading fae secrets. You can ask me for anything else."

I slumped in my seat, dejected. We chewed in silence for a few moments and I sipped at my glass of pale blue faerie wine. It was sweeter than anything I'd enjoyed in Althene, and immediately rushed to my head, filling me with the sort of boldness I wouldn't normally possess.

"Why did you kill your father?" I blurted out.

"Brave of you to ask," Declan said. "Most assume it was a thirst for power, and it serves me to allow them to believe that."

He did not elaborate further, and I didn't push for answers.

"Do you have other family?" I asked.

"My mother died long ago," he said, "And my younger brother, Sloane, is traveling the faelands currently, no doubt leaving a trail of broken hearts in his wake." Declan shook his head. "Tell me about your family."

I crossed my arms over one another. "You planted your spy at my father's court. You already know about them."

"I want to hear it in your words."

I scowled, but acquiesced.

"Well, you *met* the king," I said.

Declan smirked, no doubt thinking of how he'd nearly killed my father.

"Briefly, yes." Humor danced behind his golden eyes.

"My mother died in the birthing bed with me. I never got to know her." I sighed, gesturing toward the mis-colored hair on either side of my head that had plagued me all my life. "The midwives say I was born unlucky—under a full moon, my mother dying as I was wrenched from her body." I twirled the silver strands of hair in my fingers. "Although my father forbade them to do so, the people whisper that I wear this as a token of the three-headed goddess' disfavor against me." I sighed. "Dye doesn't cover it," I added, then changed the subject with a shake of my head. "I have two older brothers, Corbin and Wallace. Corbin's engagement ball is what you so lovingly ruined."

Declan sipped at his own wine.

"I think we made his engagement ball more interesting." He smiled. "The—*distraction* certainly gave those powdered lords something to talk about for a few weeks, although I do regret not getting to make your other brother's acquaintance as well."

"There's also Dove," I said, my heart sinking. "She's not my sister, she's my friend, but she's the best person I know and who I'll miss most. She's—joy personified." My eyes burned.

"She sounds wonderful," Declan replied softly.

I drained my glass, letting the fae wine calm my nerves in preparation for what I asked for next. I leaned forward in my seat, ready for the argument.

"I want to fight," I said.

The sentence slipped from my lips in one breath—something I'd never been allowed in Althene. The excuses I'd heard from my father my entire life bound around in my memory, clinking together.

It wasn't proper, not fit for a lady of my station. There was no need. I had knights and soldiers to protect me. I'd had enough of relying on others for protection. I was tired of empty words. No one protected me when the Seelie King came for me and plucked me from my comfortable life in Althene.

"I don't think you'd win if we fought," Declan countered.

"Not *you*," I whined with a roll of my eyes.

Declan smiled at that, and a small dimple appeared on one cheek.

Gods, he was attractive. I shook my head slightly to clear it.

This faerie wine worked quickly. My head was spinning pleasantly, the periphery of my vision slightly fuzzy and out of focus.

"I want to *learn* to fight. If I'm to live in this world of magic and power, I want the ability to defend myself." I jut out my chin, defiance coursing through my body. "You saved me from the wyrm, Declan—but I want the opportunity to save myself."

He nodded. "Consider it done. I have some business to tend to first, but we'll begin lessons soon enough."

I leaned back in stunned silence. At that moment, I realized Declan would give me anything I wished for—within reason, it seemed.

"I'm truly just to be your wife and queen?" I asked again, narrowing my eyes. "To live a life of luxury and be free to pursue whatever activities I desire?"

Declan nodded. "What sorts of activities do you desire, Princess?"

The huskiness in his voice made my breath hitch.

"Reading, mostly," I answered. Declan stared at me, and I

shifted uncomfortably under his molten gaze. "Essi mentioned the city hosts many events and entertainment during holidays. I'd enjoy seeing troupe shows and holiday festivals."

"I'll ask you to have a guard when you travel to the city, due to your high profile. You're particularly...*valuable* to me."

I nodded, having endured similar rules in Althene.

"And for reading—the palace boasts a quite impressive library. I could take you there if you'd be interested in seeing it."

My mouth fell open.

"I would love that."

Declan's returning smile transformed his face into a thing of beauty, bringing warmth into his stone-like features.

One last thought plagued my mind.

"When is the wedding to be held?"

"The first snowfall usually arrives in my court in the weeks leading up to Yule. We'll marry within the next few months, sometime in autumn to make sure we meet our deadline," Declan replied, dabbing his mouth with a napkin. "That's what was agreed, and what the treaty demands."

A few months.

In the human kingdoms, no longer than one week was needed to organize and perform wedding ceremonies, no matter how lavish the event. For the wealthy, flowers, food, and entertainment were always available.

"Why so long a wait?" I asked.

"Mere months are considered hurried by fae standards. Some may think it scandalous, but it's necessary in our case." He gestured to me. "I'm due to deliver on my promise to your father before winter arrives in earnest, as was agreed. Fae betrothals take time and are steeped in history and tradition, so we can't dawdle."

"Waiting a few months is quick?" I asked. Corbin had only announced his intention to wed Ariadni a few days before my own betrothal was announced, and his engagement ball happened less than a week later.

Declan straightened in his seat.

"Fae live for millennia. A few months are a mere blip in time to those who tread near immortality. Fae betrothals have taken as long as decades to come to fruition." He leaned back in his chair and placed his hands behind his head. "Are you that eager to jump into my bed, Princess?"

The familiar flush of crimson swept across my cheeks. The Seelie King was teasing, but hit too close to the truth. Truth I wasn't willing or ready to face.

"No!" Despite my verbal dissent, a contradicting heat curled low in my belly at the prospect of his hard body pressed against mine. I swallowed. "Only looking forward to having it be over and done with," I said, a touch too high. "Goodnight, Declan." The chair legs squeaked against the tile as I abruptly pushed my chair back and stood, wanting to be anywhere except this room with him, the air between us thick and suffocating.

"Sit back down," he ordered.

I bristled, but lowered myself back to my seat with a glower.

"What do you *want*?" I asked, irritated.

Wanting any excuse to avert my eyes from the intensity of the Seelie King's honeyed gaze, I stabbed at one of the plated vegetables with a fork, pretending it was a particularly and annoyingly attractive fae male. Declan's voice rumbled low, sending shivers across my skin.

"Our conversation is far from over, Princess. You asked a

question at the beginning of dinner that I have not yet answered."

I straightened in my chair, suddenly interested, peeking up from my nearly full plate of food.

"I asked why you brought me to the faelands—why you chose me as a bride," I said tentatively.

"Dear Princess," he said with a feline grin. "I brought you to the faelands to marry you for one very important reason." I sucked in a breath as I leaned in even closer to him.

"Why?" I asked.

My heart beat wildly in my chest as I waited for his answer.

"There is witch blood in your veins."

17
DECLAN

I waited for Roselyne's answering retort, but none came. She was finally silent, without some snappy quip readied on her tongue. Roselyne leaned back in her chair and exhaled sharply, her eyebrows creased and lips down turned. Seconds ticked by, and my unease grew.

"Say that again," she finally said.

"You are a witch. You possess *magic*." Roselyne paled. "Kera sensed it while attending your brother's betrothal tournament and reported it to me immediately. She possesses an aptitude for this sort of thing and is extremely perceptible to others' gifts."

"Oh," Roselyne said quietly.

Her expression was unreadable. My eyes flickered to her full mouth as she chewed on her bottom lip.

"How is that possible?" she asked. I watched as her fingers ticked upward and lightly touched the shell of her ears, before lightly twisting in her hair. "I'm human. Humans don't have magic."

"Most do not," I agreed. I pressed my mouth into a firm

line. "I believe you have witch blood. It's the only magic humans possess and incredibly rare. Witches are thought to be…gone."

"But would that mean my parents were witches?" She scrunched up her face. "I never knew my mother, but my father knows nothing of magic. No one in Althene does."

"It's possible you inherited the gift from your mother's side. Witch blood is passed down through either maternal or paternal line in humans. It's possible that some of the witches" —I paused—"*fled* the faelands long ago and settled among the human kingdoms."

Her eyes were wide, lips slightly parted as she sat across from me, absorbing the information.

I was surprised she was taking this news so well. "We aren't exactly sure how…but once I saw you and knew what to feel for, I sensed the power within you too."

I stood and paced the room, the nervous energy bounding within me, not allowing me to sit still any longer. I needed her to understand the magnitude of what she was—the powers she possessed. "Witches have distinct abilities fae-kind do not." I huffed a nervous laugh and watched as her face scrunched up again, fighting against the overwhelming desire to place a kiss against her nose. I shook away the interrupting thought.

"What abilities?" Her voice was small but unwavering. Her hands were folded neatly across her lap as if she had asked something as mundane as the weather.

I inhaled, unsure where to begin. "Some witches possess the sight, the ability to see the future and dream-walk, but only the extremely powerful. Witches also make use of runes and use them for conjuring, binding, and in the creations of elixirs and potions. They're able to use their magical knowledge to extend their own lives and live near an age with the fae." She nodded, and I continued, "All witches have natural aptitude with herbs and plants. Animals and magical creatures are drawn to witches and are more apt to trust them. Many say witches can see through to the very soul of a person and judge them on sight with total accuracy."

Roselyne cocked her head to the side and a spill of honey-colored hair fanned out around her shoulders. She pursed her lips.

"I think you've got the wrong princess," she said, "I've killed every plant I've ever tried to grow—and I haven't tried much because I don't care for it. I only spent time in the greenhouse because of Dove." She slumped in her chair and shook her head slightly. "As for animals?" She snorted. "A few stray cats seemed to take to me, but no more than anyone else who feeds them table scraps." She paused for a moment, then added almost wistfully, "And I am not a good judge of character." I didn't ask her to elaborate further.

Roselyne stood from her chair and crossed the room, facing the large window overlooking the grounds. Night had fallen completely, veiling the palace grounds in shadows. The trees at the edge of the property rustled in the breeze as a wolf howled somewhere within the forest. I crossed over to stand behind Roselyne, keeping distance between our bodies. She needed to understand, to accept this reality. I placed a hand on her shoulder, and she didn't flinch away from my touch. The magic trapped in her veins called to me, reaching out, but locked behind some barrier inside of her.

"Even now, I can sense the power inside of you. It's alive and wants to escape. It just needs to be accessed fully."

She shrugged, unconvinced and wary of my words. Why would she believe the Ruthless King? I was the bastard that bought her betrothal and stole her away from a home and life she enjoyed, but she still didn't know the entire truth. She needn't know about my curse—it would only further complicate things.

"There's more to know about witches," I said.

She turned to face me and arched an eyebrow in response, waiting.

"Witches are called world-walkers. They're wardens."

She frowned. "I don't understand."

"There are other realms, parallel to our own." She nodded slowly, trying to grasp my meaning. "Where beasts and demons and all sorts of monstrosities of nightmares live and thrive. Witches possessed the knowledge to conjure those beasts and harness their power and kept it closely guarded." She shivered and leaned toward me, enraptured. "Don't you see? Once I knew you were a witch—one so easily accessible—I couldn't allow anyone else to obtain you. It'd be reckless. Only Kera, Callum, and I know the truth of what you are. They are my royal council and the only ones I fully trust to know the truth. You mustn't tell anyone else."

Her beautiful face contorted into a sneer, and irritation rolled off her in waves.

"Let me understand this, Declan. You are marrying me *not* for political affiliations or physical attraction, but because if someone else married me first and realized I was a witch, it could be used *against you*?"

"Yes," I said in a clipped tone. "I couldn't have anyone else claim you for themselves when they could easily use your power against others."

Of course, I'd felt an immediate physical attraction to Roselyne, but that's not why I originally set out to marry the last witch. In truth, at that moment, I wanted nothing more than to cup her face between my hands. I longed tell her that despite my obligation to keep her power out of the hands of others, I desired her.

I wanted her lips on mine and wanted to revel in the soft press of her body. I took a step backward, creating space between us. Her brow furrowed again, creasing the skin between her eyebrows. Her mouth curved upward.

"That's not very romantic of you," she said, all irritation removed from her expression.

Some sort of primitive urge ripped a low growl from my throat.

"Do you desire more romance from me, Princess?"

Pink swept across her cheeks. She pressed her full lips into an unnaturally thin line and narrowed her eyes.

"No."

I sucked in a breath, and disappointment ricocheted through my chest.

"Very well, then."

She turned her head away, clearly uncomfortable by the turn in our conversation. I tracked the movement as she tucked a strand of hair behind her delicate rounded ear and had the most inane urge to run my own hands through her hair. I shook my head to clear it.

Get it together, Declan. She's the answer to breaking the curse, nothing more.

"Do you intend to use my magic to harm others?" Roselyne's voice betrayed her nerves, wobbling slightly as she spoke. My stomach twisted. She thought I was a monster—and why shouldn't she? In the past, I'd done exactly what she feared—used the witches' power for myself—and I was paying dearly for it now. I fought the urge to bury my head in my hands as guilt clawed at me.

I shook my head. "No, of course not. I decided to marry

you to keep you and the rest of my kingdom safe. There are no enemies that I cannot handle on my own. You've seen what I am capable of."

"If Kera sensed my power, and you can also, what's stopping anyone else? Am I to be a target for this—power?"

"Your magical signature was obvious to Kera because you were surrounded by other humans. In the faelands, magic is thick in the air, a constant all around us. Among the fae population, you'll blend in and appear an ordinary human."

She chewed at her bottom lip as she absorbed the information. I could nearly see the cogs turning inside her mind as she took all this information in stride. Roselyne lived in Solora now and would be Seelie Queen soon. She'd only benefit from knowing how our world worked.

"All fae share certain common traits as a race. We live longer, heal faster, and need less sleep, aside from that and certain physical characteristics—we are not so different from humans." She parted her lips as if to speak, but seemed to think better of it and closed her mouth, nodding toward me to continue. "Some fae are granted different abilities in addition to the racial traits we all share. Elysian gifts." She nodded. "These are passed through the family line. Kera's transfiguration into her feline form and my powers of torture are examples."

She exhaled and visibly relaxed.

"Can I learn to tap into the power within me? This witch blood? Would I have other powers—elysian gifts as you and Kera do?" she asked.

My brows lifted. She'd acclimated quickly to the idea of wielding magic and being—something more than purely human.

"Of course, you may," I said. "But it's going to be wild, untrained magic."

She leaned in closer to me and whispered in my ear, voice laced with seduction.

"I like a challenge." My cock stiffened. Roselyne smirked, as if sensing how the blood in my body had rerouted below my waistband. "Maybe I'll be more powerful than you," she said, her voice dripping with honeyed sweetness.

"Maybe you will be," I agreed.

I watched her breath hitch in her chest. There was a wire between us, pulsing and alive, and I wanted to tug against it and pull her to me. Roselyne shook her head, and her hair spilled around her shoulders.

Her mask of strong indifference slipped, and I saw her fragility for what it was. Her lip quivered. Behind all the quips, jests and shows of strength—Roselyne's life changed completely in a matter of days. I'd put too much on her too quickly.

"Hey," I called softly, "everything's going to be fine. I know this isn't the life you envisioned, but I promise—"

Roselyne's wracking sob interrupted my sentence. I watched, horrified, as tears tracked down her cheeks, and she slapped her hand to her mouth with a crazed giggle.

The dam inside of her had finally burst. The tears kept flowing, streaming down her cheeks and mixing with the black she'd used to line her eyes. I didn't know what to do or how to react. I wrapped my arms around her and pulled her against me. I ran the pad of my finger through a tear on her cheek, stopping it in its tracks. She buried her face in my chest as tears silently slid down her face, soaking into my tunic.

I told her of her magic too soon. How else could she have reacted? Roselyne pushed away from me and wiped at her face, worsening the makeup around her eyes. I fought the urge to smile—to press my lips to hers in an attempt to comfort her. *As if anything I could do would grant her solace.*

"Sorry," she mumbled, embarrassed. "Everything hit me all at once. And although I know I could marry someone much worse—" She lifted her mouth into a weak smile and shook her head, changing the trajectory of her sentence. "I wasn't given a choice in this, and it's a bitter truth to swallow. To have choice taken away, to be told I possess *magic*."

"I am not your enemy," I said. I reached toward her and ran my fingers through her hair, as I'd longed to do since I met her. She shivered but didn't move away. Roselyne's eyes fluttered closed, and her long lashes fanned against her cheeks. "I will *never* hurt you," I vowed.

The thought of harming Roselyne was abhorrent. Something inside of me detested the idea, and I wasn't entirely sure it was because I needed her to break my curse. In the short time we'd known each other, Roselyne had somehow clawed her way into my heart and nested there. I cared about her, and the thought wasn't as difficult to reckon with as it should have been.

We stood there together, not speaking, soaking in the charged silence. My hands snaked around her waist. Hers found their way to my chest, gripping the material of my clothing in her balled fists. She appeared to notice our closeness, but once again did not back away. Her gaze dipped to my mouth before meeting my eyes.

"How can I ever trust you?" she asked in a hushed whisper. "I don't even know you."

"I'll have to earn your trust. But I will," I said.

That was a promise.

If it was the last thing I'd ever do, I'd earn her trust, her respect, and if I was ever to be so lucky—her affections. A strange sensation tugged in my chest, urging me to close the gap—bring my lips to hers—but I ignored the compulsion. I was done brooding and fighting my growing feelings for Roselyne, but I'd allow her to guide if our anything between us progressed.

"I don't know why, and it's probably a terrible idea...but I want to—to believe you," she whispered through half-lidded eyes.

Her full lips were slightly parted and pink, begging to be kissed. I wanted desperately to feel them against my own. Our faces were so close. I felt her breath against my skin as she exhaled. Her pupils were huge, with only a small ring of her bright green irises still visible. Every point of contact between our bodies sent jolts of electricity pinging through me, begging for action. She cocked her head to the side and closed her eyes. This was it—finally, I'd be able to taste her.

She pulled away, and I felt like I'd been doused in water.

18

DECLAN

I still didn't know where I stood with the princess. Most times Roselyne seemed inclined to kill me, and other times as if she wished to kiss me.

I was a warrior—the Seelie King.

Ruthless.

I was not prepared for the complexities needed to navigate my burgeoning affection for the fledgling witch. She was stunning tonight, beneath the tall ceiling of the library, browsing the shelves in her green dress.

"This is amazing," she said breathlessly.

Roselyne's eyes widened as she took in the glory of the Seelie Court Library. Half underground, the library didn't appear as imposing as it truly was from its exterior. The library stood as a relic of the Seelie fae's past, with a large domed ceiling decorated with a mosaic of the sun rising in triumph over a retreating night sky. Seeing it through Roselyne's eyes for the first time put its grandness in context, and I swelled with pride thinking of the rich history of the Seelie fae.

"I've never seen anything like this before. This is incredible."

Roselyne threw her arms around my waist, and I was immediately aware of every place her body touched mine, leaving searing marks beneath my skin. I indulged for a moment and allowed myself to rest my chin atop her head. Her caramel curls tickled against the skin of my face. Roselyne had only been at the Seelie Court for less than a week, but her presence was comforting, like coming home after a long journey away. I didn't allow myself to wonder if her allure was courtesy of the prophecy that bound us together, or something else entirely.

"Of course," I mumbled. "This is your home now." I smoothed my shirt down, suddenly uncomfortable. Should I have told her about the curse and the prophecy?

Roselyne absentmindedly twisted a stray thread on her skirt as she walked through the narrow aisles of shelves. I trailed close behind, dutifully holding every book she plucked from its place.

"Where is everyone?" she asked as she navigated around a bend in the shelves.

Our footsteps echoed throughout the space.

"The Book Keepers go home at night. We're alone." She turned and faced me, euphoric and bright faced. I'd never seen her this happy. I wanted more. She grinned, her green eyes sparkling in the pale glow of the everlight orbs spaced every few feet around the library. I sighed at the show of ancient magic lingering in this place—the evidence of Seelie power at its peak, placed by powerful fae centuries ago. Perhaps soon, I would be capable of such magic and fill the court with the glimmering everlights in celebration once more.

"I've never seen this many books in one place." She sighed

dreamily. "The library in Althene is mostly full of war strategy." She crinkled her nose, and I had to stop myself from leaning forward and pressing my lips against it. *What is wrong with me?* "My father didn't think it necessary to keep the more frivolous accounts of history or fiction. I had to go into the city and buy those particulars for my own personal collection."

She frowned for a moment, then kept her browsing, handing me another book.

"What genre do you particularly enjoy?" I asked.

She paused for a moment, her step faltering.

"Romance," she said simply, before turning to walk away and down the next aisle. I didn't miss the pink tinge sweep across her cheeks.

Her finger lingered on a thick leather-bound book before plucking it from the shelf. She turned it over in her hands, and I craned over her shoulder to see what she'd chosen.

A Succinct History of Seelie and Unseelie Fae.

This book was old, the silver and gold intertwined gilding nearly faded, and the black leather of the cover worn and thin. This book certainly predated the Unseelie fae's eradication that occurred a century ago.

Roselyne thumbed through the crumbling pages quickly before returning it to the shelf. She turned and continued down the aisle, tracing her fingertips along the spines of the books as she passed them. Once more, she turned abruptly and faced me. My eyes dipped to her mouth, where she chewed her lower lip.

"What happened to the Unseelie fae, Declan?" she asked.

"They're gone now. You needn't fear them any longer."

"Kera mentioned them to me when—when I was on the ship. She said I should be grateful it was the Seelie, not the Unseelie who deigned to take me away. Where are they now?"

THE CURSE OF THE SEELIE KING

"They're all dead."

Her bright eyes went round, eyebrows creasing. I itched to kiss her worry away, to soothe her fears. The concept was jarring and unfamiliar.

"Do not pity the fate of the Unseelie fae, Princess. They were a perversion created by Umbrath, God of Death, solely to torment and antagonize the Seelie. They ruled their territory as monsters, burdened with an insatiable thirst for blood, cursed to hunt the lands and sate themselves with the killing of others to gain power. In the lands of the Unseelie, it is said the rivers ran red with the blood of their victims. It is a blessing from the divine goddess Lux that they exist no longer."

She gasped softly, and I heard the accelerating of her heart.

I'd scared her.

"They're gone now," I repeated softly.

She nodded slowly, then resumed browsing the shelves, pulling out books at random.

She chose two thinner books sitting side by side on the dusty shelf and pulled them out for inspection. I read the faded titles over her shoulder, my chest bumping against her back. She'd chosen *Siobhan: The Star-Marked* as well as *The Two Kings,* both familiar fae myths. She handed them both to me, and I added the books to the ever-growing stack I carried under my arm.

Roselyne also thumbed through a copy of *The Power of Herbs: Witching Basics* and *Greatest Achievements of Fae Women in the Last Millennia* before piling them atop her other chosen books.

"Finding inspiration for yourself as a fledgling witch and future queen?" I asked as I observed the newest titles. Her posture stiffened, and from my vantage point behind her, I could tell she was pissed.

"I'll have you know, Declan—"

She spun around with a snarl, no doubt ready with a scathing retort on her lips, but her words cut off abruptly.

Her head was at my chest level, and barely any space separated our bodies. She exhaled.

The aisle was narrow in this part of the library, my shoulders only had an inch of clearance on either side.

She craned her neck up toward me. I'd never noticed the pale dusting of freckles that swept across the bridge of her nose in tiny constellations.

Still holding her stack of books, I lowered my face closer to hers.

"For what it's worth, I'm looking forward to all the good you'll do as queen, Princess."

I watched in glee as tiny pinpricks spread all over her skin. She shivered. From this distance, I could smell the jasmine scent of her skin and hair, and I wanted to bury my face and become lost in it. I wished to be possessed wholly by this woman.

We hung there in stasis for a moment, neither wanting to be the first to acknowledge the crackling energy between us—to admit to the attraction, to accept the possibility of rejection. Whatever invisible thread connected us was very real, pulled taut, so close to snapping.

I chose vulnerability.

I released my grip on the stack of her chosen books, ancient as they may be, and they clattered to the floor, the sound echoing in this empty chamber of the library. Roselyne didn't react. As still as carved stone, she watched me, pupils dilated.

With the restraint of a better man, I splayed a hand across her abdomen and waited. Roselyne leaned into my touch and extended her neck, granting me access to the pale skin of her throat, her hair spilling across her back in gentle waves.

My lips brushed across the delicate skin, but never landed. Roselyne shivered, her eyes drawn closed. A small sigh escaped her lips.

My hands ached to touch her more, to explore every curve and dip of her body, but I couldn't rush fate.

She was the answer to breaking my curse. Our inevitability was written in the stars, our futures intertwined. I would wait as long as necessary for her.

I cradled her cheek in my palm and marveled at the softness of her skin. Her eyes opened, blazing with an intensity I hadn't seen before. I stilled—waiting, not wanting to push her too far, working to respect the boundaries she'd built between us.

Her lips parted, and the next word she spoke was my ruin.

"Yes," she whispered, and for the first time, our lips drew together.

19

ROSELYNE

Declan pressed his lips tenderly to mine for the first time, and I surrendered to him. It was a gentle touch, exploratory and asking for permission.

I'd refused to admit my attraction for the Seelie King because of who and what he was, but I would deny myself no longer. *It's only a physical attraction.* My own body starved for his. I snaked my fingers through his hair, deepening the kiss and inciting him further.

My back slammed against the shelves, and he caged me within his arms. I kissed him back with all the anger, fear, and betrayal I'd felt since our betrothal was announced. Books dropped onto the floor all around us, as if they were leaping from the shelves in an attempt to flee our impassioned embrace.

His fingers twisted against the fabric of my bodice, causing a soft moan to escape my lips.

That excited him further. I should have been terrified, but where fear formerly lived inside my body, there was now only an electric, pulsing need between my legs.

My lips parted as his tongue darted into my mouth, smooth and practiced. I couldn't help the sounds that escaped from me, small whimpers and groans from finally experiencing his body against mine. A considerable swell of hardness pressed into me from beneath his pants.

Our limbs were a tangled mess as we clawed, stroked, and palmed down each other's bodies. As he nipped and kissed at my lips, I stroked over the planes of his broad chest and shoulders before moving my hands down his abdomen toward his trousers.

I hadn't been intimate with anyone since Nolan, but my skin was flushed, and wetness pooled inside of me. *Who else better than the male I was expected to marry?*

I pawed at the laces of his pants. He caught my wrist in his hand.

"Not yet," he purred as he pressed another gentle kiss to the corner of my mouth.

The King of the Seelie Fae knelt before me, his face level with my hips, and regarded me as if I was a goddess. I shivered with anticipation.

"I want to savor you."

I was absolutely panting for him, my core pulsing with a relentless need I knew only he could sate. His expression was solemn as he slowly hitched up my skirt and spread my legs apart, baring my soaked panties to him. My legs trembled as he pressed a finger against the wet fabric, barely grazing against my swollen clit, and groaned. His own arousal only spurned mine further.

Nearby footsteps echoed against the marble floor, breaking through the haze of lust suspended over us. Declan stood abruptly, lowering my skirt as he did. My chest heaved, my nipples still hard against the fabric of my bodice, my core still dripping and unsatisfied.

My mind spun wildly, thinking of what we'd done, the line we'd crossed. I chewed my lip, thinking of how much further I'd *wanted* it to go.

Declan cleared his throat. We both stooped over, knocking into each other in a bumbling attempt to retrieve my chosen pile of books and shelve the ones knocked from their assigned places during our harried outburst of passion. Our eyes did not meet as we worked in strained silence. I apologized in my mind to the Book Keepers who'd have to correct my ministrations.

"Oh!" someone exclaimed as they rounded the corner where Declan and I knelt in the aisle, our clothes rumpled and hair mussed.

My eyes went round.

"Essi?" I asked, squinting into the dim space where she stood, trying to be sure. Essi was the last person residing in this palace I'd expect to see in the library. She held one large book in her small hands. Some runic symbol I didn't recognize was carved into its cover. She clutched it against her chest, clearly embarrassed by what scene she'd almost stumbled upon.

"Roselyne! I didn't see anything!" she assured me as she rocked on her heels and looked anywhere but at my flushed face. "I wasn't expecting anyone in the library this late."

I coughed. "I was just leaving," I said as brightly as I could muster.

I swiped the books from Declan's arms, grimacing. He recoiled, and my throat tightened at the rejection.

I cleared my throat, turning back to face my lady-in-waiting, but Essi was already gone. Her light footsteps faded away in the direction of the library entrance.

Declan and I were alone once more.

"I should go," I said quickly.

"Let me walk you to your room."

"No, that's okay—I know the way now."

I needed no pity from the Seelie King. I turned and stalked away, unsure of why tears began to fall.

20

ROSELYNE

I laid in bed trying to sleep, but memories of the kiss in the library kept me wired, awake and aching all over again. I'd slipped my hands between my legs to relieve myself from the coil of tension. Even after I reached my climax fantasizing of how far things could have escalated if Essi hadn't interrupted, my body still throbbed in protest, unsatisfied, and sleep evaded me.

I spent a few minutes flipping through the pages of one of my newest books in an attempt to inspire sleep. A light tapping came from my window, startling me from my engrossment as I read through *The Power of Herbs: Witching Basics*.

I shut the book and crossed over to the third floor window. A black falcon stood on the ledge, assessing me with beady yellow eyes. He squawked at me through the glass before tapping angrily once more with his beak. Only then did I notice the letter attached to one of his legs in an emerald-colored ribbon. I slid open the window, and the bird jumped inside my bedchamber with an irritated chirp.

"Sorry," I said to the bird. "I didn't know."

It ruffled its feathers as if I offended it and chirped again at me, extending a leg.

"Oh, okay," I said as I unfastened the ribbon. The bird nipped lightly at my fingers as I unfurled the small piece of paper.

Roselyne,
I'll be back tomorrow morning.
We'll begin your witch-studies together.
Meet me at midday in the palace library.
-Kera

I threw the letter down on my bed with an excited squeal. Kera was coming back.

I entered the library at midday and was slammed in the face with the memory of what Declan and I had done between the aisles.

"Over here!" Kera called from the center of the library.

"*Shhh*," another voice replied from far away. The infamous Book Keepers, undoubtedly.

I navigated my way to the rows of tables lining the perimeter of the large library and found Kera standing at the center of the room beneath the large mosaic sun on the ceiling.

"Follow me," Kera said, and I did.

Kera led me further into the library, into an alcove hidden away beneath an arched canopy of books. The alcove was small, about the size of Declan's intimate dining room, the walls and ceiling made entirely of books with one small table in the center. Soft orbs of everlight flanked either side of the entrance, giving off enough light to read by. Kera took a seat at the table and waved me inside.

"There's a silencing charm around this hideaway. Ancient magic placed millennia ago, similar to the everlights on the walls." My gaze drifted to the heatless flames lining the walls of the library, emitting their impossible torch-like light. Magic would never cease to amaze me. "We can speak loudly here, and none outside will be apt to hear it. We'll be away from the prying eyes and ears of the Book Keepers. Not that they'd be interested in what we're doing. Book Keepers' only love is for the texts they tend—still, it's best word didn't get out about *what* you are."

"A witch," I said.

"Yes," Kera confirmed before sitting on the small plush bench. I slid in beside her.

The alcove was cozy, filled with the comfortable scent of ancient ink on paper. Inlaid within the library, books lined the walls and ceilings in an arch, surrounding us in a cocoon of paper and leather-bound books.

"I'm glad you're back, Kera."

"I told you I wouldn't miss the betrothal ceremony. I arrived back to Solora with plenty of days to spare, it seems."

I gulped, then shook my head.

"Can you tell me where you were?"

Kera narrowed her eyes and pursed her lips.

"I was in the Western Seelie Territory. Business with the Veiled. Nothing you need to concern yourself with."

I shuffled my feet.

"What are we doing today?" I asked.

"You want to know more about witches in an attempt to access your power, yes?"

"Of course, but I don't know where to start."

"That's why we are here. To access magic you've been cut off from for so long, you must first *understand* the power you are trying to reach."

"And you're to teach me?"

"Declan has asked me to help you try." Kera nodded. "I'm no witch, but I can help you decipher your abilities and answer your questions. We'll acquaint you with the basics before attempting more—practical approaches."

"I started reading *The Power of Herbs: Witching Basics* last night," I said.

"Finish it, then we'll move on. There is more to witchery than herbology, but it's an apt place to begin. There are many secrets the witches kept of their power, and since you have no true coven leader, you must discover them for yourself. I'll leave you to it. I'm weary from travel. Good luck at the ceremony."

I groaned in a most undignified way. "You're leaving already? We just started."

She shrugged.

"I have to go into the city for work for a few days and need to rest first. Read the books, then we'll start more practical applications."

With that, Kera transformed into her black cat form and slunk away, leaving me alone in the library with my books and my thoughts.

21

DECLAN

Roselyne and I hadn't yet spoken about what happened in the library a few nights ago. The betrothal ceremony and feast were to be held soon, and I wanted to speak to her before then. Every time I went to find her in the yard or the hall, she disappeared like smoke. I meant to seek her out before breakfast, demanding we clear the air, but her room was empty when I arrived outside her bedroom door early in the morning.

A passing servant informed me Roselyne joined Essi on some errand in the city. I leaned against the wall and threw back my head. She obviously regretted our kiss in the library and was avoiding me.

The stone wall grounded me as I recounted the way Roselyne kissed me, when she'd given herself over to me—then pulled away. It was painfully obvious she regarded our passion as a momentary lapse in judgment. I slammed a fist to the door as I let the disappointment fill me before stalking off back toward my own chambers. *Why do I even care?*

I was stewing in my study when I received a letter from

Kera, sent from her post within the Soloran slums. It was two lines of text hastily scribbled on a scrap of parchment.

Sloane has returned to the Eastern Seelie Territory.
He travels toward Solora.

I only had to wait a few more hours for my brother to arrive at the palace. I had not seen him in nearly half a century. After serving on my royal council for fifty years, he'd left his position in my council to pursue his love of knowledge and learning, and if gossip could be believed, the female form.

That afternoon, my younger brother and I sat opposite each other in my private study—the study that once belonged to our father.

"You don't seem pleased to see me, Declan."

Sloane frowned for a moment as he swirled his wine around his glass, the blue liquid nearly sloshing from the rim and spilling onto the ornate rug underfoot. He appeared the exact same since we'd last seen each other—so similar to me, but lacking the jagged edges and harshness I'd earned in my time ruling as king.

As second born, Sloane didn't suffer the fate of the faelands on his shoulders, and with that, carried an air of recklessness I'd never been allowed.

"I'm ecstatic you've come back to the palace, brother," I said, truthfully. "But you left the Solora after years of serving on my council without explanation. You left without a word, and now waltz back in and expect—what exactly?"

Sloane sighed and leaned forward with his elbows on his knees. "I served on your council fifty years after the war, helping the kingdom accustom to you as their new ruler and build back up the foundation of Seelie greatness. I grew tired. I yearned instead to fill my head with magical knowledge and history as I'd always desired." His gaze flicked away for a moment, then back to me. "As for my return? I heard you'd taken a bride—a human one. It's most curious." He drank deeply and leaned forward over my desk. "It leads me to wonder if there is a particular rationale for your doing so. Althene is the poorest of the human kingdoms, the least likely to be beneficial to the fae." His forehead wrinkled. "You've never been one to make decisions without reason...I was curious, so here I am." He leaned back and crossed a leg over the other and assessed me, twirling his empty glass with his hand.

I rubbed at my temples and groaned.

"Yes, you're correct." I drained my own glass, then refilled both of ours from the half empty bottle on my desk. Sloane waited patiently for my explanation. I considered for a moment telling him the truth—of the curse and of the prophecy tying Roselyne as the answer to my weakened magic. Of my suspicions regarding the lords lying in wait to steal the throne at the first sign of weakness.

Instead, I gave my brother the lie I gave everyone else, save for Kera and Callum. "It's high time the relationship between the human kingdoms and fae are mended."

Sloane raised an eyebrow. "For what reason? And why Althene?" His nose wrinkled. "We get along fine without the human kingdoms' interference in our affairs."

I shook my head. "You grew tired of the after-effects of war, Sloane." I pressed my lips together. "Perhaps I've grown tired of being perceived as a monster."

That bit wasn't a lie, not entirely. I cared not for the opinions of the humans across the sea, but my own people trembled before me, and for years I'd used it to my advantage. No enemy would dare to strike me for fear of my wrath, and in that fear grew my own loneliness. Roselyne would be the answer to all my problems, and although she did not know it, a way to soften the hearts of the Seelie fae toward their Ruthless King.

Sloane's eyes softened. "That's—surprising," Sloane said.

"It's honest," I replied, bile rising in my throat. My brother deserved the entirety of my truth, and it pained me to keep it from him. I stood from my chair and walked around the large desk. "It's a welcome surprise to have you back at court, Sloane. You were missed in your absence. I'll take your presence at court in any way you deem to give it."

My brother stood from his chair and wrapped his arms around me in a long-due embrace.

"I've missed you too, brother."

22

ROSELYNE

I'd been in the faelands a few weeks and had settled in quite nicely. My days were spent wedding planning with Essi. In the evenings, I'd curl up in one of the large, overstuffed chairs in the library, reading about witch magic and striving to understand the inaccessible power beneath my skin. I often ended up shooting furtive glances toward the crowded aisle where Declan and I momentarily gave in to the flame of passion between us. He'd not spoken to me of the incident, and I couldn't help but wonder if I was nothing more than a plaything to him, a toy to paw at while bored.

Despite my initial misgivings toward my betrothed, the fae weren't as monstrous as I'd been led to believe all my life. I was making my peace with that, wondering what sort of other lies I'd blindly believed. Now, Finally, I was getting to go into the city proper to do some—according to Essi—*much needed* wedding shopping and preparation.

The smell of cooking meats filled the air as we strode arm in arm toward the market stalls set up in the city center. Rows and rows of vendor tents and stands lined both sides of the cobblestone streets of the city of Solora with every sort of good imaginable. Whole hairy pigs roasted on rotating spits next to a man calling out to the crowd selling fresh fruits I'd never seen before. An apothecarist sat beneath an awning of a permanent building alongside a young fae woman who could only be his daughter. A small sign hung over her head indicating specials to be had.

Essi stopped at the stall and discreetly paid for two bottles of liquid in amber vials. She turned back to me with a bright smile and continued through the market, the glass clinking together in her bag with every step.

My eyes couldn't keep up with the crowd and the variety of goods available. The entire square smelled of fresh foods and spices mixing in the air. Crowds of mostly fae and a lesser number of humans bustled past us holding large packages and bags filled to the brim with foods and trinkets. Weary mothers and fathers grabbed hold of their children's elbows and led them through the throng under the blazing sun, the pointed tips of their ears pink from the heat.

The late summer sun was directly above us in the sky, making my eyes water from the brightness. My eyes darted right to left, not knowing where to begin as I stood open-mouthed in awe.

Essi grabbed my hand and squeezed. Her golden hair was piled atop her head, similar in style to mine. We each wore breezy dresses that hit at the knee, as did many of the fae and humans around us.

Essi beamed, growing more and more excited as we took each step. The Commander of the Daylight Guard, Callum, trailed closely behind us, acting as a chaperone while Essi and I flitted about the colorful stalls like buzzing insects.

"What's going on with you and Declan?" Essi asked innocently as she turned over a glass bauble in her delicate hands. My eyes trailed over the various glittering orbs and trinkets. I plucked a tiny glass crescent moon and held it in my hands, noting how cool it felt against my skin.

"Nothing is going on," I said, embarrassed. The familiar sweep of pink colored my cheeks. *Damn it.* Would it be that terrible to admit I had the beginnings of feelings for my betrothed? I turned the moon figurine over in my hands, letting it fall through each finger.

"What I saw the other night didn't seem like *nothing* to me," Essi said. Her brown eyes sparkled mischievously in the afternoon sun. Callum had the good sense to act as if he couldn't hear our conversation from his distance a few steps behind us. "I bought an extra vial of the pregnancy protection elixir for you, you know, *just in case.*"

"I won't be needing that," I said, grimacing. Despite what I'd said, my stomach flipped in on itself at the prospect of *why* I'd need such a thing.

"Mmhm," Essi said, slipping the brown glass bottle into my bag, "Just in case."

I ignored Essi's comments and handed the vendor a handful of silver coins in exchange for the bauble. I had no idea why I bought it or what I'd do with it, but Declan granted me access to the entirety of his coffers, and I had no qualms about using them.

"Let's go," I said. "Didn't you want to see something specific?"

"Ooh, yes!" Essi said excitedly before grabbing my hand and dragging me deeper into the rows of stalls and the crowd of fae.

Callum kept pace behind us a few steps, my agreed upon escort. He was dressed casually, similar in nature to the rest of the city's patrons, but with the addition of his sword slung across his back. Even without the sunburst insignia across his chest, it was clear many passersby knew they were close in proximity to the Commander of the Daylight Guard.

Some eyed him warily as they passed, but most walked right on by, busy enough with their own errands. Callum ran his hand through his chin length blond hair and squinted up toward the sky. *Not a single cloud existed to give us mercy from the sun.*

"You ladies picked the hottest day of the year to visit town," Callum said with a teasing smile, working to keep his sweat slicked hair out of his face.

I beamed a huge grin at Callum, and Essi did the same. I couldn't help the lightness in my chest. Although I was shopping in preparation for a wedding I hadn't wished for, I was finally coming to terms with my life at the Seelie Court.

"We sure did, and it won't be the last time!" Essi quipped back, and a giggle ripped from my throat as Essi grabbed my hand once more and took off running toward a colorful market stall with a delighted squeal.

"Look, Roselyne!" she said, pointing at a tent.

Essi guided me toward a booth, with Callum close behind us. A squat, round man sat atop a cushioned stool behind the stall. All of his pale fingers were adorned with various chunky and colorful metal rings. His cheeks were pink, and his mouth was hidden beneath a thick white mustache that curled up at each end. His elongated ears were as richly decorated as his fingers, each with a row of earrings climbing his lobes all the way to their tips. He gestured over his table, which was overlaid with a velvety midnight blue cloth with dozens of glittering jewels displayed across the fabric.

"Welcome, welcome friends! Please come take a look.

Could that be the commander, I spy?" he said, nodding toward Callum. He turned his attention to me. "And *you*, so beautiful and so *human* with that exquisite bit of silver hair!" He wagged a fat, glittering finger toward my ears. "You must be the king's betrothed." The man slid into a bow from his seated position, his protruding belly making it difficult for him to hinge at the waist. "There has been a great deal of talk about how our dear Seelie King is finally taking a bride, and we are all thrilled to witness that history, none more than I."

Despite the man's earnest kindness, I left without purchasing anything. The rings for Declan and I's betrothal ceremony were chosen before I ever entered the faelands. The man smiled warmly as I turned to leave, calling out well wishes as I walked away. Every interaction with vendors went similarly. I was a known commodity all throughout the Seelie Court, it seemed, something I hadn't been prepared for. Essi and I sampled some sort of fruit I'd never seen before called dragomelon, while Callum admired swords at the booth beside the fruit stand still within earshot of us.

As we wandered the crowded aisles of tents and booths, my gaze roamed to a small purple tent. A frail fae woman sat outside atop a rickety wooden stool. Her face was gaunt, although her pale eyes still shone bright, with limp gray hair that surrounded her sunken cheeks. Her body was draped with multiple layers of deep-hued blue, green, and purple fabrics. Only her small hands and head were visible among the fabric, giving off the impression that her head and hands didn't belong to her body. I knew the fae aged impossibly slower than humans, which would make this woman undeniably ancient. She nodded as we approached the tent.

"Princess," she croaked, standing from her stool and bowing low.

"Welcome, welcome. I am Hester. I do hope you are faring well in the Seelie Court, Princess of Althene." Both her hands shot forward, clasping around my hand and shaking it. The gold and silver bracelets that adorned her arms jingled from the jerky movement. Callum moved to intervene, but I waved him off with my other hand.

The old woman continued, undisturbed by my companions, before beckoning me into her tent.

"I possess the power of divination, my lady. Let me reveal your fortune."

Essi giggled and flicked her eyes toward the old woman and back to me.

"Her fortune is pretty obvious." She rolled her eyes. "Roselyne is marrying the king. She'll be the queen soon."

Sweat unrelated to the day's heat formed on my hands, and I wiped it across my bodice. Although I'd accepted that this marriage was going to happen—I'd momentarily forgotten how drastically my life changed in the past couple of weeks.

Hester squinted at Essi with a click of her tongue.

"Skeptics are welcome."

Hester held out her hands palm up to me and motioned for me to place my palms in hers.

Essi rolled her eyes, and I nudged her with my shoulder. "Don't be rude," I whispered from the corner of my mouth, before placing my hands against Hester's and smiling politely. Her pale skin was wrinkled as parchment, and I feared it'd snag and tear, but it did not. Hester smiled at me, her eyes crinkling at the corners as she did.

In Althene, there was no magic, and no divination. The prospect of future-reading was inconceivable to me. I genuinely wanted to hear what Hester would predict—would I live a happy life alongside the Seelie King? The old woman's insight was too tempting to resist.

"Thank you. I'd love to have my fortune read."

Hester released my hands and waved us into her tent. The inside was small and cramped with a small wooden table in the center and one large shelf on the far left filled with various herbs, tinctures, and what appeared to be animal bones. Over a small fire, a kettle boiled water as steam floated through the air, creating a thick haze.

"Are you a witch?" I asked, taking in the surroundings and the sickly-sweet smell of the herbs perfuming the air.

"Of course not," Hester replied as she plucked some sort of dried leaves into a cup and poured the water into it, mixing it. "I am fae." She indicated her pointed ears. "The witches are all dead or gone. But I am old, Princess, and I was taught by many of their finest in the times before the war, when our people had peace between us." The hot water mixed with the leaves, steaming. Hester muddled it together with a stone tool as she spoke. "Much of their knowledge lives within me, although I cannot claim to be as blessed as those to whom the earth whispered directly."

Hester held the teacup out to me, and I took it in my hands. The warmth of the cup spread to my fingers in a tingly heat.

Callum stood at the tent's threshold; the space too small for all of us to enter at once. Essi wrung her hands nervously in front of her dress, standing beside me opposite Hester. The heat was stifling, and I wondered how Hester wasn't melting beneath the layers of fabric she wore. The old fae woman motioned to the two empty chairs across from her. I sat, and Essi slid into the chair beside me.

I held the cup between my two hands and blew cool air on the steaming liquid.

"Drink, drink," Hester said, her voice crooning.

Callum was still standing imposingly in the doorway, jaw ticked. I glanced to him first, and he nodded his head in affirmation.

I tipped the cup to my lips and drank the bitter liquid until Hester beckoned me to stop. Bits of leaves stuck together at the bottom of the porcelain in dark, soggy clumps.

"Enough." She motioned for me to return the cup. She swirled the empty cup and turned it over, humming softly as she did.

The sound of Essi's tapping foot and Hester's humming was the only noise to be heard inside the small tent, the sounds of the market inaudible. She turned the cup back over and peered inside, studying the clumped together tea leaves. She muttered to herself, as Essi, Callum, and I sat in silence watching.

Hester placed the cup in the center of the table between us. She clapped her hands together, bracelets jangling, and stared into my eyes with her own gray ones.

"Well," I said, "What does it say?"

Hester pointed dramatically to a wad of brown goop in the cup. "A dove." It didn't particularly resemble a dove to me, but what did I know?

"I have a friend named Dove," I offered.

Hester shook her head. I glanced sideways at Essi, who shrugged as if to say, *I don't know either*. Hester waved her arms above her head, drawing our attention back to her.

"It's a most *lucky* omen!" she said shrilly. "Signifying your success in love and affection for our dear king." She smiled at me while nodding.

I was anything but lucky, and had been all my life. My hope for some sliver of truth among the tea leaves dwindled as quickly as it appeared. I'd find no truth from Hester's reading, only false inspirations.

I sighed and shuffled my feet against the ground, waiting to hear what other magical revelations were to be found within the remnants of my teacup.

"What else is there?" I said politely, not wanting to offend the old woman.

"Most curious observations..." She paused, appraising all of us. "The crown...and the cross," she said dramatically, then frowned when none of us reacted.

She huffed, then continued a bit grumblier, realizing we weren't as impressed as she'd prefer. "The crown signifies success and honor. But the cross? An ill omen while positioned in this way." She pointed into the cup, but it truly just looked like brown blobs of tea leaves. Hester was undeterred. "A sign of trouble—perhaps even a betrayal or death!" she said, voice ringing through the cramped tent.

I winced. Hester smiled again at me.

"Don't fear, Princess. Not everything is set in stone. You have the power to change your fortune, of course."

I pasted a bland smile on my face.

"Thank you for this. How much for the reading?" I asked, digging into my pocket to retrieve fae money.

"For the human princess and future Seelie Queen, free," she said, waving my money away. "You are always welcome in my tent if you require my services."

Hester stayed behind in her tent as Callum, Essi, and I exited. The fresh air was a welcomed change from the heavily perfumed air inside the tent.

"Well, that was hogwash," Essi said, turning and squinting

down the aisle. It was still only the early afternoon and the rows of vendors were still thick with patrons. "Everyone knows Merfolk are the only *real* seers. They're sent messages by the goddess Lux herself," she harrumphed. I thought back to my time below the Lyssan Sea and suppressed a shiver. The mer Maren had spoken cryptically to me, and I'd not made sense of any of her words.

"Divination gives me the creeps," Callum said, nodding and ripping me from the memory.

"It was kind of fun." I shrugged. "There isn't anything like that where I'm from."

Essi bounced up and down on her heels and squealed, all previous irritation with the false seer evaporated.

"Look! Madam Gaelenna has a booth set up! We *have* to go see! She has the best silk on the entire continent! I know your wedding gown is already made, but we could still get something else commissioned for you! Maybe something for your wedding night!" Essi skipped off ahead of Callum and I, starry-eyed and headed toward the luxurious bolts of fabric lining the table.

Callum and I walked side by side toward the table, and I couldn't help but notice him eyeing Essi's backside as she bounded away. He caught me watching him and snapped his eyes away from Essi with a cough.

I decided I liked Callum. Things were easy with him. We walked in comfortable silence until I broke it.

"Do you know where Kera is?" I asked.

He shrugged. "Vaguely."

"She came back, but then went into the city for some other sort of job."

Callum grunted noncommittally.

I wrinkled my nose. "Can you tell me?"

He snorted. "Not unless you want the king to kick my ass." He grinned. "Not that he could," he added, easily running his hand through his thick, blond hair. "She'll be back soon. She wouldn't miss the betrothal ceremony."

He smiled, but failed to hide the worry lining his face. Although I didn't know Kera well, there was something comforting in her presence. While everyone tried to pacify me and appease me, she didn't lie to me to spare my feelings.

"Have you known Declan for a long time?" I asked as we walked toward Essi.

Callum blew out a breath. "Long to me, or you?" My face must have looked puzzled because Callum laughed, his blue eyes sparkling as he did.

"I've known Declan my entire life. My father was a part of the last king's reign. I was raised alongside Declan and Sloane. I joined the Daylight Guard as soon as I aged into it, not wanting to be anywhere else."

I absorbed his words and churned them over in my mind.

"And how old..." I began to ask.

"Three centuries," Callum answered. "Give or take a few decades."

Declan was three-hundred years old and appeared no older than thirty-five.

I'd grow old and wither away, and Declan would still appear young. I grimaced.

It was no wonder Declan wasn't fazed by taking a human bride. If I failed to learn how to wield witch magic and extend my lifespan, Declan would still have the time to marry another and spend centuries with them after my death. Jealousy snaked through me, cold and unwelcome. I hated the thought.

We reached Madam Gaelenna's booth where Essi was cooing and rubbing her cheeks along bolts of fabric while the silk-seller watched. Although the heat was blazing, Madam Gaelenna's spindly body was completely covered in a tight black dress that snaked all the way up her throat. She wore black gloves on her hands, extending to her elbows. The only section of her brown skin on display were the parts of her face not hidden beneath large, round, tinted spectacles. A black wide-brimmed hat perched atop thick copper-colored hair, cascading down her shoulders in loose waves. Lush cherry red lips parted to reveal straight white teeth. She beamed when she spotted Callum and me approaching, nodding her head in acknowledgment to me. She clasped her hands in front of her body as Callum and I stepped beneath the shade of her stall.

"Princess Roselyne. Welcome to the Seelie Court. Have a look at my silks if you desire. I can assure you that you'll find no finer quality in any corner of this world."

An array of colorful silks sat before me on individual bolts, each with an unmistakable opalescent sheen.

"They're beautiful," I murmured, running my fingers across a bolt of cream-colored fabric that transformed into a dazzling blue with the movement of my hand. The silk was impossibly soft and cool against my warm skin, a sensation more akin to liquid than any fabric I'd ever known. I gasped and glanced up at Madam Gaelenna who was watching me with a small smile playing across her lips. She was a woman who knew the value of what she possessed.

"Silk from the arachnys," she said in a silvery voice. "There's nothing quite like it."

She was right. I let the fabric ripple over my skin and closed my eyes. In my past, I'd had access to the finest garments in all the human kingdoms, and never had seen anything as fine as this. I was about to open my mouth to tell the madam how impressed I was, when Essi's sharp gasp drew my attention.

The crowded market broke out into hushed whispers as a sense of dread slipped over me. I snapped my attention toward the direction everyone had turned toward. A huge banner, the length of three men's heights, was strung across the alley between the roofs of two buildings and billowing gently in the summer breeze. I read the message, and my heart sank.

BEGONE HUMAN WHORE

23
ROSELYNE

Time slowed. Words left me as I took in the hateful message displayed in the market square for all to see. I mouthed the words silently.

Begone human whore

This was a message intended for *me*. The crowd's gazes pressed into me as the rest of the citizens of Solora realized their future queen was in their midst.

Callum drew his sword from his back as Essi grabbed hold of my arm, her nails digging in slightly and her brown eyes wild and wide. Madam Gaelenna, sensing the prospective conflict, scooped up her bolts of cloth and disappeared into the crowd with a nod to me.

The crowd buzzed like angry insects, gasping and whispering to each other as everyone took notice of the banner, and who the message was intended for. Sweat rolled down the back of my neck. Callum stepped in front of me, shielding me with his body. My cheeks flushed hot, and I wanted nothing more than to disappear. Did the Seelie fae not realize I didn't ask for this?

"Who's responsible for this?" Callum barked, his voice booming over the crowd of fae.

Gone was the friendly tone of Declan's childhood friend—Callum was currently speaking as a member of the Seelie King's royal council.

"VILE WITCH SEDUCTRESS," came a drunken yell from the back of the crowd. I froze. The buzzing of the crowd grew louder and more excited, chirping to each other and ignoring Callum's authority.

"The princess is a witch?" a woman said nearby, her voice full of glee at the rich gossip.

The man next to her huffed. "A witch in the faelands once again? Impossible!"

"It makes perfect sense! Why else would the king choose a human bride?"

"Didn't the King have a witch once before?" another voice called out.

More voices began to overlap each other into a jumble of excited words I couldn't decipher.

My heart pounded. No one was supposed to know I was a witch—Declan had made it clear the knowledge would make me a target to others.

Essi, still gripping my arm, turned her face to mine and stared into my eyes and straight to my soul.

"Roselyne?" she asked, a small frown on her lips. "Is that true? You're a witch?"

"Essi, I—"

A small explosion boomed, interrupting me and vibrating the ground beneath our feet. The crowd delved into chaos as another explosive detonated nearby, showering stone debris in the air. I stood, stunned and unable to move, the scent of burning herbs filling the air. Essi coughed beside me as she breathed in the thick plumes of smoke. In their own haste to flee, the market goers bumped into us, jostling our bodies and nearly knocking us down to the ground.

"Fuck," Callum swore. "I'm getting you out of here." He heaved me and Essi across his shoulders and bolted out of the crowd toward the palace. The rest of the market goers did the same, scooping up their crying children and loved ones, in an attempt to flee the chaos. No other explosions detonated as Callum broke through the crowd, and no one made any attempts to stop us, too concerned with their own safety. Callum turned the corner and exited the market, feet thundering along the path toward the palace at a speed I hadn't expected for a man his size.

I met Essi's eyes as Callum carried us, both still hoisted over either of his shoulders. She clasped my hand in hers, and bit her lip worriedly as she gazed back at the smoking marketplace we'd left behind. I knew it then—I wouldn't be allowed to return to the marketplace, and the secret of my witch blood was safe no longer.

Callum, Essi, and I crossed through the stone gate entering into the palace grounds, and Declan was there, fire blazing in his golden eyes that doused upon seeing me unharmed. Declan tore me from Callum's grip and scooped me into his arms, running toward the palace, leaving Callum and Essi behind in the yard. Declan was stronger than any human man I'd ever seen, cradling me easily. I remembered the last time he'd held me in his arms—when I was delirious with fever from the sea wyrm's venom. Although only mere weeks had passed, so much had changed since then.

I closed my eyes and floated weightlessly through the castle, locked in the grip of Declan's strong arms, not bothering to fight his hold on me.

Declan sat me on my bed and kneeled on the ground before me, searching for abrasions and scrapes, holding my face between his strong hands.

"Are you hurt?" Declan's voice rasped. His eyes were wild with panic, searching all over my face and body for proverbial wounds. "I heard the booms from my window. I sensed something was *wrong*." His voice cracked on his last word, full of fury and a promise of revenge.

"I'm fine," I said, shaking his hands off me and sitting upright. Declan had tended to me before, but I still wasn't used to his preening. I wasn't physically hurt, just—shaken. Shocked. Embarrassed. Heavy with despair for the fae who hated me despite not knowing me, now made aware of my greatest secret I'd barely had time to come to terms with.

I blinked away the tears that had formed against my lashes, and my chest heaved as I inhaled raggedly. At last, safe with the Seelie King, my heart began to calm.

"What happened?" he ground out, jaw clenched and golden eyes piercing. I couldn't help but squirm under his gaze, remembering the last time we were alone.

I shook my head, letting my loose hair sweep over my face, giving some separation between us. I couldn't handle the intensity of his stare. Not right now.

"Everything was fine. The people were pleasant and kind." I paused, not wanting to meet the intense scrutiny of his gaze. "Until one of them, perhaps a few—weren't as kind."

My hair tugged against my scalp as I twisted it through my fingers—a habit from my childhood I needed to break. I shook my head, trying to organize my recollection of what had occurred. It had all happened too quickly.

I recounted the banner and exclamations from the crowd and the subsequent explosions that had ricocheted throughout the market square.

Declan's eyes were black, his lips peeled back in a snarl.

He looked as much the monster as I previously believed he was, coiled with tension, a predator poised to strike—to kill. The network of veins weaving throughout his hands and arms bulged from how tightly he gripped the edge of the bed. I eyed the lines of greenish-blue that pulsed underneath his skin. He was angry, barely in control—his tether on his emotions about to snap.

"This is an insult against you, and therefore me." He stood, his rage taking up nearly the entire space of the room.

His anger pulsed in the air, alive and seeking revenge. But I was not afraid—not for myself. Not any longer. If anything, the severe set of his features made Declan somehow more striking, more beautiful. With his anger, he appeared so alike the ancient statues of warriors past, sculpted from flesh instead of stone.

"It must be related to the incident at the temple," he added, speaking more to himself than me. I chewed at my bottom lip, unsure of what he meant.

He paced the room, muttering to himself. His eyes were crazed. I'd never seen him so frenzied. He was seething, and for the first time I'd ever witnessed, Declan was unable to maintain his carefully curated image he'd always presented to me and the world.

I stood from the bed and crossed the room, placing my hands against his back to soothe his anger. Declan exhaled forcefully as I pressed my palms to his skin.

"What incident?" I asked softly, as I began rubbing soothing circles against Declan's broad back. Touching him in this way this felt...*right,* like we should have shared this intimacy long ago.

Declan slumped his shoulders and faced me. I dropped my hands, not taking my eyes from the king.

He heaved a few breaths, nostrils flaring, and set his eyes on me. I nearly melted under their intensity. I didn't shrink away. I saw him for who he was—the anger, the rage, and I was not afraid. He'd never looked less human to me—or more captivating.

He turned away from me as he spoke low, barely audible to my human ears.

"The Seelie follow other gods than the humans in their kingdoms. There are temples devoted to Lux scattered throughout all of the faelands. The Veiled—the priestesses, are caretakers of these places of worship."

I nodded my head. We had similar sisterhoods in Althene, dedicated to our three-headed goddess as well. It only made sense the fae also kept houses of worship for their own strange gods.

"The priestesses are caretakers of many ancient fae artifacts. Although only the Seelie fae remain, the Veiled were never loyal to any one kingdom. They are governed only by the whims of the goddess." His voice rumbled as he spoke low against the shell of my ear, and I shivered instinctively as gooseflesh rippled across my skin.

All of my human impulses begged me to flee. He was a predator, and I was prey—though I felt no fear, only sweet anticipation for what he'd do next.

"Someone broke into one of the temples and tore apart the place, clearly searching for *something*." My eyes darted to

Declan's hands as he clenched them into fists. "We do not yet know what they searched for, or if they found it. The Veiled Priestesses keep extensive records, and are to report to me if anything is missing—but I am beginning to fear this break-in was more than merely an attempt at petty theft."

I swallowed, mesmerized by the words he was telling me.

Declan stepped back from me, and I immediately missed the heat of his body.

"You think this has anything to do with me?" I asked, sinking back into the mattress.

My frown deepened as my heart began to race. I hadn't asked for any of this. I hadn't wanted to be a political pawn, but that's what this marriage would mark me.

"I never intended for everyone to know what you are." He paused, searching for the right words. "As my human bride, you were seen as nothing but an ornament beside my throne. A witch is a *threat*." My mouth went dry.

The mattress lurched from Declan's weight as he sat down beside me, sighing heavily.

"There is a group called Summus Nati. They believe humans should be subservient to fae as it was long ago and wish to reestablish this dynamic through any means necessary. They would not have been keen on a human queen, but it wouldn't have poised them to strike. But witches?" He rubbed at his temples. "They wrongly believe witches are humans who've somehow stolen magic from the fae, although that's impossible and not at all how witch magic works." His fingers twisted in the sheets. "I'm not certain it's them...there are others who could want you for themselves, but I can't disregard any option yet. I've sent Callum back to the city to investigate. To find out who these cowards who'd dare attack their king's betrothed are. Until we find them, you're even less safe than I previously believed. You must stay with me at all times and not leave the—"

I held up my hand, cutting off his words. "Please. I don't want to be helpless. Teach me to fight like you said you would. Allow me to protect myself."

"I can't lose you." His voice cracked on the words, and I wondered for a moment if the Seelie King had truly come to care about me as I was beginning to care for him.

My cheeks heated under his gaze, and my heart twisted inside my chest, wanting to believe he meant those words how I wish he did. A wave of bitterness surged through my veins.

"Of course," I said as I whipped my head away, so he couldn't see the redness that lined my eyes. How stupid I was to care for him. My words were staccato and forced when I spoke. "It would look bad to have your betrothed perish at the hand of your enemies and lose your witch all in one fell swoop," I snapped. He only took me as his bride so others couldn't possess my magic and use it against him—he'd told me that much himself. Magic I couldn't even *feel*, although Kera sensed it writhing inside me.

His brow furrowed, but he didn't correct me.

If not for this supposed power that flowed uselessly within me, I would mean nothing to him.

I was hot and uncomfortable from the realization and shuffled my feet against the smooth stone floor. *I shouldn't even care.*

"I will train you," Declan said softly. "Nothing else is more important."

My eyes rose to meet his, limbs tingling with nervous anticipation at the prospect of more solo time with him. Despite what I'd witnessed today, and the fear I felt, my heart leapt.

"When can we begin?" I asked, excited to learn to defend myself.

As a child, my father forbade me from even playing with my older brother's wooden practice swords. Instead, I'd been resigned to sewing and harp lessons with the other ladies of the court while my brothers got to smack each other around in the yard. He gently held my fingertips in his hand.

"Sunrise tomorrow. I will retrieve you from your bedchamber," Declan replied before pressing his lips quickly to my hand in a chaste kiss. He was out the door before I could even respond.

24

DECLAN

Time hadn't quelled the rage pumping through my body. I'd told only Kera and Callum the truth about Roselyne, and yet *somehow* others now knew what she was. As I trusted both my spy and the Daylight Commander wholly, I had no choice but to accept that a sailor aboard *The Andromeda* overheard me speaking with Kera and sold the information to the highest bidder.

My hands curled into fists, eager to hurt something. I also had to consider for what purpose whoever organized the market attack would want the truth of Roselyne's power known. It made little sense.

I'd end them all the same.

I was going to find out exactly who thought it was appropriate to intimidate my bride and spill the secrets of her witch blood. If I had been there, the city square would have been leveled, and citizens both innocent and guilty would have perished under my power. I flexed my fingers then shoved them into my pockets. Those pieces of shit had gone too far. I had hoped that the citizens of Solora would be welcoming to my

THE CURSE OF THE SEELIE KING

bride. Many were—but of course, not everyone considered it appropriate to have a human, much less a witch reigning at my side.

I could kill them. I *would* kill them.

I turned a corner toward Crossed Stars, a pleasure house located on the Street of Sins that held cells below the ground for my own personal use. A dark cowl covered my face, concealing my identity to any passerby out tonight. There were some forms of justice the Daylight Guard didn't need to be privy to.

A bell tinkled softly as I entered the thickly perfumed brothel. The air was hazy with purple smoke from the ever-burning incense the Madam kept lit during business hours. Women in various states of undress lounged on plush furniture, some reading, some sitting in men's laps, and one singing softly as she plucked the strings of a lyre. A young blonde fae woman clad in see-through wisps of cloth approached me with simulated shyness, her small breasts bobbing with every step. She smiled at me demurely, twirling her finger through her flaxen hair in what I assume was supposed to be an act of seduction.

I held my hand up and shook my head as I walked past her.

Perhaps if I was younger, I would have indulged in her services, but I had no interest in that as it were. There was only one woman I was interested in bedding as of late—and she'd made it clear she thought our near-intimacy was a mistake.

"Alaesyn, he's not here for you!" Madam Tasha barked, and Alaesyn skittered away, appearing only slightly wounded.

I nodded toward the Madam as she flashed her white teeth my way.

"Will you be enjoying your usual tonight, sir?" Madam Tasha asked me, her dark eyes glittering in the dim light, the only person inside the building who knew *who* visited them tonight.

Although I doubted any of the patrons of the brothel would know their king's voice, I didn't dare risk it, and only nodded my head.

"Follow me please," Tasha replied, beckoning me toward the narrow hallway leading to the hidden staircase I'd used hundreds of times in the past.

Tasha, of course, knew of the man chained up in her basement and why I was there. Callum delivered him earlier in the evening, and I intended to question the man before I ended his miserable life.

Madam Tasha and I shared an understanding. She allowed me the use of her basement space to dole out justice as I saw fit, and I cut her a break on the taxes owed to the crown. It was an agreement we'd had for nearly two centuries, put in place when my father still ruled as king, and the war ravaged the land.

The wooden steps creaked as I walked below the earth, unlatched the door, and entered into the familiar earthen room. It was humid and hot, and the small chamber smelled faintly of dirt.

"Who's there?" a gruff voice called out from the darkness.

My own eyes adjusted quickly to the dimness. A thin pale man was curled into a ball on the dirt floor, his hands and feet both bound by rope with a blindfold tied across his face. Dried blood was caked in his sandy hair and crusted on the side of his face. He sported a split lip, and I saw the purplish bruises around his eyes peeking out the edges of the blindfold. I smirked. It seems he put up a fight. Callum had easily rooted out who had strung the banner and insulted Roselyne. The rats in the city slums were not quite as loyal once swords were drawn by my commander. At my request, Callum brought the man responsible here to face my retribution.

"Who's there?" the man repeated.

Rage clouded my vision thinking of how scared Roselyne must have been in the market. I steeled myself. This man was going to suffer for his actions. A quick death was more than he deserved for his disrespect to what was *mine*. I ripped off the blindfold that covered his eyes.

"Your king," I said, venom dripping in my tone. I had a reputation, and this man was about to find out exactly why I was called ruthless.

"Your Majesty!" he exclaimed and began uselessly bucking against the chains that bound his arms and legs.

"You insulted my bride."

The man's eyes bulged, and the front of his pants darkened. His words were frantic as they tumbled out in a rush, hoping to save himself.

"I swear I only did it because someone paid me! My family was starving—I didn't mean any of it, I'm not like that. I already told the Daylight Commander," he pleaded.

I stepped onto his groin and twisted my heel before kneeling down beside him. The man howled like a wounded animal.

"Do *not* lie to me," I growled inches from his face, spit flying from my mouth. He cringed.

"I was paid! I was given the potions to throw and detonate! They told me only to scare her a little." Tears tracked down his face, mixing with dirt from the cell and leaving streams of brown. "I was never going to hurt her. I was instructed not to hurt her."

I said nothing as I untied the man's binds and pulled him

up to stand. He swayed on his feet and trembled, unsure of what I was doing.

"Did Summus Nati, or one of the Seelie Territory Lords hire you for this?" I asked.

This piece of shit was the reason Roselyne didn't feel safe in Solora—he'd made me a liar after I'd assured her no harm would come to her. Black hatred crept into my periphery, but I exhaled it away like smoke. He didn't deserve mercy. I was given the gift of pain by the gods, and I intended to use it. This man would give me answers, and then he would pay.

Seeing the hatred lining my face, the man began pleading.

"Summus Nati?" His face paled. "No! None!" He shook his head again, as the knowledge that his life ended tonight seemed to settle over him, "I don't know! I never saw them! I—"

His string of words was silenced as I directed my magic toward the man's throat and wrapped my invisible power around his neck and squeezed. He tried to scream, but no sound emitted from his lips. He clawed at his neck, unable to draw breath. His face turned red, then blue. After a few moments, I released him from my thrall, allowing him a brief moment of relief, and he crumpled to the floor in a heap. He took in ragged breaths as the color returned to his skin.

"Who paid you?" I asked calmly.

His chest heaved, and I could hear every beat of his racing heart. He sat up slowly, eyes darting back and forth across the dank room, searching for an exit. I blocked the only entrance with my body. There was no escape. He would die by my hand. The man seemed to sense that as well.

"I'm telling you, Highness!" he pleaded. He held his hands up in front of his body as if to stave me off. "I don't know who it was! They didn't say!" His chin trembled. Sweat peppered his hairline as the man grew more and more harried and panicked. I tried a different approach.

"So," I drawled out, as if trying to gain clarity—my words evenly spaced and calm, despite the rage near-boiling inside me. "You are not a member of the organization Summus Nati—whose aim is to create a social hierarchy that places fae ahead of all others?" I asked with feigned uncertainty.

"No! Never! Of course not! My family is starving, I had to take the job," he stammered. "Please, Your Highness, it's true! I have no qualm with witches or humans. I even bedded one once!"

Fury surged inside of me, urging me to end his miserable life and blot him from existence—but I tempered the desire. Instead, I used my power to snap one of his legs, barely gratifying my need for him to suffer. His shrieks filled the room, and he dropped back down to the ground. At that moment, I was thankful for the magical sound barrier surrounding this chamber of the Crossed Stars.

"You tried to harm what is mine," I said with a casual shrug. At that moment, I sent a wave of pain crashing through his body, searing his muscles from the inside out.

His body convulsed stiffly against the touch of my power—a wooden puppet on tangled strings. When I released him from my magic, he curled into himself along the earthen floor as blubbering sobs wracked through his body. He deserved this. He wanted to hurt Roselyne. It didn't matter if he wasn't the mastermind behind the attack. He would pay for touching what belonged to me.

"Please," he croaked.

"Give me the names of the men who paid you," I commanded.

"I don't know! They were cloaked! They approached me!"

he stammered out between tears. "I—I can contact them again! I can find out who they are! I can—"

This man was useless to me. I would send my own message to Summus Nati, or the territory lords. My statement was the same regardless of who'd ordered the attack. The future witch-queen was mine, and *untouchable*.

I stood over the man as he blubbered, tears leaking through his swollen face. Despite the curse's tamper on my magic, it only took a fraction of my power's capability to end his life. This was easy. I towered over his shivering frame and watched as his body crumpled in on itself as I shattered every bone in his body. His ribs ripped through the skin of his chest as he choked on his own blood.

The man's death hadn't cured my bloodlust. I took to the empty streets carrying the corpse of the man slung over my shoulder and dumped his body where Roselyne had been attacked. The thud of his flesh against cobblestones echoed throughout the open square, but no one was outside to hear it. I would never confirm I'd been the one to end his life, but no one else was capable of such brutality. Whoever was responsible for the attack would know who'd done this. The scum who paid the man would know exactly who left this message.

The man's glassy eyes stared toward the stars, and I asked that the Unseelie's perverse God of Death, Umbrath, spare no mercy upon him in the afterlife. Hot raindrops began to fall from the sky. I raised my face to the dark expanse above me, embracing the feel of the man's blood mixing with the rain and flowing down my body in tiny red streams.

25
DECLAN

I shut my study door behind me with a click and exhaled. I still didn't have the answers for who ordered the attack on Roselyne, but at least the man's death would send a message to those responsible. I turned and found my brother sitting in the large chair behind my desk, waiting for me, his face pale and stricken. He stood and crossed the room toward me.

"Whispers say your betrothed is a witch," Sloane said, incredulous. He sensed my hesitation for what it was—confirmation. His face fell. "It's true." He looked away for a moment, then back to me. "Who knew?"

"Let me explain."

I sat in the large wingback chair behind my desk and Sloane took a seat opposite me. He nodded as if thinking, as I uncorked a bottle of wine and poured us each a glass.

"I was under the impression all the witches are gone—or as good as."

"Yes," I said wistfully, thinking of Phaedra, the only woman I'd allowed myself to love. I shook away the memory and took a deep drink of fae wine. "I fear I must start from the beginning to explain it properly."

"Please," Sloane said with a wave of his hand. "Tell me."

I sighed. "My power, my magic—it's—I'm weaker than I once was."

"Old age," Sloane said with a joking smile. "What are you now—nearing three centuries?" He snorted.

"No—this is not natural."

"What are you saying? Your power is gone? You're basically mortal?" Sloane asked. His mouth tipped up at the corners like he couldn't believe what I spoke of and still thought it all some jest.

"No, I'm still stronger than any other fae. But I fear my power could dwindle further, leaving the throne open to attack. You know Lord Eryk has eyed the seat even before the war. He hates me for...how I ascended the throne." My mouth set in a hard line as my younger brother's smile faded. "I believe the witches cursed me for what happened to Phaedra." Saying her name out loud felt like another kind of betrayal. I didn't deserve to speak her name after what happened.

Sloane frowned and shook his head. "That was our father's doing, Declan. Not yours, and not mine."

I wanted to scream, to stand and flip the desk separating us over on its side. Nothing could quell the tempest swirling inside of me—but I kept my face expressionless. I curled my hands into fists and fought back the urge to destroy. It would do no good for others to know how the blackness threatened to swallow me whole.

"I was complicit in our father's crimes against the witches," I said, unable to hide the bitterness in my tone.

"And he paid for that—at your hand."

"Killing our father doesn't absolve me of wrongdoing. Phaedra *died*."

Sloane's eyes softened. Gone was the airy charm he typically exuded. He spoke quietly, almost reverently. "They nearly all died, Declan. The rest disappeared into the wind. Haven't you tortured yourself enough for Phaedra's death?"

A beat of silence passed between us, two brothers, and survivors of war. I balled my fists beneath the desk, grounding myself in the present. I released a breath. I was here now. Phaedra and her coven were nothing but ghosts. I sighed. There was a chance to recover my lost power, and Roselyne was the answer.

"My magical reserves are tempered somehow, growing less powerful with each passing day. For years I deluded myself into believing nothing was amiss." My mouth set in a hard line. "But it's been a century since the war, and I cannot deny what is happening any longer." I met my brother's gaze. "I believe Princess Roselyne may be my salvation."

"In what way, Declan?" Sloane brought his drink to his lips with a frown.

I spoke low, "Do you remember the prophecy the High Seer of the Merfolk brought to our father's halls before the slaughter began in earnest?"

Sloane exhaled, closed his eyes, and nodded.

The words of the elder mer woman swam in my mind, originally discarded by my father as the ramblings of an overzealous lunatic, until I could no longer ignore their merit. I recalled them to my brother.

"As the sun sets and shadows are cast,
a daughter of the earth emerges,

born rich with power beneath the shade of an eastern throne.
Bound by fate, chosen to heal the scorned, and
join with the fae warrior,
they together will restore the balance between kingdoms."

Sloane had an incredulous expression painted across his face. "You remembered the words spoken all those years ago?"

"No." I shook my head. "The scribe wrote the seer's words down before our father had her thrown from the hall. It's been sitting in the study all these years collecting dust."

Sloane cocked his head. "I don't understand. What does this mean? How is this related to your future bride?"

"When I first noticed my magic fleeing, like sand through my fingertips, I knew immediately it was the witches' doing." Sloane raised a skeptical eyebrow. "Because of my actions with Phaedra and the other witches, they died." I slammed a fist against the desk, rattling our empty glasses. "They cursed me with their last moments, knowing my lack of magic would mean my ruin." I laughed bitterly, although I could hardly blame the witches for their curse levied against me. Most days I believed I deserved it. I shook my head, clearing those thoughts, and met my brother's gaze. "I believe within this mer prophecy, therein lies a way out—a way to replenish my power."

"I'm not following, Declan..."

"Think about it, Sloane. 'As the sun sets and shadows are cast'," I repeated the first line of the prophecy. "'A daughter of the earth emerges'."

Sloane shrugged. "What is that supposed to mean to me?"

"The sun setting? It's *me*, Sloane. The Seelie King—with shadows over my powers. That's exactly how it feels. My magic is still there swirling under the surface—just veiled—inaccessible."

Sloane nodded, tentatively.

"A 'daughter of earth' could mean a human woman," he said, tilting his head and pressing his finger to his chin. "Or it could mean a witch. The third line indicates she was born of a royal line in the eastern continent."

"You see?" I asked.

He nodded, the wheels in my brother's keen mind turning. "This daughter of earth 'joining with the fae warrior'...that's your marriage," Sloane mused, nodding his head. "'Heal the scorned and restore balance between kingdoms'." He paused. "I can see how you ascribe this prophecy to you and your princess, Declan, but there's one issue."

"What?" I asked.

"There are no more witches," he said softly. "We searched for them after the war and found nothing. They're gone."

I shook my head. "Roselyne is a witch."

Sloane rubbed at his jaw, then grimaced. "The witches are *dead*, Declan. This is an impossibility."

"Yes," I agreed. "Many of the witches are dead, but perhaps some ran away to the human kingdoms? Roselyne possesses magic in her veins, her power tempered by her time in the human kingdom and cut off from the well of magic in the faelands. She was luckily unmarried and of an appropriate age, with a father whose thirst for gold and power outweighed his concern for his daughter."

"How can you be sure of this magic in her veins?"

"Kera sensed it—one of her elysian gifts," I said.

Sloane narrowed his eyes into slits, assessing me carefully.

"And you trust your spy? The one they call Widowmaker?"

"Implicitly."

He nodded. "And how does the princess feel about her role in strengthening the Seelie King's own power? Most humans and witches would have nothing but disdain for fae, for all the crimes committed against them at their hands."

"She does not know."

He quirked a brow.

I sighed. "Roselyne knows she is a witch—but not why I need to take her for my wife. Not about the prophecy, and not about what happened during the war. It makes no sense to anger her—or ruin my chances, as slim as they already are. If she knew the truth, she could refuse the marriage more easily. Human hatred for the fae runs deep. She needn't know that her acquiescence in our marriage will bring me more power."

I'd been tempted to tell Roselyne about the prophecy, to give her the entire truth. Every time I began, the words died in my throat, selfishly not wanting to spoil the semblance of affection she'd begun to show toward me.

What we'd done, or nearly done, a few nights ago only increased my feelings of guilt. I'd grown lonely in the years since the war, and the thought of someone ruling beside me was a comfort I hadn't truly allowed myself to indulge in over a century. I couldn't help but wonder if by not telling Roselyne the entire truth I'd ruined any possibility of long-term happiness with her—something I now realized I desired.

26
ROSELYNE

Beads of sweat dripped down my forehead, soaking into the silk scarf I wore covering my eyes. The muscles of my arms trembled as I held the wooden practice blade, weak from a lifetime of disuse. My thighs burned and screamed at me to sit, but I would not desist.

I'd asked for this—to be granted the chance to save myself.

"Again!" Declan's voice rang out, from the opposite end of the sparring ring. My pulse quickened in anticipation of his attack.

I could not see, but I had other senses. My feet shifted against the floor as I tried following the direction of his voice. The wind shifted as he approached, bringing with it his masculine scent, and I readied myself to parry his wooden blade.

Declan struck me on the hip and zinging pain shot up my body.

Foul words not befitting a princess spilled from my mouth in a string of profanities. I would certainly bruise.

Declan ripped the silk covering from my eyes in one smooth motion. He held my face between his two hands, his own practice blade cast away on the floor and mine hanging limply in my hand.

His fingertips burned against my cheeks like a brand—like he'd left marks I'd never be able to remove. I welcomed the sensation.

I shivered thinking of the last time Declan touched my face, remembering the reverence and veneration in which he'd beheld my body as he'd prepared to feast between my thighs.

I squeezed my legs together in an attempt to douse the dull ache growing within me despite the now-ebbing pain in my hip.

"I hurt you," he whispered, golden eyes searching mine before moving downward and assessing my body for any other indication of harm. His thumb swept across my jaw.

"Only a little," I grunted as I wriggled free of his grasp. I cleared my throat. "I'm fine—I want to learn. Getting hurt is part of the experience, I've been told."

"I never wish to hurt you."

He said the words as if he meant more than merely our blade training.

I wiped my palms against the rough fabric of the practice pants. "I grew up with two brothers, I can handle a smack on the ass." My cheeks flamed as soon as the words left my mouth.

"Oh, is that so?" He said, a knowing smirk playing about his lips.

"With a sword," I added.

We'd still not spoken regarding our—*tryst* in the library—if that's even what it could be called.

Momentary madness was more apt if I was to be asked. I chewed my lower lip.

Was madness so impermissible?

I assessed my husband-to-be.

I wanted him.

Loose tendrils of his thick black hair framed his face, fallen from where they were secured at the base of his skull. Declan's golden eyes were transfixed on me, alight with curiosity—watching my every move. His chest rose evenly with each breath he took.

His body towered over mine, broad chest and corded muscles on display with a thin sheen of sweat covering his tanned skin. The fae king was undeniably beautiful—appearing more like a god than a man.

My eyes dipped to the lines of muscles leading below his waistband before snapping my gaze back to his eyes.

He beheld my face as if I was the most beautiful woman in existence.

My body screamed out, begging me to throw myself to him—to drown myself in the honeyed pools of his eyes, to succumb to the attraction between us, to embrace the spark that would doubtlessly ignite if I allowed myself to truly care for him.

A memory held me back.

You've been hurt before, the fae king would do the same.

I took a step backward, shuffling my feet uncomfortably and eliminating the energy buzzing between us.

Footsteps echoed off the tile.

"Brother!" a voice I'd never heard before rang out.

I whirled around, wooden blade still in hand.

A man walked through the doorway, and I was immediately stunned by how alike in appearance he was to Declan. Similar in build, the man was less broad, with more wiry muscle.

"Sloane," Declan said, confirming my suspicions. "Meet Princess Roselyne of Althene, my betrothed, and as everyone in the faelands is now aware—a witch." Declan glanced at me. "Roselyne, this is my younger brother and Seelie Prince, Sloane."

Sloane approached us with a huge grin on his face. I was suddenly aware of my ill-fitting, sweat soaked clothing and the hair plastered to the back of my neck. I absentmindedly finger combed through the wild tangle of hair with a sheepish smile.

"I'm afraid you're not meeting me at my best, Prince Sloane."

"Nonsense." Sloane reached for my empty palm and placed a kiss against my knuckles. "Princess Roselyne, it is a pleasure and honor to meet you. I heard tales of your beauty as I journeyed back east, but stories pale in comparison to your radiance firsthand."

I blushed at that.

Declan nodded toward his brother, who seemed oblivious to the tense situation he'd nearly walked into.

"Will you be staying at court indefinitely, Prince Sloane?" I questioned, wondering why Declan hadn't mentioned the return of his brother.

Declan arched a brow at his brother. "A good question from my bride-to-be."

Sloane laughed warmly. "I will not lie to you, brother. I greatly enjoyed my time away, traveling and studying what exists in this realm, but I'm afraid I'm now ready to enjoy the fruits of what a life at court can give me."

Declan's face split into a grin and he embraced his brother.

"I'm expected to memorize this?" I asked.

The betrothal ceremony and feast was to be held in a few

days. Thousands of noble Seelie fae had already flooded into Solora, filling the inns and streets to bear witness to the event.

Essi pointed to the parchment. "Only this one line." She smiled. "The rest is spoken by the priestess who presides over the ceremony. There truly isn't much for you to do. The magic does the majority of the work."

"The magic?"

"Oh, yes." Essi bounced excitedly on the small pouf in my bedchamber. "Golden light supplied by the goddess Lux will bind your hands together, sealing your choice to marry." She sighed dreamily. "It's incredibly romantic." I didn't bother reminding Essi that this betrothal wasn't my choice.

We sat in my bedchambers together as Essi prepared me for the betrothal ceremony and feast. Feasting I knew how to do and what to expect, but some magical fae ceremony I'd never even witnessed? That was entirely foreign.

"What's the point of this ceremony?" I asked Essi after a few minutes of uselessly trying to speak the customary words in the ancient fae language.

"It solidifies your betrothal." She smacked her lips. "Although we already call you Declan's betrothed, under the eyes of Seelie laws, it is not entirely true until the goddess accepts the match with her magic."

I rolled my eyes. "So, it's purely ceremonial?"

"Aren't most things?" she asked with a cheeky smile.

Essi painstakingly walked me through the entirety of what to expect during the ceremony, and for that I'd forever be grateful. I'd even succeeded at memorizing the Ancient Faerie words after a few more minutes of practice. The syllables were unnatural and heavy on my tongue, but Essi assured me that my pronunciation was excellent.

"Most fae do not even speak the ancient language any

longer. Most of us only know the small bits and pieces used in ceremony. The Veiled Priestesses are the stewards of Ancient Faerie, and keep the language alive through ritual," she said.

"Everyone forgot the language?" I asked.

Essi chewed the inside of her cheek.

"Ancient Faerie was spoken *thousands* of years ago—before the Great Separation," she said.

"Separation?"

She frowned. "We don't really speak of it any longer—it was a different time then. Seelie and Unseelie lived together as one fae kingdom."

"Oh," I said, "I didn't realize."

Essi nodded solemnly. "Oh, yes, for millennia supposedly. Sloane—*ah*—the Seelie Prince told me. He's learned so much in his time away traveling, and is incredibly intelligent."

I didn't miss the tinge of pink on her cheeks.

"What happened?"

"The exact reasoning is lost to history, I'm afraid." She bit her lip. "The fae kingdom split into two, Seelie and Unseelie, and lived separately from each other for centuries in relative peace until the war."

"What happened during the war?"

"The Seelie won, and the Unseelie are gone now." Essi's lips pressed into a firm line. "Enough talk of war and the Unseelie, Roselyne." She shuddered, before recovering and wagging her eyebrow at me. "*You know*, after the betrothal ceremony is the feast."

"Yes, of course, that's the only part I'm not nervous about."

Essi sucked in a breath and grimaced.

"I don't think we've discussed what happens *after the feast*."

THE CURSE OF THE SEELIE KING

My face screwed up with confusion.

"After the feast," Essi continued, "it will be expected that you and Declan—share a bed."

"In front of everyone?"

My mouth opened in horror, although my heart thrummed at the thought of being claimed by the Seelie King in a room full of strangers. A part of me relished the thought of finally feeling the force of him move inside of me as we chased each other to climax. I pushed away the unwelcome curl of desire.

Essi laughed at that, a wheezing sound I'd never heard her make before. "No, Roselyne," she choked out between laughs. "You humans have such strange, preconceived notions about the fae." She shook her head. "No, it's expected that you move into the king's rooms and leave these ones behind as a symbol of your impending union."

I frowned and took in my now-familiar bedchambers.

"But I like my own room." I nervously smoothed my skirts and wrinkled my nose. "I don't want to share a bed with the king."

"It's fae tradition."

"I'm not fae," I snapped a bit too harshly.

None of this was Essi's fault.

She flinched. "I know that, Roselyne," she said gently. "You're a witch."

Guilt and unease mingled together in my stomach. Essi and I hadn't discussed the revelation of my witch blood. She'd found out in the market square with the majority of the Solorans.

"I'm sorry," I said quietly. "I know I must follow tradition. What else do I have to prepare for?"

Essi nodded. "Most fae nobility will be there. We can go over their names and ranks."

"Okay," I whispered, "Let's do that."

That evening, I slipped away to the small library alcove to be alone with my thoughts and perhaps read more about the magical blood pumping through my veins. In my hand, I gripped one of the large dusty tomes said to hold ancient witch wisdoms. With a dull thud, I opened the book and began at the beginning. My eyes trailed across the tiny lines of text, but I couldn't concentrate. My mind wandered, the text slid out of focus, and I found myself thinking only of how in a few days my life would change forever.

"Roselyne! Do you mind if I join you?"

Sloane's voice jolted me from my wandering thoughts. I sat upright and instinctively slammed my book shut, and turned to face the prince in this quiet carved-away place, carrying his own massive leather-bound book.

"Sloane," I said. "You know about the library alcove?"

He chuckled warmly as he stepped inside. "Of course," he said. "I was raised in the palace." Sloane ran a reverent hand down the curve of the book spines along the walls as he held his own chosen book under his arm. "I imagine I've spent as much time in this library as anyone in history."

"Right," I said, nodding. "When did you leave court again? You were part of Declan's council before, right?"

"After the war," he said, sliding into a chair beside me. His book hit the table with a thud. "Well, a half century after, at least. I helped Declan rebuild, but despite loving this place, and Solora...I needed to get away. I needed to see something *good* in the world. I'd had enough talk of blood and war to last a lifetime." His mouth set in a tight line.

I nodded my head, the sincerity of Sloane's words washing over me. Every mention of the last war left an unmistakable tightness in my chest. I imagined the horror that must have run rampant as the Seelie fae clashed with Unseelie and witches alike. I chewed the inside of my cheek.

"Do you think my presence in the faelands could cause something like that again? War?"

His expression softened. "No, Roselyne...I don't. I heard about what happened in the market...but that was the action of a few cowards, not reflective of the entirety of the fae who reside here. Most welcome humans and witches in the faelands, though not all."

I sniffed, irritated at the beginning of the tears prickling at my eyes. I tilted my face upward to stall their fall and admonished myself for the show of emotion in front of the prince I barely knew.

I swallowed. "And now everyone knows I am a witch." My voice was shaky. I turned my eyes downcast at the closed book in front of me. Strange symbols carved into the leather cover stared back. "Why do they hate the witches?" I whispered.

Sloane assessed me for a moment, then leaned forward and spoke softly.

"People hate what they fear and fear what they cannot understand."

A frustrated growl ripped from my throat as I smacked my hands against the table. "Well, they shouldn't fear me. I know nothing of the supposed power inside of me. I am no threat to anyone."

He laid a hand across mine, but not in the possessive way

Declan would have, but as a show of friendship—mutual understanding, even.

"Most of the fae will welcome you, Roselyne. Some may even call it a miracle that even *one* witch was found." Sloane lifted his hand from mine and ran it through his short, cropped hair. "My brother chose you as his bride and Solora is your home now. You belong here as much as any fae born to this land. You cannot allow fear to rule your heart."

"I know," I said, twisting my fingers together. The Seelie Prince spoke the truth. I belonged in Solora, and despite not being fae, I wanted to be here—to stay.

He leaned back in his chair. "Besides the market *incident*, how are you enjoying the faelands so far?"

A blush crept across my cheeks as I thought of the times I'd spent alone with Declan. "I'm enjoying it."

"And my brother is treating you well?"

"Yes," I said. My blush deepened. I turned away.

"Good," he said, nodding his head. "If you need someone to ever straighten Declan out, you can come to me." I met Sloane's eyes—they were a perfect match to his older brother's and just as striking, radiating warmth. "In only a few days, we'll too become family by fae law." He paused. "Or at least as close to family as possible until the actual wedding ceremony seals your and Declan's union." My heart tugged as I thought of Corbin and Wallace back in Althene. The brothers I'd left behind.

"I have two brothers in Althene as well."

"Now you'll have another." He smiled, and I felt nothing but appreciation for the fae male before me.

"Thank you, Sloane."

Although no one could replace my brothers back home in Althene, I had hope for my future in the faelands. "I think I'm going to go back to my room now." I gestured toward the book in front of me and shook my head apologetically. "I haven't been able to concentrate tonight."

Sloane also stood, glancing toward the exit. "I'll walk with you. Declan's called a council meeting, and it's primed to start soon." He scooped up the massive book he'd been carrying and tucked it beneath one of his arms. "I only popped into the library to choose a light read to have in my room in case I find myself lying awake late at night. When I can't sleep, I prefer to indulge my mind rather than stare at the ceiling." He cocked his head toward me. "But I did enjoy getting to speak with you tonight."

With my storm of anxiety quelled for a moment, Sloane and I walked together up the stairs and out of the library.

27

DECLAN

Kera, Sloane, and Callum sat around me at the large round table in our council rooms. I rapped my fingers on the large round table and my council quieted.

"I've called this meeting to make sure we are all in agreement about the state of affairs in Solora and the Seelie Court as a whole."

Callum nodded silently, while Kera and Sloane only blinked.

"As you know, the betrothal ceremony is soon."

Callum whooped and Kera rolled her eyes.

"Yes, Declan, you're to marry the beautiful princess—what of it?" she teased.

"We need security to be tighter than ever. Despite me *taking care* of the vermin who insulted Roselyne, he claimed he did not act alone." The members of my council inhaled, and I narrowed my eyes. "I'm inclined to believe there are others who may share his sentiments and wish to eliminate their future queen. Summus Nati has a history of hatred for humans, and they view witches as even worse. Someone leaked the informa-

THE CURSE OF THE SEELIE KING

tion of what Roselyne is, and the information found its way into their den."

Sloane shifted in his seat. "You think Summus Nati responsible? They haven't been active in centuries. The humans of Solora live in harmony alongside us. Why would Summus Nati act now?"

"I can't disregard the possibility."

Callum nodded. "I'll station guardsmen around the perimeter. A few hundred sets of golden armor with swords pointed at their throat would give anyone pause."

I nodded and turned to Kera.

"I know you've met with Roselyne in the library and told her the basics about witches, but it's imperative you train harder with her on accessing her magic. It's more important now than ever since the rest of the kingdom is aware of her witch blood. Roselyne needs to be able to defend herself, and a fully-fledged witch at my side could turn the tides if there was ever another war."

"Of course, Declan." Kera uncrossed her legs. "But there isn't anyone left to war with. The rest of the witches have disappeared, the Unseelie are dead, and the humans are separated from the faelands by a vicious sea they are unwilling to cross."

"There are those from my father's council who may wish to usurp me and place themselves on the throne." My mind traveled to Lord Eryk, the current Lord of the Northern Seelie Territory. After killing my father, I dismissed the entirety of the previous Seelie King's royal council and began forging my own. I'll never forget the hatred lining Lord Eryk's eyes after I crowned myself king and kicked him from his chambers in the palace. I shook away the memory. "No one can know of my weakening power," I said, frowning. "We also must speak of the temple break-ins."

Sloane leaned forward, his chin resting on his hands.

"Has there been another, Declan?" my brother asked, his mouth down turned. "You never said what was stolen from the temple in the Western Seelie Territory?"

I glanced at Kera. "Yes. Nothing was taken from the first break-in..." I grimaced. "Clearly the thieves did not find whatever they were after and moved their search onward to a different temple," I said through gritted teeth. "But, last night, a priestess was killed." Shocked faces traveled around the table. "This marks the first casualty to come of these strange occurrences, and also the first time an artifact was stolen."

"What was stolen?" Callum asked.

"I do not yet know. The Veiled did not wish to put it into writing." I turned to Kera. "I need you to go speak with the priestesses. Find out what was taken."

"Should I go now?" she asked.

I shook my head. "Leave after your lessons with Roselyne tomorrow. You could be back the next day if you ride hard."

"I couldn't miss the ceremony—Roselyne would demand your head for that." Kera said with a laugh.

"I don't intend to disappoint my bride. Be back in time for the ceremony."

I turned toward Sloane and Callum.

"Be on the alert when you travel into the city, keep your ears and eyes open for gossip regarding the princess, and report anything suspicious to me *immediately*. No one else knows of what's going on in the temples and I intend to keep it that way. We're about to have a palace full of guests of questionable beliefs, everyone needs to remain vigilant to keep Roselyne safe."

Sloane and Callum grunted in affirmation, and I dismissed my council. Sloane and Callum exited, but Kera stayed, her feet perched on the table, arms crossed over her chest.

"How are you feeling, King?"

"I'm fine, Kera."

She pursed her lips. "Is this princess no longer merely a way to break your curse? Do you care for her in earnest?"

"Yes," I said. Admitting it was easier than I'd anticipated. "I do."

"Good." She nodded. "I've grown fond of the girl and wouldn't want you to break her heart."

With that, Kera stood and left the council room, leaving me alone, thoughts swimming of only Roselyne.

28

ROSELYNE

"You're late." Kera said with a frown.

"Hardly." I sat down beside her on one of the wooden stools inside the greenhouse. The lush greenery surrounding us was a comfort, the earthy scent a distinct reminder of my home in Althene and my best friend, Dove, who waited for me there. I wondered if I'd ever see her again.

"What could possibly be more important than mastering your power?"

"I was sparring with Declan."

"Oh, now you've grown fond of spending time with your husband-to-be?"

Yes.

"No," I replied quickly.

Kera smirked as if she read my mind.

"Of course not. Let's begin."

Kera was a patient teacher. My thoughts were unfocused and difficult to reign in, as my mind wandered to tomorrow's betrothal ceremony. We sat together in the palace's muggy greenhouse among a variety of native herbs and plants.

The Seelie Court's greenhouse was grander than Castle Althene's, but the slight familiarity had me missing Dove even more than usual. Hundreds of plants I'd never seen or heard of, along with more familiar ones filled the entirety of the massive glass building. Some lined long rows full of shelves, some were suspended in the air, and some grew directly from patches of soft earth. The humidity inside was oppressively thick, and beads of perspiration rolled down my skin.

The familiar earthen scent permeated the air, reminding me of times I'd watch Dove tend her small herb garden in Althene. I'd never paid much attention to technique when she'd dig into the dirt with glee, not caring that she caked her nails with soil. I'd always been ornamental there—staying to chat and gossip about members of the court instead of sitting in my bedchamber alone. Perhaps if I'd paid better attention, I'd more easily be able to connect to the witch blood pulsing inside of me.

Two different leaves sat on the small wooden table before me. Kera sat beside me. I closed my eyes and inhaled deeply, detecting among the earthen smell of the soil, a note of fresh orange blossom. I leaned forward and stared at the leaves, trying to feel *something*. Both leaves were both completely unremarkable to me—green and dry with nothing exceptional to differentiate them from one another.

One lone vein pulsed along Kera's forehead betraying her frustration with my lack of ability.

"You can't tell the difference?" she asked, not for the first time.

I shook my head and chewed the skin of my lip. I knew this was disappointing. I tried to tap into my witch gifts, but when I reached for whatever power lay dormant inside of me, I felt nothing but hollow space.

I stared harder at the two identical leaves, willing them to whisper their secrets.

Kera grimaced. "One of these would kill you if ingested, and the other goes great in soup."

I frowned. I was supposed to possess an innate inclination to this sort of thing—a sort of instinct to support the natural well of a witch's power. My well appeared to run dry.

"I think maybe something called to me—" I pointed to the leftmost leaf. "—there."

Kera groaned and ran her hand through her black hair before dropping her head to the table with an exaggerated thud. I laughed nervously. "So, that's the poison one, I take it?"

Kera rubbed at her temples.

"It's okay, Roselyne. We don't need to push you too far. Witches of the past were surrounded by a coven who guided them beginning from childhood. You weren't given that same benefit. That doesn't mean your power is inaccessible. We'll just have to work harder. It'll happen for you."

"I don't understand what else I can do."

"Time in the faelands will help. The human kingdoms have no natural springs of magic in their lands. Perhaps your life in Althene has hindered you."

I frowned. "Maybe so."

Somewhere inside the greenhouse, insects buzzed quietly.

"I'm leaving again," Kera said.

My shoulders slumped. "Why?" I whined. "The ceremony is tomorrow." My foot began tapping nervously on the rough stone flooring. "I thought you would be there."

Kera unsheathed a small dagger from her belt and handed it to me. "Between what happened at the market and the strange occurrences in the faelands, I want you to have this—think of it as a betrothal ceremony gift."

"Is that something that's done in the faelands—betrothal gifts?"

"No." Her lip turned up at one corner. "But I hear things in the shadows. I want you to have something to protect yourself. I knew you'd begun training."

"With dull, wooden blades," I said. I turned the dagger over in my hands, admiring the delicate whorls engraved in the blade's metal.

Kera shrugged. "This one's sharp." She smirked. "I'll be back in time for your ceremony, but Declan has me checking on something else outside of town." Kera said, eyes darting toward the door leading outside.

I wiped at my skirts with my clammy hands. "Oh?" I asked, my voice an octave too high.

"It's nothing major, but one of the Temples of Lux requires attention."

My desperation showed on my face. Kera sighed.

"Don't worry, Roselyne. I won't miss the betrothal ceremony."

"Why not send Callum instead? Isn't he the head of the Daylight Guard?" I asked.

"Yes," Kera smiled. "But some of the priestesses find talking to a city authority objectionable. The Veiled govern themselves throughout the entire faelands and are loyal only to the goddess. The High Priestess has written kindly asking Declan for help. He's sending me."

My face pinched together.

"So, they'll speak with you because you're a woman?"

Kera laughed. "No, Roselyne. Unless I wish them to, they don't speak to me at all."

For a moment, Kera was still, then she transformed into the small black cat form I'd become familiar with. The cat version of Kera nuzzled into my legs, purring once, before scampering through the doorway and into the tall grass beyond.

I knew certain fae possessed inherent gifts and magical abilities—Declan's ability to touch and contort objects with only his mind, and Kera's shapeshifting ability were two such examples. Perhaps some witches, too, were granted gifts not had by others.

I stood from the small wooden chair I'd been sitting at for the past hour and groaned as I stretched my legs. My limbs were stiff from the lack of movement, and my head pounded from the intensity in which I'd been trying to access the supposed magic within me—not that it had done any good. I'd keep trying until I succeeded. I had power inside of me, and I intended to take it. I sat back down and flipped through the book Kera had lent me, a veritable tome that would hopefully help me acclimate and connect to my magical ancestry.

"Witch lessons going well?" Declan's low timbered voice gifted me rows of goose prickles along my exposed skin.

I gasped. We were alone.

I fought the urge to turn toward him, once again drawn to him like a moth to flame. I breathed in measuredly, working to control the frantic beats of my traitorous heart.

"It's going as well as it can when I'm being interrupted," I replied coolly, flipping a page.

He smiled at that.

"Did you know you bite your lip when you're concentrating? It's quite endearing."

I scowled, but kept my gaze locked on the pages of the book, ignoring him.

Nervous energy skittered through my body as memories of our previous encounter bound through my mind in flashes of perfect recall—the scent of him, the way his eyes blazed and dripped over my skin. I squeezed my eyes shut.

My body warred with itself between two opposing choices—fleeing from the greenhouse and back to the known sanctuary of my bedchamber, or wrapping my legs around Declan's middle and succumbing fully to the whims of my body.

I flipped the page with an audible sigh, and Declan chuckled darkly. I closed the book with an annoyed thud and spun to face him.

Declan was dressed in Seelie colors, a typical head-to-toe black ensemble with gold and red stitching woven throughout, but now paired with knee-high riding boots. I arched a brow at the newest addition to his attire.

His knowing smirk nearly undid me.

"Going riding with Sloane. I was going to see if you'd like to accompany us," he said, running a lone hand through his inky black hair. My breath caught in my throat as his shirt rode up slightly showing off hard tanned muscles.

I loved riding as a child and did so often alongside my brothers. But the memories I once cherished above all else grew tainted from their association surrounding my relationship with Nolan. I swallowed down the bile that crept up my throat at the memory of my ex-lover and his betrayal to me. Presented with the opportunity for a small tract of land and a noble title to give up our affair, Nolan took my father's offer.

Declan rocked back and forth on his heels as he waited for my reply, and I cocked my head.

Was the Seelie King...nervous?

A flicker of pleasure warmed my body with the knowledge that I made Declan as anxious as he made me.

"I'd love to go," I said, and it was the truth.

Recollections of riding alongside my brothers was one of

my favorite childhood memories. My heart burned as I once more thought of the family I'd left behind.

Corbin and Ariadni would have been married by now—an event the entire kingdom would have attended. I stood and brushed the loose flecks of soil from my skirts. I wasn't dressed for riding, but it was time for new memories on horseback.

29
DECLAN

Having Sloane back at the palace reminded me of better times—when our burgeoning magic grew stronger, and the Seelie Court knew no war.

Roselyne put her hands on her hips as we approached the palace's stable, digging her heels into the soft earth and stopping in her tracks.

"Where's my horse?" she asked frowning, eyeing the two tied mounts outside the stable.

I whipped around to face her. "The stable master only prepared the two for Sloane and me. I didn't know you were joining us until a few moments ago."

It wasn't the original plan, but I couldn't deny the curl of desire at the prospect of sharing a horse with the princess. Unease etched into her beautiful features. I fought the urge to kiss away the furrow of her brow. She crossed her arms over each other and chewed her lip, deliberating something behind those green eyes.

At that moment, my brother strode up to join us. He turned his charm on to Roselyne, bowing and placing a gentle kiss upon her hand. She looked down demurely in response, her dark eyelashes fluttering against flushed cheeks. I was barely able to control the low growl lodged in my throat.

"You can share my horse, Princess," Sloane offered with a friendly smile, extending his hand to help Roselyne onto the chestnut-colored stallion.

An unwelcome vine of possessiveness snaked through me. I'd be damned to the Otherrealm if another man rode with her.

Roselyne was *mine*.

"No," I snapped, interrupting whatever Roselyne was about to say. "The princess rides with *me*."

Shock registered across both Sloane and Roselyne's faces, but neither objected. All three of us mounted our horses, with Roselyne positioned in front of me atop my large black warhorse, Kez.

We joined the trail leading into the Ghostwood Forest and rode beneath the lush canopy of trees and into the dimness of the thick woods. The air was cooler beneath the trees, protected from the overbearing rays of sunlight that seemed intent to singe the skin of everyone who dared stand outside for more than a few minutes.

With every uneven step of the terrain, Roselyne's ass rubbed against my cock through the fabric of my pants. My hands tightened on Kez's reins, knuckles nearly white, as I fought back a groan of desire. I should have thought through the consequences of having Roselyne riding with me at such close proximity. I watched my brother through narrowed eyes. I shook my head. Roselyne riding with me was the better option.

In the past, women always flocked to Sloane, and I wouldn't risk my princess doing the same. He was charming, while I was moody. Sloane was wild and untamed, the uncontested life of the party, whereas I was controlled—the responsible one. I'd followed the rules that life set from me and rarely deviated. Until I killed my father and took his crown. After everything with Phaedra, I hadn't desired anyone else. I'd been content to be alone.

My cock stiffened in response to the press of her skin against mine, and the heady jasmine scent of her hair near my face. It was suffocating to want so badly. I gripped the reins tighter.

I hadn't been with a woman in years. Not since Phaedra. Sure, I'd fooled around quite a bit while I was younger. I shook my head. After I killed my father and inherited the throne, I had no more use for casual dalliances with women I didn't truly care for.

Roselyne had piqued my interest for the first time in a century. She felt different. She *was* different. She was a spark of lightning in my veins, illuminating every shadowy bit of my corrupt soul—and wholly necessary to me. It was with great difficulty I'd accepted my emotions regarding the princess, but now that I'd embraced them fully, there was no turning back.

Riding side by side, Sloane and I pointed out plants and animals to Roselyne that were not native to her homeland. Roselyne was an attentive student and paid rapt attention, squealing with joy when I pointed out a barely visible unicorn foal in the distance through the dense foliage. I'd do anything to hear that sound again.

"That's the baby," Sloane said. "The mother will be close by."

"Are there other unicorns in the forest?" Roselyne asked.

I allowed myself the indulgence of resting my chin on Roselyne's shoulder and speaking low into her ear.

"I'd imagine there's an entire herd in these woods. But

there's more living in the Ghostwood Forest than gentle creatures. I wouldn't venture into these woods alone, Princess."

Roselyne gulped and surveyed the thick vegetation before sinking closer to my body. The heat of her skin beneath the thin dress only served to cloud my thoughts. I cleared my throat and continued at a normal volume.

"Nothing will harm you with Sloane or I with you. The beasts of the forest can sense the power within our veins. Perhaps they can even sense yours. You're safe with us."

Her shoulders slumped in visible relief.

We rode on the familiar path for a few minutes longer, the underfoot crunching of leaves and chittering of the various concealed forest creatures our natural ambience.

"What have you been doing while away, Sloane?" Roselyne asked my brother, voice shining with sincerity.

"I've been doing all the things my older brother cannot," Sloane replied with a sly smile. Roselyne cocked her head and turned her body to face me as my brother answered. "Declan was born first which means he has to put up with all the menial tasks like running the kingdom, collecting taxes, and doling out punishments"—Sloane cocked an eyebrow—"but he does get the honor to marry a beautiful woman." He winked at Roselyne.

Roselyne's answering laugh vibrated the air and clawed its way into my chest, staking me in the heart.

"No one is stopping you from marrying, Sloane," I bit out, too jealous of his casual flirting.

Noticing my dark mood, Roselyne turned in the saddle and said nothing, but assessed me, her bright green eyes twinkling with mischief.

"No," Sloane said with a cheeky grin. "I'm not ready to

settle down with one woman yet. There's so much beauty in the world, and I intend to see it all."

I rolled my eyes. My younger brother could wax poetic all day long if he pleased. He spent most of his free time and coin dallying with different women each day, and the kingdom knew it. If the rumors were to be believed, he'd already made his acquaintance with the women of Stars Crossed. I was sure Madam Tasha would appreciate the coin he'd bring to the brothel.

"Where are we now in relation to the palace?" Roselyne asked me as she wiggled against me, returning to normal riding position. I bit my tongue in order to not cry out from the delicious friction between us.

Coherent thoughts were not available to me.

"We're, ah, uh, west of the palace," I said with a cough, my voice flat.

My fingers twitched from the effort it took to keep hold of the reins instead of succumbing to my desire of palming up and down the length of the princess' body.

"What's beyond the forest?" she asked. "I've never seen a map of the faelands."

Sloane interjected, his chestnut stallion riding in line with Kez. "Small villages mostly. There's an all-human settlement called Bask if you follow the main road north, and if you travel further south through the forest, you'll eventually find the ruins of the Unseelie Court."

"Unseelie?" she asked. Roselyne's body jolted and a small gasp escaped her parted lips. "Truly?"

"Remember, Roselyne. The Unseelie are gone. They've been dead a century," I said.

"Thanks to Declan," Sloane interjected. "The faelands are safer than they've ever been."

The tension in Roselyne's posture relaxed, and she leaned her back against my chest. Roselyne sighed softly, and warm satisfaction spread through my body. I chewed my lip to suppress the grin beginning at the corner of my mouth.

My heart thumped wildly, as she nestled her head against my chest, the honey and silver spill of her hair curling against my skin. Under the thick canopy of trees with Roselyne relaxed and pressed into my body—I felt peace.

Fat drops of water began to fall from above us, and I glanced up with a frown.

Through the trees, I was unable to even see the sky, so densely covered. An ominous boom of thunder sounded overhead. We'd been riding for over an hour and would need to turn back to not get stuck in a storm. Although the beasts that lurked the forest would not approach me, I didn't like the lowered visibility a storm would bring. Sloane seemed to have the same idea.

"Time to go back?" he asked, and I nodded my agreement.

We both turned our mounts around and began down the trail the direction we came. A crack of thunder boomed nearby, sending concealed birds squawking and flying out of their nests.

Roselyne shrank into me, and I curled one arm protectively around her waist. She made no protest. The sky spilled open, and all the rain that had been absent during the summer season began to fall, all at once, soaking into our clothes and drenching our bodies. Roselyne shrieked in delight and threw her head back to the clouds as they unleashed their deluge of rain.

Sloane's voice was muffled through the heavy sounds of rain.

"I'll see you two back in the palace!"

His horse took off on a gallop toward home. I half yelled in Roselyne's ear to hold on tight, and she gripped the reins below my hands, her thighs squeezing against the saddle.

Sloane was ahead of us, barely perceptible through the thick sheet of rain. Kez galloped, legs pumping, working to keep pace with Sloane's stallion, but he bore two riders instead of one.

We lost sight of Sloane as he navigated the worn trail back to the palace. Wet mud flung through the air from the force of hooves on dirt, painting our bodies in specks of brown. We kept a steady pace. I held Roselyne's body tightly against mine as Kez navigated us with expert agility through gnarled roots overgrown along the path and low-hanging branches that hadn't seemed as treacherous under better weather.

By the time Roselyne and I reached the forest edge and put Kez back in the stable, the downpour of rain slowed to a light sprinkle. Roselyne was drenched, the simple dress she'd worn stuck to her body like a second skin, outlining every tempting curve. Her hair was soaked and limp, plastered to her head. Brown mud peppered across her face with one particularly large fleck stuck to the corner of her lips.

Instead of being disgruntled by the state of her appearance and clothing, Roselyne's eyes shone with undiluted delight. She eyed me up and down, and one corner of her mouth tugged up in a smile before she burst into a fit of giggles. I'm sure I looked just as much a drowned rat as my betrothed. I couldn't help my responding grin as the sound of her laughter warmed me from within.

We walked alongside each other through the soggy grass of the palace yard, our fingers brushing together multiple times, but never fully committing to tangle together.

Although it was late summer, the air inside the palace was

cold when we stepped through the large wooden door, and she shivered from the change in temperature.

"You've said some fae have special powers? Can you warm us?" she asked as we walked toward the wing of her bedchambers.

I chuckled at that. "It's true that I was granted elysian magic, but I don't possess the powers to control flames."

"Sloane then?" she asked, jokingly as she squeezed water from her hair. I searched the room for the Seelie Prince, but he was already elsewhere.

"Sloane doesn't possess any elysian gifts," I said, then cringed. "Except for his incessant charm," I added.

"Oh."

Our boots tracked mud through the entirety of the palace, sodden socks squishing in shoes as we trudged up the stairs. Being with Roselyne like this was better than anything I could have imagined. If friendly affection was all she ever desired from me as a husband, that was what I would gladly give her. She was a ray of pure sunlight beaming down from the heavens to thaw my icy heart and broken soul. I'd do anything to keep her happy and at my side.

Too soon, we were faced with the dark wood of her bedchamber door. She curtsied, grabbing the limp fabric of her ruined dress and placed her back against her door, facing me. The outline of her stiff nipples showed through the soaked fabric of her bodice like ripe berries, begging to be tasted. I swallowed hard, averting my gaze. We were inches apart, and neither I nor her made a move to distance ourselves.

"Thank you for the ride," she breathed. Her eyes flickered to my mouth, heat in her gaze. She blinked. "And thanks to Kez, of course," she added, with a shake of her head.

"I hope the rain didn't spoil it for you," I said.

She shook her head. "Not at all." Her hair had begun to dry in stiff clumps and barely moved, too stuck together with rainwater and muck. The silvery portion of her hair was completely camouflaged by the smears of dirt and mud—and yet she'd never looked as alluring to me than she did right now.

"The betrothal ceremony is tomorrow," she said.

Her statement sounded more like a question than the fact it was. She chewed at her bottom lip awaiting my response.

"It is," I growled out. A tingle of pleasure traveled down my spine at the prospect of claiming her as mine so publicly and formally. "Are you nervous?"

"Only because I have to meet so many new people. I don't want to mess up. I think of the market sometimes. Someone clearly doesn't want me as queen." She squinted into the darkness at the other end of the corridor as if the guests had already arrived and skulked in the shadows of the palace.

"The man from the market has been dealt with. No one will ever harm you again." My lips pressed into a firm line. I wanted so badly to cradle her in my arms, as I'd done twice now. I suppressed the impulse. "You are safe with me."

She leaned her back against her door and placed a trembling palm against my chest. Our gazes locked together. She made no move to leave the hallway. The brush of her fingertips burned my skin as she swept her hand across my chest reverently. I sucked in a breath before bringing my own trembling hand to rest on hers. Roselyne's green eyes flickered to mine, full of purpose. She licked her lips.

"Declan, I—"

The door to her bedchambers swung inward and Roselyne would have fallen backward into her room had I not looped my arms around her waist and yanked her toward me.

Roselyne gasped as her body pressed into mine. My heart thundered wildly from the contact it so desperately craved.

Essi stood on the other side of Roselyne's open doorway, doorknob in hand and slack jawed. "Oh, sorry," she squeaked as she backed away from the doorway.

Roselyne pushed off from me, creating space between us. My body mourned the loss of her contact.

Roselyne wiped her hands across her dirty dress and shot a bright smile at her lady-in-waiting.

"I was just coming in, Essi. We went riding and got caught in a storm." She gestured to her ruined dress.

Essi scrunched up her face.

"Well, come in then! We've got to get those tangles out of your hair before the ceremony tomorrow," Essi tittered away, grumbling to herself. "King Declan sent all the lady's maids away, so it's my duty to get you presentable."

"I'll be right in," Roselyne said, dismissing the courtier, and Essi left the doorway to go prepare the bathing tub. "King Declan," Roselyne said formally with a small nod of her head, "I suppose I'll see you tomorrow." She rocked on her heels as she began to turn away from me.

I caught her wrist in my hand, and she turned to face me, her mouth cast in a small 'o.' I brought her hand to my lips and pressed my lips to her skin, eliciting a sharp inhale from my betrothed.

"Yes, you will," I murmured against her soft skin. "Goodnight, Roselyne."

30

DECLAN

With every piece of self-restraint in my body, I turned and walked away from the woman who'd come charging headfirst into my life and consumed all rational thought. After lying awake in my bed, tossing and turning and unable to rid my mind of Roselyne's face, I decided I needed fresh air. The air in the palace was oppressive, the sweet scent of jasmine heavy and making me dizzy. I made my way outside the palace, gulping in lungfuls of fresh air. Nightfall brought cooler air than its predecessor, a welcome respite from the heat of end of summer days. I walked off the large porch and into the grass. Insects chirped nearby. A dim glow emitted from Roselyne's window.

I needed to clear my mind. Being around Roselyne created a fog and muddied my every waking thought, making them indecipherable. Her presence clouded my judgment. When I closed my eyes, I only saw her face staring back, framed in silver. Being near Roselyne shouldn't affect me this way. But I couldn't deny the truth.

Footsteps crushed through soft grass behind me. I spun around to find Callum approaching. My friend's face was painted grim, and I realized there was no reason for him to be outside the palace this late. I frowned, sensing trouble.

"What's going on?"

Callum ran a hand through his blond hair.

"There's a dead body in town."

Fuck. A resurgence of crime is the last thing the faelands needed, especially with the betrothal ceremony tomorrow and the noble fae arriving.

"Who?"

He shook his head solemnly. "I'm not sure yet. One of the Daylight Guard sent a falcon to my tower. The body was found on the Street of Sins while she patrolled. I was on my way there when I spotted you outside. I figured you'd want to know."

I sighed and dropped my head into my hands, rubbing my forehead with slightly too much pressure to be pleasant.

"I do want to know," I said with a groan. *What was going on in Solora?* Although the city was large, until recently there was relatively no crime. For years, the humans and fae lived in relative peace side by side—until news of my betrothed began to spread. My people deserved better from me.

This was my fault. I'd been too distracted chasing Roselyne's affections. I needed to start choosing my people over my bride.

I assessed Callum. "I need to tell Sloane. I can't leave Roselyne alone."

With a quick stop to Sloane's rooms, I quickly filled my brother in on the situation in the city. He'd been asleep, with heavy-lidded eyes and a glazed expression on his face. With a yawn, he'd agreed to stay awake and keep watch over Roselyne while I was away.

I didn't believe even the worst of Summus Nati would dare attack Roselyne while in the palace. Despite that, I felt more at peace knowing my brother kept guard for her while I wasn't physically able.

A few minutes later, Callum and I made it to the crime scene. The rich scent of iron permeated the air, cutting through the haze of perfume that spilled from the Street of Sins' row of businesses. The crowd of the Daylight Guards parted, allowing their king to look upon the body of the dead.

The scene was a horror. The fae woman was nearly nude, her pale skin flayed in ribbons as if elongated claws had cut into her skin repeatedly. She lay in a pool of spilled blood, the deepest of reds surrounding her dark hair in a macabre halo. A thick trail of blood led from the street into the nearby alley, as if she'd been killed there first, then moved and placed into the open air amid the Street of Sins.

"Animal attack," Callum said with a grimace. "A bearbeast or wolf you think?"

"Her body was dragged into the street."

"Then who?" he asked. "Summus Nati?"

I shook my head. "Summus Nati only attacks humans. She's fae. It doesn't make any sense, and Summus Nati tend to claim their crimes." I thought for a moment. "It could be an animal, but it'd be something massive." I met Callum's blue eyes with my own. "Increase the nighttime patrol numbers. I don't care what it costs." He nodded.

A member of the Daylight Guard approached us, hands stiff at her sides and dark eyes shifting nervously.

"Bettany," Callum spoke low so only I could hear. "She's the sentry who found the body."

Bettany's voice trembled when she spoke aloud to me "Your...Your Highness." She bowed low. Her brown, coily hair was pulled slick against her scalp and a sword hung in a scabbard at her hip. I didn't recognize her—one of Callum's newest recruits no doubt. Her face paled as if she was about to be sick. "I found her like this while patrolling the streets. It had to have taken place in the last few hours." She smacked her lips nervously. "I immediately wrote to the commander," she said, nodding toward Callum, who grunted in affirmation.

"Did you hear anything?" I asked her.

Her eyes went wide. "No, nothing. I didn't even see her at first." She shuddered. "I stepped into her blood, otherwise—otherwise I wouldn't have noticed until sunup."

"Did you see anyone else on your patrol tonight?"

"I don't know. I didn't see a soul or hear anything."

"Have we identified the victim yet?"

"Yes." She glanced quickly toward the dead woman and back to me with a grimace. "She's the apothecarist's daughter."

"Alert her family, please. They need to know."

The guard bowed, taking the dismissal. "Your Majesty." She scuttled away, and I heard the distinct sounds of retching.

I turned to Callum. "What do you think?"

"Bettany is new to the guard, but she's a good recruit. I believe her version of this."

"Who does your gut tell you is responsible for this woman's death?"

He hesitated. "I don't know. There aren't many beasts in the forest who would breach the tree line. But the claw marks are so—"

"Animalistic?" I finished. Callum's eyebrows knit together. "Let's consider the options. Either some beast killed her, and moved her by chance, or another fae did this, and moved the body out in the open, for the sole purpose of wanting her discovered. Neither is good."

"Summus Nati only ever killed humans. There hasn't been a fae murder since the war," Callum said.

Except ones done by my hand.

My eyes trailed down the woman's broken body and Callum shifted on his feet. "*Something* killed her. Do you think it's related to the attack on Roselyne in the market?" Callum asked.

"I can't be sure. Move her body. Double the patrols of the Daylight Guard. I don't want people panicking, or anyone else succumbing to this fate. We don't yet know if the perpetrator is a fae or beast."

"The priestesses are coming to take her away and prepare her body."

"Good."

I walked back to the palace, my mind racing. It took only five minutes to get back to the grounds. As I stepped through the gates, I glanced toward Roselyne's window once more. No light was emitted from the small arched window.

Sloane was awake in the main living area of the palace's bottom floor, reading by the light of a nearby candle. He glanced up when he heard me enter the room.

"What was it?"

"A dead fae woman. Mutilated."

Sloane paled. He'd never possessed the stomach for brutality like I had.

"Who's responsible?" he asked.

"We aren't sure," I said grimacing. "Probably an animal. Nothing new here?"

"Only the sounds of night. She's been sleeping soundly. Not a peep from her room or anywhere else."

I clasped a hand on Sloane's shoulder, and he placed his hand on top of mine. "Thank you, brother."

"We'll figure this out, Dec."
"I just hope we're able to before it's too late."

31

ROSELYNE

"Just—a—little—more," Essi grunted, tugging on the golden ribbons of my bodice, cinching my waist beyond what could be considered reasonable. Even so, Essi somehow found the strength to wrench my bodice even tighter, exaggerating the already ample curves of my body.

"Perfection," she said brightly as she stepped away.

I wrinkled my nose. "This a betrothal ceremony and *feast*, correct? How am I supposed to eat if I cannot *breathe*?"

Essi didn't dignify that with a response, and instead circled around me admiring her handiwork.

"Fae fashion suits you," Essi said. "The wedding itself will be even more spectacular."

I stared into the mirror opposite me.

With only a few hours of time, Essi dressed and subsequently transformed me into the image of a proper fae-fiancée. Despite my humanity—I appeared suitable for the Seelie King.

My gown was breathtaking. The fabric was a bright gold, covered in shimmering white beads stitched into sunbursts that shone with every ripple of movement. My collarbones and shoulders dripped with golden chains adorned with red rubies and opals, while the gown's square neckline plunged low, showing off the ample curve of my breasts. The gown clung to every dip of my body, the fabric ending in a high slit in the center of one thigh in what those in the human kingdoms would surely describe as lascivious. The ensemble was completed by gossamer sleeves trailing behind my body in a flowing golden cape. Essi assured me I was dressed in the pinnacle of Seelie fashion. My lady-in-waiting wasn't aware, but beneath the layers of the gown, the dagger Kera had gifted me sat strapped against my thigh. Despite not being remotely adept with it yet, the weapon's presence gave me some pretense of control.

Half of my hair was piled on top of my head in a labyrinth of braids. The rest flowed gently over my shoulders, the silver strands of my hair on display and framing my jaw.

I looked every part the fae bride, and so unlike myself.

"This belonged to King Declan's mother," Essi said solemnly, as she revealed an ancient, golden tiara.

I realized then that I knew nothing of my betrothed's late mother and was only aware of the fact that he killed his father.

Did Declan also murder his mother in his quest for rule?

The tiara was breathtaking—somewhat similar to a laurel wreath. Gold vine-like leaves formed together to create the base of the headpiece, and small flowers made of sparkling gemstones were scattered throughout the design giving dimension to the gilded tiara.

Essi sat it atop my head, her eyes shining with delight.

"Roselyne, you're breathtaking," she said. "The king is not going to be able to take his eyes off you."

I hoped she was right. I turned away and a blush crept across my cheeks.

"Maybe not," I said.

"Are you ready for the betrothal ceremony?" Essi asked, her large brown eyes wide with concern.

I chewed my lip, smudging the cosmetics Essi applied only a few minutes ago and earning a scowl from my friend.

Humans didn't partake in betrothal ceremonies as the fae did. Since the fae lived for centuries, marriage pacts were taken even more seriously by their population. Among the nobility, a betrothal ceremony was held some time before the actual wedding ceremony. Either party had the chance to change their mind and remove the betrothal rings, so any wayward bride or groom could back out of the arrangement and face no consequence.

I exhaled, and let my shoulders relax. Essi had prepared me well for the ceremony, and I was eternally grateful to her for that.

In the past few days, my friend diligently taught me the names of major lords and ladies who'd be attending and the social niceties that differed from the human ones. I was already an outsider coming to their world to marry their king—the least I could do was not make any social gaffe and embarrass myself or Declan.

"I'm more anxious about the after the feast to be honest."

"And spending the night with the king?" Essi's eyes sparkled full of mischief. "Have you thought more of that?"

I rolled my eyes and laughed lightly, hiding the nervous pang of apprehension that settled into my chest. "If his room is set up similar to mine, I'll have the king sleep on the sofa."

Not sensing my anxiety, Essi primped herself in my mirror, smacking her lips and smiling at her beautiful reflection. "Of course, Roselyne." She swirled around to face me. "You're a romantic at heart, I can tell. There's no need to rush things with the king." She leaned forward toward the mirror, tucking a golden blonde lock of hair behind her ear, and beamed at me through the reflection. "Are you ready?"

Essi stood and smoothed her pale blue gown. The garment was constructed of a strapless fitted bodice that transitioned at her natural waist into a full flowing skirt. The icy color she'd chosen for herself would have made me appear sallow and unwell, but on her, the color somehow gave her skin a soft glow.

I steeled myself and managed a weak smile. "Yes, I am."

Essi bounced on her heels, bubbling with excitement before looping her arm in mine and leading me toward the ceremony space.

I wanted to tell Essi about my fears and reservations, but every time I began, my mouth went dry, and I found it impossible to shatter her expectations of me.

Two massive double doors swung open, and I inhaled. No amount of preparation for this ceremony would have prepared me for the sheer amount of fae packed into the great hall. Two of the six long tables stretching along the length of the room had been removed creating an aisle of sorts. Lords and Ladies from nearby Seelie territories crammed themselves on the benches, eager to witness the official betrothal of their king to an outsider—to a witch.

I took a deep breath as I entered the hall and walked down the aisle, noting the several large golden orbs hanging from the ceiling. I allowed myself a quick glance around the room. Essi's decorating was impeccable. Bright flowers covered the tables, so much there'd be barely any room to dine. Rich fabrics covered every corner of the great hall in swirls of gold, oranges, and reds as if we were located at the center of a fire.

Just a few more steps and I'd be at the newly built stairs up to the platform. The hard stares of the crowd of fae pressed against my back as I kept my feet even, one in front of the other, making my way toward the dais. My throat dried as my eyes snagged on Declan, dressed in a suit of deep burgundy embellished in gold. He was already standing on the platform, mouth pressed into a grim line, hands crossed over his front. He'd worn his hair up today, with his face neatly shaved. On his head, sat a large, spiked crown of golden sunbursts without any gemstone embellishment. Someone stood next to him, a woman I'd guess by their height—their body completely covered in a lavender cloak.

A Veiled Priestess of the Temple of Lux to perform the ceremony, I remembered.

A quick glance up toward the high rafters led me to believe Declan hired extra security for the event. I counted eight bowmen standing around the perimeter of the room, and I swallowed hard, keeping my eyes on my destination—Declan.

My heels clicked against the smooth stone floor as I passed Kera sitting near the front of the hall, her hair for once not in a braid, but loose around her shoulders. Kera smirked and nodded her head, dressed in a rich chocolate-colored gown unlike anything I'd ever seen her wear. Essi sat on the opposite side of the aisle, beaming at me. Sloane sat next to her, relaxed on the bench with his legs extended.

My gait was unsteady in these ridiculous shoes Essi chose for me. The heel of one of my heels caught on the uneven flooring and twisted. I wobbled but did not fall. The smile I plastered across my face never faltered.

I crossed the distance toward Declan, ignoring the hushed

tittering from the gathered fae. I looked up, finally at the platform. Declan's eyes met mine and his mouth parted into a reassuring smile.

The ceremony wasn't nearly as harrowing as I thought it'd be. Everything went as Essi instructed it would happen. Declan and I first drank from the large ornamental goblet supplied by the Veiled Priestess. Declan then spoke the Ancient Faerie words low so only I and the Veiled Priestess heard him. He slipped a solid gold ring around my finger. The sound of the ancient language on Declan's tongue sent shivers rippling across my skin. Next, I did the same, clunkily reciting the memorized words as I placed the twin ring to mine around Declan's finger.

Declan and I clasped our hands together, interlocking our fingers. As we did so, the priestess spoke her own words in a lilting voice, waving her hands over ours as the nobility of the Seelie Court watched. I wondered if the three-headed goddess I'd prayed to all my life observed alongside the Seelie fae's goddess Lux.

A warm golden and silver light encircled our hands and arms in thousands of shimmering threads. For only a moment, a searing pain burned where the ring lay on my finger. The light diminished, the pain was gone—and the ceremony was done. The goddess approved our union.

Until we were officially wed, Declan and I could remove our rings and forgo the betrothal if either desired without ensuring the wrath of the gods. Any time after that, we'd be divinely punished for our flightiness. As per the agreement with my father, we'd be married before the first snowfall of the season to preserve the treaty between our people.

The crowd erupted into cheers, standing from their seats and stamping their feet. A band of strings played as we walked quickly down the aisle and out the main double doors leading to the corridor. The chattering noise of the crowd grew louder as dinner was served by the few hired and vetted servants who waited in the wings. No one passed us as we stood outside the great hall—Declan and I were alone.

His warm eyes pressed into mine.

"How are you doing?" he asked.

I fidgeted with the new ring around my fourth finger. It was heavy, and I wasn't used to the weight of it.

"I'm fine," I said a bit stiffly.

His lips turned downward. "That was the worst of it, give the guests an hour, they'll all be too drunk to stand."

"That's what Essi said too." I managed a weak smile.

"When the crown supplies, it's customary to be generous. The fae wine will flow heavily tonight." He paused for a moment, rubbing his chin. "When we re-enter that room, we are considered officially betrothed. No one can contest that now. The gods have approved our union." He regarded me seriously. "Any offense to you is also considered a direct offense to me and will be managed as such."

I nodded, then glanced to the large double doors beside us. The sound of buzzing laughter and clinking glasses sounded through the thick wood of the door.

"I understand," I said.

"The party will go on until the early morning hours," he said grimly. "We aren't expected to stay the entire time. The crowd will expect us to—retire to bed after a few dances."

He coughed once and lowered his eyes down to his boots.

Was that a blush spreading along the Seelie King's face?

I considered having Declan in bed and arousal curled low in my belly.

"But of course, we won't do that." Declan added.

I bit back a frown.

"Of course not," I agreed quickly.

"I want you to be comfortable."

"Thank you," I said, feeling a strange sensation of disappointment.

Declan nodded, his golden eyes pressed into mine.

He was like staring into the sun, beautiful and dangerous, like I'd risk irreversible harm if I didn't avert my gaze. Declan clasped my hands in his and I felt a warm buzzing inside my chest from the solid contact. The doors opened wide, and we strode inside, hand in hand, officially betrothed to be married.

32

DECLAN

Roselyne's eyes shifted side to side, keeping watch of all the attendees below us on the dance floor. After the ceremony ended, servants brought out a large wooden table and raised it upon the dais for Roselyne and I to sit—future king and queen watching their subjects celebrate on our behalf. We sat beside each other on a giant throne the width of a sofa, our legs and feet concealed to the crowd below by a silken tablecloth spread atop the table.

I felt the heat of Roselyne's body, although we were not touching. Just as I'd suspected, once the drinks started flowing, my guests no longer paid us any mind, too busy getting drunk on the crown's dime to see straight.

When the sun set, the only light remaining in the great hall was the flickering of the thousands of candles, reflecting off the beads of gowns and the golden orbs on the ceiling. As night fell, the guests of the Seelie Court truly let loose. Women's intricate braided hairstyles became unruly and undone. Servants hiccupped and covered their mouths to hide their blue-stained lips and tongues. A group of fae men swayed together with sloshing cups, puffing out their chests and singing along with the musicians' instruments. Roselyne watched it all with rapt attention, while politely sipping from her own wine glass.

Two fae nobles nearby began wrestling each other, laughing and rolling around on the ground, clearly drunk off the fae wine and lager flowing freely.

"If this is only the *betrothal* feast, how will the wedding feast be?" Roselyne asked with eyes wide as saucers, watching the men.

My jaw ticked as I considered my answer.

"About the same," I said.

There was no use worrying her, but in truth, the wedding ceremony and feast would be much worse. Royal weddings in the faelands were considered kingdom-wide celebrations. At the wedding we wouldn't have the safety of being apart from the crowd. We'd be expected to engage in the revelry all day and night, and until the sun rose once more and beckoned us to sleep.

She shifted her body on our shared throne, pressing into my side. The warmth of her skin radiated through the silks of her gown and into my body, permeating my very soul. The urge to pull her to me, to claim her in front of everyone was overwhelming. I bit my tongue and squeezed my palms together.

I scanned the dance floor. Kera leaned against the wall scowling at any fae male who dared approach her to dance, looking rather striking, but perhaps uncomfortable in her gown. I snorted back a laugh. Callum danced with one of the serving women, spinning her in the air. The woman's dark hair whipped wildly around her head as she laughed, before she scuttled away, fixing her skirts. I scanned the rest of the crowd, and my eyebrows raised. Sloane danced with Roselyne's lady-in-waiting. I made a mental note to assure my brother didn't break the poor girl's heart. Roselyne seemed fond of Essi, and I didn't want one of her first friends in the faelands wanting to leave court due to needless heartbreak by my roguish brother.

"What comes after this?" Roselyne asked as she stared straight ahead. She hadn't relaxed her rigid posture at all, not even once the merriment began and the guests' attention turned away from us and to their own frivolities. I turned in my seat to appraise my bride. I saw only perfection—her caramel-colored hair, with its striking silver additions, expertly coiffed and braided, doubtlessly brushed hundreds of times by Essi before the ceremony. My gaze traveled over her face as Roselyne stared forward, noting the soft rosy pout of her lips and the smattering of pale freckles across the bridge of her sloped nose. Her eyes were bright green, concentrating on the dancing crowd, completely avoiding my gaze. She jutted her chin slightly, and I fought back a smile. She was obstinate, even now.

"Tell me when you are ready to leave, and I will escort you back to your bedchamber," I said quietly. "Tradition be damned."

I wondered if she had heard me but then saw Roselyne suppress a shiver. She faced me, and her obvious relief hit me like a punch to the gut, but I didn't allow my face to betray my own dismay.

"Thank you," she whispered, face inches from my own.

Without thinking, I took the silvery section of her hair into my hands, and I let it slip through my palm, falling through my fingers like individual beams of moonlight. She closed her eyes, long lashes fanned against her cheeks. She gasped at my touch, but made no move to pull away. I couldn't help but imagine the other sounds that I could elicit from her mouth.

I watched as the pulse point in her neck bounded uncontrollably. She was nervous.

"I'd never want to make you uncomfortable."

She bit her bottom lip, and I had the urge to do the same, to nibble on her mouth, knowing exactly how sweet her lips taste. I stifled a groan and suppressed my growing arousal.

"Thank you," she said again. Her hands twisted in her lap, the plain golden ring that now adorned her hand drawing my eye. My gaze darted to her mouth as she licked her lips. "It's not that I don't want to—"

Her words were cut off when Essi's father, the Western Seelie Territory Lord, climbed the stairs and approached us, bowing low and offering his congratulations in a string of a few rehearsed sentences. His visit seemed to signal to the other guests it was time to offer their own drunken congratulations. Roselyne and I sat together as guests came to pay homage to the new couple, wishing us well, and drunkenly telling us how ecstatic they were for the wedding. Roselyne played the part dutifully, smiling and nodding appropriately at all the strangers to her. My chest puffed with pride. She was so adaptable. The part of a king's wife was one she had been born and raised to play.

Last, Lord Eryk strode to the dais. His own lady wife was curled possessively around his arm, her face pinched like she smelled something foul, although if I recalled correctly, she may have always looked that way.

His beady eyes narrowed on me, then moved to roam across Roselyne's body, lazily drinking her in. I was filled with an irrational anger that had me wanting to rip his spine from his body and paint the walls red.

"Congratulations, my king," Lord Eryk said with a bow, voice greasy with false sincerity.

"It's so contrary to take a human wife," his wife cooed, "and a *witch* at that! Your union has created enough gossip to last the rest of the year. Everyone is wondering *why*." She laughed, then hiccupped, slapping her hand to her mouth with a giggle. Roselyne gave the woman a small smile she didn't deserve before nervously chewing at her lip and glancing at me from the corner of her eye.

"Now, now, Matilda," Lord Eryk scolded. "The king of course must have his reasons, and we are not privy to them." He faced me. "It is most impressive how you found a witch! After all that business during the war." He *tsked* and began to turn away. "We look forward to the wedding. Congratulations, again." Lord Eryk and his wife turned away and disappeared into the throng of people dancing and drinking.

The glow of the candles was dimmer now, the sun blinked completely from the sky. The flames flickered and cast shadows along Roselyne's pale face. In the dimness, she could nearly pass for fae. Even now, I sensed her innate magic thrashing within her, rolling around and trying to escape. I wondered if Roselyne experienced her unspent power as anxiety, but its presence didn't appear to bother her in the slightest.

Lord Eryk and Lady Matilda had been the only guests brave enough to mention Roselyne's witch blood, although I'm sure all my guests were aware of the potential threat that sat by my side. I glanced around the dim banquet hall. Roselyne was officially betrothed to me. No other suitor could steal her away and claim her as their own bride in a quest for her power, or they'd risk the wrath of the gods. She was mine.

"You've done so well," I said to her once we were again alone.

From the corner of my eye, I watched the corner of her mouth tip upward in a genuine smile.

All the guests were completely drunk and paid us no more attention as we sat atop the dais like gods watching over their creations.

"Fae and humans are all the same," she said, tossing her unbraided hair over one shoulder and exposing the bare, smooth skin of her neck. She leaned forward over the table in front of us.

My eyes dipped low to the neckline of her gown, appreciating how her breasts pressed together between twin panels of golden fabric, threatening to spill over. I swallowed hard.

"Oh, are we now?" My brow lifted in question.

"Yes," she said. "The men especially." Her voice was laced with seduction, dripping with a promise and challenge. *This woman would be the death of me.*

My cock stirred beneath my pants, awoken by Roselyne's ever-present taunts.

"I can guarantee, I'm nothing like the men you've known," I growled.

This woman would be my undoing. She turned to face me and leaned in close, our faces merely inches apart. I could smell the wine on her breath, mingling with her sweet jasmine scent. I watched her blue tinted tongue move in her mouth as her lips parted to form her next words.

"Then what are you like?" she asked, placing a hand on my thigh and digging in with her nails. It didn't hurt, I don't believe she meant it to, but my skin was on fire beneath her touch.

My cock jerked to attention and stiffened, pulling against the fabric of my pants. She smirked knowingly and dropped her gaze low before sucking in her bottom lip.

Was this some sort of game?

The table covered us below our chests concealing our position. To everyone else in the room, we appeared merely engaged in conversation—which I suppose was true enough.

"You don't want to play this game with me, Princess," I said, placing my own hand on her exposed knee.

Her skin was smooth and supple beneath the slit of her gown.

"Maybe I do," she whispered as she guided her hand upward toward my growing bulge. She assessed me for a split second, as if deliberating her decision, before gently squeezing my cock through the fabric.

Flashes of light exploded in my vision from her touch, erasing everything else from my vision. Nothing mattered but her hands on me, and how desperately I wanted to return her touch. I yearned to rip open her gown and take her on this very table to mark her as mine in the most primal way possible. Guests be damned.

I panted and groaned as pleasure zipped through me, as if I was some inexperienced youth. Her eyes were hazy with lust and concentration, somehow working me toward a climax with only the barest graze of her palm. I needed to regain control.

I encircled my hand around her wrist and drew her away. Her hand went limp in my own, embarrassed. With the absence of her hand on my cock, my blood flow rerouted back to my brain.

"I'm sorry," she squeaked out, looking horrified. "I thought—"

"Did you really think I'd allow you to do that?"

She looked away sheepishly, her face bright red.

No one from the crowd batted an eye toward us, too drunk to notice or care.

"I am not a selfish lover, Roselyne."

She peeked up at me through the curtain of her hair, and I leaned in closer, touching my lips to the skin of her neck, not missing the way she shivered. "Despite how much I crave your touch, I will not allow myself to succumb to pleasure without you first experiencing yours."

I smelled the arousal gathering between her legs, and the tether to my self-control nearly snapped. Her eyes fluttered closed as her breaths grew shallower.

My princess liked being in control. So did I.

Roselyne would be the one to crumble beneath me, not the other way around.

"Spread your legs and assess your subjects like the queen you'll be in a few months' time," I commanded.

For the first time since I'd met her, Roselyne followed my instruction with no hesitation.

33
ROSELYNE

I held still as stone with my legs spread apart, the slit of my gown parting to reveal my upper thigh. Too far away to see, and too drunk to care, the guests paid us no mind.

The flames of candles flickered low over every surface causing strange shadows to dance across the room. Wax melted down the sides of the candle leaving small golden and ivory drops on the table.

The blood in my veins thrummed with excitement.

I don't know what had possessed me to do it—but dallying with the Seelie King finally culminated into something tangible once more. There was no denying the attraction burning between us, and I no longer possessed the deniability to claim to myself our affair in the library was a one-time occurrence.

Declan's burning desire ignited mine. I needed him. My body was on fire with no hope for survival without his touch.

I was desperate for him, writhing for release at the hands of the Seelie King.

"Keep still," Declan said low, as he ran his nose up the sensitive skin of my neck. The masculine cedar scent of him was nearly overpowering. I fought the urge to arch into him—to turn my face and catch his mouth in mine for the only taste I craved. I was ready to submit.

The anticipation of his touch buzzed beneath my skin.

He pressed his palm to my knee then stroked his hand up the length of my thigh. His fingers brushed along my skin and stilled along the hilt of something hard.

The dagger.

I met his gaze through the corner of my eye as I continued to face forward, not daring to breathe.

He chuckled, a rumbling sound that stoked a flame of desire within me even more.

"My, my," he said, trailing a finger over the blade's concealed edge. "You don't trust me to protect you?"

His tone was playful, but his words were genuine.

I gulped and shook my head side to side, maintaining my forward-facing posture. I painted a bland smile on my face so our guests remained ignorant to the depravity their king and future queen engaged in.

Declan's golden-colored eyes grew hungry.

"No?" he asked innocuously.

His hand caressed across the blade and to the hilt, drawing closer to the center of my thighs.

"I have already killed for you, Princess. Do not think I would not *easily* do it again."

Heat surged through my veins at his admission, my heart thrashing wildly against my chest.

By all accounts, I should be horrified by his confession.

Instead, syrupy desire bloomed within me, thick and palpable and needy. My thighs parted fully below the table, and cool air kissed the exposed flesh beneath my gown.

I trembled from the anticipation.

Declan ran the pad of his finger up my inner thighs and pressed lightly against the wetness soaking through my undergarments. I inhaled sharply at his touch and bit back the urge to roll my hips into him. My core ached with a heaviness only he could fulfill.

"Don't move," he reminded, and I nodded, closing my eyes, fully and totally succumbing to the Seelie King.

In one vicious movement, he ripped through the thin fabric, destroying the white lace and ribbons Essi had chosen for me. Declan's nostrils flared as he pulled the discarded panties from beneath my skirt and set them beside us on the bench. The scraps of fabric were soaked with my arousal, overt evidence to my desires.

My eyes darted to the huge swell beneath his pants, demonstrating his own.

Our guests were none the wiser to our debauchery. They pranced and frolicked together, spinning on the dance floor, laughing and drinking with collective merriment and complete disregard for the newly betrothed couple looming above them.

His hand returned to my wetness, and he trailed the length of my slit, finding the pearl at the apex of my thighs. He caressed it softly with the pad of his finger, eliciting a jolt of electric sensation that rattled through my body.

He rubbed soothing circles as I fought to stay immobile and bit back a moan. I gripped the seat of the bench as to not scream as he plunged one finger inside of me. He began to pump in a slow rhythm, and an intense pressure began to build.

I was a bowstring pulled taut, about to snap under his punishing touch.

"You're doing so well," he cooed, adding another finger to my dripping sex. I tossed my hair back and bit down on a cry, as he explored me, the tension inside my body growing unbearable with every stroke of his hand.

I was half frenzied, driven mad with lust. My breaths were shallow panting gasps, in time with Declan's movements inside of me. My peaked nipples rubbed against the fabric of my dress making me squirm under its constraint. I wanted more of him, I *needed* more.

Flesh on flesh, I wanted to feel his full length sliding into me. I wanted to experience the heat from his body as he fucked me. I shivered.

"You're so beautiful," Declan murmured as he slipped a finger out of me and rolled it across my swollen clit, making my toes curl. Words escaped me and I could only whimper softly in response as Declan's fingers deftly circled the small bud with tender reverence before plunging back inside me. My knees buckled under the table, legs wantonly splayed open as Declan plunged into me with his fingers. A quick glance to the dance floor confirmed that no one watched us.

"Look at me, Roselyne."

I tore my eyes from the crowd and met Declan's. A fiery heat blazed in his gaze, his pupils barely visible, nearly swallowed whole in black. He circled my clit, drawing in a hitched breath from me.

"I want you to look at me when you come apart, Roselyne." His voice was stern, with no trace of humor. His dark eyes bore into me. "I want you to look into my eyes when you come, and I want you to know who did this to you."

I nodded weakly, entranced by the Seelie King. He picked up his pace, plunging his fingers in and out of me, as he swirled another finger around my clit. The musicians' music grew faster and faster, Declan's fingers keeping in time, urging me close to my inevitable climax.

The coiled tension within me reached its peak and snapped, blackening my vision. The inner walls of my sex contracted around his fingers as a rush of shuddering pleasure surged through me. I cried out in ecstasy, drowned out by thunderous applause as the musicians finished their song. Declan growled low in approval.

Aftershocks of my climax zapped through my body as Declan removed his hand. Spent, I slumped over the table, lax and immediately missing his touch. Sweat peppered my brow from the force of my orgasm, and my face flushed as I shrank away, suddenly embarrassed.

The room was stifling, my clothes too tight, too heavy on my skin. I needed fresh air, I needed to breathe. I turned to Declan, who assessed me warily as I pushed off from the bench and stood, smoothing the skirt of my gown.

"Is it appropriate timing for me to take my leave?" I asked, tight-lipped.

I don't know why I was angry, but I needed to get out of the room. My confusing emotions pinged around my brain.

Declan appraised me for a moment, his brows knit together in confusion, then nodded.

"Yes, of course. Let me escort you—"

"No," I said, holding out my still trembling palm to him. "I know the way."

With that, I left the party and made my way back to my empty bedchambers.

It was difficult getting myself out of the gown without Essi's help, but I managed. I slid a thin white chemise onto my body and unfastened my dagger from its place on my thigh before setting it down on the desk beside my bed.

I quickly undid the elaborate hairstyle and threw my hair into a loose messy braid before falling into bed and snuffing out the lone candle in my chambers. With the extinguishing of the flame, the room was immersed in darkness. I could still hear the sounds of strings and raucous laughter emitting from the great hall downstairs. The memory of Declan's fingers inside me haunted me. I'd never known pleasure like that before, and he'd only used his *hand*.

Was I embarrassed of what I'd done with Declan? I laid on my back and stared into the pitch-black space of my room, ruminating. I couldn't deny my attraction for him anymore, but something held me back—some feeling like I couldn't entirely give in. I had practically begged for release at the end. I turned over and punched the pillow into a more comfortable shape, not at all imagining it was the body of the Seelie King. I drifted to sleep with the distant sounds of music and laughter in my ears, the new gold band adorning my finger heavy as a lead weight.

34

ROSELYNE

A rough cloth pressed against my mouth, muffling my scream. My eyes flew open, wild and frantic as they worked to adjust to my dark surroundings. I jerked my body on impulse as I tried to scream, kicking my legs wildly. A man pressed himself against my legs, holding them still and binding my ankles. The sounds of the party still droned on, two flights of stairs away.

"Don't be too rough, we need her alive," a different man whispered with a slight tremor in his voice.

There were at least two of them. I fought not to panic.

I hadn't heeded the warning in the market. Someone wanted me gone from the Seelie Court and was willing to try again. Rough hands jerked my head to the side, while another pair tied a gag behind my head, muffling my screams.

I thrashed my hands wildly, scrambling to make purchase. I felt the tear of flesh under my nails.

"*Bitch*," one of the men hissed, and a fist slammed against the side of my face, the force of the hit pushing me off the bed. My body crashed against the wooden floor with a loud thud that shook the heavy furniture of my room. My head throbbed, but I held still, working to figure out how to survive this attack.

"You knocked the little whore out!" one of the men exclaimed before wheezing a laugh.

Pain flared through me. I tried to take a deep breath through the gag but was met by a searing pain along my ribs. I winced.

It was a blessing they thought I had been knocked out. My eyes adjusted to the darkness, and I made out the shapes of the two men as they began arguing quietly among themselves in hushed whispers. They were both tall and broad, and each armed by the looks of it. My heart thundered in my chest. Whoever didn't want me in the faelands had sent assassins for me, or someone to ransom me for gold.

I blinked a few more times as I grew accustomed to the pounding in my head. *How did they get into my chambers?* I could still faintly hear the roar of the drunken revelers at the feast. Were these men guests at the betrothal ceremony? That didn't matter right now, only survival did. I wriggled my toes, then my ankles.

Yes.

The binding around my ankle was loose. A spark of hope ignited within me. I turned my head toward the shapes of my attackers. My ears rang where he'd struck me. But I could hear the men, turned to face each other, still bickering.

"—said not to harm her."

"I didn't mean to! How are we supposed to get her out of the palace? I can't carry her down with her passed out like this," the other insisted with a huff. "We're on the third floor!"

"Do you think we can just carry her out of her own chamber doors?" the first man hissed through his teeth.

As they continued to squabble, I lifted my head off the wooden floor to better assess my surroundings.

A glint of metal reflected off an object on the floor.

The dagger.

It must have fallen from the table during the scuffle. Trying to not catch the attention of the men, I wiggled my foot toward the dagger—my potential savior. By the supreme grace of the three-headed goddess, I was able to reach it with one of my feet and slide it within my reach without rousing their suspicion. The two weren't very professional assassins, but that was all the better for me.

Without drawing attention to myself, I used the dagger to slash the rope that bound my wrists together. The cloth gag still covered my mouth, silencing me. I needed to think clearly about my next move.

I had barely begun to train with Declan and hadn't progressed past wooden blades. Myself against two grown fae males wouldn't be a fair fight—but one of them had let it slip that I wasn't to be seriously harmed. I had to hope they stuck true to those convictions. The men continued their arguing in hushed whispers.

I cut the gag from my mouth and gulped down a lungful of air before standing to face them, feet spread apart in the fighting stance Declan had taught me.

The two men turned to face me as realization dawned across both their faces. I could barely make out their features, but I was sure they were strangers to me.

"Come quietly girl, and we will not harm you," one man said, stretching his hand as if coaxing a wild animal to him. I backed away and held out my dagger. A chill ran down my spine, as a rush of energy thrummed throughout my body. I was only in my thin chemise, and my window was open, allowing in a late summer breeze causing goose prickles along my skin. I must have looked feral to these men who thought of humans as weak—but that wasn't me. I was a witch, and despite not accessing my magic, it lived within me.

The man lunged for me, trying to grab around my wrist, as I slashed my blade upward cutting into the flesh of his hand. He drew back with a hiss, cradling his arm as blood seeped from the open wound and dripped to the floor.

"You'll pay for that, you stupid cunt," he spat as he drew his own dagger from its holster and advanced toward me.

The other man did the same, and crept toward me, the floorboards creaking under his feet. I faced the two men as they inched closer. The door to the main corridor was only ten paces behind me. If I could get to it—I could get to the hallway, run, and find Declan.

"I'm sure they'd rather have her a little roughed up than not at all," one man said to the other before leaping toward and slashing haphazardly with his dagger. His blade bit into the skin of my cheek with a sharp slice of pain.

My training with Declan had paid off. I ducked and avoided more damage as I used all my strength to thrust my blade into his chest. *Goddess guide me.* With a force of effort I turned the blade, lodging it deep with a guttural cry.

The man had underestimated my strength, and it cost him his life. His body thudded to the floor as I withdrew my blade from his heart, my chest heaving.

I killed a man.

His partner yelped in fright and jumped backward, clearly unprepared to find a princess who fought back. The man assessed our surroundings and appeared to think better of his decisions. We circled each other, taking turns stepping over the fallen body of his partner, both our arms outstretched with our weapons poised to strike. I was still a novice, but I had killed now, and the man hesitated, unsure if he should fear me.

The clouds parted outside, and streams of moonlight shone through the open window illuminating the man's haggard face. His features were worn, his clothes little more than rags that hung limply on his thin frame. He was no blademaster, but he was a desperate. His dull eyes gleamed with determination, and his mouth sat in a grim line as he lunged toward me with his blade. It didn't matter what his original intentions were, or what his master commanded him to do. Now, this man meant to harm me. Kill or be killed.

Before either of us made a move toward each other, my door blasted open behind me with a surge of vicious power. Light from the hallway streamed in as chills spread across my skin, my hair whipping around my face from some unnatural wind. The walls of the palace trembled from the force of the terrible power. A bellowing roar of fury rang out, and I felt his presence wrap around me like armor.

Declan was here.

35

DECLAN

Rage clouded my vision. Logic didn't guide me any longer, I only possessed the insatiable urge to destroy whoever set to harm Roselyne and envelop her in the protectiveness of my power. My body thrummed with unspent energy as I focused on the bastard inside her bed chambers. I didn't know his purpose, but he would die for his transgressions. I didn't need the entirety of my power to kill him.

Twice now someone intended to harm Roselyne, and twice I would end a life on her behalf. In the haze of my bloodlust, time slowed.

My eyes darted to the piece of shit currently trembling across from my bride-to-be. The color red snared my gaze toward Roselyne. A single line of blood dripped down her cheek, but other than that she appeared mostly unharmed. There was something different in the glint of her eyes and the set of her mouth. I searched her face and found no fear—only resolute determination. With steady hands, she clung to a weapon of her own, the dagger she'd worn earlier, blood smeared across the blade.

A dead man lay on the other side of the room, blood leaking from his chest.

My princess is a warrior.

In a desperate attempt to finish his crime, the man standing opposite Roselyne frantically slashed his blade toward her. With a swell of power, I knocked the dagger from his trembling hands, and it clattered to the floor.

The assailant turned toward me. His lips parted as recognition flashed in his eyes.

He knew who I was, and what I was capable of.

The stench of piss filled the room.

Whatever he'd been offered in exchange for my bride wasn't worth the horrible death he'd endure at my hands, and he knew it.

With only a moderate effort of my power, I snapped his legs.

The sounds of the feast and music downstairs drowned out his cries of anguish. He collapsed to the floor in a tangle of broken limbs, wailing incoherently.

"*Be quiet,*" I snarled at him, with a flare of magic that silenced the man.

His lips converged, sealing themselves together. He whimpered as he attempted to drag himself away with his hands, still delusional that he'd outlive this scenario. I stepped onto his face with my boot and pressed him into the ground, using nearly the rest of my magical reserves to bind his arms to his chest.

In Roselyne's bloodied hands, she grasped her dagger and clutched it to her chest. She shook, swaying on her feet.

I wanted nothing more than to wrap her in my arms, but I needed to handle the attacker first. Roselyne dropped her dagger, and it clattered to the ground. Her hands were covered with blood—hers or someone else's, I wasn't yet sure.

I felt Callum's presence behind me.

"What's happened?"

"Someone broke into Roselyne's room," I said, twisting the heel of my boot into the man's face. He groaned incoherently, lips still sealed together by my magic. Roselyne stood tall, her green eyes flaring with light. My chest puffed with pride. "Roselyne took one down." My eyes trailed over the dead man's body as his companion tried uselessly to break the magical bonds I'd wrapped around him. I sucked in a breath. "But this one is *mine*. Callum, please take him down to the basement. I have no need of private cells of the Crossed Stars. Don't be gentle."

I crouched and spoke low to the man so only he could hear.

"I will come visit you when I am done tending to my betrothed."

The man shook with fear, eyes darting side to side. He was as good as dead and knew it. My reputation spanned the kingdoms of human and fae, and all trembled with fear at the power of the Seelie King. If the man was intelligent, he'd understand answering my questions would serve him best. I flexed my fist and stood as Callum heaved both the corpse and the still alive man over his shoulder with relative ease, leaving the room with a pinched expression.

When we were alone, Roselyne's knees buckled, and she crumpled toward the floor. I caught her before she hit the ground and wrenched her to me. She was trembling and took in a shuddering breath before leaning into me.

"Shhh," I murmured low against her hair. "You're okay."

She relaxed her posture and slumped into my chest. I wrapped my hands around her shoulders and began leading her out of her room.

"Where are we going?" she asked.

"My chambers," I replied, my voice even and calm despite the war raging inside. The insatiable thirst to kill that man tugged at me, but my magic was depleted and I wanted to make sure Roselyne was taken care of after the events that transpired.

When I questioned that man, he'd tell me everything. There was no way I'd let him out alive, but I could grant him a swifter death than what I currently had in mind. But probably not. I wouldn't lose control as I'd done with the man at the market. I'd get my answers first, then end his miserable life.

A blush spread across her face and chest.

"No, that's okay, I'm fine," she said through tight lips. "Once the blood is gone from the floor, it'll be like it never happened, I can stay with Essi tonight—"

"Absolutely not," I interrupted, with the commanding tone I used as king. "It's my duty to keep you safe, and I failed. No more sleeping apart." Her eyes went wide. "I can sleep on the sofa if you prefer, but I need to be close to protect you."

She huffed. "I did well against them."

My eyes traced the fine red line marring her cheek. "You did," I whispered. "But the only difference between the cut you received and a slice of death is less than a second in time."

She rolled her eyes, but kept in step beside me as I led her to my room.

"I need to devote more time to training. I can't access my power—at least give me a better chance to defend myself."

"Fine," I said tight-lipped.

"Fine," she agreed.

"Ow!" Roselyne hissed. "What is that?"

I dabbed the foul-smelling mixture across the thin line on her cheek.

Her nose crinkled. She was laying in my bed for the first time, although under very different circumstances than I'd allowed myself to imagine.

"It's a salve," I said. "It'll heal the cut."

"It stings," she whined.

"It's helping."

Roselyne scowled, tongue pressed hard into her cheek, letting me know with only her expression she thought I was an idiot.

Her impertinence warmed something inside of me, regardless.

"I'm fine."

I sighed, exasperated with her need to appear strong. "Let me tend to you."

She supported herself on her elbows and glowered at me for a moment before softening her expression.

"Is everyone else okay?" she asked. "Kera and Essi?" Her lip quivered as she spoke, her eyes shining with earnest fear for the fae women she'd grown to consider friends.

I held out a hand and helped pull her to sit upright.

"Kera is one of the most formidable fighters I know. She's currently securing the perimeter of the property and trying to find where these men came through. Essi, from my understanding, is asleep in her bed, unaware that this attack has even occurred. No one else was targeted, and I'm deciding how best to proceed. Please, lay back down."

Roselyne reluctantly lowered herself off her elbows and laid back onto the bed. Superficial cuts and bruises trailed all over her arms and legs. I painstakingly applied the healing balm to each one, taking care to avert my gaze from the shape of her body under the thin nightdress she wore.

For every scratch I found on Roselyne's skin, I'd vowed to crush a separate bone in that bastard's body.

I unstuck my tongue from my throat. "I'll have your belongings moved here. There's plenty of room."

She nodded slowly, accepting the only rational choice. With two attempts on her life, she was safest at my side. It could be denied no longer. Someone wanted her for themselves, or wanted her dead.

Roselyne touched her cheek. "How do you know how to make these balms? Don't you have some sort of healer on staff?" she asked me.

"When you fight in battles, it pays to be knowledgeable on different schools of magic. What good would my power be if I died from a festered wound?"

"Who taught you to heal?"

My mind wandered to Phaedra, her memory tucked into a shadowy corner of my mind, a place I didn't allow myself to wander for fear of the darkness I'd find.

"A witch," I said. "Phaedra."

Her name sounded brittle on my tongue, like I was cursed to not speak it aloud after everything that happened between the fae and the witches. Perhaps I was.

Roselyne's face pinched together before smoothing back over into an expressionless mask.

"What happened to her—to Phaedra?" she asked.

My jaw clenched. "War happened."

My father happened, and he died for his actions.

My hands curled to fists at my sides, and Roselyne and I sat in stifling silence for a few minutes, the air thick with unspoken words.

"What are you going to do to that man?" Roselyne asked quietly.

She was upright now, the balm I'd applied sank into her skin, giving her cheek a glazed flush across the already healing wound. She twisted a silver strand of hair around her fingers as she waited for my answer.

I assessed my betrothed.

"I'm going to do to him what he deserves for touching what belongs to me."

She rolled her eyes, but didn't argue, sliding herself further under the covers of my bed.

Our bed.

Whether Roselyne considered herself mine was irrelevant. My heart wholly belonged to her. She'd entered my life like a wild summer rainstorm, subverted every expectation I'd set for her, and enchanted me completely. Her soul called to mine like no other. If I was so lucky, one day Roselyne would give herself over to me, and the twin flames of our souls would intertwine completely.

Callum and I sat in my chamber's sitting room as Roselyne snored softly in the adjoining room.

Callum fidgeted in his seat, still dressed in the gilded armor he wore to the engagement ceremony. "I've confirmed no other assailants in the palace. The grounds are clear."

I pressed my mouth in a hard line and leaned forward and buried my head in my hands. This had gotten complicated. I hadn't expected taking Roselyne as a bride to have been this inciting, but clearly, I didn't know the subjects I ruled over as well as I thought. I heard the soft click of the door as Kera slipped inside and joined us on the sofa.

"No one knows about the attack. There's not even a whisper of gossip. Not even the servants are aware of it. Although I did find your brother and Essi in bed together." She scrunched up her face and shuddered, before smoothing out the expression. "Is it possible the attack was organized by one of your guests? Roselyne's assailants knew precisely which window was Roselyne's and somehow slipped past the guards." Kera frowned. "Whoever did this was invited to the ceremony, or knows the layout of the palace."

Callum shifted in his seat. "Could this be related to the temple incidents? What did the Veiled say was taken, Kera?"

"After checking the inventory, the priestesses confirmed only a tattered black book."

"A book? Someone killed a priestess of Lux over a *book*?" Callum asked, incredulous.

Kera shrugged. "The priestesses say it appeared ancient and worn, although on the inside it was completely blank—some sort of ancient un-inked journal." She sank further into the cushion. "I've no idea for what purpose someone would steal what appears to be an unused journal, but that's what the priestesses insisted."

I rubbed at my temples. "These events have to be related."

I turned to Callum, who shrugged.

"The prisoner wouldn't say or admit to anything," Callum said flatly.

I stood from the sofa and flexed my power. The small amount of unspent crackling energy rolled off my arms in thick waves in a bid to exact my revenge.

I addressed both Callum and Kera, "Stay with Roselyne tonight." They nodded in return.

I turned the handle of the door before I strode out. "He'll speak to me."

I swung open the cellar door and began descending the rickety stairs, the temperature cooling with every step as I made my way deeper below the earth. Dust covered the multitude of crates and barrels in the storeroom, long forgotten by the minimal staff I kept at court. Centuries ago, my father created cells beneath his palace, a bleak place with a bloodied history, though I typically used the ground floor of the Crossed Stars to dole out my justice. Now, my father's ancient prison was no more than glorified storage, but the cells still stood, the crimson stains and ghosts unable to be scrubbed away.

This man wouldn't make it out of the cellar alive. When I typically faced enemies, I opted to cut them down on an open battlefield. This wasn't a battle though. This man came into my home uninvited and waged another kind of war.

When the entrance to the cell creaked open, I'd been ready to hear the man beg and plead for his life. What I hadn't expected was to find his lifeless body slumped over in death behind the metal bars, his fingers clutching an empty vial.

"*No.*"

With a growl, I slammed my fist into the wall. We should have better searched his body—but I was intent on tending to Roselyne, I overlooked the obvious.

The coward killed himself with poison rather than face my wrath and answer for his crimes in blood.

I struck the stone wall again, bloodying my knuckles. I was no nearer to finding out who ordered this attack on Roselyne, or why. The only answer lay in her witch blood at the hands of

Summus Nati, or one of the Seelie territory lords, although I could not be certain. Whoever orchestrated the attack was still at large. My heart thundered with an unfamiliar sensation—fear. I needed to get Roselyne out of Solora and away from the city until I could clear my mind of what was happening in this godsforsaken kingdom.

36

ROSELYNE

Essi's voice woke me from the best night of sleep I'd had since I arrived in the faelands. The sound was muffled, and I could not fully make out her words. She spoke quickly to someone else a room or two away, clearly distraught.

I blinked open my eyes, disoriented to find myself in a room that was not my own, before remembering the attack after the feast. Declan was nowhere to be found, so I took my time in assessing his bedroom, crawling out from beneath the nest of warm blankets.

I pursed my lips. I suppose it was to be *our* bedroom now since I'd found myself a target once more. The room was richly furnished, with matching golds and reds similar to his sitting room beyond the closed door. I looked around and frowned. I had none of my belongings. I slipped off the thin chemise and felt the cool air against my bare skin. Without any clothing of my own, I chose a black tunic from Declan's wardrobe and tugged it over my head. It was loose and soft, hitting me at the middle of my thighs. His cedar smell was interwoven through the fabric and I brought the two long sleeves up to my nose and inhaled, becoming drunk on his scent.

I don't know why I was this calm about nearly being taken last night.

The attack confirmed what we'd feared—someone was out to get me, and that thought was strangely comforting. With this knowledge, I would find a solution.

I tentatively opened the door to the sitting room and found the Seelie King standing at the doorway to the corridor with his back to me. Essi, panic-stricken and disheveled, babbled nearly incoherently, her voice slipping higher and higher with every word.

"—I went there this morning, and she's not there, and there was blood—" Essi's large brown eyes snapped to me, and she pushed past Declan and into the room wrapping her tiny arms around me with a cry. "Roselyne!"

She broke the embrace and backed away, glancing up and down on my body as she took in Declan's clothing hanging off me.

"Oh," she said, before shaking her head. "Roselyne, I thought—I thought something terrible had happened! You weren't in your chambers when I came with breakfast this morning—there's something red like blood on the floor..." Her voice trailed off as she searched my face for answers.

"Someone attacked me last night, Essi," I said before turning to Declan who appraised us with a tentative expression. My heart swelled with appreciation for the fae male before me. "They tried to take me. Declan saved me. I don't know exactly what they wanted me for but—"

Essi threw her arms around me once more, and crushed me into her chest as she heaved a sob against my unruly hair, her body shaking.

I patted her on the back.

"I'm okay. Truly," I said, and I meant it. "I only need a few of my things. I'll be staying with Declan from now on."

I gave him a pinched smile as I felt a swooping sensation in my stomach.

Declan took a step forward and trailed a finger across my shoulders, and I barely concealed a shiver.

"I'll have your things brought, although I do enjoy seeing you in my clothing."

I squeezed my thighs together as a rush of warmth spread through my body.

Declan then addressed Essi, speaking in his king's voice, "Thank you for your concern, Essi, but now that she is awake, I must speak with my betrothed alone."

Essi dipped a polite curtsy and shot me a knowing wink before excusing herself from the room.

I suppressed a groan. My lady-in-waiting would expect all the sordid details later, and I wasn't sure I was prepared to give them.

Alone in the bedroom, the tension between Declan and I was palpable, like some sort of living beast in the room with us. He assessed me with his predator's gaze and I squirmed under the intense scrutiny.

"We're leaving," Declan said in a clipped tone.

I flinched. "What are you talking about?"

"It's not safe in Solora. I'm getting you out. At least until we can buy some time and figure out what's going on."

My eyebrows knitted together. "I'm not running away. You said it yourself, I'll be safe with you, I just—"

He shook his head, and my chest tightened. This wasn't a discussion—this was him *telling me.*

Just as I'd grown accustomed to my new life, he intended to uproot me once more.

Maybe it was childish, but I didn't care—I stamped my foot and pointed my finger at him, pressing against the hard muscled chest beneath his clothing.

"*No.* I am not running from those who wish me gone. That's giving into their very whims! Are you the Seelie King or not?"

What was he thinking acquiescing to the demands of a someone insistent on terrorizing those he claimed to care about?

"I'll train harder, I won't leave the palace grounds." The words tumbled out of my mouth faster than I could think. "We don't even know who did this. No demands have been given."

He pressed his lips together, unmoved by my words.

"They meant to harm you—" he gritted out through his ticked jaw, eyes roaming along my cheek and the yellow bruises that covered my body. "—and they did."

I let out a most unladylike, derisive snort and crossed my arms over each other.

Declan and I were beyond formalities now. What we'd done together and subsequently not discussed created space for us to be more genuine with one another.

"Do not treat me like some porcelain figure to keep on your shelf," I said coolly as I turned my back to him, nose in the air. "If I am to be your queen, I will not listen to blanket commands from you."

His answering growl sent shivers across my skin, but I held my ground. A few seconds ticked by until Declan spoke, breaking the tense silence.

"A compromise, then?" he asked from behind me, and the

roughness of his voice sent sparks of lightning skittering up my skin.

I turned over my shoulder and met his eyes. My eyebrow arched. "What did you have in mind?" I turned all the way around and faced him once more, arms still crossed.

"We go away." He held up a hand to stop me before I could interrupt. "We go away for *now,* for a few days, perhaps a week, until this attack blows over and we get more information."

I chewed the inside of my cheek, rolling this information around in my head. My face must have looked unconvinced, because Declan continued.

"We can train longer there, with no interruptions. The natural space could help you focus. A few days. Please." His voice cracked on the last word.

My lips parted in surprise as he moved closer to me and clasped my hands in his, Declan's large palms dwarfing mine.

"I can't lose you," he whispered.

My resolve melted away. The Ruthless King exposed all of himself to me and showed me his true vulnerability. I wouldn't take that for granted.

"Okay," I whispered. "Let's go."

37

ROSELYNE

Declan and I agreed to meet back up in an hour, giving us the necessary time to pack our bags and for Declan to rest assured his kingdom wouldn't collapse in his absence. As his heir, Sloane was charged with the day-to-day ruling of the Seelie Court for the time we were gone, with the addition of Kera and Callum's support.

Before leaving, I only wished to say goodbye to Essi. She'd been so distraught this morning, I wanted to tell her in person Declan and I were leaving and that everything was okay.

Essi's personal chambers were on the opposite wing as my old ones. I'd never made the trek there myself, instead my lady-in-waiting always came to me.

I peeked inside the room I believed to be Essi's, and found her sitting at her vanity with a variety of perfumes and cosmetics around her.

"Essi," I said, announcing my presence with a knock on the partially open door. She jerked upright, away from the mirror in her hands and her eyes found mine. Her face split into a grin.

"Roselyne!" Essi beamed. "Come in!" she called as she

swiped a pink balm across her mouth and smacked her lips together.

Essi's chambers were similar to mine and Declan's, with fine wooden furniture and rich linens. Her room was smaller, with pale pink bedding and drapes over her window. I approached and sat on the available sofa near the vanity where she perched. She finished applying rouge to her cheeks then turned to face me.

"To what do I owe the pleasure of your company?" she asked.

"Declan and I are going away for a few days, I wanted to let you know."

She frowned. "Because of last night?"

"Yes, and no," I said. "I think it'll be good for me—for us."

"Where will you go?" she asked, head cocked.

"He didn't say."

She clasped her hands together, her large brown eyes sparkling as she squealed with delight and bounced on her chair.

"Roselyne! This is incredibly romantic," she gushed. "Whisking you away? It's so dreamy."

I grimaced. It was no use telling her that this was no romantic destination, but a chance to get away before I was the victim of another attack.

By the time I made it back to the sitting room, Declan waited for me, carrying a small near-empty vial I'd seen once before—the day I arrived in the faelands.

"Lunar ash?" I asked.

Declan smirked. "You remembered."

"How could I forget?" I eyed the silvery powder with hesitation, remembering the first time I'd traveled in that manner.

Declan tossed the fine powder over our bodies as he

clutched my hand in his, interlocking our fingers. My feet no longer touched the ground, and I felt the familiar swooping in the pit of my stomach as well as the sensation of being tugged in all directions. Flashes of images whirred by, blurs and swirls of greens and browns impossible to discern at the speed in which we traveled through space. We were falling through the air—and then it was over.

Our feet landed on soft green grass that tickled my shins. I could hear the faint buzz of insects and the sounds of bubbling water somewhere in the distance. Tiny wildflowers were scattered throughout the meadow like bits of multicolored confetti as I saw the peaks of mountains in the distance. I inhaled a lungful of the fresh air and felt the sweet relief of my expanding lungs. A calming sensation of peace settled over me like a veil in this place. My ears rang from the method of travel, but the sensation faded away within a few seconds.

"Where are we?" I asked as my eyes darted around the meadow.

Lush trees and vegetation surrounded us on all sides, all variations of bright greens and with some interspersed golds and reds—a sign of the nearing seasonal change.

"North," Declan answered, as he unlaced his fingers from mine. I flexed my hand and mourned the absence of his touch. Declan looked into the distance toward a small stone cottage situated nearby, nestled among the trees.

"Only a few know, but my mother kept a country home for when she wanted to escape the city. Sloane and I would come here as boys."

His eyes were distant as he took in the surroundings. He closed his eyes and breathed in. "I haven't been back in years. Not since our mother died."

I still knew nothing about the former queen, the woman

who raised the male before me and whose title I was set to inherit in such a short time.

"What was she like?" I asked.

He frowned. "Another time, perhaps." His head snapped to the left toward a thick copse of trees. "Let's go, we need to begin your training."

38

DECLAN

Roselyne leapt toward me, sharpened blade in hand, and slashed upward toward my neck. I was distracted by her beautiful brutality, and she nearly struck me with her blade. I parried her sword at the last moment, thinking about how much she'd improved in such a short amount of time. We'd moved on from the wooden practice blades.

After the events a few nights ago, it was clear she was prepared for sharpened steel.

Our days were filled with training drills under the bright sun until her body was exhausted and spent. Each night, she'd retire to bed and fall asleep quickly. I'd curl up on the couch in the living room and lay awake, overcome with fear for the woman dreaming a room away.

I dodged another crushing blow from Roselyne, her sword instead slicing a loose thread from my tunic.

She turned with a laugh, and her hair whipped around her face. The meadow filled with the sounds of her joy. She was visibly relaxed here, all the tension that seemed to live coiled inside her body released the moment our boots hit the soft earth of the meadow clearing each morning to begin drills.

The pressures of court life, the impending marriage, and whatever was going on with our relationship had all but been erased. Neither of us dared bring it up for fear of spoiling the newfound tranquility between us.

No prying eyes watched us in this place. We were alone in nature with only the sun overhead and beasts of the wood as our companions.

Roselyne was natural with a weapon in her hand, and the fresh air had done wonders for her confidence, although we'd had no luck with accessing any of her magic. It had been an easy decision to leave Solora after the attack. I squeezed the hilt of my sword as I grit my teeth, the cool metal digging into my palms. My only regret concerning the entire event was that I didn't get to kill the bastard who attacked Roselyne myself, although my princess had fared well on her own before my arrival, despite her lack of training.

I smiled at my bride-to-be, and she stuck out her tongue and laughed again as she backed away and prepared another strike. She glowed in the nature of the Northern Seelie Territory, in her element as a witch, surrounded by the golden leaves of the forest ushering in autumn. I wished we could stay here forever and ignore our duties to the kingdom and families.

I looked south and exhaled. Although I couldn't see the tops of the brown stone buildings that made up Solora, the tug of duty was ever-present and demanding.

I shook my head and readied my stance, noting the adorable way Roselyne poked her tongue into her cheek when deep in concentration. The corner of my mouth lifted. The capital would be fine in my absence. The royal council was capable of controlling things for a few days while Roselyne and I trained together and recovered from the attack.

If any issues should arise, my council knew how to reach me using a messenger falcon.

Roselyne deviated from the repeated combination and slammed her sword down on me. I blocked her, but the force of her hit reverberated through my entire arm. I grinned and wiped a hand down my face as she breathed hard with a huge beaming smile on her face.

"I struck you," she said.

Her green eyes crinkled at the corners.

"Nearly," I agreed.

She huffed with false indignation then laughed again—my favorite sound. I glanced toward the darkening sky, the western horizon backlit with the palest of purples.

"Let's break for now."

As summer drew to its end, we had fewer hours of daylight to train, and instead spent our nights together in the cottage, with only one wall to separate us.

The leaves were already beginning their yearly transition this far north. The foliage along the trees transformed into brilliant golds and coppers dissonant to the sun who still blazed overhead in the afternoons, oblivious to the inescapable end of the summer season.

"I'm starving," Roselyne whined.

My own stomach grumbled in agreement. I scooped up her sword and slung it across my back. "I packed us food."

She arched a brow and smirked. "That was very domestic of you." Roselyne bound after me with a noticeable spring in her step. "*Very* impressive."

"Come on," I said with an over-exaggerated eye-roll.

"There's something I haven't taken you to see yet. It's beautiful. We'll eat there."

Her green eyes flicked upward. She nodded and followed me past the cottage and through the opening in the trees. If she feared the forest, Roselyne showed no signs of it. Her shoulders were relaxed, and she possessed an air of serenity.

We walked beside each other in comfortable silence with only the chittering of small forest creatures and the whispers of the trees keeping us company. Her eyes darted back and forth, but not from fear, instead, shining with intrigue and curiosity at the sounds of this foreign-to-her land.

"Where are we going?" Roselyne asked after a few minutes of walking. She glanced pointedly toward the small wicker basket I carried as I heard the rumblings of her stomach.

"Just a few more minutes," I replied. I hadn't visited this place in centuries. Not since my mother died.

We padded along the barely visible path, clearly untouched since my last visit. The vegetation grew thicker, and the trail narrowed, causing Roselyne and I's shoulders to knock together. Unruly roots grew over the path covering the soft trail.

As I remembered, the thick trunks of the trees parted to reveal a small grassy field beside a lagoon and waterfall. Roselyne's face lit with joy, her smile spread wide across her face as she took in the turquoise bubbling water and the wildflowers surrounding its shore.

Seeing the world through her eyes was like seeing it anew, colors brighter and smells sharper.

"It's beautiful," she whispered as she knelt to touch the petals of a small pink flower. It was one of thousands that spanned the sea of grass in tiny pinpricks of bright purples, pinks, and whites against a backdrop of green. Nearby, the waterfall poured into the bright blue lagoon with a thunderous roar.

We sat down on the soft grass, me with my legs crossed, Roselyne with her body outstretched on her side supported by her elbows, cradling her face in her hand.

"You really prepared all this?" she asked as she appraised the spread of jams, breads, and cheeses as I pulled each item from the basket.

"I did," I replied, fighting a smile as I continued to empty out the basket. "I'm a fairly capable male."

She rolled over to her back and closed her eyes with a soft sigh, basking in the diminishing rays of the setting sun.

I allowed myself the small indulgence of studying her face, committing every detail to memory. Her cheek was unmarred, the line from the assailant's blade faded away as if it never existed. Her caramel hair with her shimmering silvery strands pooled across the soft grass. Roselyne looked so serene despite everything she'd been through—what I'd put her through. Roselyne proved time and time again that she was stronger and more resilient than she'd been given credit for.

Roselyne hadn't left my mind since I'd seen her the evening of the Althenean ball. The night in the library and our betrothal ceremony were forever seared into my mind, unable to be blinked away. There was so much more pleasure I wished to wring from her, but she'd made no indication that's what she wanted.

I would accept this half-life with her, if only to stay near her always. The prophecy, and breaking the curse was nothing but a distant buzz in my ears. I wanted her in earnest now, not for the witch blood in her veins that would return me to my height of power. In the meantime, I'd train her, all the while tempering my ever-growing desires for her.

After we ate, I stripped off my sweat-drenched tunic and took a place beside Roselyne in the grass and turned my gaze to the darkening sky overhead. We laid together side by side in the grass on our backs, limbs outstretched toward each other but never allowing our bodies to touch. It was some sort of game we played together, an illusion of intimacy, a hint so neither one of us were truly susceptible to rejection.

Roselyne's back was pressed against the grass. The tall stalks folded around her body cocooning her in a soft shell of greenery, parting as if allowing her space to lay among the tiny white and pink blooms of wildflowers. Our weapons lay in the grass a few feet away.

This was peace. I could lay in this meadow with her forever. Forget the crown, forget Summus Nati and the Seelie Territory Lords. I could live a simple life with her in the forest cottage where no one else could find us. I turned my head and rested my cheek against the grass to better gaze at Roselyne. Her eyes were closed. She breathed in softly through her nose, her chest rising in perfect rhythm to my own.

I felt so in sync with her, as if she were celestially designed for me—*destined* for me, and in a way she was. Prophecies do not work in absolutes, but I was certain everything pointed toward our union. The gods knew I'd need to break the witch's curse at this exact time in history with this exact human woman. *Perhaps she's my fate-bound mate.*

I shook my head and cleared it of the notion. Such a thing was a rarity among the fae, even more so across races, although not unheard of. Roselyne opened her eyes, no doubt sensing the heat of my gaze and smiled, before squinting up at the sky. Night had fallen in earnest during our time here, and millions of glittering stars hung in the sky among the ever-present moon and its silver light.

Roselyne lifted herself up onto her elbows and nodded toward the nearby spring of turquoise water, now nearly black in the darkness.

"Is it safe to swim in?" she asked as she absentmindedly twirled a lock of her hair around her finger.

"It's spring fed, so it's quite comfortable year-round," I said. "But many say the water this far north is steeped with the goddess Lux's magic as it pours directly from the earth. They say you are unable to speak falsities while submerged within its depths, so be wary of those you swim with, for fear of knowing unpleasant truths."

Her face brightened at that, and the image knocked the wind from my chest.

"I'll never tire of magic," she said, sitting upright.

Roselyne stood and began to strip off her sweat soaked pants with an unabashed smile. She wiggled the brown fabric over the curve of her hips and down to her ankles revealing her pert ass and thighs before I had the good sense to avert my gaze and turn away from her.

Sweat peppered my brow that had nothing to do with the temperature of the forest glen. Roselyne was trying to kill me. I heard a loud splash of water and droplets misted against the bare skin of my chest. I turned to see the previously still water, rippling where Roselyne submerged herself beneath the crystalline depths lit only by the round moon hung low in the sky.

A few seconds later, Roselyne's head breached the surface, her hair slicked down against her pale face. The vision of her body was refracted through the water as she pumped with her arms and legs easily, keeping herself afloat.

"Well?" she asked as her mouth pulled into a playful curve. "Aren't you joining me?"

39

ROSELYNE

I hadn't been sure Declan would join me in the lagoon. I didn't know what possessed me to strip and sink into the bubbling water, but I had, and pleasure curled low in my belly at the prospect of the Seelie King joining me.

The warm temperature of the water contrasted deliciously with the night air's cool breeze. Time held still. With only my eyes above the waterline, I watched Declan undress himself and sink his body into the lagoon. Declan swam to me without speaking, and I suddenly realized we were both naked. My eyes darted to the bundles of our sweaty practice clothes at the shoreline, mine jumbled in a pile, and Declan's neatly folded.

I'd expected the familiar rush of shame and apprehension to wash over me, but it did not. Only tingles of anticipatory excitement thrummed deep in my core. I felt the press of the stars' watchful gazes, observing Declan and I like we were on the precipice of something inevitable.

My toes scraped along the sandy bottom of the small body of water as I swam to Declan. He offered me a hand which I grasped, making it easier to tread the deeper water beside him.

A large waterfall roared behind us, making it difficult to hear. My eyes scanned the darkened tree line imposing along the water's edge. Yellow and green pinpricks of light floated within the trees, just far enough away I could not make out their shape. Declan followed my gaze.

"Sprites," Declan said, their light dancing in the reflections of his eyes. "Curious creatures of pure magic."

The glowing light of the sprites bobbed along the forest line, floating with no apparent consistency, bumping into each other, and drifting on the air. I stilled in the water.

"Sprites?" I asked.

"Older than anyone can recall. The sprites have always been here, the wardens overseeing the land of magic." The sprites kept their distance, opting to watch us from the tree line. "They do no harm."

We watched the dancing lights of the sprites for a few minutes until they faded away, moving on to another part of their domain. I faced Declan in the water.

"Thank you for taking me here. It's—special." I chewed my lip. "Maybe you were right about going away for a while."

"I was?" He grinned.

"I just...having this time away has been really—it's been nice." A blush spread across my cheeks.

Declan swam closer to me, his face only inches from mine, the tips of his dark hair dipping into the lagoon. I dared not look down through the nearly translucent water to his body below.

Declan's eyes softened, and he whispered to me, barely audible above the roar of the waterfall. "I'd want to share it with no one but you."

My cheeks burned, my body crying out for me to throw my arms around him and close the gap between our bodies.

Instead, I slapped the water, sending a torrent of bright blue splashing at his face. Declan threw his head back with a laugh.

"Did you *splash* the Seelie King?" he asked, a playful glint shining in his eyes, the water dripping down his face.

"And what if I did?" I sniffed with fake indignation, throwing a wet mass of hair behind my shoulder in a show of cheekiness.

His mouth curved upward in a devilish smile. "That'd be very unwise of you and deserving of punishment. Attempted regicide is frowned upon in the faelands."

Declan turned away and swam toward the waterfall with long graceful strokes.

His feet barely reached the bottom of the lagoon that far out, the water rising up to his chin. He beckoned to me with a hand. "Come here, I want you to see something."

I paddled to him. When I reached the waterfall, my feet no longer touched the bottom of the lagoon, instead, I was surrounded on all sides by the warm caress of water on my skin. Declan noticed and offered me his arm to steady myself in the deeper water. Liquid beaded and dribbled off the hard planes off his square jaw before disappearing into the blue. I licked my lips before averting my gaze.

Reluctantly, I took hold of him, careful to keep space between our nude bodies. Declan stood in the water facing the opaque sheet of waterfall as it pummeled into the lagoon, roaring in our ears with its intensity.

"Well?" I asked.

"Do you trust me?"

I clung to Declan's arm, considering the question for a moment before the word left my lips.

"Yes," I whispered, barely audible above the roar of the rushing water.

I did trust him. Somewhere between our meeting in Althene and the kidnapping attempt, my heart had softened toward the Seelie King. I trusted him, wholly and implicitly—maybe I always had.

He grabbed behind my head, his fingers tangling in my wet hair, and I thought for a moment he might kiss me again. Instead, he pulled my body to his and cradled me in his arms, one hand hooking behind my knee, the other supporting my shoulders, floating in the water. My heart beat against my chest, my entire body abuzz with lightning at our proximity and nudity.

"Close your eyes," he instructed.

I did as I was told.

"*Now* you listen to me." He chuckled low.

I kept my eyes closed, but stuck out my tongue, earning another laugh from the fae king.

Declan moved forward in the lagoon, parting the water around him, and I glided in his arms. The waterfall grew louder in my ears as he drew nearer. The thick sheet of water slammed into the top of my head, threatening to drown me. The sound of the falls roared in my ears—then, as soon as it began, it was over.

With my eyes still closed, I clung harder to Declan's skin and felt the water level begin to recede until my shoulders stuck out from the top of the waterline. Declan's legs pushed through water with ease—it must only be chest high.

"Open your eyes, Roselyne." Declan's rumbling voice spoke low in my ear.

Goosebumps spread across my skin despite the warm temperature of the lagoon. I opened my eyes and gasped. Thousands of glowing crystals grew from the walls and ceilings of the cave we'd entered, at every angle, encrusting the walls and illuminating the cavern in hues of greens, blues, and purples. The crystals pulsed in harmony, as if each individual cluster were linked together, part of one living creature.

I'd never seen anything so spectacular. I craned my neck toward the direction from which we came.

The waterfall hid the entrance of the cave from the outside world.

A grin spread across Declan's face, but he wasn't surveying the beauty of the cave—he watched only me.

He released his grip on me and gently set me into the waist deep water of the cave before backing away a few steps. The air inside the cave was warmer than its counterpart on the other side of the waterfall, the water here the comfortable temperature of a hot bath. Tiny bubbles floated up in lines from the bottom of the lagoon, tickling my skin. The crystals twinkled in synchronicity, casting jewel-colored shadows across Declan's face as they oscillated between colors.

I faced Declan, lips parted in awe.

"This is—this is incredible," I said, eyes drawn upward. "What are they?"

Declan strode toward me in the water bare-chested. I drank in the sight of his body as water parted around him. Broad chest, hardened muscles, thin scar across abdomen—I vowed to remember it all. My eyes traveled lower. A line of dark hair trailed from his navel below the water. I tore my gaze away, remembering my own nudity. The level of the water reached my waist, my breasts exposed to the cave air and bathed in the faint glow of the crystals.

For once, I would not run away from my feelings. I wanted Declan to see all of me. I would deny this no longer, the bitterness in my heart be damned.

"Colstellite," he answered, his gaze unwavering from my face.

I'd recalled a singular line I'd read in a book while curled up in the large armchair of the Seelie Court Library.

"I thought all the faelands' colstellite had been mined and traded?"

"Not all of it," Declan said, tearing his gaze from mine, and taking in the glowing cave.

We walked side by side as the water grew shallower until we reached a rock shelf in the water, situated against the wall of the cave. We sat beside each other, neither daring to acknowledge our shared nudity.

"Thank you," I breathed. "I've never seen anything like this." I turned toward Declan, but he was already watching me. I kicked some water toward him with my feet and a warm sensation curled up inside me. "How did you know about this?"

"I found it by accident as a child," he said. "Sloane and I were bickering while here with my mother and father." His eyes went glassy for a moment. "I decided to go for a swim to clear my head. I leaned against what I presumed would be a wall of rock beneath the waterfall." He chuckled at the memory. "Instead, I fell through and found myself trapped under the force of the falls, body twisting beneath the water, struggling to find the surface. I was too small, you see, and I was alone. I couldn't reach the bottom. I thought I would drown. When I clawed my way back to the surface and emerged from the water, gasping for air, I was no longer outside in the lagoon where I'd been swimming—I was here."

He leaned back against the craggy rock and rested his arms behind his head.

"I told no one. I knew what I had found was special, and selfishly I wanted to keep this one thing of beauty for myself."

I leaned against the edge of the rock and gazed upward to the ceiling. The colstellite crystals pulsed as if they too listened and corroborated Declan's recollection. A bead of water dripped from one of the crystal formations, the liquid glowing bright as it landed on the skin of my neck. Declan trailed a finger through the liquid, dragging it across my collarbones in a delicate caress. My breath hitched.

"And yet you showed me," I said, trying to appear at ease, working to mask the fluttering sensation that had overtaken my body.

"Roselyne, when I saw your face for the first time, I realized never before in my life had I witnessed true beauty. The first time you smiled at me—at the ball in Althene, I felt it even then. A jolt, a push from the universe guiding me to you. But I ignored it."

I stared at him, enraptured.

"You hated me once you knew the truth of who I was, and why wouldn't you?"

He shook his head, and I wanted to shake him, to make him understand I didn't feel that any longer, but he kept speaking.

"The hate in your eyes burned through me, twisting like snakes poised to strike. At the time, I didn't recognize what that feeling was…" He looked down for a moment, then met my eyes once more. "Time went on and I denied what I felt, not allowing myself to indulge in the emotions I was clearly developing."

I sat upright, pulling my knees to my chest as Declan continued.

"We were to be married, yes, but only to serve a purpose.

'*Marry the witch*,'" he said wistfully. "I was never supposed to *feel* anything for you." He chuckled. "It's incredible isn't it—what we can convince ourselves of, how our minds can be so blind to what's right in front of us. At first, I thought it was merely a physical attraction burning between us, scorching me with every scowl of your face. It couldn't possibly evolve into anything more. I was your abductor, a monster who stole you away from the only home you've ever known and burdened you with the truth of your power. How could you ever desire me?" He threw his head back to the thousands of glittering gems above, eyes closed, and whispered. "But then you kissed me in the library, and like flint to stone, an ember of hope sparked to life within me for the first time. I fully realized the extent of my affections for you after the attack in the market. The thought of someone harming you nearly drove me to madness. I told myself my rage was because I viewed the attack against you as an affront to me, but deep down I knew that wasn't the truth." He searched my face, his eyes wide and pleading.

"You are everything to me," he said, agony etched along his beautiful face. "Every day I wake up without you beside me, and I mourn. I've tried to stay away, tried to guard my heart against your charm, but I cannot do it any longer. I can barely stand to look at you, knowing you do not suffer to feel the same way I do." He turned away.

"Declan," I said, breathless, my mind racing with possibilities.

"I never experienced the sunrise until you smiled at me for the first time. You—" He hesitated for a moment, "You mean everything to me. You are everything. I could not imagine keeping the truth of my feelings from you any longer."

I sat in stunned silence, stupefied as his words washed over me in waves.

"I love you," he said quietly. The colstellite glowed brighter at his admission, twinkling dots of color sprinkled all over the walls and ceiling. Brightening and dimming in unison as if they nodded their figurative heads. "I believe I have for some time now."

Declan loves me. It should be impossible. We'd only known each other a few months, but I saw nothing but sincerity within the Seelie King's gaze.

We sat facing each other, legs crossed inside the lagoon. His hand clasped mine, interlocking our fingers as my heart hammered heavy in my chest, threatening to burst.

My lips parted, too entranced by the words he continued to weave.

"When you came into my life, a film was removed from my eyes, allowing me to see clearly for the first time. Although I do not deserve your affections, I want to share in the knowledge that you are everything to me." His thumb stroked a small circle on the back of my hand. "I don't expect you to feel the same way, but I can't keep this inside me any longer, suffocating as it is. Despite who I am, and the evils I've committed, I belong to only you."

I inhaled sharply, unsure how to respond.

"Roselyne, for as long as my wretched heart beats—it is yours."

Declan stared at me, his eyes focused on my throat as it bobbled. I searched for the words I wanted to say to him. He waited for my response. I suddenly felt the jitters of vulnerability settle inside of me. I shivered despite the warmth of the cave.

"I never wanted this," I whispered.

Devastation crossed Declan's face for a moment before he schooled his features into a hardened mask. He pressed his mouth into a firm line as he withdrew his hands from mine, skin ashen in the bright blue glow of the colstellite.

"Let me explain," I whispered, squeezing his hands in my own.

He nodded once.

I took in a deep breath. "When I was brought to the Seelie Court, I was aware of the transactional nature of the marriage. I've been told all my life the way I'd best serve my family would be in what could be given to Althene in exchange for my betrothal, be it soldiers, ships, or gold."

Declan opened his mouth to protest, but I pursed my lips and cut him off with a glare before he could begin. I fidgeted with a loose piece of rock on the shoreline.

"Let me say this before I lose my nerve," I whispered.

Declan nodded again, completely enraptured in what I was saying, leaning forward toward me.

I smiled weakly before continuing. "I'd allowed myself to experience this...*feeling* once before. It ended poorly." My face flushed crimson. "Despite my bitterness toward men and notions of romance, I yearned for it still."

Declan remained still as stone.

My eyes trailed upward toward the sparkling gems overhead. "I knew it was foolish considering my position—but I cannot help what my heart desires." I closed my eyes, unable to meet Declan's intensity. I exhaled. "And then I found out my father had finalized a match for me...It happened so quickly. I wondered who my father chose for his only daughter. I'd had dozens of suitors in my lifetime, and I'd turned them all away. He tired of that, and took the choice away from me. What was I *worth*?" I scoffed lightly at the memory, a time when I was ripe with fear and uncertainty—before I knew the truth.

"Then my father announced who I was to be married to, and my hope for a marriage of—*affection* died." I sighed, remembering the fear I felt at that time, and how out of place that fear was, and how my own ignorance colored my views.

Declan sucked in a breath and I met his gaze.

"'*The Ruthless King*' they called him."

Declan winced at the moniker—the title bestowed upon him by those that only knew to fear him.

"But that's not what you are at all."

His jaw ticked, and I fought the urge to run my hands down his beautiful face, to make him look at me, to realize what he meant to me.

"That is who I am," he gritted out, turning away from me.

My mouth twisted into a frown. "You are not," I said through clenched teeth.

Declan shook my head, and pressed his hands to his temples, rubbing them in circles.

"Don't you realize, Roselyne? Although the degree to which I care for you and desire you...You are too good for me, I couldn't—" His voice was strained as he spoke, as if his words caused him physical pain.

Irritation flashed through me, and I scoffed, effectively cutting him off mid-sentence. How dare he decide this on my behalf. Hadn't he heard me? All I had ever sought in my life was to be able to make my own choices. Moments ago, Declan told me he loved me, but now he was saying we couldn't truly be together? For fear of what? Sullying me in some way? I'd find it laughable, if I wasn't so incensed. I may be human, and he fae, but I was not some frail thing that needed tending to.

Despite the strange block on my powers, I was a witch, and I was capable of making my own choice.

I snarled, thrusting my finger against his chest. His eyebrows shot up. I was on my knees, water dripping from my arms as I held them above the water. Declan stayed sitting cross-legged, a dazed expression on his face.

I relaxed my pointer finger, splaying my hand out across the hard muscles of his chest. His heart hammered beneath my touch. I softened my voice, barely above a whisper.

"Declan Danchev, King of the Seelie Fae, if you believe me unstained and pure, this is a formal plea begging for you to ruin me. For now that I've known you, and had parts of you, I know for certain I cannot live without you. If that is what it takes to have you in earnest, please, corrupt my body and soul, for I see exactly who you are, and I will not run away. *You* are who I want, and who I choose."

Beneath the glow of the colstellite crystals, I laid my soul exposed and bare, all traces of uncertainty erased. I'd made it perfectly clear my desires. Declan rose to his knees matching my stance and tipped my chin up with the pad of his finger. I closed the distance between our faces and pressed my lips to Declan's, and he did not pull away.

40
ROSELYNE

For only a moment after our lips touched, Declan was still and unmoving as if he were stone, unable to fathom or believe the change between us.

Tenderly, Declan placed his hands on either side of my face and deepened the kiss, the warmth of the water comparably frigid to the heat unfurling between my legs.

He wrapped the back of my hair around his fist and pulled gently, exposing my neck. The stubble of his jaw tickled my skin as he trailed kisses around my throat with devout reverence. I arched into him, seeking more.

"Tell me you're sure you want this," he growled low against my skin, his mouth traveling lower and pressing kisses along the way. "Tell me to stop and I will, and we'll never speak of this madness again."

A small gasp escaped my lips as he kissed lightly against my collarbones, the heat from his mouth searing against my too-sensitive skin. My eyes fluttered closed.

"I want this—you. More than anything,"

It was the truth I'd run from, too scared of feeling that hurt again, but I was done running. I shivered under the press of his lips.

"I've dreamed of you," he murmured low against my skin before sweeping his tongue over the hard bud of my nipple and taking it in his mouth. My body bucked from the intensity, seeking friction. I could only whimper in response, my hands grasping and tangling through his dark hair as he rolled his tongue over the sensitive skin. I clenched my thighs together, aching with need.

"Declan, please," I gasped.

He pressed a delicate kiss to the skin between my breasts. He was straddling me on the earthen bench of the hot spring. I caught a glimpse of his hardness beneath the water and sucked in a breath.

Even in the dim light, I could tell he was considerably large. My mouth watered in anticipation of the sweet stretching burn of the fae king filling me that I'd craved for so long. Declan moving inside of me would be the solace to curb the pool of longing inside of me.

"Yes, Roselyne?" he asked with a sly smile as he trailed soft kisses back up to my lips.

My mouth parted beneath his as he swept his tongue into my mouth with expert deftness. My body was pulled taut, desperate for the sensation of him inside of me. I met him with my own tongue swirling around his own as I pressed my body into his. Explosions of light and colors burst behind my eyes. This was bliss.

"Ruin me," I breathed out between kisses.

He obliged.

Showcasing his fae swiftness, Declan lifted me in his arms and carried me out of the water. He gently lowered me to the ground, my upper body supported by the cavern wall. The

Seelie King sank between my legs and spread them wide, his eyes ravenous as he discovered the arousal slicked between my thighs.

"I've dreamed about the taste of your pleasure since I first laid eyes on you. I've fantasized of savoring you as you ripen and burst against my tongue."

My breaths were shallow rapid pants as Declan's face drew nearer to my throbbing entrance. He pushed my thighs further apart, and my legs trembled in anticipation. Declan ran his tongue down the length of my folds and stars burst forth, peppering my vision. His low growl sent vibrations shooting across my skin, his next words rough and unhurried as they dripped from his mouth like honey.

"I intend to wrench every ounce of pleasure from your body and leave you limp and languid and ruined for anyone else."

Declan traced his tongue through my wetness, savoring my arousal as if it was the sweetest elixir, before swirling around the swollen bud at the apex of my thighs. I moaned, shuddering from the pleasure that bound through my body, the tension inside of me coiled tightly. I'd never experienced anything like this. I'd been with men of course, but none had ever ventured to put their face between my thighs and embraced the slick heat inside of me with such skilled devotion.

My nails raked against the crumbling cavern floor, digging into the earth, searching for something to ground me in reality as Declan swept his tongue inside of me with a groan. My back arched off the stone, overwhelmed from the sensation of the vibrations. My head swam with headiness and desire, my body pounding with desperate need. Declan pulled away from me for a moment, my arousal evident and dripping from his chin as he assessed my expression. I had no shame and wantonly spread my legs further apart.

"You taste better than I imagined," he groaned, burying his face between my thighs once more.

My body writhed from the intensity, causing the stone floor to press into my back, but I didn't care. Nothing else in the world mattered except this uncompromising pleasure.

His hot mouth sucked against my clit as he slid a finger into my entrance and began rhythmically rubbing a place deep inside of me. The familiar sensation of pressure began to build. With only a few movements, Declan had my body on the brink of losing all control. His mouth worked in tandem with his fingers, sucking and licking with his tongue as his fingers swirled around my clit. My body jerked involuntarily from the intensity of his touch. I was a puppet, and he was my master, manipulating my body to the most all-consuming pleasure. If he didn't stop soon, I was going to come.

I lifted my head and met Declan's heated gaze as he slid another finger inside of me, my body wet and slick. I shuddered, throwing my head back from the intensity as the walls of my core squeezed around the welcome invasion of his fingers. I threw a hand over my mouth, muffling the sounds as I tried not to cry out.

"Don't hold back with me," Declan growled.

I chanced a quick glance down toward my lower body. One of Declan's hands fucked me, while the other gripped my upper thigh, squeezing the fleshy skin between his fingers. I swallowed, mouth watering.

Declan's cock dripped with his own arousal, and I desperately ached to feel him fully sheathed inside of me. Declan picked up speed with his tongue, and I felt my climax approaching quickly. With one more expert plunge of his fingers, my building climax crested and waves of pleasure skittered through my body, zaps of lightning all through me.

After, I slumped against the cool stone, spent, chest heaving with a sheen of sweat glistening across my body. The colstellite twinkled overhead. Declan rose to his knees, his mouth and jaw wet from my arousal, eyes flashing with that same insatiable hunger. My voice trembled when I spoke.

"That was—"

Declan kissed me, silencing my words, and I tasted myself on his tongue.

"I'm not done with you, yet."

I gulped and my eyes went round. My body was completely lax, the waves of energy faded, but still pinging through my body.

At the fae king's hungry expression, desire bloomed within me again, a tingling sensation emanating from my core outward to my fingertips and toes. Anticipatory chills spread across my skin as Declan leaned forward to nuzzle against my hair, inhaling deeply. I closed my eyes and sighed, his masculine cedar scent intoxicating me as my legs fell apart wholly baring myself to him. Declan sucked in a breath.

"Roselyne, now that I've tasted you, nothing else could ever satisfy me."

I blushed. I'd never been this unabashed with a man before, but everything between Declan and I felt inevitable and natural.

This was supposed to happen. *We* were supposed to happen. The crystal clusters twinkled overhead as if they too agreed.

"I want you inside of me," I said, voice rough.

Declan kissed me again, slow and sensuous before positioning himself over me, lining his hardness up with the opening of my body. My limbs vibrated with anticipation. I arched into Declan as he fully sheathed himself within me in one thrust. The wetness between my thighs eased the bite of pain as my body stretched to accommodate his size. My eyes rolled back at the intense sensation of pressure as his cock filled me. Declan began moving in and out of me, slowly at first, then building up to a quick rhythm. He bent down to meet my lips, and my nails raked down his back, tearing into his skin. I cried out, my body overwhelmed with devastating pleasure as he pressed a kiss to my jaw.

Tiny stars popped across my vision as he dragged the head of his cock out of me, rubbing against the sensitive spot inside of me before slamming it back inside of me. My toes curled, and the pressure began to build anew. He bit and sucked at the skin of my neck before moving to press a bruising kiss to my lips. He swept his tongue into my mouth as he pumped into me. I moaned into his mouth as he slammed back into me with ruthless abandon, the pleasure inside of me growing tauter as my body tumbled toward another climax.

He growled low in my ear as his body collided with mine again and again.

"Do you know how many nights I've laid awake in bed thinking about the sounds that would leave that pretty mouth as I fucked you?"

I moaned into his open mouth, catching his lips in a kiss as he continued pumping in and out of me.

"Do you know how many times I've spilled myself thinking of you, searching for any modicum of relief? Your very presence haunts me. You're a wraith—unable or unwilling to leave my mind. I thought I was going mad. You consume my thoughts day and night. There is no reprieve."

His confession swept through me.

"Maybe I've done the same," I said, pushing Declan off me and onto his back. His face was shocked for a moment before he smirked, ready and accepting for whatever I choose to do. I straddled him and inched my way down his length, as he closed his eyes, groaning from pleasure.

I began to wriggle my hips, riding him. From this angle, the pressure quickly began to build again. Declan gripped the flesh on my hips, grinding me onto his length. I'd never known pleasure like this all my life. I threw my head back in ecstasy, my hair wild around my face as my breasts bounced in time with every movement of my body on Declan's cock.

I bent forward and raked my nails down the skin of his hard chest as he pounded into me, earning a hiss of satisfaction from the fae king. His heart beat wildly under my hand before he grabbed my palm and kissed at the tender flesh of my wrist.

We were a frenzy of flesh on flesh, him completely buried inside of me, as I controlled the tempo of our passion, grinding on his hardness and tumbling toward oblivion. The pressure built, and my body clenched around his cock as I reached my crest. I toppled over the edge, as a rush of bliss washed over me. Declan slammed my body down on his length once more, reaching his own peak and erupted inside of me as aftershocks of pleasure spasmed through my body squeezing around his cock.

The force of his orgasm shook the cave, dislodging some of the smaller clusters of colstellite from the ceiling. A small dusting of the glowing mineral fell down on us like mist.

I collapsed onto his chest, panting and sweat soaked, completely spent. Declan turned me over and laid beside me, softly stroking my hair, sticky from the humidity of the cave. My body ached with a pleasant soreness, a welcome memento of our passion.

I don't know how long we laid side by side afterward. Long enough for our heartbeat to slow to a normal rhythm. We were holding hands, our fingers intertwined, and a resounding sense of peace swept over me.

I no longer cared if Summus Nati or someone else didn't think I belonged at the Seelie Court or deserved to be their queen. I would train every day so I could protect myself, and access the witch magic trapped within my veins. I refused to be a liability to Declan or the Seelie fae any longer.

Although being with Declan had been forced upon me in the beginning, I now needed him like the very air I breathed. The prospect of a life without him was an impossibility I couldn't dare face.

Declan turned to face me, and I smiled at the warmth in his gaze, my heart fluttering madly in my chest. His thumb swept across the skin of my hands, comforting and warm, and pressed a delicate kiss to each hand, similar to how he'd done when we first met.

"I meant what I said before, Roselyne. My soul is yours to possess. I may be King of the Seelie Fae, but I surrender to you."

Under the soft glow of the crystals, I believed him.

41
DECLAN

In all, we shared over a week at the cottage in the Northern Territory. In the mornings, half asleep and heavily lidded, our bodies would come together, melding in movement until we both were spent, wrung completely of pleasure, our appetites for each other momentarily sated.

Afterward, Roselyne would sit outside and try to communicate with nature in an attempt to rouse the wild magic in her veins. The afternoons were dedicated to training outdoors with weapons, and Roselyne had made incredible progress. At Roselyne's request, in the evenings, by candlelight, we'd sit in chairs at the small round wooden dining table of the cottage and pour over old texts regarding the history of the Seelie Court.

"I am not content to be some gilded figure upon a throne. If I am to be queen, I should have knowledge about the court I am to serve."

We did so now, flipping through the pages of some book she'd chosen, stealing kisses from each other every few minutes of silence while a small fire blazed in the hearth. Roselyne sighed at something as she flipped a page, her brows creasing together in the most adorable way.

I fought the urge to take her again atop the table.

"This book makes mention of witches and their ability to open realms and speak into other worlds…We've spoken about that before, but…" She hesitated for a moment. "This book also states the Danchev line as a credit to the witches' eradication."

She turned her large green eyes on me, unwavering and questioning.

I frowned and took the book from her hands as she pointed out the small paragraph. I squinted at the minuscule text of the book. "That's a mistranslation, I'm sure." I flipped a page. "I had nothing to do with the disappearance of the witches. It was war." The lie felt oily on my tongue. "As far as world-whisperers, yes, I knew of that magic. The power in the hands of the witches was too much though. They destroyed themselves in their quest for power. There are dangers beyond our world, it's best they are here no longer to practice such things."

Roselyne took the book back in her hands. She nodded once, then buried her nose back between the paper-thin pages, her fingers trailing over the faded words.

I felt guilty for the lie, but Roselyne wasn't there all those years ago. I hadn't made the final call, but I hadn't stopped it either. She couldn't possibly understand why I'd made the decisions I had, and I did not want to burden her with the knowledge.

Something tapped at the small window beside our chairs and the hair along my neck prickled.

Another *tap, tap, tap* against the glass had me standing and striding over to the intrusion.

A bluish gray falcon pressed its beak against the glass and squawked, clearly irritated that I hadn't slid open the glass yet, its beady eyes set on me. A red ribbon attached a letter to one of its feet.

"Hey there girl," I said, sliding open the glass as the bird of prey hopped inside and atop the table, ruffling its feathers and holding out a leg. It nipped at my fingers and chirped with contempt as I unrolled the small scroll that was affixed to her.

Roselyne cooed at the falcon, running her fingers through its blue feathers as I scanned the letter written in Callum's handwriting.

The ever-present noose tightened around my neck as I read through my commander's messy scrawl. Roselyne stopped her doting on the messenger bird and studied me, eyes swimming with concern.

"What's happened?" Roselyne asked, dropping her hand from the bird's neck, earning a loud squawk of protest from the falcon.

I drug my hands down the skin of my face, not eager to delve into this.

I didn't want to have to leave this cottage and our small bubble of peace. Away from the capital, it was easy to pretend the outside issues of the Seelie Court didn't exist, but my council had done as I requested, and informed me of strange happenings in my court.

"There's been a murder," I said stony-faced. Roselyne's eyes widened. "Callum says it appeared similar to an animal attack, but the council determined it requires my assistance."

Roselyne covered her mouth with her hand, horrified. "We need to go back," she whispered.

"It appears so," I said frowning, resigned and duty bound.

"Immediately," Roselyne agreed, her eyes blazing. That

wasn't fear shining through her expression, but raw determination. Roselyne was to be my queen, and this was her subject that lay slain.

We left a few minutes later after packing up the few possessions we brought with us. We stepped outside the cabin into the crisp night air, autumn's greeting to us. I took Roselyne by the hand and threw the remaining lunar ash over our bodies and we were transported back to Solora.

The streets were quiet tonight. With Roselyne's hand in mine, we walked quickly, dodging muddy puddles pooling along the uneven cobblestone streets. Here in the business district, no everlights shone. Our only light source was the pale moon, bathing the streets in its eerie glow, reflecting off the wet streets. I silently thanked the goddess for the cloudless night as I led Roselyne around a dark corner and splashed into a puddle. We were nearly there. I scented it on the wind—death and bloodshed. Droplets of the earlier rain dribbled off the canopies of market stalls, collecting and pooling on the ground. I gripped Roselyne's hand in my own.

"I should have brought you back home first," I said.

She jutted her chin, eyes flashing full of defiance, as if daring me to try.

"Well, we're almost there now," I said flatly. "Just—if it's too much for you, please tell me, and we'll leave."

Roselyne nodded. "I will."

Callum spoke nearby, the words too low to be deciphered. Roselyne and I turned another corner and found the commander facing away from us, the back of his blond head dipped low and speaking to another member of the Daylight Guard.

We approached him, and Callum's pointed ears pricked beneath his hair. He turned and faced me, then noticed Roselyne, and his face drained of all color.

"You shouldn't be here, Roselyne."

Roselyne scowled and crossed her arms.

"If I am to be Queen of the Seelie Fae, those slain are to be *my subjects*. I am not some delicate flower plucked from the earth to sit idly in a vase," Roselyne snapped.

A chilly breeze blew, lifting all the small hairs along her arms. Roselyne's body shivered, her posture stiff, shoulders nearly to her chin. I pressed against her shoulders, and she relaxed them, then sagged against my chest. I hugged my arms around her, cocooning her in the warmth of my body.

Callum's eyes tracked the movement, but he did not speak on our newly minted affections. Roselyne's hair tickled my chin as it blew in the breeze, diffusing the air with its jasmine scent as I kissed the crown of her head. I closed my eyes and breathed in her scent. Steeling myself, I slid my arms from Roselyne's body and took a step toward the crime scene.

A small blanket shrouded the body. Callum grimaced as he pulled back the white covering revealing the nude corpse of a fae man. His large eyes stared up, face forever etched in an expression of horror. His skin was ashen in death, all color leached from his cheeks, his lips the faintest blue. My eyes tracked down his body toward his abdomen. Dried blood covered every inch of his body, his skin torn into ribbons and hanging limply. A huge, jagged gash took up the length of his chest and stomach, his entrails spilling out over his navel and onto the ground.

My people were being torn to shreds, and I hadn't any idea how to stop it.

"What sort of beast kills in this manner?" I asked Callum.

"I don't know," he said, shaking his head. "It keeps happening, though." His mouth pressed into a hard line as he glanced to Roselyne, then back to me. "There's thought that it could be—otherworldly. *Demonic*," Callum said. "The people are frightened, Dec."

Roselyne's gaze flitted to mine, her large eyes round, and her brows creased.

I shook my head. "The doors between worlds remain closed. No demons hunt in this realm any longer, and haven't for centuries," I said. "If demons hunted in the faelands, there'd be more bodies than a handful. Certainly, our assailant is some bold beast emerging from the tree line, then slinking back into the shadows once they've sated their bloodlust."

Roselyne's eyes darted toward the trees, swaying at the edge of the city. I looked to my betrothed as a Daylight Guard covered the dead man's body once more, the blood seeping through the white cloth.

I took Roselyne's hand in mine. "I'm taking you home immediately."

I turned toward Callum and frowned.

"Starting now, Solora has a curfew. I'll not have my citizens needlessly mutilated. Spread the word, anyone caught outside after nightfall will be fined handsomely. Gather volunteers from your guard. Tomorrow, we set out into the forest. There will be a hunt. We'll find and kill the beast haunting our kingdom. Solora will be safe again."

42

ROSELYNE

Declan, Sloane, and Callum left before dawn to hunt the beast terrorizing Solora. Declan snuck from our room with a light press of his lips on mine. When I woke, his side of the bed was cold, and I had a sinking sensation in the pit of my stomach. Chalking it up to hunger, and with nothing else to do with Declan gone, I went to have breakfast.

"Did you enjoy your time away with the king?" Essi asked as she slid in beside me at the large table in the center of the palace's dining room. I swallowed the eggs I'd been chewing and blushed crimson.

"Yes," I said, "we trained a lot. I'm getting quite good."

Essi leaned in toward me.

"Anything else?" she asked.

"I don't kiss and tell."

She shrieked at that, slapping my shoulder. I couldn't help but smile.

"I knew it!" She bounced in her seat. "Ooh, Roselyne, that's amazing!"

"Yeah." I sighed. "I wish we could have stayed longer, but..."

"The attack brought you back?" she said frowning. "The Seelie Prince told me about it."

"It did."

Essi straightened her posture. "Well, I'm glad you're back as is. We have last minute plans to go over for the wedding."

"I thought you planned everything already."

"Most things, yes, but your input is vital. You're going to be Queen of the Seelie Court, everything has to be perfect."

"Let me at least finish breakfast before we begin."

It was strange planning a wedding, considering the state of affairs in Solora. Less than twelve hours ago, I'd stared into the eyes of a dead man's mutilated corpse.

Now, I sat next to Essi in the palace's formal dining room choosing table arrangements and florals. Sunlight beamed in through the multicolored glass window, sending rainbows of light all over the table. Wedding planning seemed so trivial in comparison to everything else happening. Essi held up two different shades of golden shimmering fabric.

"Which do you prefer?"

"For?"

"To cover the tables and hang from the walls," Essi said.

With a sigh, I motioned toward the cooler, less yellowed tone. "That one."

Essi sensed my hesitation and frowned.

"The king and his men will sort out this nastiness, Roselyne. It won't overshadow your big day."

I managed a weak smile. Being *overshadowed* wasn't my concern, but it'd do no good to voice.

Essi looked up. "Maybe this beast will have a beautiful pelt, and you can make a rug of it for all the devastation it's caused."

I wrinkled my nose. "Gods, I hope not." I shuddered. "I'm just worried about Declan and the others today. I've seen firsthand what the beast can do to a person."

Essi clicked her tongue. "The king and his men will be fine. Declan has his brother and the commander at his side. There are none better qualified to fell this beast."

The thought did bring a small amount of comfort to me. I rested against the back of the chair.

I arched a brow and leaned in toward my friend.

"Speaking of Declan's brother…"

Essi's face flushed scarlet, a stark contrast with her golden hair.

"What's going on with you two?"

"Only a dalliance," Essi said quickly. "A flirtation. Nothing more."

I dropped the conversation. It wasn't my business, regardless. Essi was grown and knew the prince's reputation. Her heart was hers to decide what to do with.

Essi and I spent the next few hours finalizing menus, choosing entertainment, and selecting which flowers I wanted weaved into my hair and placed along the aisle.

We'd settled on burgundy dahlias and roses, with yellow accents to represent the Seelie motif of sunlight throughout the ceremony space.

She squealed with excitement. "It's going to be beautiful, Roselyne!"

The back door swung open. I jumped from my seat and ran toward the sound, desperate to see Declan and make sure he was unharmed, with Essi at my heels. In strode Declan, Callum, and Sloane, all covered in mud…and blood.

I inhaled sharply, eyes razing down Declan's body. "Are you hurt?" I asked.

Sloane clapped his brother on the back. "We're all fine, the beast is dead. It was a massive one."

I sighed, relieved.

Callum laughed. "Sloane dealt the killing blow."

Sloane grinned. "An arrow to the eye, but Declan and Callum certainly roughed him up for me."

Essi wrinkled her nose. "You all smell terrible."

Despite her words, she bit her lip while assessing the Seelie Prince.

"What was it?" I asked, "the creature?"

"A bearbeast. The largest I'd ever seen," Declan said. "Just as we suspected. There was a den of cubs nearby, but they're taken care of now. The city will sleep soundly tonight."

Declan frowned at me. "You're tense."

"I'm fine." I nuzzled into the crook of Declan's arms as we lay together in bed. "I just have a bad feeling."

Declan stroked my hair. "Well, you *are* a witch," he said, "so I'm liable to trust your intuition." He smiled down at me. "But the monster is gone."

"What if that wasn't it?" I asked.

"We'll keep the curfew for a few nights to make sure."

That admission helped ease the gnawing worry in my chest, but I still felt fidgety, full of nervous unspent energy.

"Can we train tomorrow?" I asked. Hitting things would help me. "I have plans for witching lessons with Kera in the afternoon already. I'm so close to a breakthrough."

"Will Essi allow it?" He chuckled. "I know she's kept you busy with planning for the wedding."

"The majority of the planning is done. Tomorrow I'm free of wedding plans."

His voice rumbled low. "The morning, then."

Declan pressed a soft kiss to my brow, and my eyes fluttered closed with a soft sigh. His hand trailed down the center of my chest, and my breath hitched under his gentle caress.

He spoke low in my ear. "Soon, I'll make you my bride."

I ran my fingers across the smooth golden band on my left hand, a reminder of our promise to each other, and bit my lip. In less than two months, we'd belong to each other entirely and in accordance with the fae gods.

"Soon," I said, smiling.

Declan brought his lips to mine, and our bodies came together between the sheets, as we whispered promises of forever to each other.

43

ROSELYNE

For the next two weeks, the streets of Solora were still and peaceful. No mangled bodies decorated the streets and alleys, and the citizens of Solora breathed a sigh of relief that their looming monster was slain.

When Declan and I made our way to the sparring ring of the palace, Callum and Sloane were already there, dulled practice blades in hand and swinging at each other. I sat beside Declan on the floor just outside the training ring, my head resting on his shoulder, as the Seelie Prince and the Commander of the Daylight Guard sparred together.

"We can't afford to get rusty, now can we?" Sloane joked as he ducked a blow from Callum.

Callum huffed, a thin sheen of sweat lining his brow. "Aren't you supposed to be the bookish type?" He lunged at the fae prince who sidestepped him easily. "Bookish *and* a rogue, that's what I've heard."

Sloane's eyes twinkled.

"Those accusations may both be true, but there's something to be said of a man with a sword in his hands." Sloane hit

Callum with the flat of his blade, striking against the commander's hip. "Point," he said, before continuing. "Although I don't truly care for fighting with weapons. I much prefer wordplay." He threw a wink my way before turning and ducking a slash from Callum. "Although fair maidens love a man wielding a sword, intent on protecting their honor."

Callum snorted at that, a sly smile lining his mouth, before raising his blade above his head and bringing it down toward Sloane, and smacking the prince against the shoulder. "Point," Callum said with a grin. "I don't believe protecting maidens' virtues is what you're *known for*, Prince Sloane," Callum said.

Sloane grinned, his white teeth fully on display, before throwing his head back and howling with laughter.

"Alright, that's enough of you two," Declan said, rising to stand. "You two can go whack each other around in the yard, Roselyne and I require use of the ring."

The two men lowered their blades.

Sloane tossed his to the ground outside the ring. "I'm done sparring for today. I have business to attend to in the city proper," he said.

Declan raised an eyebrow. "Business?"

"Well." Sloane's eyes glanced at me, then back to his brother. "Your upcoming wedding and subsequent monetary promises to Althene are quite taxing to the crown. I'm meeting to see what we'll need to adjust and prepare for, going forward."

I fingered a silver strand of my hair, wrapping it around my finger. It wasn't my fault, and Sloane hadn't insinuated so, but it was true that upon Declan and I's marriage, the Seelie Court would owe Althene an insurmountable amount of gold, as was agreed upon.

Callum shifted his feet. "I need to go check on the new

recruits. Although the beast is dead, we've kept the increased number of patrolling guards at night just in case there are more nearby."

The two men exited, and Declan and I were alone in the echoing room.

"Training with swords or daggers today?" Declan asked.

Declan tucked the errant strand of hair behind my ear and cupped my cheek, tilting my chin upward toward him.

"Surprise me," I said.

"I'm not sure you're ready for the kind of surprises I have in mind for you."

A ripple of desire fluttered through me, but I stamped it out. I wanted to be proficient with blades, not delve into a frenzy of lust every time Declan and I found ourselves alone.

"Swords then," I said.

With a chuckle, Declan nodded his head, retrieving two practice swords and handing one to me.

After training, Declan left to hold court, and I walked the short distance to the edge of the palace property toward the greenhouse to meet Kera. I felt as if I was on the precipice of unlocking my powers, the supposed hum of energy beneath my skin waiting to be released upon the world. I joined my friend in the greenhouse, the air outside cool and dry thanks to the changing seasons, the sweat of my skin drying in the chilled air.

"Close your eyes," Kera instructed, leafing through some old book I'd never seen.

I did as she commanded, but no answering magic beckoned me toward it.

I frowned. "Should I be feeling something by now? We've been trying for weeks."

"Have patience, Roselyne. Even being among the earth can help attune you and bring your magic to the surface." I opened one eye, and found Kera's face gazing toward the outside tree line of the Ghostwood Forest, face lined with worry.

"Aren't there other things witches can do? It's not all herbs, potions, and poisons, right? There are other things..."

Kera flicked her dark eyes back to mine. "It's not," she said, "but that's what I'm most familiar with. Witches kept their magic to themselves, closely guarding their secrets, rightfully fearful of what others would do with its knowledge. It's by design we're having trouble getting you to connect to your power."

"Oh," I said, sinking into my chair. "Is there something else I can try?"

Kera's mouth twitched. "Witches have inherent healing abilities."

"How does that work—?"

Before the full sentence was out of my mouth, Kera whipped a concealed dagger from its sheath at her thigh and sliced the blade down her forearm from wrist to elbow. Crimson bloomed from the cut and spilled across her arm, falling to the earthen ground of the greenhouse and mixing with the dirt.

I leaped from my chair, startled. "Kera, why would you do that?" I began frantically searching around the greenhouse for anything to stanch the bleeding.

More blood gushed from the wound. "I only have so much time, Roselyne. A cut this deep?" She whistled low. "I'll bleed out in minutes."

"Kera, please." I grabbed her forearm and yanked it to me, assessing the damage. The slice was deep, but clean. Kera was an expert with a blade and was careful not to deal herself lasting damage. A few stitches and she'd be fine, no unattainable magical healing necessary. Her blood smeared on my hands and under my fingernails as I pressed my palms the length of her forearm, working to cut off the flow of blood.

Kera *tsked* and snatched her arm from my hands. "Magic *only*."

Her normally tanned skin was paler, nearly a match for mine beneath the smears of red.

"Kera, I can't." I reached for her again, and she pulled away again, more slowly this time. "Please, let me get someone—"

Her dark eyes narrowed. "You want to access your magic? Then do it."

Tears swam in my eyes and my heart pounded in my chest. I did as Kera commanded, searching deep within myself, but found no magic reaching back for me to stitch my friend back together. "There's nothing there, Kera." I reached for her again, pleading with her to heal herself, but she pulled away once more, wobbling as she did. Her lips were the palest blue—her dark eyes clouded, but defiance still burning bright behind them.

"Magic," she whispered, her mouth barely moving to form the words.

Kera stumbled and began to fall. I caught her before she hit the pavers of the greenhouse, slick with her blood, and guided her to the ground, noting the rapid and shallow rise and fall of her chest. I pressed my palms into her bleeding arms and screamed, hoping one of the few servants would hear me. I couldn't leave her like this—she would die, and it would be my fault.

44

DECLAN

"Are you demented, Kera? You could have died." Kera shifted to sit upright. Dried blood crusted her arm. I'd barely made it in time to heal her before she succumbed to her wound, only roused by Roselyne's screams carried to me on the wind. All that remained of the self-inflicted wound was a quickly fading pink line. I'd sent Roselyne back to our room, while I stayed in Kera's, knowing we needed to discuss what happened without the ears of my betrothed present.

Kera scowled. "Don't seek to lecture me, Declan. Roselyne has made no advancements in accessing her power. I thought perhaps, I could force it to appear."

I ground my teeth. "By traumatizing her and nearly killing yourself in the process?"

She frowned, tracing her fingers across the raised line on her skin. "I thought it would work. I'm still not convinced it wouldn't have."

I shook my head and inhaled deeply, trying to dampen the growing rage inside of me. "You don't get to decide that."

The mark on Kera's skin faded fully away, erased completely as if it had never happened. The dried blood smeared across her forearm told another story.

Kera met my eyes with hers. "You put me in charge of helping Roselyne access her gifts, Declan, but she's made no progress. If I didn't sense the magic in her, I'd believe I was wrong, and she wasn't a witch at all. She has zero inherent knowledge of herbs and poisons"—Kera held up her arm—"and clearly doesn't possess the ability to heal under pressure."

"She needs time," I snapped. "Roselyne is the answer to breaking this curse the witches bestowed upon me."

"What if there isn't a curse, Declan?"

My nostrils flared, and if I possessed elemental gifts, I swore I would have breathed fire. It took everything in me to not scream at my council member, my spy, my *friend*.

"What are you saying?" I asked her. "I know you were not there when it was spoken, but you've seen the prophecy written."

With a groan, Kera rose from the sofa, and stood before me, fidgeting with her fingers. She hesitated for a moment, holding out her palms to me.

"What if instead of a curse, it's guilt gnawing at you? Weakening you? Have you considered that? I know you weren't the one who lit the pyre, but I can imagine how you must feel—"

I interrupted her, tired of hearing Kera's attempts at understanding me, on turning this entire situation on its head. "You will never know what I felt—what I *feel*," I gritted out. "You are the one who nearly killed yourself to prove a point."

"And that's my choice to make, isn't it?" Kera stood taller, fire dancing behind her dark eyes. "You've sent me into wolves' dens when it served you, Declan." She let loose a mirthless laugh, a joyless sound I'd never heard from her lips. "But when

I try something on my own, suddenly I am the problem? Seems just as so. Callum and I have paused our entire lives in order to *serve you*, and now your brother has rejoined the council and done the same. But you never thank us, you are never grateful for what we do for you."

My hands balled into fists at my sides. "You are a part of my council, it is your *duty*," I said through clenched teeth.

Kera's eyes narrowed on me as she pursed her lips. "A duty I do for my friend as well as my king. I suppose I need to better separate you from your two identities," she said, voice laced with poison, before crossing her arms.

"Get out," I said, regretting it the moment the words left my lips. "Wait—"

But it was too late—Kera had already transformed into her black cat form and jumped from the open window, landing on the soft grass below. With feline quickness, she darted across the yard and into the forest line, no doubt going back to the apartment she kept in the city.

My anger subsided, replaced immediately by a knot of regret. Kera had been at my side for half a century, joining me after the war, and we'd never bickered this way. I collapsed into the pristine gray sofa of her bedchamber and ran a hand through my hair, catching on snarls and tangles.

She'd be back soon. She had to be. The wedding was soon, and Roselyne would be gutted if Kera didn't show. After a few moments, I collected myself and walked back to mine and Roselyne's bedchambers, my heart heavy with unease.

I clicked the door shut behind me, and Roselyne peeked up from her book. After the incident with Kera today, she'd opted to take a break from her studies, and instead curled up on the sofa and read something for leisure for a change.

"How's Kera doing?" Roselyne asked, her brows knit together.

"Completely healed," I said, and Roselyne sagged in relief.

She closed her book. "I'm going to go see her. Which way is her bedchamber? I haven't actually ever been there before, but I figured now's as good as ever."

"She's not there," I said.

Roselyne's eyes went round.

"What do you mean?"

"She left," I said through clenched teeth.

"Why," she asked. "Where did she go?"

"It's nothing. We bickered."

Roselyne narrowed her eyes. "About what happened today?"

"Of course, Roselyne," I said, exhausted. "Kera was wrong for doing that to you, for traumatizing you."

"I can be mad on my own behalf if I need to, Declan," Roselyne said. "You don't need to act like some savior and protector on my behalf. I was never in harm's way. *Kera* was."

"Well, I—"

"What exactly happened?" She snapped her book shut. "After nearly bleeding out, you kicked Kera out into the streets?"

"She has an apartment," I mumbled, but Roselyne acted like she hadn't heard me.

"You're so—pigheaded!" An angry flush crept up her neck. "I'm not that delicate, Declan. If I want to be mad at Kera, I will be, but I don't need you fighting my battles on my behalf."

She stood and strode to the door, her hand on the knob.

"Where are you going?" I asked.

"To see Essi," she replied, her face full of scorn. "Is that alright with you, *King Declan*? Do I need a chaperone?"

"No," I said, taken aback. "Roselyne, I didn't mean to upset you."

She shook her head. "Look, I care deeply for you, but I'm angry right now. I want to go elsewhere and not be around you for a moment. Please allow me that courtesy."

I nodded, unsure of how this fight had even begun, as I watched the woman I loved walk out the door.

45

ROSELYNE

I knocked softly on Essi's door to no response. Not wanting to go back to our bedchambers yet, I decided to walk to the library and spend some time among the books and crackling hearth of the giant fireplace.

The library was as impressive as it always was, the dimming sky above showing off whorls of pinks and purples through the windows of the entrance. I descended the stairs into the lower levels and watched as the everlights began to glow brighter, naturally cued by the setting sun.

I quickly found myself immersed in the familiar scent of ink on paper as I aimlessly wandered through the aisles, my hands tracing along the book spines. Done with their duties, the Book Keepers left to go back to their homes, leaving me alone in the library. I curled into one of the overstuffed chairs in front of the fireplace and allowed myself to get lost in a book. I was entranced in the magical word of fantasy and whimsy when I saw something flicker from the corner of my eye. The fire glowed brighter for a moment and I thought I saw movement within the flames, but I blinked and it was gone. I went back to reading.

Sometime later, I heard a cough behind me, startling me from the depths of my novel I'd read half of.

"Hello?" I said into the darkness beyond the glow of my half-burned candle.

There was no movement in the dim glow cast by the everlights lining the walls or the fire in the hearth, now only a few flickering embers.

I whirled around in my chair and found Sloane sitting at the study tables behind me, legs crossed and grossly immersed in a book, scribbling notes onto parchment.

My movement roused him from whatever thought he'd been lost in.

His eyes snapped from his book and met mine. "Roselyne! You're up late I see."

I rubbed my eyes. "Time got away from me, I suppose." I got up from my chair and sat beside him at his table.

Sloane shut the book he was reading. It was old and weathered, with the title completely faded away. I could only make out a few strange shapes in the cover, barely recognizable as some sort of ancient runes.

"What's that?" I asked, motioning toward the ancient book and the scribbles on paper.

"Another language." He said. "Although I'm back on Declan's council, I can't quench the thirst for knowledge I've always had. Did you know it's possible to learn other schools of magic not usually supplied to fae?" His mouth turned down in a frown, his expression softening. "I heard about Kera—about how Declan kicked her out of the palace."

I squirmed in my seat. "I know what she was trying to do, and I understand why. My powers are blocked by something.

Even her nearly dying couldn't get them to appear. I'm disappointing everyone."

Sloane tapped his finger against his chin. "It's a shame Declan needs you to access your magic to break his curse, otherwise you wouldn't feel such pressure."

I sucked in a breath. *Curse?* I'd always been told accessing my magic was my own choice, and not something Declan required of me—a way for me to feel powerful in this place of magic and deception.

"What do you mean?" I asked.

At my incredulous expression, Sloane's face became stricken, as he stared open-mouthed at me. "You still don't know..." his voice trailed away, and he shook his head. "It's just a hunch, nothing definite. Forget what I've said."

I began trembling, unnerved by what he'd revealed. "Explain."

"It's not my secret to tell, Roselyne," Sloane said, refusing to meet by eyes. "Please go talk to Declan if you need answers."

"*Sloane,*" I said, half begging the man I'd begun to consider a friend.

He sighed. "I thought with the—*shift* between you two, Declan would have told you everything, would have filled you in. I'm sorry."

My chest tightened, and I struggled to take in a deep breath. My hands trembled, as I placed them on the table, gripping the edge to ground myself to the present.

"What curse?" I asked quietly.

"It's not my place to tell you, Roselyne."

"Please," I said, "Do me this courtesy. What is going on?"

Sloane dragged his hands down his face, a mixture of guilt and defeat in his expression. "I will only tell you because it's your right to know. You're marrying my brother and deserve the entirety of the truth."

My heart beat wildly in my chest. "Please," I said.

"Did Declan tell you about the war?"

"Some," I said, thinking of the few times I'd asked about the Unseelie fae and their destruction, and what little I'd read in books. "A century ago, the Seelie fae triumphed over the Unseelie after centuries of skirmishes, decimating their armies."

"Yes," Sloane said, nodding his head. "And do you know *how* the Seelie fae achieved this great victory?"

I chewed my bottom lip. I'd never asked. I'd assumed like all war, the Seelie victory came to them on a battlefield of sweat and blood.

Sloane leaned forward. "Witches," he said.

The candlelight flickered, casting Sloane's face in shadows as he unraveled everything I'd come to know about the war.

"What does this have to do with me?" I asked, my voice shaking with every word.

"The witches performed their spells under duress," he said. "Declan believes they cursed him for his betrayal to his lover, Phaedra."

Phaedra. The name was familiar. Declan mentioned her to me once. He'd betrayed her? I leaned back in my chair as what I'd heard swept through me.

"And I am...?"

"The answer to breaking his curse." Sloane said. I swallowed, but nodded, and Sloane continued. "There is a prophecy...Declan believes marrying a witch—marrying *you* will break the witches' curse upon him, and he will return to his full strength once more."

"Full strength?" I asked, voice wavering.

"His magic is fading. My brother is only a fraction as

strong as he once was. He's still incredibly powerful and a force to be reckoned with, but he fears it will only worsen if he does not break the curse bestowed upon him soon. He fears his territory lords plot against him and would move to take the throne if they smelled a whiff of weakness."

"That's why he proposed marriage between us?" I said.

I slumped in my chair, although my heart was racing as the truth of Declan and I's relationship washed over me. *He was using me.*

I was merely a means to an end, a way to break a curse. He didn't care about me, and if he did, it was only for what I could do for him. Why else deceive me this way? Hot tears burned at my eyes.

"I'm sorry for burdening you with this, Roselyne."

"No," I said, holding back the tears, "Thank you for telling me." I managed a weak smile at Sloane. "I'll speak with Declan."

He assessed me with a worried gaze, and resembled his brother so much in that moment, I averted my face away from his scrutiny.

Declan used me. The sentence repeated in my mind, louder than any words being spoken aloud. *Declan used me.*

Suddenly, the comforting aisles of the library only served to oppress, towering and imposing over me. I needed out of this library, this palace, and this city. I needed a chance to work through the truth of what I'd been told *alone* and without interference. At this moment in time when I realized I could truly trust no one in the faelands, I missed Dove the most.

"I think I'm quite ready for bed," I said, my voice full of false sunshine. I stood, brushing down my gown and turning to retreat toward the ground floor of the library and toward the palace.

"Goodnight, Princess," Sloane said. I receded into the darkness, and finally allowed the tears to fall.

I sat on the front steps of the palace, my mind numb, and my body shivering as the breeze blew through my hair, the silver and light brown strands dancing together under the pale moonlight. I buried my head in my knees and let my despair wash over me.

I couldn't go back and lay beside Declan and pretend everything was fine, knowing the depths of his deception toward me. I choked back the tears, my breath exiting in a puff of visible air in the chilled weather.

I chewed at my bottom lip, unsure of whether to trust my feelings for the Seelie King as truth. If Declan was capable of such a betrayal, what else would he lie about?

I squeezed my eyes shut, willing my reality to shift backward to when I was merely angry that Declan sent Kera away in a show of overprotectiveness. I silently begged my memories to regress to when I wasn't burdened with the knowledge of that damned curse and prophecy. The tears spilled over from both of my eyes and tracked down my cheeks in twin streams.

Although I hadn't yet said the words aloud, I loved Declan. Though I wondered if that love burning through me was merely a concoction of my mind, slipped to me as a fae glamour as easily as the pregnancy prevention elixir I took with each cycle of the moon. I wiped at my eyes with a sniffle. How could I trust anything I thought was true?

The choice was painful, but easy to make. I scribbled a note on the scraps of parchment I'd found in the pockets of my cloak, and stuffed it under the doorway of our bedchambers before returning to the yard. Only a few members of the Daylight Guard patrolled tonight, their numbers more concentrated on the tree line near the city—they'd be easy enough to get past while exiting the property.

Under the cover of darkness, I snuck to the stables, saddled my own mount, and began riding toward the all-human settlement outside Solora, my heart cleaved completely in two.

46
DECLAN

Sunlight streamed through the window of Roselyne and my shared bedchambers, waking me from my fitful sleep on the sofa. I stretched and blinked as the room slid into focus. My eyes drifted to the bed, expecting to see my betrothed snoozing softly, our quarrel of yesterday long forgotten. Instead, the covers were thrown back, the sheets ice cold. I ran my hand down my face with a groan. Roselyne never came back to our room last night.

My heart felt heavy in my chest as I scanned the room, thinking of the assailants who'd previously tried to abduct Roselyne. Dread spread throughout my body. Something was wrong. Someone had taken her from me. I ground my teeth, vowing to kill them all. My power flared through me, hot and primed to strike, though sluggish. I stood, readying myself to level the palace in an attempt to locate Roselyne, when I spotted it—a note, folded neatly and located inside the threshold of the door.

My name was written in a familiar soft looping script—Roselyne's. My hands trembled as I unfurled the paper and scanned the letter. My heart shattered into thousands of shards, slicing me apart from the inside out upon seeing the brief message written in my betrothed's own hand.

Declan,
I know the truth. I am leaving of my own volition. Please do not look for me.
-R

I exhaled. *The truth? Leaving?* Roselyne's penned words pulled out my heart and twisted it in her small hands. I shook my head, re-reading the letter, desperately searching for some clue that she didn't do this.

She *couldn't* have done this.

A howl of grief and pain burst from my lips as I sank onto my knees. She'd left me, and where my heart once beat, only a hollow shell remained.

I barely noticed my brother enter, eyes alight and scanning the empty room, as Essi stood wide-eyed and open-mouthed in the doorway to the bedchamber.

"What's happened?" Sloane asked as he tugged against my arm, pulling me from my knees to stand. He held me by the shoulders and shook me. "Where's Roselyne?" his eyes scanned the room again, and his mouth turned downward.

"Gone." My voice was barely audible, as if my mouth refused to speak the word.

Sloane dropped his arms to his sides and assessed me with a confused expression. I jerked my head toward the open letter cast aside on the floor. I shook my head, desperate, but unable to wake up from the nightmare that plagued my reality. I didn't even care about the curse any longer. Let my powers fade and someone else take the damned throne. I wanted to marry Roselyne because I loved her and couldn't imagine a life without her by my side.

Who was I ever kidding, thinking I was worthy of love? It was laughable. The sins of my past would always catch up with me, and ruin anything poised to make me happy.

Sloane read the letter and swore. I could barely hear him. A soft buzzing hummed in my head, buffering all noise outside of my body. He instructed something to Essi, who scurried away closing the door as she exited.

"Can she even *do this*?" Sloane asked, holding the wretched letter aloft. The dark swirls of ink mocked me before he folded it back over. Only my name was visible on the outside of the parchment, and I envied the pen she'd used to ink the message.

I ran a hand down my face. "If she takes her ring off before our wedding, yes. The gods will not punish a changing mind if decided in earnest before the marriage is sealed. There's nothing I can do."

"But the treaty?" Sloane asked. "The agreement with Althene?"

"I would never harm them for Roselyne's decision to break the betrothal if she so chooses. She would only despise me further."

Surely this pain was some divine punishment from the goddess herself, shaming me for gross misuse of my powers of torture, or perhaps even another facet of the witches' curse. Cursed to love a witch—to make me fall in love, and have her leave, taking my soul with her as she did.

"Declan, I fear this may be my fault," Sloane said, eyes wary as he held the letter like it burned him.

"Speak now," I commanded.

Sloane poured both of us a drink and handed one to me. My hands shook slightly as I grabbed for the glass. The warm liquid burned my throat as I swallowed. I deserved this pain. I'd relish in it.

"I mentioned the prophecy to Roselyne, and the curse...I thought she knew, but upon seeing her face—" His voice trailed off.

"*Why* would you say anything to her?" I roared. My power flared to life in my chest, desperate to lash out—to kill. "I told you she didn't know about the curse." Guilt gnawed at me for that, for the deception I could have easily avoided.

"She asked, and I told her the truth, Declan. She deserved that much," Sloane said.

My vision narrowed. Without thinking, I crossed the room and punched my brother in the jaw.

"You had no right to interfere," I said, seething. I wanted to pummel him, to make him share in some of the hurt burning inside of me.

Sloane rubbed his jaw, but made no moves to strike me back, despite having every right. The familiar tendrils of shame crept up my neck. Sloane didn't deserve my ire. This pain I felt was my own doing. *I* was the liar. If I had been honest from the beginning everything would be different. I curled my hands into fists and breathed deeply, working to calm the rising tide of desperation inside of me.

"Did she say where she was going? I can find her, I can—"

"She did not share with me her plans. I did not know the extent of her distress." He frowned. "Do you truly care for the girl?"

"Yes," I said, voice tight. My eyes burned.

"Ah."

How could I explain what Roselyne meant to me? I was a damned fool to have allowed her into my home and heart, and an even bigger fool for not being more deserving of her affections.

No one, least of all I, expected me to fall in love with the princess. But I had.

I had fallen and landed among thorns, and bore their scars upon my heart.

"Sloane, please leave me. I'd like to be alone," I said quietly as I sipped the amber liquid from the glass. From the window, I could see the sun had fully risen, but I only felt myself slipping further into the darkness.

"I'm sorry brother. Truly," Sloane said, as he slipped outside the room with a polite bow of his head, heeding my wishes. The door clicked closed behind him.

I exhaled. Roselyne was gone. Although every ounce of my body screamed at me to retrieve her, I forced myself immobile. She'd chosen this. To leave. The glass of warm liquor shattered in my hand, the force of my grip too much. Tiny cuts sliced into my skin but I did not wince at the bite of pain, I welcomed the distraction to the bleakness of my thoughts. This was nothing compared to the devastation wrought upon my soul.

I do not know how long I sat on the small sofa alone with my sorrow. A cloak of protective numbness swept over me as I sat unblinking. The sun eventually sank below the horizon and the shadows of the room grew long and narrow. I shook my hand and the pieces of glass dislodged and clattered to the floor. I flexed my fingers. My accelerated healing erased all evidence of the broken glass, and only tiny pink lines remained as tangible proof of my heartbreak. I tipped my head back over the edge of the sofa. I closed my eyes and sank into oblivion, allowing the darkness to consume me. Sometime later, my door creaked open. I opened my eyes.

A small black cat strolled into my open bedchamber door. I

rubbed at my eyes to be sure of what I saw. Kera stood in front of me in her fae form, a worried expression etched across her small face, our previous disagreement forgotten.

"Essi wrote me," she said, before I'd even been able to ask the question. She crossed the room and clicked her tongue. "I've allowed you to wallow long enough. Are you ready to do something about it?"

"She asked me not to follow her," I croaked, voice hoarse from disuse and a lack of water. "And I don't know where she is. She's *gone*, Kera."

"Males are such petulant children, content to sulk and brood." She sighed impatiently. "Roselyne asked to not follow her because she is *hurt* and *angry with you*."

I nodded, oblivious to whatever point Kera was trying to make.

She sighed again. "You love her, don't you?"

"Yes," I said immediately.

"Then go to her."

"I don't know where she's gone. What if she doesn't want me there? Maybe she's seen how wretched I am and has left in earnest."

Kera rolled her eyes. "As far as the dynamics between the two of you—I am no relationship expert, but I have eyes. She loves you. Regarding *where* she'd go—" Kera shrugged. "Roselyne is a human woman in the faelands. Where do you *think* she'd go if she wanted to feel comfortable away from her *fae* betrothed?"

"The human village," I said. It was so obvious.

To her surprise, I gripped Kera in a tight hug. She patted me awkwardly on the back for a moment before I broke the embrace and bound out of the room toward the stables intent on bringing my betrothed back to me.

47

ROSELYNE

It took hours by horseback to reach the all-human village of Bask, but there it was as promised, along the main road heading north. No one paid much attention as I rode through the small gates leading into the village, my wine-colored cloak drawn tightly over my face. I had the distinct feeling the villagers of Bask were used to the odd traveler through their town. The air was thick with mist as the sun began its daily creep above the horizon, the ground still spongy from yesterday's rainfall, heavier in the countryside than its city counterpart.

A rickety three-story building sat near the entrance of the town, with a small stable in the back. The building's chimney puffed gray smoke, filling the street with the scent of roasting meats. A faded sign hung from the awning, identifying this place as the Sunburst Tavern and Inn. Golden ivy crept up the side of the inn, overtaking grimy stained windows, and climbing toward the roof. The inn was quaint and comforting, looking similar to those I'd seen while traveling through the crowded city where I'd grown up.

Yearning to stretch my legs after riding all night, I stabled my stolen horse in the small building behind the inn and walked to the entrance. My boots squished in the mud, misting my calves with flecks of brown.

A small bell tinkled as I slunk through the door of the inn. I drew the hood of my cloak more tightly around my face. Prying eyes would surely recognize the Seelie King's bride despite my tear-stained puffy eyed appearance, and I wasn't keen on being found out so easily. The hours of riding through the night hadn't unburdened my heart. Instead, on my journey, I played through every moment we shared, every tender memory between Declan and I, and tasted bile.

All lies to further his own power.

The inn's common room was scarcely filled. Specks of dust floated through the air, shimmering in the sun, reminding me of the sprites we'd seen in the Northern Seelie Territory while in the lagoon. My stomach roiled at the memory, tainted with the truth that every sweet word from Declan's lips only existed to further his own power.

I scanned the patrons as they sat at plain wooden benches spooning heaps of porridge into their mouths. For the first time since I arrived on this side of the sea, I was surrounded by humans. Rounded ears poked out beneath hair all around me, but the sight was no comfort, I only felt the aching sorrow of Declan's absence at my side.

A woman appeared to run the inn, a similar age to my father, plump of body, with tanned skin and curling brown hair. I approached her, fiddling with the sapphire clasp on my cloak. I bent the jewel from its prongs and plucked it from its setting.

The woman smiled warmly as I approached, her brown eyes crinkling at the corners as she did.

"Welcome to the Sunburst, traveler," she said, wiping her hands across her dingy apron. "I'm Magda. What can I do for you?"

"How many nights can I get for this?" I asked, uncurling my hand to reveal the coin-sized sapphire.

The woman arched her brow, but made no comment inquiring where I'd procured such a gem.

"Two weeks," she said.

I nodded and dropped the sapphire into her outstretched palm. She shoved it into a hidden pocket lining her skirt before drawing a key from beneath her bodice.

"I'm afraid your room is on the top floor, little mouse, but that's all I got for tonight. Breakfast starts at sunup until it's gone."

Without waiting for a response, the innkeeper turned away to yell at one of her barmaids.

Exhausted from riding all night, I bypassed breakfast and walked up the rickety wooden stairs to my newly acquired room. Two weeks was more than adequate time to find passage to Althene. *Did I even want to go back to Althene?* In the time since I'd arrived, the faelands had begun to feel like home.

Thoughts of returning to my kingdom of origin did nothing to dull the hollowness in my chest, but I didn't belong in the faelands—not if Declan didn't truly love me.

He'd tricked me for his own nefarious purpose. *It was all a lie. Every kiss, every caress, and every pretty word whispered in my ear.* The Seelie Court was never my home, not truly, and I was a fool for thinking it ever could be.

I slipped my dress over my head, then removed the dagger from my thigh, placing it beneath the thin pillow. The mattress groaned as I sank into it, hard and full of lumps. It would suffice for my time here.

Despite my best attempts, sleep did not find me. I laid on my back and stared through the small black holes of the straw roof until the sun rose, listening to the sounds of outside insects. Eventually, tiny beams of sunlight streamed through the cracks of the thatched roof, heralding in a new day.

I strapped my dagger to its holster on my thigh, then pulled on the gray woolen dress and cloak I'd worn yesterday. I could buy new clothes once I returned to Althene. My heart clenched as I thought of leaving the faelands behind. *At least I'd see Dove and my brothers soon.*

The wooden stairs creaked underfoot as I descended into the dining hall of the inn, stirring up puffs of dust with each step. It was loud this morning in the dining room. The inn was bursting with human men and women, red faced from the crisp morning air, getting soup and sustenance, all served by Magda and her staff.

I sank onto one of the simple wooden benches of the common tables lining the large room, not knowing where to begin my journey back home, making sure to keep my face and hair covered. The scent of rosemary and thyme hung thick in the air, and a slight barmaid brought me a pint of ale and a bowl of the food.

"Comes with the room," she said, voice squeaking as she placed the steaming bowl in front of me with a nervous smile.

I cleared my throat. "Could you direct me to where I could book passage to the human kingdoms?"

She nodded her head, wispy flaxen hair bobbing with the motion. "Heath's your guy. He's one of the regulars." She scanned the packed tavern hall. "I don't see him yet, but I'll send him your way when he comes in."

"Thank you," I said. I took a seat at the crowded wooden bench and sipped at my soup, tasting nothing but ash.

48
DECLAN

Despite its location situated on a main pathway leading toward Solora and firmly within the boundaries of the Seelie Court, I'd never bothered to venture to the human village of Bask. With a glamour concealing my true fae features, I rode Kez through the open gates and soon found myself approaching an unimpressive and crooked building. The masonry was lopsided, like the upper levels weren't original to the infrastructure, the topmost story so askew, it appeared as if it would topple over in a heavy rainstorm. A shabby sign indicated the building as an inn.

My ears pricked as I focused in on the sound of Roselyne's voice through the thin walls of the building. Someone else was with her, a man, and they spoke in hushed whispers. I may have been disguised as a human, but I was still fae, and I heard it all.

"A deposit," Roselyne said from inside the inn. "For passage to Althene."

A bitter taste filled my mouth. She meant to leave in earnest. My heart began to race, dismayed. I needed a chance to explain. I could salvage this—*us*. Nothing else mattered. Fuck the curse and my diminishing power. *I only wanted her. She had to understand.*

Roselyne's companion replied, a low male voice that sent a rush of irritation through me.

"We leave tomorrow."

"Alright," Roselyne whispered.

I couldn't take it any longer.

Blood pounded in my ears, urging me to act.

I tugged a cloak over my head and stepped into the crowded inn. A few patrons eyed me warily as I crossed the threshold. Even appearing as a human, I towered over their tallest men, nearly at a height with the peeling door frame.

I watched as Roselyne's back retreated up the rickety stairs.

I followed, making sure to keep my head covered and my true identity concealed.

A barmaid watched as I ascended the stairs, but made no move to stop me.

The door to Roselyne's inn room stared back at me. I could smell her within the walls, her jasmine scent as intoxicating as ever, and leading me straight to her.

With the loud crowd of people in the common room, no one would hear me.

I kicked the door open in one motion, not willing her to deny me entry.

I frowned. Her room lay empty.

Something sharp pierced the skin of my upper arm, drawing a hiss from my lips. I swiveled my head to face my attacker, and the hood pooled around my neck, revealing my identity.

Roselyne stared at me, the blade buried in the flesh of my arm, her hands still gripping the hilt.

"Oh," she said, before releasing the dagger from her hand

and backing away. The dagger clattered to the floor, my blood still on the blade. "I thought a thief followed me."

"And your first inclination is to stab?" I asked, incredulous.

Crimson soaked through the sleeve of my shirt, but I was already healing, my skin threading back together neatly. Roselyne scurried to retrieve the dagger and wiped the blood on the skirt of her dress.

"Yes," she snapped. "Better them than me. *You* taught me that."

"I did," I said softly.

Roselyne smiled for a moment before her face twisted into a sneer, like she remembered she was angry with me. "Why are you here, Declan? *To lie to me*? To make me more the fool? How *dare* you show your face to me." Her green eyes blazed, furious and red-rimmed.

I needed to make her understand. "I never lied to you."

Her face contorted into a snarl.

Shit. That was the wrong thing to say.

She shook her head. "You withheld information from me. You failed to tell me that our marriage would garner you more power, breaking some curse you *very well* may deserve. You lied to me...made me believe you wanted to be with me. *I believed you.*" Her voice cracked on her last sentence, taking my heart with it. Tears streamed down her face. *"I—cared for you."* She wiped her eyes with the back of her hand. "I will not be some pawn in this game you play, Declan—some ornament that only exists to give you power. I've learned the truth. I am leaving, and you cannot stop me." She turned her back to me.

A low growl rose in my throat. "You know I can."

"But you won't," she challenged. "My passage to Althene is booked. I leave tomorrow and soon, I'll be *home* and you will be nothing but a memory. A mistake to scrub from my skin."

I winced at the venom in her tone. "You don't know everything," I pleaded. "Let me speak, please."

"Oh, there's more?" she said, full of derision, her back still facing me.

"I love you," I said.

Her answering laugh was hollow.

In that moment, I'd never hated myself more for making her doubt the earnestness of my affections.

She half turned to face me, arms still crossed over her chest. "Just another lie."

"No, it's not. Please believe me."

"How can I believe anything you say to me?" she spat. "Why not be honest with me?"

"You're right," I agreed. "I thought you were some vapid princess. I was wrong. I never expected to feel—*this*. I should have been honest from the beginning and saved ourselves the pain of misunderstanding. Please, Roselyne—I've made so many mistakes in my life, but losing you would be the worst."

She turned away from me once more, arms still crossed.

"Because you need me to keep your throne."

"I don't care about that any longer." I needed her to understand. "Please," I rasped. "How can I prove this to you?"

She remained silent, posture stiff with her chin tilted upward and defiant. "Tell me the truth," Roselyne said quietly. "All of it."

Roselyne turned her body to face me all the way, her gaze down turned and lashes wet, staring at the dusty wooden boards of the floor.

I crossed the room, and she tentatively allowed me to take her hands in mine. She continued looking down, avoiding my eyes, and stared at our intertwined fingers. Our matching rings shimmered in the low light. She hadn't taken it off. I allowed myself one flicker of hope.

I took in a deep breath and began. "What Sloane told you is true. The prophecy is real. I set out to Althene to retrieve you, believing a marriage between us would break the curse and restore the strength of my power."

She still didn't meet my eye. My heart thundered in my chest. *No, no, no.* I had to make her understand. Although I'd hidden the truth from her, everything I said now was the most honest I'd ever been. A life without Roselyne was unfathomable, not because of the witch blood, but because of *her*.

I squeezed her hands in mine. "Roselyne, what I feel for you dwarfs anything I've ever felt for anyone else. You are the sun blazing in the sky, and I worship you despite the prophecy and curse." I exhaled a ragged breath.

She tore her hand from mine. "I already booked my passage. You can't come here and spin more lies to convince me to stay. I'm returning to Althene, and there's *nothing* you can say to stop me. I told you I didn't want to be a pawn, Declan—but that's exactly what you've made me."

"Roselyne, please—"

"No!" she shrieked, and I took a step backward.

"I will *not* be made a fool again." Her eyes were swimming with tears, though none fell. "How *dare* you make me—care about you." She scoffed. "Every soft touch, every gentle kiss—a lie." She turned away from me. She couldn't be more wrong.

I was desperately in love with Roselyne. She consumed the entirety of my being, but I feared if I said the wrong thing right now, I'd lose her forever. I curled my hands into fists, angry with myself for creating this divide between us and causing her pain.

I'd made many mistakes in my lifetime. I'd been quick to

anger and relished in others' agony. I'd taken lives, both guilty and innocent. But if I lost Roselyne now, and she returned to her homeland across the sea, it'd be the greatest regret of my life.

I dropped to my knees, stripped of all pride and ready to beg Roselyne to understand.

She turned back to face me with a startled expression that quickly transformed into a sneer as she looked down at me kneeling before her. "Well, let's hear it," she said, voice wobbling. "Let's hear what other lies you can spew."

"Roselyne, you're right." Her posture relaxed, only slightly. "I didn't tell you the entirety of the truth, and for that, I'm sorry. You deserved better. But you need to know that everything I've said to you...my love for you? That's the truth."

She exhaled, but allowed me to continue, staring down at me with intense green eyes.

"Before you, I had no interest in love...but you reignited that part of me and chased away the shadows of my past. I was content to be a monster until I met you. I know I don't deserve you, but I'll work the rest of my life to earn your trust once more. I won't stop you if you decide to return to Althene, but know if you do this—"

"How am I supposed to believe you?" she asked quietly. "If you've withheld the truth once, how can I know you won't do it again?"

I felt myself losing her all over again.

"Tell me what to do," I said, voice cracking. "Please."

In the hundreds of years I'd been alive, I'd never begged for anything. Everything I'd earned was through brutality and violence. Roselyne deserved softness. I'd happily kneel at her feet if that's what she desired. She was a goddess, and I'd worship at her altar daily if she'd allow it. I would do anything to restore her faith in me.

She said nothing, and my heart shattered once more as she slipped further away from me. I closed my eyes and steadied myself for what I was about to say, desperate that she'd believe the sincerity of my words.

"Don't marry me," I said.

She hadn't expected that.

"What?" she said, confused, assessing me through her hair.

I stood and held her by the shoulders. "*Don't marry me,*" I repeated.

She tilted her head to the side but remained silent, allowing me to continue, her lips pursed and eyes wary.

"But stay with me," I said. "I will gladly live with this diminished power as penance for my sins. I only want you by my side."

Her lower lip trembled. "What will happen to you," she asked, "if you don't break the curse? Could you lose your power entirely?" Fear and uncertainty lined her eyes.

I shook my head. "I don't know for certain. But anything that happens to me is better than losing you."

"How can I forgive the lies?" she asked quietly.

"I was wrong," I said. "But know I *never* lied about my love for you. Please give me the opportunity to make things right." I brushed her hair behind her ear, and she shivered. "For so long I have feared allowing myself to love. I didn't think I was capable any longer," I said.

She stared at me.

I knitted my fingers through her hair, and she allowed me to bring her face close to mine. "I was a fool." I shook my head. "We need not marry, Roselyne, if that's what it takes for you to be certain my affection for you is genuine. I would burn it all down for you. The palace, Solora, the *entirety of the faelands.*" She inhaled sharply, her gaze boring into mine. I could not tell what she was thinking behind those eyes. "You are all that matters to me now," I said, pleading for her to understand.

She gripped my arms and drew closer.

"*Never* lie to me again."

She brought her mouth close to mine and her eyes fluttered closed. Electricity danced between our lips, only a breadth apart.

"Never," I promised. "Do not run from me again."

As long as I lived on this wretched earth, I'd do everything to repair her trust in me.

"Do not give me a reason to run and I won't," she said with a slight nod of her head. "But if you ever lie to me again, Declan—know it will be the last time you do so."

She gripped the backs of my arms, nails digging in, and pressed her mouth against mine.

49

ROSELYNE

Our kiss was not gentle. Declan poured every bit of anguish, hurt, and betrayal into our embrace, and I obliged, kissing him back wildly, my nails raking across the skin of his broad shoulders as he pressed his body to mine. I writhed against him, the hard swell of his cock wanting to burst free from his pants. Heat pooled between my legs. Declan groaned into my open mouth as we licked, bit, and sucked at each other with the fervor and intensity of the sun. Neither of us relented, continuing the game of push and pull we'd been playing for months. We were a frenzy of tangled limbs, clawing and grasping at each other's bodies, mad with primal lust and the promise of forever. Every nerve under my skin vibrated with untamed anticipation of Declan fully sheathing himself within me and laying claim to the throbbing heat between my legs.

"How did you find me?" I gasped out in between kisses.

He nipped hard on my bottom lip as he squeezed the curve of my ass, his fingers digging into the soft flesh. My core throbbed in response, desperate to be filled. He spoke low against my lips.

"There's nowhere you could go that I would not find you." The thought was thrilling, and I believed him.

In one fluid motion, Declan gripped me by the hair and twisted it around his fist, wrenching my head backward to press scorching kisses upon the delicate skin of my neck. I relented, allowing my body to go lax under his touch. My eyes fluttered closed as I gave myself over entirely to the Seelie King.

He bit down, drawing a pinprick of pain and eliciting a gasp from my parted lips.

As if he could wait no longer, Declan ripped through the laces of my bodice and it dropped to the floor in a muddled heap. Hands weaved over hands as we undressed each other and toppled backward onto the cheap, straw mattress.

We were both naked, the heat of his skin a pleasant scorch against mine. The smooth hardness between his legs pressed against my stomach, and I involuntarily bucked my hips, seeking the friction only him filling me would bring.

The tendrils of Declan's powers slid over me, restraining my hands and feet in invisible bonds at each corner of the mattress.

Instead of his cock, Declan dipped two fingers into me, curving them and rubbing against my sensitive flesh, guiding me toward climax. My body squeezed around his fingers, desperate to feel him inside of me. My breaths were shallow pants, my skin flushed and nipples hard as I lay splayed helplessly across the bed, a toy for Declan's amusement.

"Please," I said with a sigh, and he obliged, dipping his fingers back inside me once more and rubbing slowly, driving me mad.

I bucked my hips, meeting the thrust of his fingers in a shameless display of wanton need.

"Tell me what you need, Princess."

I could barely hear him, so driven wild with lust as he swirled his fingers around my clit and back inside of me. I arched my back against the bed, clamoring for more.

"Do you want my mouth on your cunt, or my cock inside of it?"

A low sort of strangled sound escaped my lips as his fingers worked inside of me. My thoughts were incoherent, barely tangible under the haze of arousal Declan inspired within me, but I was able to moan out one singular word. "Cock."

Declan withdrew his fingers and pushed himself upright.

My mouth watered at the sight of his swollen cock, already glistening with pearly wetness at the tip. My body was shaking, trembling to be filled, and unable to move due to the delicious snare of his magic.

In a show of more power, Declan spread my legs further apart. He lined himself up to my entrance and claimed me in one punishing thrust.

Stars peppered my vision. I moaned from the feel of him, the intense fullness every time he withdrew and slid inside. His pace was brutal, and I rocked in time with him, meeting his cock with every thrust.

"Never leave again," Declan growled as he moved inside of me.

"I won't." I promised. "Don't ever lie to me again."

"Never again," he said.

He palmed my breasts, rolling my nipples in his fingers before pinching them, eliciting another gasp from me. His hungry eyes traveled to the golden ring adorning my left hand.

"You didn't take your betrothal ring off," he said, as his

cock slid into me, the satisfying fullness making me squirm beneath his body. The ends of his dark hair tickled the skin between my breasts as he bent forward and took a nipple into his mouth, rolling his tongue over the hard bud as he continued to move inside of me. His breath was hot on my skin as Declan brought his face closer to mine speaking against the shell of my ear. "With the rings on, we still belong to each other in accordance with fae marriage laws." He pressed a kiss to my jaw, and I turned and caught his lips with mine. "Was this your plan all along? Did you want me to find you here, Roselyne? Did you want our fight to end with me fucking you in this inn?" He moved inside of me and I moaned into his open mouth.

"I was going to sell the ring," I lied. "I was going to use the money from it to pay for the rest of my passage *away from you*."

I had other jewelry available to use to pay for my passage, but I couldn't help the lie, knowing it would only incense Declan further.

He withdrew his cock from me and flipped my body around, positioning me on my hands and knees, with my ass bared to him. The familiar kiss of his magic swirled around my wrists and ankles, locking me into place. My body quivered with anticipation, dripping with need.

"You were going to sell the ring?" Declan asked, lightly tracing his fingertips along the curve of my ass. "You'll need to be punished for that transgression."

I arched into him, needing more of his touch. I nodded my head, my entire body vibrating with desire.

I heard a crack, then registered the stinging burn of my ass cheek. Before I could comprehend what happened, Declan placed his hand on my ass, dampening the delicious bite of pain and kneading my flesh in his hands. Liquid pooled inside of me, wet and wanting more.

Declan's voice was low and level. "Did you like that, Princess?"

"Yes." I moaned at the sensation of his large hands rubbing my body, the tease of him so near my entrance, but ignoring that part of my body desperately craving his touch. One of his fingers dragged up my center, slick with my arousal and I shuddered, eyes drawing closed.

"Who do you belong to?" he asked me, voice low.

"You," I said, "And what about *you*, Seelie King?"

"I am yours," he said, as he lined his length up to my entrance. I met him with my body as he slid inside of me with a groan. "I am yours wholly and evermore."

50

ROSELYNE

The passing days flew by in a haze of lazy mornings with Declan, bodies melding together beneath our sheets, before I went to the greenhouse to continue working to access my magic with Kera. In the afternoons, Declan and I would train with our practice blades, with Sloane and Callum sometimes joining us, while Essi filled my free time with court gossip and camaraderie. No one spoke of how I'd run away intent on returning to Althene.

Declan made it abundantly clear that we did not need to get married, but I chose to continue to go through with the ceremony. We'd argued the point for a few days, but Declan ultimately conceded to my wishes. The thought of him potentially losing his power and becoming vulnerable to attack left a bitter taste in my mouth. He'd suffered enough already, and I'd made it clear I'd leave him if he was ever dishonest again.

With Declan and I in agreement, we continued to plan and prepare for the faelands' most anticipated ceremony and event. Every time I looked down at my left hand and saw the golden ring on my finger, I felt a rush of apprehension and excitement at the prospect of our upcoming marriage.

Late summer transformed fully to autumn in a tide of changing leaves and cool breezes. Instead of the lush, jeweled green that greeted me upon my arrival to the faelands, the forest outside the castle perimeter now shone like the sun itself. The foliage transformed into a dazzling myriad of oranges, reds, and golden leaves adorning the ancient trees as they'd done in the Northern Seelie Territory. Although the beast attacking the town was slain, Declan still forbade me to enter the forest for fear of more monsters lurking within the woods. We also still weren't sure who had tried to steal me away.

Sunlight streamed through the stained glass of the dining room, a mosaic of colored tiles in the shape of the sun hanging high in the sky. Essi sat across from me in the handsome room, scribbling with her quill, lips pressed together in concentration as she picked at her breakfast. Her golden tresses were slicked back away from her face, held with an ornamental pearl clip. She muttered to herself, scowling over the seating chart. I stuffed a bite of poached eggs in my mouth and swallowed.

"Is it truly of such importance where each lord and lady sit?" I asked.

Surely, it could not matter this much.

Essi's affronted expression told me that I was clearly ignorant to the nobility of fae society, and I couldn't disagree with her assessment.

"*Roselyne,*" she admonished.

I groaned and rested my head against my wooden table. "Surely there's someone else who can do this?" I said, lifting my head and giving my friend my best attempt at innocence.

Essi's stern expression broke and her face split into a smile as she rolled her eyes. "Somebody *could*, I suppose, but I've got a knack for this sort of thing. Besides, it's horribly important that no one is offended by their seat mates! You don't want any fights to take away from your big day, do you?"

"You're right," I agreed halfheartedly, tapping my fingers on my chin and staring wistfully out the large window.

I didn't care if a seating arrangement offended some unnamed lord. If they squabbled, every guest would surely gawk, and it'd be fewer eyes on me.

I sighed once more, drawing a brief scowl from Essi.

I loved attending parties and banquets, but being stared like some sort of anomaly was another thing entirely. The betrothal ceremony was difficult enough, with the press of lords and ladies all preening for a glimpse at the witch-bride as if I was some prized calf to send to slaughter.

Not everything was bad at the ceremony, however. I smiled at the memory of Declan's hand between my legs, and how everything had changed between us so soon afterward.

"Roselyne!" Essi snapped, breaking me from my daydream.

I straightened my posture and leaned toward my friend and self-appointed lady-in-waiting. "I'm paying attention."

"Sure, you are," she said, dragging out the syllables, an exasperated smile played about her lips.

By some mercy of the gods, Kera walked in, saving me from eternal boredom at the hands of wedding planning. She leaned against the doorway and appraised Essi and I at the table, parchment spread all around us with the former scribbling madly and muttering to herself.

Kera arched a black eyebrow. "Having fun?"

I shrugged, not deigning to answer, and Essi didn't lift her head, instead opting to wave Kera off dismissively and utter some sort of noncommittal grunting noise.

"I see," Kera said, with an amused grin. She put her hands

in the pockets of her tight black pants. "Well, Roselyne, come find me when you're done. I need to speak with you."

Essi's head popped up. "I can finish up, Roselyne. No worries."

"Really?" I asked Essi, "You don't need me?"

Essi waved me away. "I enjoy this sort of thing." She waved me away with her hands. "Go practice magic or read tea leaves or whatever it is you two do together for hours in that greenhouse."

Essi went back to scribbling, and I jumped out of my chair, face grinning and skipped toward Kera as we walked together out the large patio doors and into the winding garden path.

The air in the gardens was chilled, even though it was midafternoon. I wrapped my arms around myself as my skin prickled in the cool weather. We passed by a plot of aster flowers, bright pinks and oranges straight from the sunset, and sat on one of the many intricate, iron wrought benches scattered throughout the palace gardens.

"What did you want to speak with me about?" My eyes darted back and forth, checking that we were truly alone. No one else was nearby. I lowered the volume of my voice to barely above a whisper, regardless. "Is it about the prophecy?"

Kera shrugged innocently. "Oh, I was giving you an 'out' from wedding planning. I could hear from the other side of the palace how dull it was." Her mouth curved into a feline grin, and I couldn't help the surprised chuckle that emitted from my own lips. "It's a beautiful day, you shouldn't spend it cooped up inside around some small table doing things you hate."

A small nagging sensation tugged at me. I swirled the heel of my boot into the dirt path, guilt gnawing at me.

"I shouldn't have left Essi alone to deal with that," I said.

Kera scoffed.

THE CURSE OF THE SEELIE KING

"Are you kidding me? Essi lives for this sort of thing. Since she's arrived, she's been begging every new season to throw balls and host parties. Trust me, she's fine."

"How long has Essi been at court?"

Kera clicked her tongue as she recalled. "Nearly a century, I think. Sometime after the war." She touched her fingers to her chin. "She blended in with the other courtiers when the palace was full, but I was never interested in the social aspect of court life. Essi volunteered herself to stay at the palace when Declan sent everyone away, knowing you'd need friends in the palace."

Movement across the yard caught my eye. Six large men with carts began erecting some sort of wooden totem in the center of the yard in front of the palace.

"What is that?" I asked Kera.

"The blood moon is tomorrow," she said. "Do you not celebrate them in the human kingdoms?"

I shook my head. "Blood moon? What is it?"

"That makes sense," she said, nodding. "Blood moons are rare, and treated as major holidays in the Seelie Court. The moon will rise, full and red in the sky, a symbol of how the Seelie defeated the Unseelie. The moon transforms into the color of blood to evoke the memories. Declan opted for a smaller observance this time." Kera frowned. "We still don't know who tried to steal you away at the betrothal feast, and Declan wishes to keep as many guests out of the palace as possible unless necessary. The servants you see down there are setting up the bonfire."

I eyed the massive pile of wood. "A bonfire?"

She grinned. "It's customary. We thank the goddess Lux for her help in triumphing over the Unseelie and their wicked god of darkness and death, Umbrath. The darkness does not owe the Seelie loyalty, but during the blood moon, even the night shows reverence for the Seelie victory over the monstrous Unseelie. Tomorrow evening, every hearth will be lit in honor of the goddess."

I shivered, and it was silent for a moment, with only the hum of bees and rustle of leaves in the air. I shuffled my feet against the stone path, unsure if I should ask the question on my mind.

"What happens if I can't access my powers, Kera? We've been at this since I arrived in the faelands, and I've made no progress."

Kera leaned back against the bench, crossing her small legs. She sighed, as if deciding whether to spare my feelings or not.

"If what Declan believes is true, his powers will continue to weaken, leaving him susceptible to usurpers and enemies," Kera said, and I recoiled at her candid words ringing with nothing but truth. "That will never happen, of course. Even diminished as they are, Declan remains stronger than any other fae, and no one has cause to suspect otherwise. His curse is a closely guarded secret only his royal council is aware of, unlike the secret of your witch blood."

I chewed the inside of my cheek. "And if I am able to access my magic? Able to harness the powers of the earth and land and the two of us wed?"

Kera's gaze burned through me before she opened her mouth to speak.

"Declan would regain his strength, and you as a pair with your combined schools of magic would be unstoppable."

51

DECLAN

Insects buzzed outside as the sun and moon began their nightly dance across the sky and evening turned to lavender twilight. Roselyne and I sat outside on a patch of grass on the palace grounds each with a book in hand. We'd been laying together for hours, but I had no intention of leaving yet. The bonfire would be lit soon, and the sounds of revelry would float up to us from the city streets, and the celebration would begin in earnest. The moon's red glow would come later in the night. For now, I'd soak in the bliss of her company.

She sat leaned against a thick trunk of one of the property's massive oak trees, flipping through a novel deep in whatever fantasy world was written between the pages. As the sunlight dimmed, she held the book closer to her eyes, desperate to finish before we lost all light.

I laid my head across her lap, enjoying the rhythmic movement of her breathing in and out. Oftentimes, when Roselyne turned a page, she'd absentmindedly stroke my hair. Lounging with her was peace.

Roselyne looked downward and peered around her book, before setting it beside us on the soft grass.

She tipped forward and met her lips with mine in a chaste kiss. Her hair spilled over my face, tickling my skin.

"So, do they live happily ever after?" I asked, nodding toward the discarded book. Roselyne rolled her eyes with a small smile and shifted herself to lay beside me, our backs against the blanket, and eyes turned upward toward the darkening sky.

She snuggled into me as I knit my fingers into hers. Her answering squeeze of my hand made my stomach flip in on itself.

She clicked her tongue and turned her face toward me. "I'm not at the end yet," she said, eyes bright in the dim light. She shrugged. "Who's to say about how it'll turn out."

She bit her lip as I reached forward and pulled her on top of me. She shrieked happily, her laugh ringing through the air as I sat up and pressed soft kisses to her cheeks, traveling down to her exposed collarbones. She leaned her head back and moaned softly, letting her hair cascade down her back and allowing me more access. I pressed gentle kisses along her skin, noticing as a ripple of gooseflesh spread across her arms as she sat in my lap.

"Just a bit longer until we're husband and wife," I said, pressing soft kisses to her lips in between words.

"I can't wait," she said, and my heart soared.

Her skirt rode up her thighs, revealing creamy skin, and my cock stirred to life.

With a mischievous smile, Roselyne brought her mouth to mine again in a scorching kiss. She twisted her hands through my hair and raked her nails across my back, before breaking our kiss and trailing her mouth down the center of my chest, placing searing kisses every few inches. I curled my hands around her waist, trying to hold her in place, but she wiggled out of reach. She shimmied down the length of my body and positioned her face in line with my throbbing cock. Her gaze was hungry and feral, and my breath caught in my throat at the sight of the unchecked lust in her.

"What are you doing?" I asked, glancing beyond the tall grass that surrounded us, surveilling for intruders that would ruin our slice of divinity that Roselyne and I carved together in the yard the past evening. It was dark outside—the moon had won its nightly battle with the sun and was currently positioned high in the sky, bathing the land in a soft silvery light. She tugged at the laces of my breeches and looked up at me from beneath her lashes.

"What I've wanted to do since I first saw you at that damned ball when we were only strangers—or so I thought," she replied with a newfound huskiness to her voice. She paused for a moment, not touching me—as if waiting for me to grant her permission.

I nodded my head at her, puzzled.

Since the ball she'd wanted me?

Eyes heavily lidded with her own lust, Roselyne swept her hand over the hard swell that ached to burst forth from beneath my pants and squeezed lightly. I bucked my hips instinctually and bit back a groan at her featherlight touch. I wanted to strip her out of that damned dress she wore and claim her right here, below the ancient oak tree, and mark this place forever ours.

She deftly unlaced my pants, and my hardness sprung forward, ready for whatever she'd do. I'd never get enough of her. She eyed my cock with unmistakable desire, and I couldn't stifle the groan that escaped my lips as Roselyne placed her bee-stung lips around the head of my cock and sucked.

Stars burst across my vision, competing with their predecessors hanging in the sky as Roselyne sucked at my cock, swirling her tongue around the tip with robust enthusiasm. My hips jerked of their own accord and my fingers dug into the grass, as my cock thickened and grew larger in her mouth. She moaned, and the vibrations sent waves of pleasure down my length. She moved to take me deeper into her mouth, working me with her hands as she bobbed up and down my shaft. A familiar pressure began to build below the base of my cock.

"Fuck, Roselyne," I groaned out, which only incited her more.

Roselyne pressed her mouth further down my shaft and met my eye with a wicked grin. The vision of her mouth wrapped around my cock and the untempered lust in her eyes had me ready to spill myself right then and there.

With one fluid motion, Roselyne bobbed back down on to the base of my cock expertly taking me entirely within her mouth as if she were starved for me. She sucked in slow languid sweeps of her tongue, her silken mouth squeezing around my length, as she stroked me with her hands. The coiled tension inside of me grew taut and snapped. With a grunt, my hips bucked into her mouth, and I moaned, spilling all of myself into her. Roselyne didn't balk as my arousal filled her mouth. Instead, she devoured every last drop, swallowing everything before lifting her lips from my cock, a pearly string of wetness dripping from her swollen lips.

I reached down to bring her to me, and she acquiesced and nuzzled her face into the crook of my neck with a soft sigh. I closed my eyes and breathed in the smell of her jasmine scent being carried on the autumn air.

Before Roselyne came tearing into my life, I never thought I'd have this—or be worthy of it, but she'd seen every ugly damaged dark part of me and chose to stay—*chosen me*. I didn't deserve her, but here she was.

We laid there together beneath the stars, not speaking, the steady rise and fall of our chests in sync with one another. All the hateful things I've ever said to myself, the thoughts that seemed to endlessly bound around in my head were finally silenced.

52

ROSELYNE

The bonfire blazed against the backdrop of the black sky, fifty feet high and shooting sparks of flame upward into the night.

After we'd enjoyed our dinner, Declan, Essi, Sloane, and I sat together on wooden logs surrounding the fire, as was customary on any evening of a blood moon. Callum was overseeing the Daylight Guard, while Kera had chosen instead to celebrate the Seelie victory in solitude at her home in the city proper, something Declan informed me she does each blood moon.

The flickering of the towering flames cast everyone's faces in dancing shadows, illuminating them in an eerie glow and morphing everyone's features. Essi and Sloane shared one log, as did Declan and I, Essi's legs bent toward the prince, wrapping a foot around one of his calves. Although I could not see their hands in the darkness, it appeared their fingers were intertwined.

Although I found Prince Sloane kind and amusing, he had the reputation of being an overt womanizer, and I hoped he'd

THE CURSE OF THE SEELIE KING

be gentle with Essi's heart. I leaned into Declan and he wrapped his arm around my shoulders.

"I wish Callum and Kera were with us," I said.

A particularly long ember burst from the top of the orange flames and dissolved into a puff of ash. Declan dipped his head in acknowledgment and agreement.

Essi leaned forward. "It is such a shame," she agreed, before pursing her lips and assessing the towering flame as we sat listening to the crackling of the fire.

"Do you celebrate blood moons in the human kingdoms, Roselyne?" Sloane asked.

"No, but Kera told me about the traditions and the history." I gestured toward the tower of flames.

Sloane waved a hand. "Kera no doubt told you about the traditions of bonfires and feasts, giving thanks for our triumph over darkness—but there's more to a blood moon than just merriment."

The wind blew, and Essi trembled. Sloane absentmindedly put his arm around her, giving her warmth.

"Oh?" I asked, eyeing Declan. "What do I not know?"

Sloane smiled.

"The veil between realms is at its thinnest on this night and angry spirits walk this world, disoriented as to how they died and where they find themselves on this plane."

I pursed my lips.

Declan wrapped his arm around my shoulder and brought me closer to his body, and I was thankful for the warmth.

"Yes," Declan said, "But it's a time of gratitude toward the goddess of life and light, Lux. She conquered the darkness of Umbrath, as the Seelie conquered the Unseelie." He squeezed my shoulders and placed a kiss there. "Your presence is a blessing from the goddess herself." He pressed another kiss to the top of my head, and I nuzzled into his chest, content.

One of the few servants currently working in the palace approached us tentatively.

Declan sat up, alert, and the small mousy girl bowed clumsily.

"Milord," she mumbled as she handed him the slip of parchment. "A red ribbon falcon arrived a few moments ago." Declan assessed the rolled-up paper with a stony face, his finger trailing the wax sealing the document.

"Thank you," Declan said through tight lips as he began to unfurl the scroll. The serving girl took that as her leave and bowed again before scurrying back toward the palace.

Declan's brow furrowed as he read through the note. Sloane and Essi leaned forward with curiosity, watching as Declan's posture grew tighter and more rigid.

Sloane cleared his throat and stood, craning his neck to read the letter from behind Declan's back.

"Who's writing so late?" he asked with a slightly pinched expression on his face.

Essi wound her golden hair around her fingers nervously as she eyed the red ribbon.

"Another temple was broken into, and it seems the thieves were after more than just a blank journal this time," Declan said tight-lipped. "The High Priestess has asked me to come immediately. The Veiled once again didn't wish to put details in a letter for fear of someone intercepting it." He lowered the parchment. "I fear something far more powerful than that book could have been taken from them this time."

Declan rubbed at his forehead and looked at me with apology, sighed, then kissed the top of my head. "It's a couple hours ride to this temple—" He gazed upward toward the sky and the high hanging moon before darting toward the stables with a sigh. His eyes met mine. "I'll be back by sunrise."

I stood and tilted my head and pressed my lips to his. "I'll be waiting for you," I whispered low so only he could hear. Declan's returning smile made my stomach flutter.

Sloane stood and walked toward us and Declan handed his brother the letter. Sloane frowned as he read the black inked words.

"Do you want me to come with you?" His foot tapped nervously against the ground, a dull thud on the short grass, as Essi eyed us from her seat. The fire popped and crackled as a wolf howled somewhere behind the tree line of the forest. A shiver ran down my spine.

Declan shook his head. "No, I'll be quicker alone."

With that, Declan strode away, readied his mount, and left the palace grounds as a feeling of unease settled over me.

It's just because of the blood moon. Everything is fine.

I excused myself from the bonfire and retreated to Declan and I's bedchambers, clicking the door shut behind me. I sank into a hot bath and scrubbed away the smell of smoke and fire that clung to my skin and hair. It did nothing to ease the knot of worry in my chest.

My hair hung loose and wet around my shoulders as I padded through the corridor toward Essi's rooms. My bath had done wonders to soothe my worries, but it wasn't late enough for sleep, and I wanted to see if Essi wanted to have a drink with me.

The candle I'd used to light my way down the corridor was half burned. The ivory wax dripped onto my hands, burning against my skin for only a moment until the wax cooled and hardened against my wrist. I tipped my ear toward the door and only silence greeted me. I rapped my knuckles softly on the wood but received no reply.

Essi was probably with Sloane in his chambers. I crinkled my nose. Essi was besotted with the traveling prince, and a hopeless romantic at that, and I feared she'd fall in love with the man and get her heart broken.

Dejected, I walked back to my own rooms and slunk into bed, the sheets unnaturally cool against my skin without the hard press of Declan's body against mine for warmth. I pulled his pillow to my chest and breathed in deeply. The Seelie King's familiar cedar scent comforted me, and I closed my eyes drifting toward sleep, awaiting the return of my lover in only a few hours.

Someone banged against my door, pounding with their fists against the thick slab of wood frantically.

I sat upright, startled, and blinked a few times as my eyes adjusted to the darkness. I fumbled on the side table searching for a match to light, but only found the hardened glob of wax from the candle I'd burned earlier in the night. My fingers groped at the nightstand. I palmed my dagger and held it close to my chest as I padded to the door, not knowing who or what waited for me there. Thoughts of another attempt at a kidnapping flashed through my mind.

"Roselyne!" Essi's frantic voice rang out. It was muffled through the door, but it was her, to be sure. With a sag of relief, I wrenched the door open. Her eyes were wild and frantic, nearly bulging out of her face as they darted around the dark room behind me searching for some invisible assailant.

"What's wrong?" I cried out, gripping her shoulders.

She shook, her teeth chattering together as tears streamed down her face.

I'd never seen her in such an emotional state. Fear flooded me. She bounced on her heels and fidgeted with her fingers. Her typically polished and neatly filed nails were now chewed bloody.

"Dec- Declan—" she stammered before darting down, then back up at me with a terrified expression on her face.

My heart sank.

I shook her, too concerned to be gentle with my friend. "What's happened to Declan?" I asked sharply.

If something had gone wrong at the temple, if the thieves were still there and waiting for him...I shook my head, dismissing the thought and looked to my friend. She blubbered through her tears.

"What's going on?" I begged.

Her voice was barely a squeak, and her words came out in a rush.

"Declan's been injured. He's hurt in the forest."

Something resolute snapped in me, and all I could focus on was getting to Declan. He was hurt, and by the sound of Essi's voice, he needed my help.

"Alert Sloane," I said as I elbowed past her and began running down the corridor and toward the double doors. "Write Callum and Kera immediately."

A ragged sob tore from her throat as I rounded the corner and took the stairs down two at a time. Goose pimples rippled across my skin as a gust of chilled air blasted me as I swung open the front entrance. The world was bathed in red. I hadn't seen the intensity of the blood moon before I retired to my bedchambers, but now, it hung high in the sky, a beacon of past bloodshed illuminating the grounds in its crimson light.

    My thin nightdress swayed in the breeze—I hadn't the time to dress myself. Declan needed me. The long grass tickled against my bare feet as I began sprinting toward the forest line toward Declan, in whatever condition he may be.

53

DECLAN

Although Kez's hooves pounded against the dirt with practiced expertise, a thick mist rolled into the main road, slowing my journey to the southern temple. Once I arrived at the forest bordering the Disputed Lands, I cut my way through hanging vines and gnarled roots navigating my way to one of the Veiled Priestess' Temples of Lux.

The temple was massive, a building of smooth white stone set among a backdrop of still-green brambles and branches. Autumn's kiss had yet to visit the faelands this far south. Thick columns surrounded the cylindrical temple, supporting the weight of the marble building and its large copper domed roof, now the color of sea-foam after centuries of exposure to the elements. Ancient everlights dotted the perimeter, emitting a faint glow. The front of the temple was open to the air, with a large, erected statue of the Goddess Lux in the center. Behind the statue, a spiral staircase led below the earth, and into the temple proper.

The age of the temples was lost to history long ago, their time of construction unrecorded. They have always been. As I dismounted Kez and approached the temple, I felt the faint buzzing of magic surrounding the ancient place of worship. Some scholars still claimed the gods themselves constructed the temples, before shedding their mortal bodies, and leaving to rest in their celestial realm among the stars where they watch us from a distance, behind a veil of clouds and smoke.

I ran my hand down the smooth exterior, tracing one of the gray veins running through the marble in branching patterns, reminiscent of lightning strikes. The color reminded me so much of the silvery strands framing Roselyne's face. Nocturnal forest critters chittered nearby, rustling tree leaves as they leapt from branch to branch. All was calm outside the temple. I saw no evidence of the urgent danger the High Priestess referred to.

I crossed beneath the threshold toward the stairs leading down and glanced at Lux's likeness etched in stone. She was veiled, depicted in her mortal body, hands outstretched to her left as if another statue should be filling the empty space beside her. The ceiling was inlaid with thousands of tiny colored fragments of glass, pieced together to create an image of dawn transforming into a glittering night sky.

My shoes clicked against the black and white tile as I stepped behind the statue toward the stairs. The pale steps were a different stone than the exterior, some crumbling from their age. The steps led down where relics were stored and the priestesses worked and lived, and to where I would find the High Priestess who wrote requesting my aid.

"Are you sure?" I asked, wiping the ornamental oil from my hands against the fabric of my shirt.

High Priestess Inez cocked her head, the beads of her lilac veil tinkling softly.

"Yes, King Declan. May I see?"

She extended a tanned wrinkled hand to me, and I placed the letter in her palm. Inez unrolled the letter and studied the broken wax previously sealing the parchment. She nodded once. Her face was covered as it always was by the opaque veil all priestesses of her order bore, but I imagined her own expression matched mine—bewilderment.

"This is our seal, yes, but neither I nor any of my priestesses wrote to you tonight." She handed the letter back to me.

"Are you sure?"

"Although I am old, I still have my wits about me and would remember writing to the reigning monarch of the land in which our temple resides."

A chill crept up my spine.

She tipped her head in polite acknowledgment of my title, but not in submission. The Veiled Priestesses were only loyal to their goddess, and that was something the faelands learned to accept millennia ago. "Since another temple's burglary a few weeks ago, there has not been a shadow of trouble or disturbance among the priestesses—Lux grant us safety," she said, although I noticed the way her shoulders tensed. "We initially believed the thief stole only the blank journal, but I see now, the impression of our seal was taken, perhaps in preparation for this very night."

A feeling of impending doom blossomed inside of me, spreading toward my lungs and squeezing. Something was horribly wrong. My eyes shifted, readying for attack, but inside the temple, there was no movement, only a calm stillness in the presence of this sacred space.

Although her face was enshrouded in the draping fabric, I

saw Inez's posture stiffen. She clutched my forearm as she spoke to me, her long nails digging into my skin through my shirt.

"Although the Veiled Priestesses take no part in conflicts of the kingdoms of fae and others…" Inez lowered her voice and leaned in close to me. I could barely hear her over the thundering of my heart. "On this night of the blood moon when this realm of the living straddles lands of shadows and death—I cannot think that this is merely a simple misunderstanding." She leaned back. "Go to your bride, Seelie King, and may the goddess grant you swiftness."

With only my terror for Roselyne guiding my steps, I ran up the stairs two at a time, my pulse bounding. I breathed in lungfuls of fresh air as I crested the temple entrance. My legs pumped underneath me, the sound of my frantic steps echoing across the tiled entrance of the temple as I made my way to Kez.

Someone tricked me, and I was a fool for not seeing it. Someone duped me and lured me away with a false letter, leaving Roselyne completely vulnerable to another attack. I was hours away, nowhere near the palace to protect her. A rush of air propelled me toward my war horse. The hair on the back of my neck stood, the overwhelming feeling of being watched closing in on me. I had no time for this. I rushed away from the temple, swung my leg over Kez, and rode like mad beneath the moon's red glow. As Kez's hooves pounded against the path, I begged the gods that the High Priestess was mistaken and that Roselyne was safely asleep in our bed.

54
ROSELYNE

By the time I reached the trees lining the forest edge, the rush of energy guiding my legs began to sputter out. I whirled in a circle, searching for Declan through the thick fog settled low along the ground. I called out for him, my voice echoing through gray mist and beyond the tree line to the forest—the echo of his name growing softer each reiteration.

Chills crept up my spine. My eyes strained as I tried to see through the thick mist, but saw only shapes of densely packed trees and shadows. The hair on the back of my neck stood on end, and I felt the prickly sensation of being watched.

"Declan?" I called out again, my voice shaky. I took another step into the forest, my bare feet crunching on the dead leaves scattered along the ground, freshly dropped from their homes in the trees. Only the rustle of leaves and the humming of insects answered. My breath turned to fog in the cold air, mingling with the unnatural mist on every exhale. If Declan was hurt, I needed to find him.

Love was not easily frightened. I entered into the forest, determined to locate my betrothed, my king, my everything.

The snap of a branch sounded from behind me and I whirled around to see the silhouette of a figure through the bleak grayness further into the thicket of trees.

"Declan," I exclaimed breathlessly as I ran forward to him, desperate to be wrapped in the warm embrace of his arms. He moved away, and I followed him deeper into the trees. "Declan, I'm right here," I called out again.

I found myself deeper in the forest, and the tightly packed trees opened up to reveal a small glade. Declan's indistinct shape waited for me on the other side of the glade behind the wall of mist. A blanket of fog grew thicker with every step I took deeper into the forest. I tripped over a tree root and slammed to the ground, skinning my knees.

I stood to take another step toward the figure, but when I tried lifting my leg, my foot refused to move from its place on the ground. I tried again with the same result. I slammed my fists into an invisible barrier, surrounded on all sides. I was trapped within some magical circle, bound to the ground by unseeable chains.

Spots burst in my vision from the panic that threatened to overtake me. This was not the gentle caress of my lover's magic. This was constricting and suffocating and painful. My eyes narrowed on the figure that stalked closer to me.

Through the hazy air, I realized the figure was not Declan at all, but someone taller, more slender. My eyes widened as I took in the image of Declan's brother walking toward me in the mist.

"Sloane," I said, relieved. I struggled against the invisible vines that rooted my feet in place. "Something's trapped me, I can't go further." I banged my fists against invisible barriers. "Declan is in trouble, he's—"

As Sloane approached me, I could see him clearly. The hair

on the back of my neck raised. He was disheveled, his golden eyes bright, edged with some sort of energy I couldn't place.

"Roselyne..." he clicked his tongue. "I'm sorry it has to be this way, truly." He walked around me in a circle and I turned my head, following him with my eyes, desperate to understand. "I did grow to like you, but after all, you are but a means to an end."

"What's the meaning of this?" I asked a bit too loud, my voice unwavering so as to not betray my fear. "Is this meant to be some trick? It's not amusing. Where is Declan?"

"It's no jest, Roselyne. The runes have done their purpose." He winked and gestured toward my feet. "Can't have you running off now, can I? Not when I've been planning this for so long."

I looked down. Strange symbols were carved into the forest floor surrounding my body and holding me in place, familiar jagged lines and slashes I didn't understand but had seen before in the ancient witch texts. A small wooden bowl filled with dark purple herbs sat on the uneven ground, just outside the symbols and impossible for me to reach.

My head snapped back toward the man I'd begun to consider a friend and found no remorse in his hardened gaze. He resumed his walk around me as I stood, still unable to break past the magic tethering me to this spot.

"You will serve a great purpose for me tonight, and after it is done—the faelands will rejoice."

All color drained from my face. At that moment I was sure —Sloane intended to harm me.

"Essi knows where I am. She'll write to Declan, to the Daylight Guard and the other members of the council—" I started, but Sloane interrupted me with a cruel laugh that sent a spike of fear through me.

"Essi?" he scoffed. "Essi sent you *to me*, all wrapped up in a pretty little bow. Her infatuation with me finally proven fruitful." Sloane sneered. "Your Commander of the Guard is currently keeping watch in the slums of Solora. The so-called Widowmaker is at her home in the city, none the wiser, and my older brother is hours away on a fool's errand." Sloane smiled. "No one is coming to save you."

His eyes razed my barely clothed body, and the realization of Essi's betrayal washed over me, stinging more than the prospect of Sloane's plans.

I crossed my arms over my chest, covering my near nudity. Sloane rolled his eyes. On the streets, people whispered that Declan was ruthless, but I knew the truth. The monster was Sloane. I saw through the cracks in his mask into the ugly hateful soul below. My hands balled into fists.

"Was it you then? Who hired those men to steal me away at the betrothal feast? Are you leading Summus Nati?" I sneered. "Do you despise the prospect of a witch-queen that much?"

"Summus Nati exists, or did long ago," he said. "Although I tried, I could not locate them." He glanced at the bowl of herbs on the ground for a moment, before meeting my eyes once more. "But there are still some who share many of their beliefs. Did you know that although the Seelie Court is the most powerful and wealthy in all the world, there are those who live among us that are *starving*." He clicked his tongue. "*Ruthless King*, indeed. It was too easy to find those desperate enough for coin to aid in ridding the faelands of the king's newest distraction—the witch whore would-be queen."

My face contorted with disgust, and he shrugged.

"Their words, not mine." Sloane placed a palm to his heart. "I'm not a bigot, Roselyne."

I scowled, slamming my body against the invisible barrier.

Sloane gave me a pointed look. "I have no qualms with humans or witches residing in the faelands. When I'm king, I'll lord over them all."

"Declan is the king," I hissed.

Sloane flipped his hand dismissively.

"For a few more hours, yes." He sighed as if he was inconvenienced. "It's the curse of second born sons that I intend to break."

I tried to take a step forward once more and was stopped by the same unseeable barrier.

"Ancient runes—do you like them?" Sloane asked, assessing his nails. "Some knowledge I picked up during my years of travel. The witches actually first harnessed their power, can you believe it? Only a few remaining minds even know of their existence—and who would refuse to teach the Seelie Prince to yield them?"

My lips peeled back into a snarl.

"What does this have to do with me?" I asked through bared teeth.

"As I said before, my grievance isn't with you," Sloane said without elaboration.

He glanced toward the sky and extended his neck allowing the reddish glow of the blood moon to pour over him. He turned back toward me.

"My brother *truly* loves you, you know. There's immense power in love."

I jut out my chin defiantly. "Declan and my union will break the witches' curse. He will become even more powerful, and he will *destroy* you."

Sloane clicked his tongue.

"There is no curse, Roselyne." He chuckled.

"What do you mean?" I asked, eyes narrowing.

Sloane scoffed and ran his hand through his mess of dark hair, so similar to his brother's.

"*I* have been weakening my brother." He chuckled. "It's laughable to think the witches could have done what I have. With what power would they have achieved this? The witches' magic was drained from their bodies during the war, and they were tossed aside when their use ran out."

"How?" I asked, my voice barely a whisper on the wind. It made no sense. Sloane possessed no elysian gifts to make this magic possible.

"Why do you all think I traveled across the faelands for decades? Whoring and a thirst for knowledge are wonderful excuses to hide my true intentions," He said. "I've been learning. Yes, studying all matters of ancient magic in order to defeat my brother. I've even studied witch magic."

My eyes grew round.

He waved a hand. "Not the healing and the herbs and all the things you're probably imagining." He smiled. "Hexes— among other things. A slow, steady fade on my brother's magic was not difficult to devise, and it went years without his notice. Declan was eager to believe he was cursed. The only curse was his own paranoia and a refusal to take accountability for his actions during the last war." He shrugged. "All the better for me."

My breath caught in my chest. The witches' curse wasn't real. It was Sloane all along. For decades plotting against his own flesh and blood.

"You've done this to Declan? Weakened him?"

Sloane flexed a hand. "Yes, but it *still* wasn't enough. I am smarter than my brother, but even I can still admit he is physically stronger, despite my attempts." He rubbed at his jaw. "I knew I needed something else to tip the scales in my favor. And then how convenient for me, he finds himself a witch to marry...I didn't believe her at first when Essi told me through the two-way mirror, but she insisted. The girl is a horrible gossip, but it proved useful." He smiled. "I came back to Solora immediately, of course, and here you are, a living, breathing *witch*—capable of so much more than they'd allowed you to learn."

"What about the prophecy?" I asked. "I've seen it written myself. *You* showed it to me. Declan told me the truth of it."

He scoffed. "I wouldn't rely so heavily on the merit of mer prophecy, Roselyne." Sloane leaned forward. "I value *real* power. Tactile magic you can see and touch—not the musings of half-mad half-fish who live below the sea." He straightened his spine. "Do you know the *true* power of witches, Roselyne? The things history has long forgotten due to their nature and possibility for misuse?"

"I am a witch," I bit back, uncertain.

"Yes, but your tutor wouldn't let you learn what I have learned. To do what I must do. There are still some magics inherent to only witch-kind, and as such, why I have use of you."

"I don't understand."

He seemed pleased by that, eager to explain to a captive audience.

"Conjuring and binding, Roselyne."

The words felt like an oily caress against my skin. I shuddered at the sensation, remembering how Declan told me about the world-walkers when he first explained to me of the magic in my veins. A gust of chilled air blew, whipping my hair into a tangled mess, my feet still anchored in place as Sloane explained further.

"Witches possessed the ability to reach and communicate

with other realms. Worlds you cannot see but exist near and in conjunction with our own. Places of great and terrible beauty—and ripe with power. Imagine possessing the ability to conjure a demon and bind its own strength to you, to bend it to your will." He sighed. "Of course, the practice was eventually forbidden among witches, but what are witch laws to a fae prince?" Something sinister glimmered in his golden eyes. "But I've done it. Conjured. Perfected the art of it, and allowed the demons to test their powers on a few unfortunate Soloran citizens." He scoffed. "As if a *bearbeast* could do such damage." He tipped his head. "But without witch blood, I cannot *bind* what I've conjured to me. That's where your part comes to play, Roselyne."

"Impossible," I said.

"Nothing is impossible," he corrected. "I traveled the faelands, visiting every academic institution this side of the Lyssan Sea, *searching* for how to access this ancient and powerful magic. I was successful. I translated their grimoire, and right now, with you, a witch, I hold that very power within my grasp."

My eyes darted to his hand as he pulled something from within his jacket—an unremarkable tattered black book. I watched as he opened the book and revealed blank pages.

"What do you intend, Sloane?"

"Exactly what I've learned. This is where your relevance enters, dear Roselyne. Reaching through worlds to conjure another exacts a heavy toll—a life." He paused. "But I am willing to pay." Sloane turned the book's blank pages toward the sky for a few moments, and the parchment filled with symbols written in swirling red ink. He took a step toward me, and I could not shrink away, glued to the spot by the power of the ancient runes. His expression softened, almost in apology. "I've checked multiple times. To bind myself to the demon I conjure—it has to be a witch. For this I am sorry."

Sloane unsheathed a small, jeweled dagger I hadn't noticed he wore and spun it in his hand. I realized then what part I was to play in his wicked plan. I thrashed uselessly against the invisible bonds.

"Declan is stronger than you," I snarled. "He'll *kill* you."

I stared down the prince with my head held high, but Sloane was completely unaffected by my threats.

"Right now, my brother's power exceeds my own, but with your sacrifice, Roselyne—it will not."

My heart thrashed against my chest. My body screamed at me to move—to get away, but my feet stayed rooted firmly in place, trapped within the runic circle. Sloane approached me holding the steel blade in one hand and the grimoire in another.

Sloane tucked the grimoire under his arm and rolled up the sleeve of his shirt. He touched the tip of the blade to the skin of his inner wrist, wincing as blood swirled around the edge. He pressed the blade further into his skin, and groaned as he began carving various runes I didn't understand into the flesh of his arm, marking his skin with a constellation of strange symbols. Crimson fell to the ground in large drops, sizzling on impact and burning through the dead leaves.

Sloane withdrew the book from under his arm, flipped to another page marked with a piece of leather and began to recite words in a language I couldn't understand. Involuntarily, my arms shot down to my body, restrained by my side just as my feet were planted to the earth. Sloane crouched down, dipping his fingers into the herbal mixture in the bowl beside me and stood. His blade was still held in his other hand, red-tipped with his blood. I jerked against my invisible bonds, working uselessly to break loose.

"Now, hold still, I don't want to mess this up," he chided lightly, as if I was a child sneaking sweets, and not about to be forced to participate in some forbidden ritual. He pressed some of the mixture to my forehead and face in swirls and dots I couldn't see. I spat in his face and jerked my head from his grasp.

Sloane slapped me across the cheek with the back of his hand and wrenched my chin back to face him. The taste of iron filled my mouth. He continued painting my body with the herbal mixture until my chest and arms matched my face, covered in smears of purple.

A twig snapped nearby. My eyes darted side to side, but I saw no one else with us in the glen.

Sloane stepped away from me, held the grimoire up high, and began reciting more of those strange and rhythmic ancient words. I hadn't time to comprehend what was about to happen before it was done.

In one motion, Sloane slashed his blade across my throat.

The spell tethering me in place broke as my body hit the ground. I clutched at my neck, but it was of no use. Blood poured from my neck in thick spurts with every sluggish beat of my heart, creating a puddle of crimson beneath me. My body was too weak to move, and I felt myself fading out of consciousness. The familiar scent of wet earth was a comfort as I began to die.

As if manifested by the gods themselves, Declan burst through a break in the trees, hands outstretched toward his brother. The two began hacking and slashing at each other as Sloane's arm continued to drip red rubies of blood into the earth.

An unnatural chill filled the air. My body began to convulse and my vision grew hazy. The blood-soaked dirt beside me began to ripple and morph, creating a whirlpool in the wet soil, causing tiny fissures along the ground that spread across the wooded glen like cracked glass.

The brothers made no notice, too engrossed in their own fight.

The spiral of soil and earth vibrated as the dirt coiled tighter and tighter until the ground began to sink in on itself. I'd lost too much blood, and despite the bonds of magic being broken, found I hadn't the strength to move. I shivered against the cold earth, no longer able to feel my arms or legs.

The scent of blood in the air was cut with something else—a musk of amber and something spicy.

As the brothers continued their duel, from the ground, a figure slowly rose. Taller and broader than Declan, the conjured demon had arrived at last, primed to submit its power to Sloane. The two brothers, engrossed in their fight, hadn't noticed. Some black tarry substance completely covered the demon, and sweeping shadows indicative of its infernal realm of origin shrouded its features. The demon opened his eyes—a striking silver that met mine. He quirked his head, and the corner of his mouth lifted.

I tried to open my mouth to cry out, to warn Declan of the demon's arrival, but instead, blood bubbled from my lips as I began to sputter and cough. I was dying.

The demon unfurled two large batlike wings, and spread them wide. Clumps of black muck dropped to the ground as he stretched his membranous wings before shooting directly up into the air and disappearing against the night sky.

Black crept in from the corners of my vision and closed in over me, embracing me in the silky dark.

55
DECLAN

Kez's hooves pounded against the path faster than he'd ever galloped in all his years as my warhorse. It was as if my steed could sense the potential fragility and direness of our circumstances and pushed himself beyond his limits, bringing me back to the palace.

When I swung open the door to my bedchambers and found the mattress cold and empty, I knew right then that something terrible was underway. I rushed in the corridor and knocked into Essi, her eyes rimmed in red and her appearance harried and flighty.

"Declan," she gasped as she backed away from me, her dark eyes shifting side to side. She knew something.

My voice shook the palace as crackling power flicked from my hands, "Where is my betrothed?"

She held her hands up and trembled at my display of power. Essi had always been a welcome addition to my court, but I would end her if she withheld information, and the fear in her eyes told me she knew exactly that.

"Rose- Roselyne is in the forest," she stammered out.

THE CURSE OF THE SEELIE KING

Essi released a loose sob, but I held no pity for the woman. "I don't know what he's going to do," she whispered. Her eyes went round, and she pressed herself against the wall as I stalked past her without a word quickly navigating outside toward the forest. Whatever had befallen Roselyne would determine how I'd deal with the Western Lord's daughter. I had no use to waste any of my dwindling power on Essi.

Mist swirled around the grounds, gathered low near the earth and unnaturally thick. The air smelled of blood and herbs, as the moon shone its light down in beams of red. I rushed toward the faint murmurings of voices, traveling as quietly as possible.

This couldn't be right.

The coverage of trees concealed my body as I saw but could not comprehend the scene before me. Sloane's back was to me, facing Roselyne. She was unharmed, but she was in only her thin nightdress and bare feet, strange symbols painted on her skin.

I took a step, snapping a twig underfoot as I went to confront them.

In a flash, Sloane swiped a dagger I didn't know he was holding across Roselyne's throat and she collapsed to the ground. Her body convulsed as she grabbed at her throat trying to stifle the torrent of crimson flowing from her neck—the dark blood a stark contrast against her pale skin. My mind blanked, as I allowed rage and my power to guide me. I had no time for lamentations. An emotional response wouldn't save Roselyne. But my rage could kill my brother.

I burst from the shadows, sending a blast of power hurtling toward Sloane, but he ducked the blow and withdrew a long darksteel sword from the scabbard at his back. To my left,

Roselyne gurgled, her body convulsing as she lay bleeding in the dirt.

I unsheathed the sword at my back and stood, ready to fight my brother.

"What have you done?" I screamed, slashing my blade at Sloane.

Sloane ducked the blow and laughed, high and cold.

"It's too late," Sloane said, "Your would-be bride has given me a gift. For once you will face me, and I will be your better."

I stole a glance at Roselyne on the ground, but forced my face back to my brother.

Her skin was ashen, her lips nearly white. She lay on her back in a pool of her blood. Her green eyes were wide open and glazed, facing the stars. Her chest rose in rapid, shallow breaths.

For now, Roselyne lived. I turned back to my brother.

"Why?" I roared, hacking at him again.

Sloane parried my sword with his own as if it were nothing to him.

His eyes glinted full of malice. "You are a coward, brother, and not fit to rule as Seelie King." He huffed a laugh. "Just because you burst from our mother's cunt before me does not make you more adept to wear the Seelie Crown."

He slashed at me, and I jumped backward, narrowly missing a slice to my ribs.

"I've never cared about ruling."

Sloane barked a laugh.

"Never cared? You are not the good little king you'd have your whore believe," he spat. "You've told her naught of the Unseelie's demise and subsequent disappearance of witch-kind. You lust for power just as much as I—only I will make the kingdom a better place, a stronger place for fae. You're too soft on the humans and the others—they forget their place." He hacked again. "A witch-queen in the faelands, Declan? The Seelie Court would fall into ruin under your rule. I do this for the good of the faelands."

He readied his stance to strike again, but I instead opted to blast him with my magic, concentrating on cracking his bones. I wanted this over quickly so I could help Roselyne. She still lived—I could sense it. She would not die. I would not allow it.

The ground trembled as I channeled all my rage into striking my brother—I concentrated and sent a torrent of pain his way, unleashing the majority of my energy at his chest.

Nothing happened.

Sloane smirked at me, his own sword still raised. He yelled at me from the small distance between us.

"That won't work on me right now brother. I am rich with witch-kind knowledge long extinct from the world, resurrected and translated to serve only me," he cried out, mad with glee. "The elysian magic you've lorded over me our entire lives is null against me now—so pick up your sword and fight me as equals." He moved his weight from foot to foot. "Your princess doesn't have much longer, it seems."

I snuck a glance behind me—Sloane was right.

"What sick magic is this?" I cried out.

"I've reached through realms, Declan." He licked his lips. "Things long thought impossible are easily accessed if you only possess the patience. A demon of the Otherrealm is bound to me now—and its strength will be your undoing."

"Abomination," I yelled as I ran at him, sword raised, ready to cleave my younger brother in two.

Sloane smiled, a wicked grin that told me he held no fear for me.

"Did I strike a nerve brother?" he asked innocently before he brought his own sword down on my shoulder.

Pain radiated through my chest. Blood bloomed beneath the thin fabric of my shirt. I winced, but readied my stance once more.

It would take more than a cut, even from a darksteel blade, to fell me. Roselyne's life hung in the balance. I tightened my fist around my pommel, using the pain of the wound to urge me forward. I hadn't bothered to put on armor, favoring speed over protection as I rode to the priestesses. I'd only brought the sword as a precaution, not knowing what foe I'd be facing when I arrived at the temple.

Our swords clashed midair, and a flurry of bats flew from the canopy of the trees that hung above us. Sloane had never been good with weapons—not like this. In his time away, he'd been working at it—practicing, all for this moment when he'd strike me down.

I welcomed Sloane back with open arms when he arrived to court after his travels, but I understood—it was all a ruse. My brother would die for this, and Roselyne would live. Now that I knew what love was, and experienced it firsthand, a life without Roselyne was not worth living—if Roselyne died, I would follow her into the abyss.

But not yet. I needed to kill Sloane first.

I snuck a glance at Roselyne. Her body was still, the blood no longer pouring from the wound in her neck.

She was too still.

"No," I whispered.

With a howl of pain, I hacked at my brother, narrowly missing his face. He stumbled backward and fell to his ass as his sword flung away from him, his face the image of stunned disbelief.

I stood over him, my sword held over his chest. Instead of

irreparable rage, I felt the deepest sense of grief and loss for the brother I once had.

A single tear rolled down my face as I held the tip of my sword to his chest, readying myself to plunge my blade into the heart of my younger brother. Memories of our shared adolescence flashed through my mind, working to give me pause, but I shook them away.

Before I moved to kill my brother, the earth shifted and knocked me off my feet.

My momentary distraction was enough for my brother to regain the upper hand. He rolled out from beneath me, stood, and threw the dagger he'd used to cut Roselyne's throat, aiming for my heart.

56

ROSELYNE

I remembered nothing.
    I was an untethered spirit, drifting alone in the inky black. I possessed no body, so no pain found me as I floated in space, held in the gentle caress of complete and total darkness. From a distance far away, a tiny pinprick of white light appeared, before it began hurtling toward me, growing larger with every second.

The light slammed into me, knocking me backward. I hit the ground with a thud, suddenly aware of my body. My eyes flew open. Instead of the familiar cocoon of never-ending black—a blinding white light seared against my vision. I stood, wincing from my fall. The light faded to reveal a meadow. Dewdrops still coated the grass, glistening in the soft dawn light, or perhaps it was twilight. A gentle breeze blew, ruffling my hair and sending a shiver down my spine. I was dressed in a silvery gown, inlaid with gold beading and shimmering threads, although my bare feet squished against the spongy earth. Here, in this place, it was as temperate as spring, although I was not aware of where I found myself, in the strangest of dreams.

To my left, black mountains rose over the horizon in steep peaks capped with snow, a stark comparison to the warmth found in the meadow. To my right, a large metallic hourglass, the height of two fae men and ancient in appearance, sat idly on grass, tiny grains of sand falling to the lower chamber with gentle clinks.

A feminine figure stood a few paces from me, clad in billowing lilac robes spilling around the grass in puddles, her entire body and face concealed by a hood. The cloaked figure approached me, her feet leaving no indentation as she glided through the morning dew, tiny white wildflowers springing from the earth where she passed.

"Where am I?" I asked.

Flashes of memories flooded through me, and I remembered it all. Sloane's lies, the truth of the curse, the bite of a dagger slicing across my throat.

I reached for my neck—but felt only unmarred skin where the press of Sloane's blade kissed my flesh.

"The Aether," the figure answered as she clasped her hands together in front of her body. "The realm between."

She spoke as a chorus of ethereal harmonies, a multitude of echoing voices in tandem.

"Am I dead?" I asked. "Or is this a dream?"

My eyes snagged on another cloaked figure, taller, and more slender. He stood at the tree line, just outside the meadow, watching us, although I could not discern more about him.

"Time moves differently here," she replied, in that dreamy voice of thousands, as her eyes followed my gaze.

"Sloane killed me," I said, unsure.

She nodded. My chest deflated. I didn't want to die, I wanted to be with Declan. I wanted to see Dove and my brothers again. She lifted her hands to her hood, uncovering her face.

A gasp slipped from my lips. This woman was not human, or fae, or mer. She was something else entirely and not of this world.

Her skin was the color of midnight with a constellation of glowing white freckles dotted across the bridge of her nose and cheeks. Her eyes lacked irises; instead, glowing bright white and matching the hair cascading down her shoulders in tight spiraling curls. I scrambled to take a step backward. But, for however terrified I was of her, I could not deny she was beautiful and awe-inspiring, and I trembled before her terrible power.

"Yes, Roselyne. You are dead at the hands of the Seelie Prince," she said, "But it is not necessary you stay that way."

My breath hitched.

"How is that possible?" I asked, my voice barely above a whisper.

The woman smiled. "I foresaw your death before your birth. It is by design that you find yourself with me"—she gestured toward the other cloaked figure in the distance—"With *us*, at this pivotal moment in time."

"I don't understand. Who are you?" My gaze shifted to the cloaked man in the distance, unmoving and watching us still.

"Those of your world call me Lux—Goddess of Daylight and Life." She gestured toward the other figure. "And he is Umbrath, my lover, God of Death, and the Shadow of Night."

My eyes widened.

Lux continued. "Upon your birth, together, Umbrath and I bestowed you with a great and terrible power." She frowned slightly. "And for that I am sorry."

"What power?" I asked, "My witch magic?"

THE CURSE OF THE SEELIE KING

The goddess frowned for the first time—her ethereal beauty undiminished by the downward turn of her full lips.

"No," she said. "You are not witch-kind. You are something else entirely." From the corner of my eye, I watched as Umbrath began crossing the meadow and approaching us, tendrils of dark shadows licking at his heels. He reached us and slid an arm around Lux's waist, his face and body still concealed by the black cloak he wore and the shadows wrapped around him. "You are imbued with a kernel of each of our powers, should you choose to yield them," Lux said. "Just as we are not entirely of this world, neither are you, Roselyne Vaughn."

I frowned. The realization didn't slam into me as hard as anticipated. I wasn't a witch. Of course, I wasn't. Nothing about witch magic had come easily to me in the hours I'd spend trying to access the power with Kera.

"Then what am I?" I asked, eyes round. "Is the prophecy false, then? As Sloane thought?" At the mention of Declan's brother, I began to turn wildly around the meadow, searching for an exit, a way back from the Aether and to the Seelie King. I found only the half empty hourglass staring back. "Is Declan alright? I need to get back to him, I—"

Lux spoke again, silencing me. "There is truth in prophecy, Roselyne." I opened my mouth to interrupt, but Lux held up a hand, stopping me. "As for what you are? You are Star-Marked, chosen by fate to repair the balance of this world and right the wrongs of the past. You bear this mark upon your crown." A gentle wind blew and the silvery strands of my hair danced in the breeze.

I sucked in a breath. *Star-Marked.*

The term felt familiar, resonating deep within my chest, although I didn't know what that meant.

"Why? For what purpose would you do this?" I asked.

"This world is out of balance, and you are the deliverer of truth, decided eons ago. Every action has a price, and the forces of nature require justice."

I shook my head. "You knew I was going to die?"

"Yes," Lux replied. "Certain events have been put into action, and the gods cannot interfere directly. You have been celestially designed to deliver justice and *balance*."

"How am I supposed to do that? What's out of balance?"

Lux looked into the distance, gaze fixed on the hourglass. More grains of sand filled the bottom chamber than the top. Umbrath stood silently, but even through the thick cloak concealing his face, I felt his eyes boring into me.

"I cannot say everything I wish to. I've interfered enough as is, and fate is watching." She slid from Umbrath's embrace. "But know this—there is a side to every coin. Good and evil. Day and night. Life and death. All necessary in this world."

"I don't understand what you'd have me do," I said, irritated. I needed to get back to Declan, to help him fight off his brother, to somehow kill Sloane for his betrayal. "Why not do it yourself?" I snapped. "I only have a portion of your power, surely you could do this task." A quick glance to the hourglass told me only a few handfuls of sand remained in the topmost chamber.

"Umbrath and I are trapped in this realm, and cannot interfere further. Even now, communication is limited and we are running out of time in this liminal space between life and death."

Umbrath lowered his hood, and I suppressed a gasp. His face was sharp angles on pale skin. Like Lux he lacked irises, but instead of the bright white glow the goddess possessed, Umbrath's eyes were an abyss of black, seemingly endless and devoid of all light. Despite lowering his hood, he still did not speak, instead turning his head and communicating with Lux in silence. Lux nodded and tightened her grip on my hands as she glanced at the hourglass. Only a few grains of sand remained.

"Make your choice, Roselyne. Stay or go. Accept your fate, or do not. You must choose."

"Will it hurt?" I asked, "To go back?"

"Most certainly," Lux said. "The best things do."

"What about—" I began, but Lux held up a hand in answer.

"No more time for questions. Our time has ended. You must choose now. Live, and accept your fate—or die, and find all the answers you've desired?" she asked.

"I want to go back—to live," I said placing my hand into hers. My fingers trembled as my skin made contact with the goddess', and I gasped at the heat radiating from her flesh. A bright sphere of swirling pale flames erupted from my hand and floated midair between Lux, Umbrath, and me. The last grain of sand hit the bottom of the hourglass.

"Then go," she said.

The ball of energy exploded, filling the meadow with pure white light.

57

ROSELYNE

The air smelled of iron and looming death.

My head throbbed. The hard ground beneath every part of my body was sore. Something sticky and wet coated my skin. I blinked my eyes open, remembering it all.

I am alive.

It appeared no time had passed, the two brothers hacking and swinging at each other with reckless abandon, still immersed in their dance of death. Declan's movements were sluggish, and he held his non-dominant hand pressed against his chest as he continued swinging at his brother.

A dark red stain seeped from his shirt and a grim expression of pain marred his features.

Sloane had the upper hand. Panic washed over me.

I stood, shaking uncontrollably, some newfound sensation inside of me beating against the confines of my body, trying to free itself.

Sloane thrust his sword at Declan, aiming to cleave his older brother in two. Sloane's eyes met mine, and all color drained from his face. I must have resembled a wraith standing there—barefooted in the damp soil, wearing only my chemise, and soaked in blood—the evader of death.

At Sloane's expression, Declan turned, and his eyes locked on mine. His expression was one of disbelief, then apprehension. His mouth began to tip upward into the beginnings of a hopeful smile.

Sloane thrust his sword into his brother's stomach and twisted.

Declan sank to his knees and dropped his own blade, as the rivers of blood soaking through his shirt and puddling around him. An unnatural scream tore through my throat as Declan collapsed into the dirt.

With swiftness not granted to humans, I ran to Sloane with my hand outstretched. Only blind fury guided me. A swell of energy surged within my body, and whatever barrier dampened my power finally snapped. Unfettered raw magic skittered through my veins, equal parts terrifying, exhilarating, and wild.

I had no control over the pale flames that burst forth from my palms as they licked up my arms, and engulfed me completely. The strange fire burned through my clothing and jewelry, melting the golden betrothal band from my finger, but I felt no pain. Nude and consumed in flame, the untamed magic unleashed from my fingertips and hurtled toward Sloane, striking him in the chest. He reached to clutch at his heart with a bewildered expression that matched my own.

With a terrible scream, Sloane's body also burst into matching white flames, but unlike me—he shrieked in pain as his skin began to bubble and slough off. It took only a few moments until he turned to ash before my eyes. The wind blew gently, and the remains of Sloane floated away as if he never existed.

My chest heaved. *I killed Sloane.* With magic. I was no

longer human, or a witch, I was—something else. Chosen by fate and marked by the stars.

The flames dissipated, and I was left standing nude in the forest clearing, breath heavy from the force of expelled energy. My eyes darted to where Declan lay on the ground. He was impossibly still, his normally tanned skin paler than I'd ever seen. With wobbling legs, I staggered to him, the man I'd chosen—not because of some agreement between our kingdoms, or to break some false curse—but for ourselves.

He would not die.

Declan did not move, but I was unconvinced. I steeled myself. Lux was the goddess of light and life—there must be some part of me—some part of the magic that could heal him despite my lack of training.

My body screamed in protest, completely spent as I crawled on my knees toward the man who'd reignited my belief in love.

I flung myself across his body and pawed at his ruined shirt with my hands. The blood was slick and wet as I tore through the fabric and placed my hands on the jagged wound where Sloane's sword had found its mark.

Declan inhaled shakily as his glazed eyes locked on mine. His lips moved as if to speak, but no sound passed. I pressed both of my hands against his chest, working to stanch the blood that spurted from the deep slash, desperate to keep him alive. His breath was a wet rattle in my ears.

"You don't get to die," I cried out, tears streaming down my face and blurring my vision.

My hands slipped in the slickness of the blood, smearing it on his chest.

The blood flow slowed as Declan drew nearer to death. My face twisted in agony as I pressed my entire body against the ruined flesh of his chest.

"You don't get to make me love you, then leave me alone," I cried out.

I collapsed onto Declan's body with a sob, still working to slow the bleeding that never seemed to end.

If I was to be burdened with this power, should it not suit my purpose? If I'd know what I'd return to, I would have chosen death. I groaned as I put more pressure on Declan's wounds.

Declan could not die. He would not die. If I was forced to bear a part in the will of the gods, I would only do so with the fae king at my side.

Soft droplets of rain began to fall from the sky, as if the gods in their celestial realm heard my pleas but took no further action. The rain grew heavier, drenching my naked body and mixing with the blood pooled on the ground and diluting it down. I turned my face toward the sky, and screamed into the blackness—at the stars, at Lux, at Umbrath, and any other gods who observed what happened in the realm of the living.

My voice cut through the sound of the rain falling in heavy sheets, pelting against my bare skin like hail. "You can't have him!" I screamed into the unanswering sky.

If Declan's death was willed by the gods, I would defy them. I laid my head down on my love's chest as his shallow breathing ceased, and a stifling heaviness washed over me.

An uncontrolled wail tore from my throat. Tears streamed from my eyes, blinding me with their abundance, stinging my skin as they trailed along my cheeks, and spilled onto Declan's ruined chest, tasting of salt and despair. I wept for unfulfilled promises, bitterness for the future, and for the lifetime I'd have to endure without Declan at my side.

58
DECLAN

I woke the evening after the blood moon with Roselyne at my side, curled up beside me in our shared bed. She slathered my chest with thick paste on my new scar trailing from my heart to my navel. Sloane had marred me with a darksteel blade, and because of that, I'd wear the evidence of my brother's betrayal on my body for the rest of my life.

By all accounts, I should be dead from the wound I received, but Roselyne saved me. Her raw magic had somehow stitched me back together—or the gods themselves had intervened and allowed me to live on her behalf. Either way, because of Roselyne, I was still alive. For the first time in nearly a century, the full extent of my power thrummed in my veins.

What Roselyne told me should have been impossible. She was Star-Marked, a condition only believed to have existed in myths of old. She'd recounted how Lux and Umbrath visited her in the Aether as she straddled life and death. Roselyne told me of how she was called to bring balance back to the world, but given no further instruction on how to achieve this. She recalled how the witches' curse never existed, but was a concoction fueled by my brother's hatred for me, exacerbated by my own guilt.

I only accepted the truth of her words when she'd parted her hair, revealing elongated fae-like ears.

"How?" I asked, reaching out to touch the tip. Her eyes fluttered closed with a breathy exhale as I stroked the new tapered skin.

"Kera believes my human body burned up from the force of my power, and the magic created this new one." She smiled fully at me, and I stared at her pointed ears. She looked *fae*. "I'm a bit taller," she added with a shrug.

I sucked in a breath. "Star-Marked," I said, more to myself than Roselyne.

She nodded.

If Roselyne was imbued with the power of Lux and Umbrath, she was potentially more powerful than anyone in the entire realm, containing powers held by the gods of both the Seelie and Unseelie fae.

"Where is Sloane?" I asked, sitting upright.

"Dead," she said quietly.

"Good."

"I killed him," Roselyne said in a small voice. She turned away from my face.

"And Essi?" I asked softly.

Roselyne shook her head. "Gone," she whispered. Her lips flattened into a straight line. "By the time Kera found us in the forest, Essi had already fled the palace. She could be anywhere by now."

I tugged Roselyne's body against mine, relishing in the comfort of her presence. "I'm sorry I didn't protect you."

We stayed there for a few moments before she pulled away.

"There's something else you need to know." She chewed

her bottom lip. "Sloane failed in his attempt to bind a demon to himself, but it was summoned and did appear. He"—she hesitated—"*it* looked at me and flew away." She fiddled with a loose thread on the bed linen for a moment before meeting my eyes. "It's still out there somewhere. Kera and Callum scoured the city last night, but found no trace of it—or Essi."

I wasn't sure what to make of that.

"A demon is easily handled, by me and my council, my love."

I brushed a soft kiss against her jaw. Roselyne and I had escaped death, some hellish fiend from the Otherrealm was no match for the full strength of my power. She didn't look convinced, instead assessing me with furrowed brows.

"In the past, demons slipped into this realm through small fissures and cracks between worlds before they were sealed permanently centuries ago. I'll take care of it, as fae lesser than I have done many times before."

I pressed my lips to hers, gripping her waist and bringing her closer to me. My hand traveled through her hair and settled on her cheek as I deepened our kiss and squeezed her hand in mine. I brushed my fingers over hers and noticed she wasn't wearing the golden ring binding us together on her finger.

She followed my gaze and pulled away, flexing her hand. "It burned away when I accessed my magic. There was nothing I could do."

I pressed my lips to her unadorned finger. "The marriage bond is broken," I murmured against her skin. "You removed the ring before we wed. We're no longer betrothed. You're free to walk away from our union without stoking the wrath of the gods. So, think long and hard about whether you want to spend your life alongside the Seelie King."

She snorted. "The gods should be more concerned with *my*

wrath," she said. "They've tasked me to restore balance in the world and given me no guidance." She turned her eyes on me, and I was momentarily breathless. "Do you not think that could be our wedding? The unification of fae and men? Separated for centuries, our union joins two worlds." She positioned herself on her knees and settled between my legs. "Besides, I'm beginning to grow accustomed to the idea of a marriage to you."

I arched a brow. "Just now?"

She grinned. "Maybe for a while."

"I love you," I said. My love for Roselyne was the most implicit truth in this world.

"I love you too," she replied, eyes sparkling.

Warmth radiated through my body, tugging a grin across my face. She's never said those words to me. I leaned forward to kiss Roselyne properly, and my cock stirred to life, not aware of how narrowly we'd escaped death. She grinned up at me through thick eyelashes.

"You don't want to wait for the wedding night?" she asked with a laugh. I groaned and moved her body to straddle mine.

"I think we're past that, Princess."

She squealed in delight and squeezed her thighs around my waist, careful not to touch the wound across my chest. Her hair tickled my skin as she leaned down and pressed her lips to mine in a chaste kiss. The bed groaned in protest as I threw Roselyne onto her back, her fits of laughter, filling the room.

It was the most pleasant sound I'd ever heard—a testament to the ordeals we'd been through, and how we'd fought to stay alive for each other. Roselyne and I would unite the kingdoms, and make this world a better place for humans and fae alike. I gripped her chin with one hand while the other trailed down between her legs. She snapped her thighs shut.

"I don't want to hurt you," she said, eyeing the angry red line slashed across my chest.

"It does not pain me. I had an excellent healer," I said, to which she smacked me lightly against the arm with a wry smile.

"Declan Danchev, none of that until you're all the way healed," she said, placing a kiss atop my brow before slipping from the bed and walking to the door. "I'll let the others know you're awake."

59

ROSELYNE

I unfurled my fingers, coaxing the tiny white flame to appear. It danced in my palm for a moment before growing too large and singeing my skin. I snapped my fist shut with a wince.

"You'll get the hang of it," Declan called from across the room. "But perhaps it's not best to practice your magic surrounded by ancient irreplaceable texts." He smirked.

We'd not told anyone the truth of what transpired the night of the blood moon, instead allowing the Seelie fae to believe Sloane died in a tragic accident.

The city and kingdom mourned for their prince, all festivals and ceremonies would be held until the thirty-day mourning period lapsed, including the royal wedding and any related plans. None save for Declan's royal council and myself knew the truth of how the prince had died, and the Seelie fae would be better for it.

During this time, Declan, Kera, and I spent our days within the palace's massive library reading about myths involving gods intervening and gifting divine power to mortals, working to understand the scope of the magic I'd been granted.

It was not something that happened often.

I flipped a page, barely registering any of the text and let my eyes glaze over. I slept all night, but exhaustion tugged at my eyelids beckoning them to close.

"Yesterday was our original wedding date," Declan said with a pinched expression, snapping his book shut.

I sat upright and uncrossed my legs. Kera quirked a brow and assessed me before burying herself back within the pages she held, her legs curled up beneath her.

Had it been that long already? Since my death, I walked through each day in a haze, never fully aware of where I was, or the truth of my reality. I grew frailer with each new day, perhaps some consequence of the newfound magic within me, but refused to worry Declan by telling him. Night terrors plagued me while I slept, but when I woke in the mornings, all memories of my time dreaming fell through my fingers like sand. I kept this to myself.

I rubbed fingers along my pounding forehead.

"Already?" I asked.

"Mhm," he replied. "And we still have a few more days left of the mourning period. We'll choose a new date—I don't want our celebration of love to be overshadowed by that traitor's death."

I nodded once and smiled at my betrothed. We'd fought for each other and came out the other side still standing, hands clasped together and victorious.

A rogue snowball slammed into the back of my already pounding head. I quickly turned to see familiar paw prints pressed into the top of the snow leading away from me. With a laugh, I bent down and scooped up a handful of snow and packed it into a tight ball.

I couldn't see Kera in the snow, but her black fur in her catlike form wouldn't be difficult to spot among the sea of white. I followed the prints, tossing the snowball in my hand, readying myself to aim.

I followed the paw prints around the side of the castle to the frozen garden. Icicles dripped from petals of blue roses. The shimmering palace sat in the background, appearing more like a winter kingdom than the seat of the Seelie Court. Althene rarely froze like this, and I adored the fluffy snow and frost that covered every building and walkway as if it belonged beneath the sea.

Kera said this season brought the earliest snow in the faelands' history, and I thought perhaps the gods sent this weather to cleanse the grounds of all the evils that occurred here. I walked through a canopy of white flowering vines, frozen in place to the iron trellis it climbed.

Now that the mourning period was over, Declan reinstated all the servants in the castle, and the only place we were truly alone was in our bedchamber. I enjoyed having more people around. The bustle of the servants distracted from Essi's absence. I'd avoided her rooms altogether since the incident, finding it too painful to be in proximity of her things and the memories associated with our time spent together giggling and gossiping throughout the palace halls.

The trail of tiny paw prints stopped abruptly and continued as small, Kera-sized boot prints in the snow, leading further into the palace gardens.

I chuckled to myself, tossing the snowball in my hand and catching it. The Widowmaker of the faelands was giving an easy chase. I followed the trail until I gasped at the sight before me.

Instead of finding Kera, Declan waited for me in the center of the palace gardens.

Thousands of flowers lined the walkway leading to him, varieties of hellebores, winter roses, and snowdrops in multiple shades of blue and white. I dropped the snowball against the ground.

A spectacular fountain sat behind him, the water frozen to create a sculpture of ice. I approached Declan with a flutter of apprehension.

Declan's hands were behind his back, and he wore fine clothes of burgundy. The bright golden embroidered Sunburst of the Seelie was sewn into his coat and seemed to radiate heat enough to thaw the grounds. The cold wind blew, tousling his dark hair. He nervously pushed it away from his face and cleared his throat.

I chewed the inside of my cheek. "Declan, what is this?" I asked as I approached him.

His face split into a toothy grin. He held out his hands for me, and I placed my palms in his.

He dropped down to one knee.

I gasped.

"Princess Roselyne Vaughn," he began, "Would you do me the honor of entering into a betrothal commitment with me for the sole purpose of melding our souls together...to never be parted again in this lifetime, or the next?"

A whisper of a smile crossed my lips.

"Declan, you know we're already betrothed. We had the ceremony already...even if my ring did melt off," I teased.

He was undeterred.

"We didn't get a choice in that." He turned his gaze toward the frozen earth, then back into my eyes. "I am choosing you, Roselyne. Not because of a curse, or a deal between our kingdoms, but because I never want to know another day without you at my side. I wish for you to rule beside me as Queen of the Seelie Fae—if you desire it." He swallowed. "I told you before, and I meant what I said. I bow to no one but you, Roselyne." His hands trembled slightly as he held a ring, another plain golden band, this one adorned with a ruby the size of a quail egg. "Will you wear this ring and rule beside me as Seelie Queen?"

He looked nervous for a moment, waiting for my response.

"Yes, of course!"

I laughed before reaching and pulling him to stand. He slipped the ring onto my finger. No swirl of magic surrounded our hands as it had during the official betrothal ceremony and feast, but we didn't need the gods' approval. We chose this for ourselves.

"It was my mother's," he said softly, sweeping his fingers across my own.

"It's beautiful."

He wrapped me in his arms and kissed me—deeply, passionately, and like he owned me—and in some ways he did. My soul belonged to the Seelie King, and his to me. Our union would heal the fractured relationship between humans and fae, foreseen centuries ago and written in prophecy.

It was only too poetic that we also fell in love.

60

ROSELYNE

Solora settled into a new normal in the weeks following the blood moon. With all the servants back in the palace, I grew accustomed to the ever-present hum of conversation filling the corridors. The taste of Essi's betrayal still stung, and I wanted nothing to do with any of the plans she'd made regarding the wedding ceremony.

Even though Declan insisted we needn't marry according to Seelie Tradition, I was adamant Declan and I marry as the Seelie fae would expect of their new queen. We hadn't yet chosen a new date, and instead basked in the knowledge we had survived everything, and the belief that our union would heal the rifts between human and fae.

As such, my days were spent in a whirlwind of working to access the newly awakened powers within my veins and sparring, until eventually falling into bed at night, dizzy and too exhausted for much else.

Many nights while the moon still hung high, I'd wake drenched in sweat, full of dread, but remembered nothing of my dreams. Instead, I'd kiss Declan across his brow while he slept, then lay awake with a pounding heart until the sun rose and filled our chambers with its light. The feeling of unease never truly left me even with the rising sun.

Today, Declan and I were enjoying a much-needed break from any sort of training or responsibilities to the kingdom. We holed away in our bedchamber, curled up together in one of the overstuffed armchairs, stealing kisses between turned pages. A hearty fire crackled and popped in the white marble mantle, warming the chilled room. It had snowed again last night, and the palace grounds were covered in a thick blanket of white.

Kera stalked in the room, her mood grim and lips pressed into a firm line. Her eyes found mine and narrowed.

"There's a messenger for you, Roselyne." She tapped her foot. "From Althene."

I glanced at Declan with an expression of bewilderment. His face matched my own. I wiggled off his lap and stood, craning my neck to see behind Kera and into the corridor behind her.

"Who?" I asked.

"Roselyne!" a familiar voice squealed in delight.

I only saw a blur of reddish hair before I was tackled to the ground.

I sat upright and blinked. My previous, and very human, lady's maid slid into focus, kneeling at my eye level, her head cocked to the side and studying me.

"Dove," I said, throwing my body against hers, and pulling her into a tight embrace. "How are you here?" I asked as I squeezed her against me. She was *here*. It should have been impossible.

We separated, legs still tangled together on the ground. She grinned at me, her bright blue eyes sparkling, before she pulled back her expression into one of solemnity and stood, dusting off her pale green traveling dress. I grasped her outstretched hand, and she helped pull me to my feet.

"You seem well, Rosie." My oldest friend smiled tentatively at me, darting her eyes toward Declan as she rocked on her heels. "Wallace is here as well, but the...*security* would only let one of us through."

Kera scowled and crossed her arms. Declan's furrow between his brow grew deeper.

I squeezed Dove's hand in mine. She was real, and she was here. How many days I'd longed for her company, and by some divine intervention here she was, as if the gods' favor had finally turned in my benefit.

"I've missed you so much, Dove."

Tears welled in her eyes and she quickly wiped them away with a tentative smile.

"I've missed you too." She chewed her lip for a moment as she took in the plush furnishings in our bedchamber. "Are you...happy here?" She met my gaze, her own blue eyes open wide and hopeful.

"I am, truly," I said.

I tucked a stray lock of hair behind my ear, and Dove's eyes widened as she stifled a gasp.

"Rosie...what *happened*?"

My cheeks flamed as I pulled the hair back over to cover my new fae ears and fidgeted with the strands, wrapping them around my fingers. "I'll tell you everything once I know the meaning of your visit," I said.

Dove rocked on her heels. "I wish I came bearing better news." She shook her head and steeled herself, and a strange sense of formality swirled in the air. Dove inhaled deeply, her eyes darting between mine and Declan's as she spoke. "I've been sent to the faelands on business as an official envoy of the Althenean Crown, escorted by Prince Wallace of Althene."

My face scrunched into a frown. *Prince Wallace? Why the formality? What news would carry one of my brothers and my best friend across the sea?*

Declan crossed the room and stood behind me, snaking a possessive hand around my waist.

Dove tracked the movement with her eyes and chewed on her bottom lip. Her hands trembled slightly as she handed me a neatly tied scroll, sealed with the navy wax seal of the King of Althene, still clutching another in her hands. "I'm sorry, Rosie," she whispered.

I took the letter from her, but did not rip through the seal to open it. The parchment felt heavy in my hands, for I knew it bore no good tidings.

"Tell me, Dove," I said.

She inhaled slowly before speaking, her expression one of sympathy. "Your father, the king, is dead." She grimaced.

I flinched. I hadn't expected that. Declan's grip on my waist tightened, but I barely registered the change in pressure, my mind reeling instead.

My father was not a young man, but neither elderly by human standards. He was the type of man I'd imagine living forever, a figurehead who'd led Althene for decades—and the kingdom anticipated he'd continue for many more. Even in his fifth decade of life, my father was still adequate with a sword and hammer and rarely found himself confined to a sickbed, even during the winter months.

Dove cleared her throat before speaking again with her eyebrows knit together in apology. "Your brother Corbin has been crowned the King of Althene and"—she hesitated, eyes darting first to Kera then Declan before bringing her gaze back toward mine—"brings demands to the faelands."

"How did he die?" I asked, my voice far away.

"What *demands*?" Declan interrupted in a rough growl.

Declan pulled me closer to him, his body anchoring me in reality. My head pounded, but not from grief as I'd expected, but from some other emotion I couldn't quite place. My father was dead. I thought he'd live forever.

Dove's gaze slid from Declan to me, unsure of who to answer.

"It was strange how it happened," Dove said. "A wild beast was spotted on the outskirts of the city. Some giant black wolf, the townspeople said. Unnatural in size." She studied her feet for a moment before continuing. "The king and his men organized a hunt. Corbin and Wallace were there. The men spotted the beast in the wood and surrounded it, plying it with arrows. It was dying. The king intended to land the killing blow. He raised his hammer to strike, but instead, when he was within reach, the beast lashed forward, and with a giant claw, sliced through your father's mail like butter before fleeing deeper into the forest, pelt still full of arrows."

"And this is what killed him?" I asked, tears welling in my eyes. "None of his men helped their king? Not his own sons?" My fists balled at my sides. I knew I was being unfair. It wasn't unheard of for men to die in a hunt, but my father? It was laughable. He was stronger than men twenty years his junior and had been on countless hunts in his lifetime.

"They tried," Dove said gently. "I was in the castle when they brought him in. I saw the wound myself. It was not deep, but the fever began immediately, and the cut did not heal." She took a step forward as if to comfort me, as she'd done countless times in years past. Instead, Dove's gaze darted to Declan, and she shifted back on her feet and shook her head. Her voice was barely a whisper as she continued. "It was as if the wolf's claws were tipped with poison. The wound, while shallow, refused to heal, and festered, turning black and branching further across his skin. The healers thought it...most suspicious. Althene's brightest healers called it a death unlike any previously seen in the human kingdoms."

Dove turned her attention to Declan and cleared her throat, undeterred by his clenched jaw and rigid expression.

She tentatively held out the other parchment toward him, her hands trembling. He snatched it from her and ripped through the seal in one motion. Declan's already present scowl deepened as he read the words penned by my eldest brother.

"No," he snarled, crumpling up the letter before I had the chance to read it.

Dove held her chin high despite the fact the top of her head only reached Declan's chest.

"Those are the king's demands," she said, voice wavering.

Declan turned away and threw the paper into the roaring fire of our sitting room, anger pouring off him in dark waves.

I wrapped my hands around Declan's forearms, working to calm the furious energy inside of him to no avail. His skin was hot like a flame. I tried to send some of Lux's soothing magic to him, but only hit invisible barriers.

"What demands did Corbin send, my love?" I asked.

Declan untangled his arm from mine and stepped away, shaking his head, dark hair spilling into his eyes.

"The boy-king believes I had your father killed. The castle healers have whispered tales of magic into your brother's ears, and the new king thinks me responsible." He ran a hand down his face with a groan, and Kera's posture stiffened in my peripheral vision.

"You had nothing to do with that!" I said before turning to Dove. "Declan has been with me the entire time. He had no reason to harm my father," I said, willing her to understand. But it didn't matter what Dove believed. She was sent here on her king's orders. "Our marriage will heal the rift between kingdoms of fae and men. It was recorded in prophecy long ago and willed by gods," I pleaded with my friend who was in no position to help me, begging her to understand. "Declan and I are destined to be together, bound together by fate."

"There's more," Dove said quietly, not meeting my eye. "According to the agreement between our kingdoms," she swallowed, and her voice came out in an apologetic whisper, "You were supposed to be married before the first snowfall." She grimaced. "The magic binding the marriage treaty is void."

"*So?*" I said. "What does that matter?"

Declan took a step forward, and the air in the room thickened around us, static charging and poised to strike. He turned to face me, features drawn tight before speaking.

"The new King of Althene demands the return of their princess." His lip curled into a snarl. "And threatens war."

Need to know what happens next?

Book 2 is coming soon

FOLLOW CHLOE ON SOCIAL MEDIA AND JOIN THE CONVERSATION TO STAY UP TO DATE WITH ALL THE BOOKISH NEWS

facebook.com/chloeeverhart
instagram.com/chloeeverhart.author
tiktok.com/@chloeeverhart.author

Printed in Great Britain
by Amazon